Praise for

DEAD LIKE YOU

"Possibly the most engrossing thriller since Thomas Harris's *The Silence of the Lambs*." —*The Washington Post*

"Sinister and riveting. Peter James is one of the best in the world." —Lee Child

"A terrific thriller . . . *Dead Like You* is a haunting page-turner that seamlessly blends psychological suspense with police procedure, echoing the heart and voices of such authors as P. D. James and Ian Rankin at their best." —Jeffery Deaver

"Peter James creates worlds as familiar as your backyard, but doubly spicy, smart, and entertaining. Danger and drama leap from every page, as the master delivers precisely what every reader wants: plenty of sizzle and emotional clout. *Dead Like You* makes for a terrific read. Don't miss this one." —Steve Berry

"U.S. readers deserve to know what the rest of the world has known for years—Peter James is one of the best crime writers in the business." —Karin Slaughter, *New York Times* bestselling author of *Broken* and *Undone*

"Thrilling . . . will leave readers eager for the next installment." —*Publishers Weekly*

DEAD MAN'S GRIP

PETER JAMES

MINOTAUR BOOKS ✠ NEW YORK

DEAD MAN'S GRIP. Copyright © 2011 by Really Scary Books / Peter James. All rights reserved. Printed in the United States of America. For information, address St. Martin's Press, 175 Fifth Avenue, New York, N.Y. 10010.

www.minotaurbooks.com

The Library of Congress has cataloged the hardcover edition as follows:

James, Peter, 1948–
 Dead man's grip / Peter James.
   p. cm.
 ISBN 978-0-312-64283-9 (hardback)
 1. Grace, Roy (Fictitious character)—Fiction. 2. Police—England—Sussex—
Fiction. 3. Stalking—Fiction. I. Title.
 PR6060.A472D427 2011
 823'.914—dc22

                                                                2011027083

 ISBN 978-0-312-64321-8 (trade paperback)

First published in Great Britain by Macmillan, an imprint of Pan Macmillan, a division of Macmillan Publishers Limited

First Minotaur Books Paperback Edition: September 2012

D 10 9 8 7 6 5 4 3 2

TO EVA KLAESSON-LINDEBLAD

DEAD MAN'S GRIP

1

On the morning of the accident, Carly had forgotten to set the alarm and overslept. She woke with a bad hangover, a damp dog crushing her and the demented pounding of drums and cymbals coming from her son's bedroom. To add to her gloom, it was pelting with rain outside.

She lay still for a moment, gathering her thoughts. She had a chiropody appointment for a painful corn and a client she loathed would be in her office in just over two hours. It was going to be one of those days, she had the feeling, when things just kept on getting worse. Like the drumming.

'Tyler!' she yelled. 'For Christ's sake, stop that. Are you ready?'

Otis leapt off the bed and began barking furiously at his reflection in the mirror on the wall.

The drumming fell silent.

She staggered to the bathroom, found the paracetamols and gulped two down. I am so not a good example to my son, she thought. I'm not even a good example to my dog.

As if on cue, Otis padded into the bathroom, holding his lead in his mouth expectantly.

'What's for breakfast, Mum?' Tyler called out.

She stared at herself in the bathroom mirror. Mercifully, most of her forty-one-year-old – and this morning going on 241-year-old – face was shrouded in a tangle of blonde hair that looked, at this moment, like matted straw.

'Arsenic!' she shouted back, her throat raw from too many cigarettes last night. 'Laced with cyanide and rat poison.'

Otis stamped his paw on the bathroom tiles.

'Sorry, no walkies. Not this morning. Later. OK?'

'I had that yesterday!' Tyler shouted back.

'Well, it didn't sodding work, did it?'

She switched on the shower, waited for it to warm up, then stepped inside.

2

Stuart Ferguson, in jeans, Totectors boots and company overalls on top of his uniform polo shirt, sat high up in his cab, waiting impatiently for the lights to change. The wipers clunked away the rain. Rush-hour traffic sluiced across Brighton's Old Shoreham Road below him. The engine of his sixteen-wheel, twenty-four-ton Volvo fridge-box artic chuntered away, a steady stream of warm air toasting his legs. April already, but winter had still not relaxed its grip, and he'd driven through snow at the start of his journey. No one was going to sell him global warming.

He yawned, staring blearily at the vile morning, then took a long swig of Red Bull. He put the can into the cup-holder, ran his clammy, meaty hands across his shaven head, then drummed them on the steering wheel to the beat of 'Bat Out of Hell', which was playing loud enough to wake the dead fish behind him. It was the fifth or maybe the sixth can he had drunk in the past few hours and he was shaking from the caffeine overdose. But that and the music were the only things that were keeping him awake right now.

He had started his journey yesterday afternoon and driven through the night from Aberdeen, in Scotland. There were 603 miles on the clock so far. He'd been on the road for eighteen hours, with barely a break other than a stop for food at Newport Pagnell Services and a brief kip in a lay-by a couple of hours earlier. If it hadn't been for an accident at the M1/M6 interchange, he'd have been here an hour ago, at 8 a.m. as scheduled.

But saying *if it hadn't been for an accident* was pointless. There were always accidents, all the time. Too many people on the roads, too many cars, too many lorries, too many idiots, too many distractions, too many people in a hurry. He'd seen it all over the years. But he was proud of his record. Nineteen years and not one scrape – or even a ticket.

As he glanced routinely at the dashboard, checking the oil

pressure, then the temperature gauge, the traffic lights changed. He rammed the gear lever of the four-over-four splitter box forward and steadily picked up speed as he crossed the junction into Carlton Terrace, then headed down the hill towards the sea, which was under a mile away. After an earlier stop at Springs, the salmon smokery a few miles north in the Sussex Downs, he now had one final delivery to make to offload his cargo. It was to the Tesco supermarket in the Holmbush Centre on the outskirts of the city. Then he would drive to the port of Newhaven, load up with frozen New Zealand lamb, snatch a few hours' sleep on the quay and head back up to Scotland.

To Jessie.

He was missing her a lot. He glanced down at her photograph on the dashboard, next to the pictures of his two kids, Donal and Logan. He missed them badly, too. His bitch ex-wife, Maddie, was giving him a hard time over contact. But at least sweet Jessie was helping him get his life back together.

She was four months pregnant with their child. Finally, after three hellish years, he had a future to focus on again, instead of just a past full of bitterness and recrimination.

Ordinarily on this run he would have taken a few hours out to get some proper kip – and comply with the law on driver hours. But the refrigeration was on the blink, with the temperature rising steadily, and he couldn't take the risk of ruining the valuable cargo of scallops, shrimps, prawns and salmon. So he just had to keep going.

So long as he was careful, he would be fine. He knew where the vehicle check locations were, and by listening to CB radio he'd get warned of any active ones. That was why he was detouring through the city now, rather than taking the main road around it.

Then he cursed.

Ahead of him he could see red flashing lights, then barriers descending. The level crossing at Portslade Station. Brake lights came on one by one as the vehicles in front slowed to a halt. With a sharp hiss of his brakes, he pulled up, too. On his left he saw a fair-haired man bowed against the rain, his hair batted by the wind, unlocking the front door of an estate agency called Rand & Co.

PETER JAMES

He wondered what it would be like to have that sort of job. To be able to get up in the morning, go to an office and then come home in the evening to your family, rather than spend endless days and nights driving, alone, eating in service station cafés or munching a burger in front of the crappy telly in the back of his cab. Maybe he would still be married if he had a job like that. Still see his kids every night and every weekend.

Except, he knew, he'd never be content if he was stuck in one place. He liked the freedom of the road. Needed it. He wondered if the guy turning the lock of the estate agency door had ever looked at a rig like his and thought to himself, I wish I was twisting the ignition key of one of those instead.

Other pastures always looked greener. The one certainty he'd learned in life was that no matter who you were or what you did, shit happened. And one day you would tread in it.

4

3

Tony nicknamed her Santa because the first time they made love, that snowy December afternoon in his parents' house in the Hamptons, Suzy had been wearing dark red satin underwear. He told her that all his Christmases had come at once.

She, grinning, gave him the cheesy reply that she was glad that was the only thing that had come at once.

They had been smitten with each other since that day. So much so that Tony Revere had abandoned his plans to study for a business degree at Harvard and instead had followed her from New York to England, much to the dismay of his control-freak mother, and joined her at the University of Brighton.

'Lazybones!' he said. 'You goddamn lazybones.'

'So, I don't have any lectures today, OK?'

'It's half eight, right?'

'Yep, I know. I heard you at eight o'clock. Then eight fifteen. Then eight twenty-five. I need my beauty sleep.'

He looked down at her and said, 'You're beautiful enough. And you know what? We haven't made love since midnight.'

'Are you going off me?'

'I guess.'

'I'll have to get the old black book out.'

'Oh yeah?'

She raised a hand and gripped him, firmly but gently, below his belt buckle, then grinned as he gasped. 'Come back to bed.'

'I have to see my tutor, then I have a lecture.'

'On what?'

'Galbraithian challenges in today's workforce.'

'Wow. Lucky you.'

'Yeah. Faced with that or a morning in bed with you, it's a no-brainer.'

'Good. Come back to bed.'

5

'I am so not coming back to bed. You know what's going to happen if I don't get good grades this semester?'

'Back to the States to Mummy.'

'You know my mom.'

'Uh huh, I do. Scary lady.'

'You said it.'

'So, you're afraid of her?'

'Everyone's afraid of my mom.'

Suzy sat up a little and scooped some of her long dark hair back. 'More afraid of her than you are of me? Is that the real reason why you came here? I'm just the excuse for you to escape from her?'

He leaned down and kissed her, tasted her sleepy breath and inhaled it deeply, loving it. 'You're gorgeous, did I tell you that?'

'About a thousand times. You're gorgeous, too. Did I tell you that?'

'About ten thousand times. You're like a record that got stuck in a groove,' he said, hitching the straps of his lightweight rucksack over his shoulders.

She looked at him. He was tall and lean, his short dark hair gelled in uneven spikes, with several days' growth of stubble, which she liked to feel against her face. He was dressed in a padded anorak over two layers of T-shirt, jeans and trainers, and smelled of the Abercrombie & Fitch cologne she really liked.

There was an air of confidence about him that had captivated her the first time they had spoken, down in the dark basement bar of Pravda, in Greenwich Village, when she'd been in New York on holiday with her best friend, Katie. Poor Katie had ended up flying back to England on her own, while she had stayed on with Tony.

'When will you be back?' she said.

'As soon as I can.'

'That's not soon enough!'

He kissed her again. 'I love you. I adore you.'

She windmilled her hands. 'More.'

'You're the most stunning, beautiful, lovely creature on the planet.'

'More!'

'Every second I'm away from you, I miss you so much it hurts.'

She windmilled her hands again. 'More!'

'Now you're being greedy.'

'You make me greedy.'

'And you make me horny as hell. I'm going before I have to do something about it!'

'You're really going to leave me like this?'

'Yep.'

He kissed her again, tugged a baseball cap on to his head, then wheeled his mountain bike out of the apartment, down the stairs, through the front door and into the cold, blustery April morning. As he closed the front door behind him, he breathed in the salty tang of the Brighton sea air, then looked at his watch.

Shit.

He was due to see his tutor in twenty minutes. If he pedalled like hell, he might just make it.

4

*Click. Beeehhh . . . gleeep . . . uhuhuhurrr . . . gleep . . . grawwwwwp
. . . biff, heh, heh, heh. warrrup, haha . . .*

'That noise is driving me nuts,' Carly said.

Tyler, in the passenger seat of her Audi convertible, was bent
over his iPhone playing some bloody game he was hooked on called
Angry Birds. Why did everything he did involve noise?

The phone now emitted a sound like crashing glass.

'We're late,' he said, without looking up and without stopping
playing.

Twang-greep-heh, heh, heh . . .

'Tyler, please. I have a headache.'

'So?' He grinned. 'You shouldn't have got pissed last night.
Again.'

She winced at his use of adult language.

Twang . . . heh, heh, heh, grawwwwpppp . . .

In a moment she was going to grab the sodding phone and
throw it out of the window.

'Yep, well, you'd have got *pissed* last night, too, if you'd had to
put up with that prat.'

'Serves you right for going on blind dates.'

'Thanks.'

'You're welcome. I'm late for school. I'm going to get stick for
that.' He was still peering intently through his oval wire-framed
glasses.

Click-click-beep-beep-beep.

'I'll phone and tell them,' she offered.

'You're always phoning and telling them. You're irresponsible.
Maybe I should get taken into care.'

'I've been begging them to take you, for years.'

She stared through the windscreen at the red light and the
steady stream of traffic crossing in front of them, and then at the

8

clock: 8.56 a.m. With luck, she'd drop him off at school and get to her chiropody appointment on time. Great, a double-pain morning! First the corn removal, then her client, Mr Misery. No wonder his wife had left him. Carly reckoned she'd probably have topped herself if she'd been married to him. But hey, she wasn't paid to sit in judgement. She was paid to stop Mrs Misery from walking off with both of her husband's testicles, as well as everything else of his – correction, *theirs* – that she was after.

'It really hurts, still, Mum.'

'What does? Oh, right, your brace.'

Tyler touched the front of his mouth. 'It's too tight.'

'I'll call the orthodontist and get you an appointment with him.'

Tyler nodded and focused back on his game.

The lights changed. She moved her right foot from the brake pedal and accelerated. The news was coming up and she leaned forward, turning up the radio.

'I'm going to the *old people* this weekend, right?'

'I'd rather you didn't call them that, OK? They're your *grand-parents.*'

A couple of times a year Tyler spent a day with her late husband's parents. They doted on him, but he found them deadly dull.

Tyler shrugged. 'Do I have to go?'

'Yes, you have to go.'

'Why?'

'It's called *servicing the will.*'

He frowned. 'What?'

She grinned. 'Just a joke – don't repeat that.'

'Servicing the will?' he echoed.

'Forget I said it. Bad taste. I'll miss you.'

'You're a lousy liar. You might say that with more feeling.' He studiously drew his finger across the iPhone screen, then lifted it.

Twang . . . eeeeeekkkk . . . greeeep . . . heh, heh, heh . . .

She caught the next lights and swung right into New Church Road, cutting across the front of a skip lorry, which blared its horn at her.

'You trying to get us killed or something?' Tyler said.

'Not us, just you.' She grinned.

9

'There are agencies to protect children from parents like you,' he said.

She reached out her left arm and ran her fingers through his tousled brown hair.

He jerked his head away. 'Hey, don't mess it up!'

She glanced fondly at him for an instant. He was growing up fast and looked handsome in his shirt and tie, red blazer and grey trousers. Not quite thirteen years old and girls were already chasing him. He was growing more like his late father every day, and there were some expressions he had which reminded her of Kes too much, and in unguarded moments that could make her tearful, even five years on.

Moments later, at a few minutes past nine, she pulled up outside the red gates of St Christopher's School. Tyler clicked off his seat belt and reached behind him to pick up his rucksack.

'Is Friend Mapper on?'

He gave her a 'duh' look. 'Yes, it's on. I'm not a baby, you know.'

Friend Mapper was a GPS app on the iPhone that enabled her to track exactly where he was at any moment on her own iPhone.

'So long as I pay your bill, you keep it on. That's the deal.'

'You're overprotective. I might turn out to be emotionally retarded.'

'That's a risk I'll have to take.'

He climbed out of the car into the rain, then held the door hesitantly. 'You should get a life.'

'I had one before you were born.'

He smiled before slamming the door.

She watched him walk in through the gates into the empty play area – all the other pupils had already gone inside. Every time he went out of her sight, she was scared for him. Worried about him. The only reassurance that he was OK was when she checked her own iPhone and watched his pulsing purple dot and could see where he was. Tyler was right, she was overprotective, but she couldn't help it. She loved him desperately and, despite some of his maddening attitudes and behaviour, she knew that he loved her back, just as much.

She headed up towards Portland Road, driving faster than she should, anxious not to be late for her chiropodist. The corn was giving her grief and she did not want to miss the appointment. Nor did she want to get delayed there. She badly needed to be in the office ahead of Mr Misery and, with luck, have a few minutes to catch up with some urgent paperwork on a forthcoming hearing.

Her phone pinged with an incoming text. When she reached the junction with the main road, she glanced down at it.

I had a great time last night – wld love to see you again XXX

In your dreams, sweetheart. She shuddered at the thought of him. Dave from Preston, Lancashire. Preston Dave, she'd called him. At least she had been honest with the photograph of herself she'd put up on the dating website – well, reasonably honest! And she wasn't looking for a Mr Universe. Just a nice guy who wasn't 100 pounds heavier and ten years older than his photograph, and who didn't want to spend the entire evening telling her how wonderful he was, and what a great shag women thought he was. Was that too much to ask?

Just to put the icing on the cake, the tight bastard had invited her out to dinner, to a far more expensive restaurant than she would have chosen for a first encounter, and at the end had suggested they split the bill.

Keeping her foot on the brake and leaning forward, she deleted the text, decisively, returning the phone to the hands-free cradle with no small amount of satisfaction.

Then she made a left turn, pulling out in front of a white van, and accelerated.

The van hooted and flashing its lights angrily, closed up right behind her and began tailgating her. She held up two fingers.

There were to be many times, in the days and weeks ahead, when she bitterly regretted reading and deleting that text. If she hadn't waited at that junction for those precious seconds, fiddling with her phone, if she had made that left turn just thirty seconds earlier, everything might have been very different.

5

'Black,' Glenn Branson said, holding the large golf umbrella over their heads.

Detective Superintendent Roy Grace looked up at him.

'It's the only colour!'

At five foot, ten inches, Roy Grace was a good four inches shorter than his junior colleague and friend, and considerably less sharply dressed. Approaching his fortieth birthday, Grace was not handsome in a conventional sense. He had a kind face with a slightly misshapen nose that gave him a rugged appearance. It had been broken three times – once in a fight and twice on the rugby pitch. His fair hair was cropped short and he had clear blue eyes that his long-missing wife, Sandy, used to tell him resembled those of the actor Paul Newman.

Feeling like a child in a sweet shop, the Detective Superintendent, hands dug deeply into his anorak pockets, ran his eyes over the rows of vehicles on the Frosts' used-car forecourt, all gleaming with polish and rainwater, and kept returning to the two-door Alfa Romeo. 'I like silver, and dark red, and navy.' His voice was almost drowned out by the sound of a lorry passing on the main road behind them, its air horns blaring.

He was taking advantage of the quiet week, so far, to nip out of the office. A car he'd liked the look of on the *Autotrader* website was at this local dealer.

Detective Sergeant Branson, wearing a cream Burberry mackintosh and shiny brown loafers, shook his head. 'Black's best. The most desirable colour. You'll find that useful when you come to sell it – unless you're planning to drive it over a cliff, like your last one.'

'Very funny.'

Roy Grace's previous car, his beloved maroon Alfa Romeo 147 sports saloon, had been wrecked during a police pursuit the previous autumn, and he had been wrangling with the insurance company ever since. Finally they had agreed a miserly settlement figure.

'You need to think about these things, old-timer. Getting near retirement, you need to look after the pennies.'

'I'm thirty-nine.'

'Forty's looming.'

'Thanks for reminding me.'

'Yeah, well, the old brain starts going at your age.'

'Sod off! Anyhow, black's the wrong colour for an Italian sports car.'

'It's the best colour for everything.' Branson tapped his chest. 'Look at me.'

Roy Grace stared at him. 'Yes?'

'What do you see?'

'A tall, bald bloke with rubbish taste in ties.'

'It's Paul Smith,' he said, looking hurt. 'What about my colour?'

'I'm not allowed to mention it under the Racial Equality Act.'

Branson raised his eyes. 'Black is the colour of the future.'

'Yep, well, as I'm so old I won't live long enough to see it – especially standing here in the pissing rain. I'm freezing. Look, I like that one,' he said, pointing at a red two-seater convertible.

'In your dreams. You're about to become a father, remember? What you need is one of those.' Glenn Branson pointed across at a Renault Espace.

'Thanks, I'm not into people carriers.'

'You might be if you have enough kids.'

'Well, so far it's just one on the way. Anyhow, I'm not choosing anything without Cleo's approval.'

'Got you under her thumb, has she?'

Grace blushed coyly. 'No.'

He took a step towards a sleek silver two-door Alfa Brera and stared at it covetously.

'Don't go there,' Branson said, stepping along with him, keeping him covered with the umbrella. 'Unless you're a contortionist!'

'These are really gorgeous!'

'Two doors. How are you going to get the baby in and out of the back?' He shook his head sadly. 'You have to get something more practical now you're going to be a family man.'

Grace stared at the Brera. It was one of the most beautiful cars he'd ever seen. The price tag was £9,999. Within his range – although with rather high mileage. As he took a further step towards it, his mobile phone rang.

Out of the corner of his eye, he saw a salesman in a sharp suit, holding up an umbrella, scurrying towards them. He glanced at his watch as he answered the phone, mindful of the time, because he was due for a meeting with his boss, the Assistant Chief Constable, in an hour's time, at 10 a.m.

'Roy Grace,' he said.

It was Cleo, twenty-six weeks pregnant with their child, and she sounded terrible, as if she could barely speak.

'Roy,' she gasped. 'I'm in hospital.'

6

He'd had enough of Meat Loaf. Just as the railway-crossing barrier began to rise, Stuart Ferguson switched to an Elkie Brooks album. 'Pearl's a Singer' began to play. That song had been on in the pub the first time he'd gone out with Jessie.

Some women on a first date tried to distance themselves from you, until they knew you better. But they'd had six months of getting to know each other over the phone and the Internet. Jessie had been waiting tables in a truck stop just north of Edinburgh when they'd first met, late at night, and chatted for over an hour. They were both going through marriage bust-ups at the time. She'd scrawled her phone number on the back of the receipt and hadn't expected to hear from him again.

When they'd settled into the quiet side booth, on their first proper date, she'd snuggled up to him. As the song started playing, he'd slipped an arm around her shoulder, fully expecting her to flinch or pull away. Instead she'd snuggled even closer and turned her face towards him, and they'd kissed. They continued kissing, without a break, for the entire duration of the song.

He smiled as he drove forward, bumping over the rail tracks, mindful of a wobbly moped rider just in front of him, the wipers clunking. His heart was heavy with longing for Jessie, the song both beautiful and painful for him at the same time. Tonight he would be back in her arms.

'In one hundred yards turn left,' commanded the female voice of his satnav.

'Yes, boss,' he grunted, and glanced down at the left-angled arrow on the screen, directing him off Station Road and into Portland Road.

He indicated and changed down a gear, braking well in advance, careful to get the weighting of the heavy lorry stabilized before making the sharp turn on the wet road.

In the distance he saw flashing headlights. A white van, tailgating a car. Tosser, he thought.

7

'Tosser,' Carly said, watching the white van that filled her rear-view mirror. She kept carefully to the 30mph speed limit as she drove along the wide street, heading towards Station Road. She passed dozens of small shops, then a post office, a curry house, a halal butcher, a large red-brick church to the right, a used-car showroom.

Immediately ahead of her was a van parked outside a kitchen appliance shop, with two men unloading a crate from the rear. It was blocking her view of a side road just beyond. She clocked a lorry that was coming towards her, a few hundred yards away, but she had plenty of space. Just as she started pulling out, her phone rang.

She glanced down at the display and saw to her irritation that it was Preston Dave calling. For an instant she was tempted to answer and tell him she was surprised he hadn't reversed the charge. But she was in no mood to speak to him. Then, as she looked back up at the road, a cyclist going hell for leather suddenly appeared out of nowhere, coming straight at her, over a pedestrian crossing on her side of the road, just as the lights turned red.

For an instant, in panic, she thought it must be her who was on the wrong side of the road. She swung the steering wheel hard to the left, stamping on the brake pedal, thumping over the kerb, missing him by inches, and skidded, wheels locked, across the wet surface.

Empty chairs and tables outside a café raced towards her as if she was on a scary funfair ride. She stared, frozen in horror, gripping the wheel, just a helpless observer as the wall of the café loomed nearer. For an instant, as she splintered a table, she thought she was going to die.

'Oh shittttttttttt!' she screamed as the nose of her car smashed into the wall beneath the café window and a massive explosion numbed her ears. She felt a terrible jolt on her shoulder, saw a blur of white and smelled something that reminded her of gunpowder.

Then she saw glass crashing down in front of the buckled bonnet of the car.

There was a muffled *barrrrrrrrrrrpppppppppp*, accompanied by a slightly less muffled banshee siren.

'Jesus!' she said, panting in shock. 'Oh, God! Oh, Jesus!'

Her ears popped and the sounds became much louder.

Cars could catch fire, she'd seen that in films. She had to get out. In wild panic, she hit the seat-belt buckle and tried to open her door. But it would not move. She tried again, harder. A baggy white cushion lay on her lap. The airbag, she realized. She wrenched the door handle, her panic increasing, and shoved the door as hard as she could. It opened and she tumbled out, her feet catching in the seat belt, tripping her, sending her sprawling painfully on to the wet pavement.

As she lay there for an instant she heard the banshee wail continue above her head. A burglar alarm. Then she could hear another wailing sound. This time it was human. A scream.

Had she hit someone? Injured someone?

Her knee and right hand were stinging like hell, but she barely noticed hauling herself to her feet, looking first at the wreckage of the café and then across the road.

She froze.

A lorry had stopped on the opposite side. A huge artic, slewed at a strange angle. The driver was clambering down from the cab. People were running into the road right behind it. Running past a mountain bike that had been twisted into an ugly shape, like an abstract sculpture, past a baseball cap and tiny bits of debris, towards what she thought at first was a roll of carpet lying further back, leaking dark fluid from one end on to the rain-lashed black tarmac.

All the traffic had stopped, and the people who had been running stopped too, suddenly, as if they had become statues. She felt she was staring at a tableau. Then she walked, stumbling, out into the road, in front of a stationary car, the high-pitched howl of the siren almost drowned out by the screams of a young woman holding an umbrella, who was standing on the far pavement, staring at that roll of carpet.

Fighting her brain, which wanted to tell her it was something different, Carly saw the laced-up trainer that was attached to one end.

And realized it wasn't a roll of carpet. It was a severed human leg.

She vomited, the world spinning around her.

8

At 9 a.m. Phil Davidson and Vicky Donoghue, dressed in their green paramedic uniforms, sat chatting in the cab of the Mercedes Sprinter Ambulance. They were parked on a police bay opposite the taxi rank at Brighton's Clock Tower, where they had been positioned by the dispatcher.

Government targets required that ambulances reached Category-A emergencies within eight minutes, and from this location, with a bit of aggressive driving, they could normally reach anywhere in the city of Brighton and Hove well within that time.

Ninety minutes into their twelve-hour shift, the rush-hour world passed by in front of them, blurred by the film of rain on the windscreen. Every few minutes Vicky flicked the wipers to clear their view. They watched taxis, buses, goods vehicles passing by, streams of people trudging to work, some huddled beneath umbrellas, others looking sodden and gloomy. This part of the city didn't look great even on a sunny day; in the wet it was plain depressing.

The ambulance service was the most constantly busy of all the emergency services and they'd already attended their first call-out, a Category-B emergency shout to attend an elderly lady who had fallen in the street outside her home in Rottingdean.

The first life lesson Phil Davidson had learned, from his eight years as a paramedic, was very simple: *Don't grow old. If you have to, don't grow old alone.*

Around 90 per cent of the work of the paramedics was attending the elderly. People who had fallen, people who were having palpitations, or strokes or suspected heart attacks, people who were too frail to get a taxi to hospital. And there were plenty of wily old birds who knew how to exploit the system. Half the time, much to their irritation, the paramedics were nothing more than a free big taxi service for lazy, smelly and often grossly overweight people.

They'd delivered this particular lady, who was a sweetie, into the care of Accident and Emergency at the Royal Sussex County Hospital and were now on standby, waiting for the next call. That was the thing Phil Davidson most liked about this job, you never knew what was going to happen. The siren would sound inside the ambulance and trip that squirt of adrenalin inside him. Was it going to be a routine job or the one he would remember for years? The job's category of emergency, ranging from A to C would appear on the screen on the console, together with the location and known facts, which would then be updated as further information came in.

He glanced down at the screen now, as if willing the next job to appear. A rainy rush hour like today often produced accidents, particularly traffic *collisions*, as they were now known. They were not called *accidents* any more, because it was always someone's fault; they were known as Road Traffic Collisions.

Phil liked attending trauma cases best. The ambulance's lockers were packed with the latest trauma technology. Critical haemorrhage kits, Israeli military dressings, a combat application tourniquet, an ACS – Asherman Chest Seal – standard equipment for the British and US military. The benefits of war, he often thought cynically. Little did some victims of terrible accidents, who recovered thanks to the paramedics' work at the scene, realize they owed their lives to the medical advances that came out of battlegrounds.

Vicky nipped out to have a quick pee in the Starbucks just beside them. She'd learned always to grab the opportunity to use a loo, because in this job you never knew when you were going to get busy and there might not be another chance for hours.

As she climbed back behind the wheel, her crewmate for the day was talking on his phone to his wife. This was only her second time out with Phil and she had enjoyed working with him a lot the last time. A lean wiry man in his late thirties, with his hair shaven to stubble, long sideburns and several days' growth of beard, he had the air of a movie bad guy about him, although he was anything but. He was a big-hearted softy who doted on his family. He had a reassuring manner, a kind word for everyone he treated and a true passion for this work, which she shared with him.

Finishing his call, he looked down at the screen again.

'Unusually quiet, so far.'

'Not for long, I don't expect.'

They sat in silence for a moment as the rain pattered down. During her time with the ambulance service, she'd discovered that every paramedic had his or her own particular favourite field of work and seemed by some quirk of fate to attract that particular call-out. One of her colleagues always got mentally ill patients. She herself had delivered fifteen babies over the past three years, while Phil, in all his career, had yet to deliver one.

However, in her two years since qualifying, Vicky had only attended one serious road accident, and that had been on her first ever shift, when a couple of teenage boys had accepted a lift home in Brighton from a drunk driver. He'd hit a parked car, at 80mph in the centre of town. One boy had been killed outright and another had died at the roadside. Despite the horror of that incident, she found her work incredibly rewarding.

'You know, Phil,' she said. 'It's strange, but I haven't been to a road fatality in almost two years.'

He unscrewed the cap from a bottle of water. 'Stay with this job long enough and you will. In time you get everything.'

'You've never had to deliver a baby.'

He smiled sardonically at her. 'One day—'

He was interrupted by the high-pitched *whup-whup-whup* siren inside the ambulance. It was a sound that could dement you sometimes, especially during the quiet of the night. The sound of a call-out.

Instantly he looked down at the screen mounted between their seats and read the Incident Review information:

Emergency Inc: 00521. CatB Emergency

Portland Road, Hove.

Gender unknown.

Three vehicle RTC. Bicycle involved.

He tapped the button to acknowledge the call. It automatically loaded the address into the satnav system.

The target response time for a CatB was eighteen minutes – ten minutes longer than for a CatA, but it still called for emergency action. Vicky started the engine, switched on the blue lights and siren, and pushed her way carefully out over a red traffic light. She turned right and accelerated up the hill, past St Nicholas's Church, pulling out into the right-hand lane and forcing oncoming traffic to brake. She switched between the four different tones of the ambulance's sirens to get maximum attention from the vehicles and pedestrians ahead.

Moments later, peering hard at the incident screen, Phil updated her. 'Situation confused,' he read out. 'Several calls. Upgraded to CatA. A car crashed into a shop. Oh shit, cyclist in collision with a lorry. Control not sure of situation, backup requested.'

He leaned through the bulkhead for his fluorescent jacket and Vicky felt a tightening in her gullet.

Screaming down towards the clogged-up Seven Dials round-about, concentrating hard on her driving, she said nothing. A taxi driver sensibly pulled over on to the pavement to let them through. Fuck me, Phil thought, a cabbie who was actually awake! He unclipped his seat belt, hoping Vicky didn't choose this moment to crash, and began wriggling into his jacket. At the same time he continued watching the screen keenly.

'Age unknown, gender unknown,' he updated her. 'Breathing status unknown. Unknown number of patients involved. Oh shit – high mechanism. SIMCAS en route.'

That meant the Accident and Emergency doctor had been summoned from the hospital to the scene.

Which meant the status of the incident was worsening by the minute.

That was confirmed by the next update on the screen. 'Limb amputation,' Phil read out. 'Ouch! Bad day for someone.' Then he turned to her and said, 'Sounds like you might be getting your wish.'

9

Hospitals gave Roy Grace the heebie-jeebies and particularly this one. The Royal Sussex County Hospital was where both his parents, at a few years' interval, had spent most of the last days of their life. His father had died first, at just fifty-five, from bowel cancer. Two years later, when she was only fifty-six, his mother had succumbed to secondaries following breast cancer.

The front façade, a grand Victorian neoclassical edifice with an ugly black metal and glass portico, used to give him the impression of an asylum whose portals you entered once, never to leave.

Stretching out beside it, and up the hill behind the front entrance, was a massive, messy complex of buildings, new and old, low- and high-rise, joined by a seemingly never-ending labyrinth of corridors.

His stomach knotted, he drove his unmarked silver police Ford Focus estate up the hill to the east of the complex and turned into the small parking and turning area for ambulances. Strictly speaking, this area was for emergency vehicles and taxis only, but at this moment he did not care. He pulled the car up to one side, where he wasn't causing an obstruction, and climbed out into the rain.

He used to pray as a child, but since his late teens Roy had never had any religious convictions. But he found himself praying now, silently, that his darling Cleo and their unborn child were OK.

He ran past a couple of ambulances backed up to the entrance to Accident and Emergency, nodding greetings to a paramedic he knew who was standing beside a NO SMOKING IN HOSPITAL GROUNDS sign, grabbing a cigarette under the awning. Then, bypassing the public entrance, he went in via the paramedics' emergency doors.

Early in the day it was always quiet in here, in his experience. He saw a youth sitting in a chair, in handcuffs, a thick bandage on his forehead. A woman police officer stood by him, chatting to a nurse. A long-haired man, his face the colour of alabaster, lay on a trolley, staring vacantly at the ceiling. A teenage girl sat on a chair, crying. There was a strong hospital smell of disinfectant and floor polish. Two more paramedics he knew wheeled an empty trolley out past him.

He hurried along to the admittance desk, behind which were several harassed-looking people, most on them on phones, urgently reading forms or tapping at computer terminals. A male orderly with a thin fuzz of blond hair and wearing blue scrubs, was writing on a large whiteboard on the wall. Grace leaned over the desk, desperately trying to catch someone's attention.

After an agonizingly long minute the orderly turned to him.

Grace flashed his warrant card, not caring that he was on a personal matter. 'I think you've just admitted Cleo Morey?'

'Cleo Morey?' The man looked down at a list, then at the whiteboard on the wall. 'Yes, she's here.'

'How do I find her?'

'She's been taken to the labour ward. Do you know your way around here?'

'A little.'

'Thomas Kent Tower.' He pointed. 'Down there and follow the signs – they'll take you to the lift.'

Grace thanked him and ran along the corridor, following it left, then right, passing a sign that read X-RAY & ULTRASOUND. ALL OTHER BUILDINGS. He stopped for a moment and pulled his phone out of his pocket, his heart a lead weight in his chest, his shoes feeling like they had glue on them. It was 9.15 a.m. He dialled his boss, ACC Rigg, to warn him he would be late for his 10 a.m. meeting. Rigg's MSA – his Management Support Assistant – answered and told him not to worry, the ACC had a clear morning.

He passed a WRVS Coffee Shop, then ran on along a corridor lined with a mural of swimming fish, following more signs, then reached two lifts with a parked mobility scooter near them. He stabbed the button for a lift, debating whether to take the stairs, but the doors opened and he stepped in.

It climbed agonizingly slowly, so slowly he wasn't even sure if it was moving. Finally he stepped out, his heart in his mouth, and

opened a door directly in front of him labelled LABOUR WARD. He
went through into a bright reception area filled with rows of pink
and lilac chairs. There was a fine view out from its windows across
the rooftops of Kemp Town and down to the sea. A photocopier
sat in one corner and in another there were several food and
drink vending machines. Racks full of leaflets had been fixed to the
walls. On a modern television screen was the gaily coloured word
KIDDICARE.

A pleasant-looking woman in a blue smock sat behind the large
reception counter. 'Ah yes, Detective Superintendent Grace. They
phoned from downstairs to say you were on your way.' She pointed
along a corridor with yellow walls. 'She's in Room 7. Fourth door on
the left.'

Grace was too churned up to say anything beyond a mumbled
thank you.

10

The traffic ahead of them was braking and further along Portland Road Vicky Donoghue could see that it had come to a complete halt in both directions. Phil Davidson pulled on his surgical gloves, mentally preparing himself for the task ahead.

A lorry was facing them, the driver's door open, and several people were gathered towards its rear offside. On the other side of the road a black Audi convertible had ploughed into the side of a café. The driver's door of that was open, too, and a woman was standing near it, looking dazed. There was no sign of any other emergency vehicles here yet.

She raced the ambulance past the line of vehicles, on the wrong side of the road, keeping her eyes peeled for anyone who hadn't heard them coming. Then she braked, slowing to a crawl, killing the siren, and halted in front of the lorry. Her stomach tightened and her mouth felt suddenly dry.

The digital display read six minutes, twenty seconds – the length of time taken to get here from when the call came in. Comfortably inside the CatA eight-minute target. That was some small relief. Phil Davidson switched the emergency lights to stationary mode. Before jumping down from the vehicle, both of them briefly absorbed the scene.

The woman standing near the Audi, who had wavy blonde hair and was wearing a smart raincoat, was holding a mobile phone some distance away from her head, as if it was a ball she was about to throw to a batsman. Smashed and upturned tables and chairs lay around the car, but there was no immediate sign of any casualties there, and no one, apart from a youth in a cagoule, who was photographing the scene with his mobile phone, seemed to be taking any notice. The concentration seemed to be around the rear wheels of the lorry.

The two paramedics climbed out, looking around carefully,

continuing to take in as much as they could and making sure there was no danger from any passing traffic. But everything had very definitely stopped.

A short, stubby man in his mid-forties, in jeans and overalls, holding a mobile phone, hurried towards them. From his pallid face, wide staring eyes and quavering voice, Vicky could see he was in shock.

'Under my lorry,' he said. 'He's under my lorry.' He turned and pointed.

Vicky noticed, a short distance further along, a bicycle lamp, a saddle and a reflector lying in the road. Then, near them, was what looked at first like a length of denim tubing with a trainer attached. Her gullet constricted and she felt a rush of bile, which she swallowed back down. She and Phil hurried through the rain towards the rear of the sixteen-wheel articulated lorry, gently edging back the crowd to give them space.

A young woman was kneeling under the truck, but moved out the way for them. 'He has a pulse,' she said.

Nodding thanks, both paramedics knelt down and peered under the vehicle.

The light was poor. There was a stench of vomit from somewhere nearby, mixed with the smells of engine oil and hot metal, but there was something else too, that sour, coppery tang of blood that always reminded Phil Davidson of going into butcher's shops with his mother, when he was a kid.

Vicky saw a young man with short, dark hair streaked with blood and a lacerated face, his body contorted. His eyes were closed. He was wearing a ripped anorak and jeans, and one leg was wrapped around the wheel arch. The other was just a stump of white bone above the knee surrounded by jagged denim.

The anorak and layers of T-shirt around his midriff were ripped open and a coil of his intestines lay in a pool of fluid on the road.

Followed by her colleague, Vicky, who was smaller, crawled forward, beneath the lorry, smelling oil and rubber, and seized the young man's wrist, feeling for a pulse. There was a very faint one. The two paramedics were getting covered in oil, road grime and blood, which was soaking into their trousers and elbows and coating their gloves, turning them from blue surgical coverings into bloody, grimy gauntlets.

'*Fubar Bundy*,' Phil Davidson whispered grimly.

She nodded, swallowing acrid bile. It was a term she had heard before, at the fatal accident she had attended previously, only a short distance from this location. The gallows humour of the paramedics – one of their mental survival mechanisms for coping with horrific sights. It stood for: *Fucked Up Beyond All Recovery But Unfortunately Not Dead Yet*.

With internal organs exposed and on the tarmac, there was very little chance of the victim's survival. Even if they got him to hospital still technically alive, infections would finish him off. She turned to her more experienced colleague for his guidance.

'Pulse?' he asked.

'Faint radial,' she replied. A radial pulse meant that he had enough blood pressure to maintain some of his organs.

'*Stay and play*,' he mouthed back, knowing they had no option, as they couldn't move him because his leg was trapped in the wheel. 'I'll get the kit.'

Stay and play was one step above *Scoop and run*. It meant that although the victim's chances were slim, they would do all they could – try their best until he was dead and they could stop. Going through the motions, if nothing else.

She was aware of the scream of an approaching siren getting louder. Then she heard Phil radioing for the fire brigade to bring lifting gear. She squeezed the young man's hand. 'Hang on in,' she said. 'Can you hear me? What's your name?'

There was no response. The pulse was weakening. The siren was getting louder still. She looked at the stump of his severed leg. Almost no blood. That was the only positive at this moment. Human bodies were good at dealing with trauma. Capillaries shut down. It was like the accident she had attended two years ago, when one of the young lads was dying but was hardly bleeding at all. The body goes into shock. If they could get a tourniquet applied, and if she was careful with his intestines, then maybe there was a chance.

She kept her fingers pressed hard on his radial artery. It was weakening by the second.

'Hang in there,' she said. 'Just hang in there.' She looked at his face. He was a good-looking kid. But he was turning increasingly paler by the second. 'Please stay with me. You're going to be OK.'

The pulse was continuing to weaken.

She moved her fingers, desperately searching for a beat. 'You can make it,' she whispered. 'You can! Go for it! Go on, go for it!'

It was personal now.

For Phil he might be a *Fubar Bundy*, but for her he was a challenge. She wanted to visit him in hospital in two weeks' time and see him sitting up, surrounded by cards and flowers. 'Come on!' she urged, glancing up at the dark underbelly of the lorry, at the mud-encrusted wheel arch, at the grimy girders of the chassis. 'Hang on in there!'

Phil was crawling back under the lorry with his red bag and his critical haemorrhage kit. Between them, they covered everything that modern medical technology could throw at a trauma victim. But even as Phil tugged the red bag open, displaying pockets filled with vials of life-saving drugs, apparatus and monitoring equipment, Vicky realized, in this particular situation, it was mere cosmetics. Window-dressing.

The young man's pulse was barely detectable now.

She heard the whine of the EZ-10 bone drill, the fastest way to get the emergency cannula in. Every second was critical. She assisted Phil, locating the bone inside the flesh of the good leg, just below the knee, the professional in her kicking in, pushing all emotion aside. They had to keep trying. They *would* keep trying.

'Stay with us!' she urged.

It was clear that the poor young man had been dragged right around the wheel arch after the wheel had gone over his midriff, crushing him and splitting him open. Phil Davidson was calculating the likely damage to his internal organs and bones as he worked. It looked as if one of the wheels had shattered his pelvis, which in itself was usually sufficient to cause massive internal bleeding and almost certain death – on top of everything else that was probably going on in there.

This lad's best hope, he thought grimly as he worked on, would be to die quickly.

11

Roy Grace was shocked to see how pale Cleo looked. She lay in a high bed, in a room with pale blue walls that was cluttered with electrical sockets and apparatus. A tall man in his early thirties, with short, thinning brown hair, dressed in blue medical pyjamas and plimsolls, was standing beside her, writing a measurement on a graph on his pad as Roy entered.

She was wearing a blue hospital gown, and her blonde hair, cascading round her face, had lost some of its usual lustre. She gave Roy a wan, hesitant smile, as if she was happy he had come, but at the same time embarrassed that he was seeing her like this. A forest of electrode pads were attached to her chest and a monitor, like a thimble, covered her thumb.

'I'm sorry,' she said meekly, as he took her free hand and squeezed it. She gave him a weak squeeze back.

He felt a terrible panic rising inside him. Had she lost the baby? The man turned towards him. Grace could see from his badge that he was a registrar.

'You are this lady's husband?'

'Fiancé.' He was so choked he could barely get the word out. 'Roy Grace.'

'Ah, yes, of course.' The registrar glanced down at her engage-ment ring. 'Well, Mr Grace, Cleo is all right, but she's lost a lot of blood.'

'What's happened?' he asked.

Cleo's voice was weak as she explained, 'I'd just got to work – I was about to start preparing a body for post-mortem and I suddenly started bleeding, really heavily, as if something had exploded inside me. I thought I was losing the baby. Then I felt terrible pain, like cramps in my stomach – and the next thing I remember I was lying on the floor with Darren standing over me. He put me in his car and drove me here.'

Darren was her assistant in the mortuary.

Grace stared at Cleo, relief mingled with uncertainty. 'And the baby?' His eyes shot to the registrar.

'Cleo's just had an ultrasound scan,' he replied. 'She has a condition that's called placenta praevia. Her placenta is abnormally low down.'

'What – what does that mean – in terms of our baby?' Grace asked, filled with dread.

'There are complications, but your baby is fine at the moment,' the registrar said, pleasantly enough but with foreboding in his voice. Then he turned towards the door and nodded a greeting.

Grace saw a solidly built, bespectacled man enter. He had dark hair shorn to stubble, a balding pate, and was dressed in an open-necked blue shirt, grey suit trousers and black brogues. He had the air of a benign bank manager.

'Mr Holbein, this is Cleo's fiancé.'

'How do you do?' He shook Grace's hand. 'I'm Des Holbein, the consultant gynaecologist.'

'Thank you for coming in.'

'Not at all, that's what I'm here for. But I'm very glad you've arrived. We're going to have to make some decisions.'

Roy felt a sudden stab of anxiety. But the consultant's business-like attitude at least gave him some confidence. He waited for him to continue.

The consultant sat down on the bed. Then he looked up at Roy.

'Cleo came in for a routine ultrasound scan five weeks ago, at twenty-one weeks. At that time the placenta was very low but the baby was normal-sized.'

He turned to Cleo. 'Today's scan shows your baby has hardly grown at all. This is unusual and cause for concern, to be honest with you. It signifies that the placenta is not working well. It's doing its job just about enough to keep the baby alive, but not enough to enable it to grow. And I'm afraid there's a further complication that I don't like the look of. It's a very rare condition known as placenta percreta – the placenta is growing much further into the wall of the uterus than it should.'

From feeling a fraction upbeat seconds ago, Roy's heart plunged again. 'What does that mean?'

Des Holbein smiled at him – like a bank manager approving a loan, but with tough strings attached. 'Well, one option would be to deliver the baby now.'

'Now?' Grace said, astounded.

'Yes. But I would really not be happy to do this. Although 50 per cent of normal babies would live if delivered at this time – and probably a little more than that – the survival rate for one that has not grown since twenty-one weeks is much, much lower. In another month that would increase substantially – if we can get your baby's growth normalized, we'd be looking at above 90 per cent. If we could get to thirty-four weeks, that would rise to 98 per cent.'

He looked at each of them in turn, his face placid, giving nothing away.

Roy stared at the consultant, feeling sudden, irrational anger towards him. This was their child he was talking about. He was gaily reeling off percentages as if it was something you could put a spread bet on. Roy felt totally out of his depth. He had no idea about any of this. It wasn't in any of the books he had read; nor was it in *Emma's Diary* or any of the other booklets Cleo had been given by the NHS. All of those dealt with perfect pregnancies and perfect births.

'What's your advice?' Grace asked. 'What would you do if it was your child?'

'I would advise waiting and monitoring the placenta very closely. If Cleo suffers further blood loss, we will try to keep the baby inside by transfusing against that loss. If we deliver now and your baby does survive, the poor little thing is going to have to spend several months in an incubator, which is not ideal for the baby or the mother. Cleo seems otherwise healthy and strong. The ultimate decision is yours, but my advice is that we keep you here, Cleo, for a few days, and try to support your circulation and hope that the bleeding settles.'

'If it does, will I be able to go back to work?'

'Yes, but not immediately and no heavy lifting. And – this is very important – you will need to take a rest at some point during the day. We'll have to keep a careful eye on you for the rest of the pregnancy.'

'Could this happen again?' Grace asked.

'To be truthful, in 50 per cent of cases, no. But that means in 50 per cent of cases, yes. I run a *three strikes and you're out* rule here. If there's a second bleed, I will insist on further reductions to your fiancée's workload, and depending on how the percreta condition develops, I may require Cleo to be hospitalized for the rest of her term. It's not only the baby that is at risk in this situation.' He turned to Cleo. 'You are too.'

'To what extent?' Grace asked.

'Placenta percreta can be life-threatening to the mother,' the consultant said. He turned back to Cleo again. 'If there is a third bleed, there is no doubt about it. You'll have to spend the rest of your pregnancy in hospital.'

'What about damage to our baby?' Grace questioned.

The consultant shook his head. 'Not at this stage. What's happened is that a part of the placenta is not working so well. The placenta is an organ, just like a kidney or a lung. The baby can lose some placenta without a problem. But if it loses too much it won't grow well. And then, in extreme cases, yes, he or she can die.'

Grace squeezed Cleo's hand again and kissed her on the forehead, terrible thoughts churning inside him. He felt sick with fear. Bloody statistics. Percentages. Fifty per cent was crap odds. Cleo was so strong, so positive. They'd get through this. DC Nick Nicholl had been through something similar last year with his wife and the baby had ended up strong and healthy.

'It's going to be fine, darling,' he said, but his mouth felt dry.

Cleo nodded and managed a thin, wintry smile.

Grace glanced at his watch, then turned to the doctors. 'Could we have a few minutes together? I have to get to a meeting.'

'Of course.'

The doctors left the room.

Roy nuzzled his face against Cleo's and laid his hand gently on her midriff. Fear spiralled through him and he had a terrible sense of inadequacy. He could do something about criminals, but it seemed at this moment that he couldn't do a damned thing for the woman he loved or their unborn baby. Things were totally out of his hands.

'I love you,' he said. 'I love you so much.'

He felt her hand stroking his cheek. 'I love you, too,' she replied. 'You're soaking wet. Is it still raining?'

'Yes.'

'Did you see the car? The Alfa?'

'I had a brief look. I'm not sure if it's practical.' He stopped himself short of saying *with a baby*.

He held her hand and kissed the engagement ring on her finger. It gave him a strange feeling every time he saw it, a feeling of utter joy, yet always tinged with foreboding. There was still one big obstacle in the way of their actually getting married: the minefield of formalities that had to be gone through before his wife, Sandy, missing for ten years now, could be declared legally dead.

He was being scrupulously careful to tick every box in the process. On the instructions of the registrar, he had recently had notices placed in the local Sussex newspapers and the national press, requesting Sandy, or anyone who might have seen her in the past ten years, to contact him. So far, no one had.

A fellow officer and friend, and his wife, were both sure they had seen Sandy in Munich, while on holiday there the previous summer, but despite alerting his German police contacts and travelling over there himself, nothing more had come of it, and he was increasingly certain that his friend and his wife were mistaken. Nevertheless, he had declared this to the registrar, who had requested that he also place notices in the appropriate German newspapers, which he had now done.

He'd had to swear an affidavit listing all the people he had made enquiries with, including the last person who had seen Sandy alive. That had been a colleague at the medical centre where she worked part-time, who had seen her leaving the office at 1 p.m. on the day she vanished. He'd had to include information about all police enquiries and which of her work colleagues and friends he had contacted. He'd also had to swear that he had searched the house after she had gone and had found nothing missing, other than her handbag and her car.

Her little Golf had been found twenty-four hours later in a bay at the short-term car park at Gatwick Airport. There were two transactions on her credit card on the morning of her disappearance, one for £7.50 at Boots and the other for £16.42 for petrol from the local branch of Tesco. She had taken no clothes and no other belongings of any kind.

He was finding the process of filling in these forms therapeutic in a way. Finally he was starting to feel some kind of closure. And with luck the process would be complete in time for them to get married before their child was born.

He sighed, his heart heavy, and squeezed her hand again.

Please be OK, my darling Cleo. I couldn't bear it if anything happened to you, I really couldn't.

12

In his eight years' experience with the Road Policing Unit, PC Dan Pattenden had learned that if you were the first car to arrive at a crash scene, you would find chaos. Even more so if it was raining. And to make matters worse, as he hurtled along Portland Road on blues and twos, because of budget cuts, he was single-crewed.

The information he was receiving on his screen and over the radio was chaotic, too. The first indication that the accident was serious was the number of people who had phoned to report it – eight calls logged by the Control Room so far.

A lorry versus a bicycle; a car also involved, he had been informed.

A lorry versus a bicycle was never going to be good news.

He began slowing down as he approached, and, sure enough, what he observed through the rain-spattered windscreen was a scene of total confusion. An articulated refrigerated lorry facing away from him and an ambulance just beyond it. He saw, lying in the road, a buckled bicycle. Broken reflector glass. A baseball cap. A trainer. People all over the place, most frozen with shock but others snapping away with their mobile phone cameras. A small crowd was gathered around the rear offside of the lorry. On the other side of the road a black Audi convertible, with a buckled bonnet, was up against a café wall.

He halted the brightly marked BMW estate car at an angle across the road, the first step to sealing off the scene, and radioed for backup, hoping to hell that it would arrive quickly – he needed about twenty different pairs of hands all at once. Then, tugging on his cap and his fluorescent jacket he grabbed an Accident Report pad and jumped out of the car. Then he tried to make a quick assessment of the scene, remembering all the elements that had been drummed into him from his initial training, his refresher courses and his own considerable experience.

A rain-drenched young man in a tracksuit ran over to him. 'Officer, there was a van, a white van, that went through a red light, hit him and drove off.'

'Did you get the van's licence number?'

He shook his head. 'No – sorry – it all happened so fast.'

'What can you tell me about the van?'

'It was a Ford, I think. One of those Transit things. I don't think it had any writing on it.'

Pattenden made a note, then looked back at the young man. Witnesses often disappeared quickly, especially in rain like this. 'I'll need your name and phone number, please,' he said, writing the information in his pad. 'Could you jump in the car and wait?'

The young man nodded.

At least he might stay around if he was warm and dry, Pattenden reasoned. He passed the information to the Control Room, then sprinted over to the lorry, clocking a severed leg lying in the road but ignoring it for the moment, and knelt beside the paramedics. He looked briefly at the mangled, unconscious cyclist and the coiled intestines on the road, and the blood, but was too wrapped up in all he had to deal with to be affected by it at this moment.

'What can you tell me?' he said, although he barely needed to ask the question.

The male paramedic, whom he recognized, shook his head. 'Not looking good. We're losing him.'

That was the only information the police constable required at this moment. All road fatalities were viewed as potential homicides, rather than accidents, until proved otherwise. As the only officer present, his first duty was to secure the area around the collision as a crime scene. His next was to try to ensure that no vehicles were moved and to stop witnesses from leaving. To his relief, he could now hear the distant wail of sirens as, hopefully, more vehicles approached.

He ran back to his car, calling out at everyone he passed, 'Please, if you witnessed the incident come over to my car and give me your names and phone numbers.'

He opened the tailgate and dragged out a folding POLICE ROAD CLOSED sign, which he erected a short distance behind his car. At the same time he shouted into his radio that there was a potential hit and run and he needed the fire brigade, the Collision Investigation Unit, the inspector and backup PCSOs and uniformed officers.

Then he grabbed a roll of blue and white POLICE LINE DO NOT CROSS tape, tied one end around a lamp post and ran across the road, securing the other end around a parking sign on the pavement. As he was finishing he saw two more officers from his unit running towards him. He instructed them to tape off the road on the far side of the lorry and grab names and phone numbers from anyone else who might be witnesses.

Then, inside the taped cordon, he pulled off his reflective jacket and threw it over the severed leg, wanting both to spare people the horror of it and to stop one particular ghoul in a raincoat taking any more photographs of it.

'Get the other side of the tape!' he shouted at him. 'If you're a witness, go to my car. If not, move along please!'

More emergency vehicles were arriving. He saw a second ambulance and a paramedic car which would be bringing a specialist trauma doctor. But his main focus now was on identifying the drivers of the lorry and the Audi from the mass of rubberneckers and potential witnesses.

He saw a smartly dressed woman with rain-bedraggled hair standing near the open driver's door of the Audi. She was staring, transfixed, at the lorry.

Hurrying over to her, he asked, panting, 'Are you the driver of this car?'

She nodded, eyes vacant, still staring over his shoulder.

'Are you injured? Do you need medical assistance?'

'He just came out of nowhere, came out of that side street, straight at me. I had to swerve, otherwise I'd have hit him.'

'Who?' Surreptitiously he leaned forward, close enough to smell her breath. There was a faint reek of stale alcohol.

'The cyclist,' she said numbly.

'Were there any other vehicles involved?'

'A white van was right behind me, tailgating me.'

He had a quick look at the Audi. Although the bonnet was

crumpled and the airbags had deployed, the interior of the car looked intact.

'OK, madam, would you mind getting back into your car for a few minutes?'

He gently took her shoulders and turned her round, away from the lorry. He knew that if drivers of vehicles involved in an accident stared at a serious casualty for too long, they would become traumatized. This woman was already partway there. He steered her over to the Audi and waited as she climbed in, then with some difficulty pushed the door, which seemed to have a bent hinge, closed.

As he did so, he saw a PCSO running over towards him. 'Any more of you around?' Pattenden asked him.

'Yes, sir.' The man pointed at two more Police Community Support Officers approaching, a short distance away along the pavement.

'OK, good. I want you to stay here and make sure this lady does not leave her vehicle.'

Then he ran towards the two PCSOs, delegating each of them to scene-guard at either end of the crash site and to log anyone crossing the police line.

At this point, to his relief, he saw the reassuring sight of his inspector, James Biggs, accompanied by his duty sergeant, Paul Wood, coming, grim-faced, through the rain towards him, both men holding a reel of police tape and a police traffic cone under each arm.

At least now the buck no longer stopped with him.

13

Carly sat numbly in her car, grateful for the rain which coated the windscreen and the side windows like frosted glass, at least making her invisible and giving her some privacy. She was aware of the dark figure of the PCSO standing like a sentry outside. Her chest was pounding. The radio was on, tuned as it always was to the local news and chat station, BBC Radio Sussex. She could hear the lively voice of Neil Pringle, but wasn't taking in anything he said.

The image of what was going on underneath the lorry behind her was going round and round inside her head. Suddenly Pringle's voice was interrupted by a traffic announcement that Portland Road in Hove was closed due to a serious accident.

Her accident.

The car clock said 9.21.

Shit. She dialled her office and spoke to her cheery secretary, Suzanne. Halfway through telling her that she did not know when she would be in and asking her to phone the chiropodist, she broke down in tears.

She hung up, debating whether to phone her mother next or her best friend, Sarah Ellis. Sarah, who worked at a law firm in Crawley, had been her rock after Kes's death five years ago in an avalanche while skiing in Canada. She dialled her number, then listened to the phone ringing, hoping desperately she was free.

To her relief, Sarah answered on the fifth ring. But before Carly could get any words out, she started sobbing again.

Then she heard a tap on her window. A moment later, her car door opened and the police officer she had seen earlier, the one who had told her to wait in her car, peered in. He was a sturdy-looking man in his mid-thirties, with a serious face beneath his white cap, and was holding a small device that resembled some kind of meter.

'Would you mind stepping out of the car please, madam?'

'I'll call you back, Sarah,' she spluttered, then climbed out into the rain, her eyes blurry with tears.

The officer asked her again if she was the driver of the car, and then for her name and address. Then, holding a small instrument in a black and yellow weatherproof case, he addressed her in a stiffer, more formal tone. 'Because you have been involved in a road traffic collision, I require you to provide a specimen of breath. I must tell you that failure or refusal to do so is an offence for which you can be arrested. Do you understand?'

She nodded and sniffed.

'Have you drunk any alcohol in the past twenty minutes?'

How many people had an alcoholic drink before 9 a.m., she wondered? But then she felt a sudden panic closing in around her. Christ, how much had she drunk last night? Not that much, surely. It must be out of her system by now. She shook her head.

'Have you smoked in the last five minutes?'

'No,' she said. 'But I bloody need a fag now.' She was shaking and her throat felt tight.

Ignoring her comment, the officer asked her age.

'Forty-one.'

He tapped it into the machine, then made a further couple of entries before holding the machine out to her. A tube wrapped in cellophane protruded.

'If you could pull the sterile wrapper off for me.'

She obliged, exposing the narrow white plastic tube inside it.

'Thank you. I'd like you to take a deep breath, seal your lips around the tube and blow hard and continuously until I tell you to stop.'

Carly took a deep breath, then exhaled. She kept waiting for him to tell her to stop, but he stayed silent. Just as her lungs started to feel spent, she heard a beep, and he nodded his head. 'Thank you.'

He showed her the dial of the machine. On it were the words *sample taken*. Then he stepped back, studying the machine for some moments.

She watched his face anxiously, shaking even more now with nerves. Suddenly, his expression hardened and he said, 'I'm sorry to tell you that you have failed the breath test.' He held the machine up so she could read the dial again. The one word on it: *fail.*

She felt her legs giving way. Aware that a man was watching her from inside the café, she steadied herself against the side of her car. This wasn't possible. She could not have failed. She just couldn't have.

'Madam, this device is indicating that you may be over the prescribed limit and I'm arresting you for providing a positive breath sample. You do not have to say anything, but it may harm your defence if you do not mention when questioned something which you may later rely on in court. Anything you say may be given in evidence.'

She shook her head. 'It's not possible, she said. 'I didn't – I haven't – I was out last night, but—'

A few minutes ago Carly could not have imagined her day getting any worse. Now she was walking through the rain, being steered by the guiding arm of a police officer towards a marked car just beyond a line of police tape. She saw two ambulances, two fire engines and a whole host of other police vehicles. A tarpaulin had been erected around the rear section of the lorry and her imagination went into hyperdrive, guessing what was happening on the far side of it.

There was a terrible, almost preternatural stillness. She was vaguely aware of the steady patter of the rain, that was all. She walked past a fluorescent yellow jacket lying on the road. It had the word POLICE stencilled on the back and she wondered why it had been discarded.

A tall, thin man with two cameras slung around his neck snapped her picture as she ducked under the tape. 'I'm from the *Argus* newspaper. Can I have your name please?' he asked her.

She said nothing, the words 'I'm arresting you' spinning around inside her head. She climbed lamely into the rear of the BMW estate and fumbled for the seat belt. The officer slammed the door on her.

The slam felt as final as a chapter of her life ending.

14

'Dust. OK? See that? Can't you see that?'

The young woman stared blankly at where her boss was pointing. Her English wasn't too good and she had a problem understanding her, because the woman spoke so quickly that all her words seem to get joined together into one continuous, nasally undulating whine.

Did this idiot maid have defective vision or something? Fernanda Revere strutted angrily across the kitchen in her cerise Versace jogging suit and Jimmy Choo trainers, her wrist bangles clinking. A slightly built woman of forty-five, her looks surgically enhanced in a number of places and her wrinkles kept at bay with regular Botox, she exuded constant nervous energy.

Her husband, Lou, hunched on a barstool in the kitchen's island unit, was eating his breakfast bagel and doing his best to ignore her. Today's *Wall Street Journal* was on the Kindle lying beside his plate and President Obama was on the television above him.

Fernanda stopped in front of twin marble sinks that were wide enough to dunk a small elephant in. The vast bay window had a fine view across the rain-lashed manicured lawn, the shrubbery at the end and the dunes beyond, down to the sandy Long Island Sound beachfront and the Atlantic Ocean. On the floor was a megaphone which her husband used, on the rare occasions when he actually asserted himself, to shout threats at hikers who tramped over the dunes, which were a nature reserve.

But she wasn't looking out of the window at this moment.

She ran her index finger along one of the shelves above the sinks and held it up inches in front of her maid's eyes.

'See that, Mannie? You know what that is? It's called *dust.*'

The young woman stared uncomfortably at the dark grey smudge on her boss's elegant manicured finger. She could also see the almost impossibly long varnished nail. And the diamond-encrusted Cartier watch on her wrist. She could smell her Jo Malone perfume.

Fernanda Revere tossed her short, peroxide-blonde hair angrily, then she wiped the dust off the finger on the bridge of her maid's nose. The young woman flinched.

'You'd better understand something, Mannie. I don't allow dust in my house, got that? You want to stay here working for me or you want to go on the next plane back to the Philippines?'

'Hon!' said her husband. 'Give it a break. The poor kid's learning.'

Lou Revere looked back up at Obama on the television. The President was involved in a new diplomatic initiative in Palestine. Lou could do with Obama's diplomacy in this house, he decided.

Fernanda rounded on her husband. 'I don't listen to you when you wear those clothes. You look too dumb to say anything intelligent in them.'

'These are my golf clothes, OK? The same as I always wear.'

The ones that made him look ridiculous, she thought.

He grabbed the remote, tempted to turn the sound up and drown her voice out.

'Jesus, what's wrong with them?'

'What's wrong with them? You look like you're wearing a circus clown's pants and a pimp's shirt. You look so – so . . .' She flapped her hands, searching for the right word. 'Stupid!'

Then she turned to the maid. 'Don't you agree? Doesn't my husband look stupid?'

Mannie said nothing.

'I mean, why do you all have to dress like circus clowns to play golf?'

'It's partly so we can see each other easily on the course,' he said defensively.

'Why don't you just wear flashing lights on your heads, instead?' She looked up at the clock on the wall, then immediately checked her watch: 9.20. Time for her yoga class. 'See you later.' She gave him a quick, loveless wave of her hand, as if she were brushing away a fly.

They used to embrace and kiss, even if they were only going to be apart for half an hour. Lou couldn't remember when that had stopped – and in truth he didn't care any more.

'Seeing Dr Gottlieb today, hon?' he asked.

'He's just so stupid, too. Yes, I'm seeing him. But I think I'm going to change. I need a different shrink. Paulina, in my yoga class, is seeing someone who's a lot better. Gottlieb's useless.'

'Ask him for stronger medication.'

'You want him to turn me into a zombie or something?'

Lou said nothing.

15

Carly sat in the back of the police car, trails of rain sliding down the window beside her, tears sliding down her cheeks. They were heading up a hill on the A27. She stared out at the familiar grassy landscape of the Brighton outskirts, which were blurred by the film of water on the glass. She felt detached, as if out of her body and watching herself.

Scared and confused, she kept seeing that cyclist underneath the lorry. Then the white van in her rear-view mirror that had disappeared, like a ghost.

Had she imagined the van? Had she struck the cyclist? The past hour was as fogged in her mind as the view through the glass. She clenched and unclenched her hands, listening to the intermittent crackle and bursts of words that came through the radio. The car smelled of damp anoraks.

'Do you – do you think he's going to be all right?' she asked.

PC Pattenden replied to something on the radio, either not hearing or ignoring her. 'Hotel Tango Three Zero Four en route to Hollingbury with suspect,' he said, indicating left and taking the slip road.

Suspect.

She shivered, a knot tightening in her stomach. 'Do you think the cyclist is going to be OK?' she asked again, more loudly this time.

Pattenden glanced at her in the mirror. His white cap was on the front passenger seat beside him. 'I don't know,' he said, shuffling the wheel through his hands as he negotiated a mini-roundabout.

'He came out of nowhere, just straight at me. But I didn't hit him, I'm sure.'

They were heading downhill now. His eyes were on her, briefly, again. There was kindness in them behind the hardness.

'I should warn you that everything that's said in this car is recorded automatically.'

'Thank you,' she said.

'Let's hope he'll be OK,' Pattenden said. 'What about you? Are you OK?'

She was silent for a moment, then she shook her head.

He braked as they passed a vaguely art deco building that always reminded Carly of the superstructure of a tired old cruise ship. Several police cars were parked out the front. Ironically, she knew a lot about this building. There were photographs of it on the wall of the firm of quantity surveyors, BLB, for whom she had done legal work at the start of her career, when she'd been a trainee solicitor. The firm had managed the conversion of the premises from an American Express credit card manufacturing plant to its current use as the HQ CID for Sussex Police.

At the end of the building PC Pattenden slowed and turned sharp left up a driveway, then halted in front of a green reinforced-steel gate. There was a high spiked green fence to their right and behind it was a tall, drab brick structure. They had stopped beside a blue sign with white lettering announcing BRIGHTON CUSTODY CENTRE. The officer reached out of the window and swiped a plastic card. Moments later the gate began sliding open.

They drove up a steep ramp towards a row of what looked like factory loading bays at the rear of the brick building, then turned left into one of them, and into semi-darkness, out of the rain. Pattenden climbed out and opened the rear door, holding Carly's arm firmly as she stepped from the car. It felt more like he wanted to stop her running away than to support her.

There was a green door ahead, with a small viewing window. He swiped his card on a panel, the door slid open and he ushered her forward into a bare, narrow room about fifteen feet long and eight wide. The door closed behind them. At the far end of the room was another identical door. The walls were painted a stark, institutional cream and the floor was made of some speckled brown substance. There was no furniture in here at all, just a hard, bare bench with a green surface.

'Take a seat,' he said.

She sat down, resting her chin against her knuckles, feeling badly in need of a cigarette. No chance. Then her phone rang.

She fumbled with the clasp of her handbag and pulled the phone out. But before she could answer the officer shook his head.

'You'll have to switch that off, I'm afraid.' He pointed at a sign on the wall which read: NO MOBILE PHONES TO BE USED IN THE CUSTODY AREA.

She stared at him for a moment, trying to remember what the law was about making calls when you were arrested. But she'd only done a tiny bit of criminal law in her studies – it wasn't her area – and she didn't have the will at this moment to argue. If she complied, just did everything she was told, then maybe this nightmare would end quickly and she could go to the office. As for her particularly demanding client, she'd have to see him another day, but she absolutely had to be in the office for 2 p.m. for a conference with the barrister and another client, a woman who was due in court tomorrow morning for a hearing about financial matters in her divorce. Missing that meeting was not an option.

She switched off the phone and was about to put it back in her bag when he held out his hand, looking embarrassed.

'I'm sorry, but I'm going to have to take that phone off you for forensic analysis.'

'My phone?' she asked, angry and bewildered.

'I'm sorry,' he repeated, taking it from her.

Then she stared at the bare wall in front of her. At another laminated plastic notice stuck to it: ALL DETAINED PERSONS WILL BE THOROUGHLY SEARCHED BY THE CUSTODY OFFICER. IF YOU HAVE ANY PROHIBITED ITEMS ON YOUR PERSON OR IN YOUR PROPERTY TELL THE CUSTODY AND ARRESTING OFFICER NOW.

Then she read another: YOU HAVE BEEN ARRESTED. YOU WILL HAVE YOUR FINGERPRINTS, PHOTOGRAPH, DNA TAKEN RIGHT AWAY.

She tried to think exactly how much she had drunk last night. Two glasses of Sauvignon Blanc in the pub – or was it three? Then a Cosmopolitan at the restaurant. Then more wine over dinner.

Shit.

The door beyond her slid open. The officer gestured for her to go through, then followed, staying close to her. His prisoner.

She walked into a large, brightly lit room dominated by a raised semicircular central station made from a shiny, speckled grey composite and divided into sections. Behind each section sat men and women dressed in white shirts with black epaulettes and black ties. Around the edge of the room were green metal doors and internal windows looking on to what were probably interview rooms. It felt like another world in here.

In front of one section she saw a tall, balding, slovenly man in a shell suit and trainers, with a uniformed police officer wearing blue rubber gloves at his side, searching his pockets. In front of another, there was a gloomy youth in baggy clothes, hands cuffed behind his back, with an officer on either side of him.

Her own officer steered her across to the console and up to the counter, which was almost head-high. Behind it sat an impassive-looking man in his forties. He wore a white shirt with three stripes on each epaulette and a black tie. His demeanour was pleasant but he had the air of a man who had never, in his entire life, allowed the wool to be pulled over his eyes.

On a blue video monitor screen, set into the face of the counter, at eye level, Carly read:

DON'T LET PAST OFFENCES COME BACK TO HAUNT YOU.

A POLICE OFFICER WILL SPEAK TO YOU ABOUT ADMITTING OTHER CRIMES YOU HAVE COMMITTED.

She listened numbly as PC Pattenden outlined the circumstances of her arrest. Then the shirt-sleeved man spoke directly to her, his voice earnest, almost as if he was doing her a favour.

'I am Custody Sergeant Cornford. You have heard what has been said. I'm authorizing your detention for the purpose of securing and preserving evidence and to obtain evidence by questioning. Is that clear to you?'

Carly nodded.

He passed across the counter to her a folded yellow A4 sheet that was headed SUSSEX POLICE NOTICE OF RIGHTS AND ENTITLE-MENTS.

'You may find this helpful, Mrs Chase. You have the right to have someone informed of your arrest and to see a solicitor. Would you like us to provide you with a duty solicitor?'

'I'm a solicitor,' she said. 'I'd like you to contact one of my colleagues, Ken Acott at Acott Arlington.'

Carly got some small satisfaction from seeing the frown that crossed his face. Ken Acott was widely regarded as the top criminal solicitor in the city.

'May I have his number?'

Carly gave him the office number, hoping Ken was not in court today.

'I will make that call,' the Custody Sergeant said. 'But I am required to inform you that although you have a right to see a solicitor, the drink-driving process may not be delayed. I am authorizing you to be searched.' He then produced two green plastic trays and spoke into his intercom.

PC Pattenden handed Carly's phone to the sergeant and stepped aside as a young uniformed woman police officer walked across, snapping on a pair of blue gloves. She studied Carly for a moment, expressionless, before beginning to pat her down, starting with her head and rummaging in each of her coat pockets. Then she asked her to remove her boots and socks, knelt down and searched between each of her toes.

Carly said nothing, feeling utterly humiliated. The woman then scanned her with a metal detector, put that instrument down and started emptying out her handbag. She placed Carly's purse, her car keys, a packet of Kleenex, her lipstick and compact, chewing gum and then, to her embarrassment, as she saw PC Pattenden eyeing everything, a Tampax into one of the trays.

When the woman had finished, Carly signed a receipt, then PC Pattenden led her into a small side room, where she was finger-printed by a cheery male officer, also in blue gloves. Finally he took a swab of her mouth for DNA.

Next, holding a yellow form, PC Pattenden escorted her out, past the console, up a step and into a narrow room that felt like a laboratory. There was a row of white kitchen units to her left, followed by a sink and a fridge, and a grey and blue machine at the far end, with a video monitor on the top. To her right was a wooden desk and two blue chairs. The walls were plastered in notices.

She read: NO MORE THAN ONE DETAINEE IN THIS ROOM AT A TIME, THANK YOU.

Then: YOU'LL COME BACK.

Next to that was a sign in red with white letters: WANT TO GO THROUGH THIS AGAIN?

PC Pattenden pointed at a wall-mounted camera. 'OK, what I must tell you now is that everything seen and heard in this room is recorded. Do you understand?'

'Yes.'

The officer then told her about the breath-test machine. He explained that he required her to give two breath specimens and that the lower of the readings would be taken. If the reading was above 40 but below 51 she would have the further option of providing a blood or urine sample.

She blew into the tube, desperately hoping that she was now below the limit and this nightmare – or at least this part of it – would be over.

'I can't believe it. I didn't drink that much – really, I didn't.'

'Now blow again for the second test,' he said calmly.

Some moments later he showed her the printout of the first test. To her horror it was 55. Then he showed her the second reading.

It was also 55.

16

Roy Grace's phone rang in the hospital room. Releasing his grip on Cleo's hand he tugged it out of his pocket and answered it.

It was Glenn Branson, sounding in work mode. 'Yo, chief. How is she?'

'OK, thanks. She'll be fine.'

Cleo looked up at him and he stroked her forehead with his free hand. Then she suddenly winced.

He covered the mouthpiece, alarmed. 'You OK?'

She nodded and smiled thinly. 'Bump just kicked.'

Glenn Branson said, 'We've had a call from Inspector James Biggs, Traffic. A fatal at Portland Road. Sound like a hit and run. They're requesting assistance from Major Crime Branch as it looks like death by dangerous driving or possibly manslaughter.'

As the duty Senior Investigating Officer for the week, Roy Grace was in charge of any Major Crime inquiries that came in. This would be a good opportunity for Glenn, whom he considered his protégé, to show his abilities, he decided.

'Are you free?'

'Yes.'

'OK, organize a Crime Scene Manager for them, then go down yourself and help the rats. See if they've got everything they need.'

Rats were known to eat their own young and traffic officers had long been known as the *Black Rats*. This dated back to the time when all police cars were black and was because of their reputation for booking other police officers and even members of their own family. Some of them today wore a black rat badge with pride.

'I'm on my way.'

As Grace put his phone back in his pocket, Cleo took his hand.

'I'm OK, darling. Go back to work,' she said. 'Really, I'm fine.'

He turned and looked at her dubiously, then kissed her on the forehead. 'I love you.'

'I love you too,' she said.

'I don't want to leave you here.'

'You have to get out there and catch bad guys. I want them all locked up before Bump is born!'

He smiled. She looked so frail, so vulnerable, lying in this bed. With their child inside her. Cleo's life and the life of their unborn child hanging on a thread more slender than he wanted to think about. Cleo was such a strong and positive person. It was one of the thousands of qualities about her that he had fallen in love with. It seemed impossible that things could go wrong. That their child could be threatening her life. She would get through this. She would be fine. Somehow. Whatever it took.

It was Cleo who had given him his life back after the years of hell following Sandy's disappearance. Surely she could not be taken away from him?

He stared at her face, her pale, soft complexion, her blue eyes, her exquisite snub nose, her long, graceful neck, her pursed-lip grin of defiance, and he knew, he absolutely *knew*, it was all going to be OK.

'We'll be fine, Bump and me!' she said, squeezing his hand, as if reading his mind. 'Just a few teething problems. Go back to your office and make the world a safer place for Bump and me!'

*

He stayed for another hour, waiting to get a chance to speak privately to Mr Holbein, the consultant gynaecologist, but the man was not able to add much to what he had already said. It was going to be a case of taking things one day at a time from now on.

After saying goodbye to Cleo and promising to return later in the day, he drove out of the hospital and down to Eastern Road. He should have turned left and headed around the outskirts of the city back to his office. But instead he turned right, towards Portland Road and the accident.

Like many colleagues in the Major Crime Branch, murders fascinated him. He'd long become immune to the most grisly of crime scenes, but road fatalities were different. They almost always disturbed him – a tad too close to home. But what he needed right now was the solace of his mate, Glenn Branson. Not that the DS, who was going through a marriage break-up from hell, was exactly a comfort zone much of the time at the moment, but he had at least been in a cheerier mood this morning than Grace had seen him in for a while.

What's more, Grace had a plan to lift him from his gloom. He wanted Glenn to try for promotion to Inspector this year. He had the ability and he possessed that most essential quality for all good coppers: a high degree of emotional intelligence. If he could just lift his friend out of his screwed-up mental state over his marriage, he was convinced he could get him there.

The mid-morning Brighton traffic was light and the rain had eased to a thin drizzle. Portland Road, with its shops and cafés, surrounded by large residential areas, was normally busy at most times of the day and night, but as Grace turned the silver Ford Focus into it, it was as quiet as a ghost town. A short distance ahead he saw a Road Policing Unit BMW estate parked sideways in the middle of the road, with crime scene tape beyond it, a uniformed PCSO scene guard with his log and a gaggle of rubberneckers, some snapping away with cameras and phones.

Beyond the tape was a hive of quiet, businesslike activity. He saw a large articulated lorry, its rear section screened off by a green tarpaulin. A black Audi convertible on the opposite side of the road against a café wall. A fire engine and the dark green coroner's van, beside which he noticed the slim, youthful figure of Darren Wallace, Cleo's Assistant Anatomical Pathology Technician, as the deputy chief mortician was known, and his colleague, Walter Hordern, a dapper, courteous man in his mid-forties. Both were smartly dressed in anoraks over their white shirts, black ties, black trousers and black shoes.

Further along was another tape across the road, a scene guard and another RPU vehicle parked sideways, with more rubberneckers just beyond. Alongside it were a VOSA – a Vehicle and Operator Services Agency – inspection van and a Collision Investigation Unit van.

He saw several police officers he recognized, including the uniformed Road Policing Unit Inspector, James Biggs, and a SOCO photographer, James Gartrell, working away methodically. Some of them were combing the road and one senior Road Collision Investigation Unit officer he knew well, Colin O'Neill, was walking the area and taking notes, while talking to Glenn Branson, to Tracy Stocker, the Major Crime Branch Crime Scene Manager, and to the Coroner's Officer, Philip Keay. Unlike at most crime scenes, none of those present was wearing protective suits and overshoes. RTC sites were generally considered already too contaminated.

A buckled bicycle lay on the road, with a numbered yellow crime scene marker beside it. There was another marker next to some debris that looked like a broken bicycle lamp. A short distance behind the lorry he saw a fluorescent jacket covering something, with another marker beside that. More markers were dotted around.

Before he had a chance to hail Branson, suddenly, materializing out of the ether, as he seemed to do at every crime scene Grace attended these days, was Kevin Spinella, the young crime reporter from the local paper, the *Argus*. In his mid-twenties, with bright eyes and a thin face, he was chewing gum with small, sharp teeth that always reminded Grace of a rat. His short hair was matted to his head by the rain and he was wearing a dark mackintosh with the collar turned up, a loud tie with a massive knot and tasselled loafers.

'Good morning, Detective Superintendent!' he said. 'A bit nasty, isn't it?'

'The weather?' Grace said.

Spinella grinned, making a curious movement with his jaw, as if a piece of gum had got stuck in the wrong place.

'Na! You know what I'm talking about. Sounds like it could be a murder from what I hear – is that what you think?'

Grace was guarded, but tried to avoid being openly rude to the man. The police needed the local media on their side as they could be immensely useful. But equally, he knew, they could at times bite you hard and painfully.

'You tell me. I've only just arrived, so you probably know more than I do.'

'Witnesses I've spoken to are talking about a white van that went through a red light and hit the cyclist, then accelerated off at high speed.'

'You should be a detective,' Grace said, seeing Glenn Branson making a beeline towards him.

'Think I'll stick to reporting. Anything you'd like to tell me?'

Yes. Fuck off, Grace thought. Instead, he replied pleasantly, 'Anything we find out, you'll be the first to know.' He nearly added, You always are anyway, even if we don't tell you.

It was an ongoing cause of irritation to Roy Grace that Spinella had a mole inside Sussex Police that enabled him always to get to the scene of any crime way ahead of the rest of the press pack. For the past year he had been quietly digging away to discover that person's identity, but so far he had made no progress. One day, though, he promised himself, he would hang that creep out to dry.

He turned away, signed his name on the log and ducked under the tape to greet Glenn Branson. Then they both walked off towards the lorry, safely out of earshot of the reporter.

'What have you got?' Grace asked.

'Young male under the lorry. They've found a student ID card. His name's Anthony Revere, he's at Brighton Uni. Someone's gone there to get his full details and next of kin. From what the Collision Investigation Unit's been able to piece together so far, seems like he came out of a side road – St Heliers Avenue – turned right, east, on the wrong side of Portland Road, causing that Audi travelling west to swerve on to the pavement. He was then hit by a white van that had gone through the red light, a Transit or similar, that was behind the Audi, also travelling west. The van flipped him across the road, under the wheels of the artic, which was travelling east. Then the van did a runner.'

Grace thought for a moment. 'Anyone ID the driver?'

Branson shook his head. 'There are a lot of witnesses. I've got a team covering the area for any CCTV footage. I've put an alert out to the RPU to stop any white van within two hours' driving distance of here. But that's kind of needle in a haystack territory.'

Grace nodded. 'No registration?'

'Not yet – but with luck we'll get something from a CCTV.'

'What about the drivers of the Audi and the lorry?'

'Woman Audi driver's in custody – failed a breath test. Lorry driver's in shock. Colin O'Neill from the Collision Investigation Unit's had a look at his tachometer – he's way out of hours.'

'Well, that's all looking great, then,' Grace said sarcastically. 'A drunk driver in one vehicle, an exhausted one in another and a third who's scarpered.'

'We do have one piece of evidence so far,' Branson said. 'They've found part of a damaged wing mirror that looks like it's from the van. It has a serial number on it.'

Grace nodded. 'Good.' Then he pointed along the road. 'What's under the fluorescent jacket?'

'The cyclist's right leg.'

Grace swallowed. 'Glad I asked.'

17

Specially trained Family Liaison Officers were used whenever possible but, depending on circumstances and availability, any member of the police force could find themselves delivering a death message. It was the least popular duty, and officers of the Road Policing Unit tended, reluctantly, to get the lion's share.

PC Tony Omotoso was a muscular, stocky black officer with ten years' experience in the unit, who'd once had his own brush with death on a police motorcycle. Despite all the horrors he had seen, and experienced personally, he remained cheerful and positive, and was always courteous, even to the worst offenders he encountered.

His first task had been to make next-of-kin enquiries from the information that he'd found in the victim's rucksack, which had been lying underneath the lorry. The most useful item in it had been the deceased's student card from Brighton University.

A visit to the registrar's office at the university had revealed that Tony Revere was a US citizen, twenty-one years old and cohabiting with another student, Susan Caplan, who was English, from Brighton. No one had seen her on campus today and she wasn't due to attend any lectures until tomorrow, so it was likely that she was at home. The university had the contact details of Revere's family in New York, but Omotoso and the registrar made the decision that Susan Caplan should be informed first. Hopefully she would have more details about him and would be able to formally identify his body.

As much for moral support as anything else, Omotoso drove back down to the incident scene and collected his regular shift partner, PC Ian Upperton. A tall, lean officer with fair hair cropped to a fuzz, Upperton had a young family. Bad accidents were a part of his everyday routine, but those involving youngsters, such as this, were the ones he took home with him, like most officers.

He greeted PC Omotoso's request to join him with a resigned

shrug. In the Road Policing Unit you learned to get on with the job, however grim. And once a week, on average, it would be really grim. Last Sunday afternoon, he had found himself sweeping up the body parts of a motorcyclist. Three days later he was now heading off to deliver a death message.

If you allowed it to get to you, you were sunk, so he tried as hard as he could never to let it. But sometimes, like now, he just couldn't help it. Particularly as he himself had recently bought a bicycle.

They were both silent as Tony Omotoso drove the marked police car slowly down Westbourne Villas, a wide street that ran south from New Church Road to the seafront. Both of them peered out at the numbers on the large detached and semi-detached Victorian properties. Every few seconds the wipers made a sudden *clunk-clunk* against the light drizzle, then fell silent. Ahead of them, beyond the end of the street, the restless waters of the English Channel were a dark, ominous grey.

Like their hearts.

'Coming up on the right,' Upperton said.

They parked the car outside a semi-detached house that looked surprisingly smart for student accommodation, then walked along the black and white tiled path to the front door, tugging on their caps. Both of them looked at the Entryphone panel with its list of names. Number 8 read: *Caplan/Revere*.

PC Omotoso pressed the button.

Both of them were secretly hoping there would be no answer.

There wasn't.

He pressed the buzzer again. Give it a few more tries, then they could leave and with any luck it might become someone else's problem.

But to his dismay there was a crackle of static, followed by a sleepy-sounding voice.

'Hello?'

'Susan Caplan?' he asked.

'Yes. Who is it?'

'Sussex Police. May we come in, please?'

There was a silence lasting a couple of seconds but felt much longer. Then, 'Police, did you say?'

Omotoso and Upperton shot each other a glance. They were both experienced enough to know that a knock on the door from the police was something that was rarely welcomed.

'Yes. We'd like to speak to you, please,' Omotoso said pleasantly but firmly.

'Uh – yuh. Come up to the second floor, door at the top. Are you calling about my handbag?'

'Your handbag?' he said, thrown by the question.

Moments later there was a rasping buzz, followed by a sharp click. Omotoso pushed the door open and they went into a hallway which smelled of last night's cooking – something involving boiled vegetables – and a faint hint of old wood and old carpet. Two bicycles leaned against the wall. There was a crude rack of pigeon-hole mail boxes and several advertising leaflets for local takeaways were lying on the floor. The exterior might look smart, but the common parts inside looked tired.

They walked up the manky, threadbare stair carpet and, as they reached the top of the second flight, a door with flaking paintwork directly in front of them opened. A pretty girl, about twenty, Omotoso estimated, parcelled in a large white bath towel and barefoot, greeted them with a sleepy smile. Her shoulder-length dark hair was in need of some attention.

'Don't tell me you've found it!' she said. 'That would be amazing!'

Both men courteously removed their caps. As they entered the narrow hallway of the flat, there was a smell of brewing coffee and a tinge of masculine cologne in the air.

Tony Omotoso said, 'Found what?'

'My handbag?' She squinted at them quizzically.

'Handbag?'

'Yes. The one some shit stole at Escape Two while we were dancing on Saturday night.'

It was a nice flat, he clocked, walking into the open-plan living area, but untidy and sparsely furnished, in typical student fashion. It had polished bare oak flooring, a big flat-screen television, expensive-looking hi-fi and minimalistic but tatty dark brown leather furniture. A laptop on a desk near the window overlooking the street was switched on, showing a Facebook homepage. Strewn haphazardly around the floor were a pair of trainers, a screwed-up cardigan, female panties, a single white sock, piles of paperwork, a half-empty coffee mug, several DVDs, an iPod with earphones plugged in and the remains of a Chinese takeaway.

It had been Ian Upperton who'd had to break the news last time they had done this, so they had agreed between them that today it was Omotoso's turn. Every officer had their own way of doing it and Omotoso favoured the gentle but direct approach.

'No, Susan, we haven't come about your handbag – I don't know about that, I'm afraid. We're from the Road Policing Unit,' he said, registering her sudden look of confusion. 'According to the records from Brighton University, you are living with Tony Revere. Is that correct?'

She nodded, eyeing each of them with sudden suspicion.

'I'm afraid that Tony has been involved in a road traffic accident on his bicycle.'

She stared at him, suddenly fixated.

'I'm sorry to say, Susan, that following the injuries he received he didn't survive.'

He fell silent deliberately. It had long been his policy to let the recipient of the message come out with the words themselves. That way, he found, it sank in better and more immediately.

'You mean Tony's dead?' she said.

'I'm very sorry, yes.'

She started reeling. PC Upperton caught her arm and guided her down, on to the large brown sofa opposite a glass coffee table. She sat there in silence for some moments, while the two officers stood awkwardly. There was never an easy way. Each time the reaction was different. Susan Caplan's was to fall silent and then start to shake, little tremors rippling through her body.

They remained standing. She was shaking her head from side to side now. 'Oh shit!' she said suddenly. 'Oh shit.' Then she seemed to collapse in on herself, burying her face in her hands. 'Oh shit, please tell me it's not true.'

The two officers glanced at each other. Tony Omotoso said, 'Do you have someone who could come round and be with you today? A girlfriend? Any member of your family you'd like us to call?'

She closed her eyes tight. 'What happened?'

'He was in a collision with a lorry, but we don't have all the details.'

There was a long silence. She hugged herself and began sobbing.

'Susan, do you have a neighbour who could come round?' Omotoso asked.

'No. I – I don't – I – we – I – oh shit, shit, shit.'

'Would you like a drink?' Ian Upperton asked. 'Can we make you a cup of tea or coffee?'

'I don't want a sodding drink, I want my Tony,' she sobbed. 'Please tell me what happened?'

Omotoso's radio crackled. He turned the volume right down. There was another long silence before eventually he said, 'We're going to need to make sure it is Tony Revere. Would you be willing to identify the body later today? Just in case there's been a mistake?'

'His mother's a control freak,' she blurted. 'She's the one you're going to have to speak to.'

'I'll speak to anyone you'd like me to, Susan. Do you have her number?'

'She's in New York – in the Hamptons. She hates my guts.'

'Why's that?'

'She'll be on the first plane over, I can tell you that.'

'Would you prefer her to identify Tony?'

She fell silent again, sobbing. Then she said, 'You'd better get her to do that. She'd never believe me anyway.'

18

Tooth was small. It was an issue he'd had to deal with since childhood. He used to be picked on by other kids because of his size. But not many of them had ever picked on him twice.

He was one of the tiniest babies Brooklyn obstetrician Harvey Shannon had ever delivered, although he wasn't premature. His mother, who was so off her face with junk she hadn't figured out she was pregnant for six months, had gone to full term. Dr Shannon wasn't even sure that she realized she had actually given birth, and staff at the hospital told him she kept looking at the infant in bewilderment, as if trying to figure out where it had come from.

But the obstetrician was worried about a bigger problem. The boy had a central nervous system that seemed to be wired all wrong. He appeared to have no pain receptors. You could stick a needle in the tiny mite's arm and get no reaction, while all normal babies would bawl their lungs out. There were any number of possible causes, but the most likely, he figured, was the mother's substance abuse.

Tooth's mother died from a rogue batch of heroin when he was three, and he spent most of his childhood being shunted around America from one foster home to the next. He never stayed long because no one liked him. He scared people.

At the age of eleven, when other kids began taunting him about his size, he learned to defend himself by studying martial arts and soon responded by hurting anyone who angered him, badly. So badly he never stayed in any school for more than a few months, because other kids were too frightened of him and the teachers requested he be moved.

At his final school he learned how to make a buck out of his abnormality. Using his martial arts skills of self-control, he could hold his breath for up to five minutes, beating anyone who tried to challenge him. His other trick was to let kids punch him in the stomach as hard as they liked, for a dollar a go. For five bucks they could stick a ballpoint pen into his arm or leg. Letting them do this was the closest he ever came to any of his fellow pupils. He'd never had an actual friend in his life. At the age of forty-one he still didn't. Just his dog, Yossarian.

But Tooth and his dog weren't so much friends as *associates*. Same as the people he worked for. The dog was an ugly thing. It had different-colour eyes, one bright red, the other grey, and looked like the progeny of a Dalmatian that had been screwed by a pug. He'd named it after a character in one of the few books he'd read all the way through, *Catch-22*. The book started with a character called Yossarian irrationally falling in love, at first sight, with his chaplain. This dog had fallen irrationally in love with him at first sight, too. It had just started following him, in a street in Beverly Hills four years ago, when he was casing a house for a hit.

It was one of those wide, quiet, swanky streets with bleached-looking elm trunks, big detached houses and gleaming metal in the driveway. All the houses had lawns that looked like they'd been trimmed with nail scissors, the sprinklers *thwack-thwacking* away, looked after by armies of Hispanic gardeners.

The dog was wrong for the street. It was mangy and one eye was infected. Tooth didn't know a thing about dogs, but this one didn't look much like any recognizable breed and it didn't look designer enough to have come from this area. Maybe it had jumped out of a Hispanic's truck. Maybe someone had thrown it out of a car here in the hope of some rich person taking pity on it.

Instead it had found him.

Tooth gave it food, but no sympathy.

He didn't do sympathy.

19

'What – what happens now?' Carly asked the police officer.

'I'd like you to sign your name here,' Dan Pattenden said, handing her a long thin strip of white paper, which was headed SUBJECT TEST. Halfway down it had her name, date of birth and the words SUBJECT SIGNATURE. Below was a box containing the words *Specimen 1: – 10.42 a.m. – 55* and *Specimen 2: 10.45 a.m. – 55*.

With her hand shaking so much she could barely hold the pen he gave her, she signed her name.

'I'm going to take you to a cell where you'll wait for your solicitor to arrive,' he said, signing the same form along the bottom. 'You will be interviewed with your solicitor.'

'I have a really important meeting with a client,' she said. 'I have to get to the office.'

He gave her a sympathetic smile. 'I'm afraid that everyone involved in the incident has something important to do today, but it's not up to me.' He pointed to the door and gently, holding her right arm, escorted her towards it. Then he stopped and answered his radio phone as it crackled into life.

'Dan Pattenden,' he said. There was a brief silence. 'I see. Thank you, guv. I'm up at Custody now with my prisoner.'

Prisoner. The word made her shudder.

'Yes, sir, thank you.' He clipped the phone back in its holder on his chest and turned to her. His expression was blank, unreadable. 'I'm sorry, but I'm now going to repeat the caution I gave you earlier at the collision scene. Mrs Chase, I'm rearresting you now on suspicion of causing death by driving while under the influence of alcohol. You do not have to say anything, but it may harm your defence if you do not mention when questioned something which you may later rely on in court. Anything you say may be given in evidence.'

She felt her throat constricting, as if a ligature was being tightened. Her mouth was suddenly parched.

'The cyclist has died?' Her words came out almost as a whisper.

'Yes, I'm afraid so.'

'It wasn't me,' she said. 'I didn't hit him. I crashed because I was – because I avoided him. I swerved to avoid him because he was on the wrong side of the road. I would have hit him if I hadn't.'

'You'd best save all that for your interview.'

As he propelled her across the custody reception floor, past the large, round central station, she turned to him in sudden panic and said, 'My car – I need to get the RAC to collect it – I need to get it repaired – I—'

'We'll take care of it. I'm afraid it's going to have to be impounded.'

They began walking down a narrow corridor. They stopped at a green door with a small glass panel. He opened it and, to her horror, ushered her into a cell.

'You're not putting me in here?'

His phone crackled into life again and he answered it. As he did so, she stared at the cell in bewilderment. A small, narrow room with an open toilet and a hand basin set into the wall. At the far end was a hard bench, with a blue cushion behind it propped up against the wall. There was a sanitized reek of disinfectant.

PC Pattenden ended the call and turned back to her. 'This is where you will have to wait until your solicitor gets here.'

'But – but what about my car? When will it go to be repaired?'

'That will depend on what the Senior Investigating Officer decides, but it could be months before your car gets released.'

'Months?'

'Yes, I'm sorry. It will be the same for all the vehicles today.'

'What – what about my stuff in it?'

'You'll be able to collect personal belongings from the car pound it's taken to. You'll be notified where that is. I have to get back now, so I'm leaving you. OK?'

It was not OK. It was so totally not OK. But she was too shocked to argue. Instead she just nodded lamely.

Then he shut the door.

Carly stared up at a CCTV camera staring down at her. Then she turned towards the bench and looked at the frosted, panelled window set high above it. She sat down, not bothering with the cushion, trying to think straight.

But all she could focus on was the accident, replaying over and over in her mind. The white van behind her. The image of the cyclist underneath the lorry.

Dead.

There was a knock on the door and it opened. She saw a short, plump woman in a white shirt with black lapels and the word *Reliance Security* embroidered across her chest. The woman had a trolley laden with tired-looking paperback books.

'Something from the library?' she asked.

Carly shook her head. Her thoughts suddenly flashed to Tyler. He was staying late after school, having a cornet lesson.

Moments later the door shut again.

She suddenly felt badly in need of a pee, but there was no way she was going to squat here with a camera watching her. Then she felt a sudden surge of rage.

Sodding Preston Dave! If he hadn't been such a tosser she wouldn't have drunk so much. She hardly ever got smashed. Sure, she liked a glass of wine or two in the evening. But she never normally drank the way she had last night.

If only she had said no to him.

If only she had dropped Tyler at school just a few minutes earlier.

So many damned *if onlys*.

Dead.

The cyclist was dead.

One instant he had been riding straight at her. He'd come out of nowhere. Now he was dead.

But she had not hit him, she was sure of that.

He was on the wrong fucking side of the road, for God's sake! And now she was being blamed.

Suddenly her door opened. She saw a tall, thin man in a white shirt with black epaulettes. Standing next to him was the suave figure of one of the senior partners at her firm, Ken Acott.

Several of her colleagues said that the criminal lawyer reminded them of a younger Dustin Hoffman and at this moment he certainly looked like a movie star hero. With his short dark hair, sharp grey pinstripe suit and small black attaché case, he exuded an air of authority and confidence as he strode forward into the cell, the buckles of his Gucci loafers sparkling.

Acott had a well-deserved reputation as one of the best in the business. If anyone could sort out this mess she was in, he could.

Then the look of reassurance on his face cracked her up and, losing all her composure, she stumbled forward, towards him, her eyes welling with tears.

20

DEAD MAN'S GRIP

Shortly before 5 p.m., Roy Grace sat in his first-floor office in the Major Crime Branch of Sussex CID, sipping his mug of tea. It was almost stone cold, because he had been concentrating on searching on the Internet for anything he could find about Cleo's condition.

He didn't mind the tea, he was used to cold food and tepid drinks. Ever since he had joined the police force in his late teens, over twenty years ago, he had learned that getting anything to eat or drink at all was a luxury. If you were the kind of person who insisted on freshly ground coffee beans and healthy home cooking, you were in the wrong profession.

His mountain of paperwork seemed to grow of its own accord, as if it was some fast-breeding organism, and it seemed today that emails were pouring in faster than he could read them. But he was finding it hard to focus on anything other than Cleo. Since leaving the hospital this morning, he had made repeated calls to check. The ward sister was probably starting to think he was some kind of obsessive compulsive, but he didn't care.

He looked down at a thick file that was open on his desk. In his current role as Head of Major Crime, in addition to being an active Senior Investigating Officer, Grace was familiar with all the current cases in the entire Major Crime Branch. For some police officers, the work ended with the arrest of the suspect, but for him, that was merely the first stage. Securing convictions was in many ways far harder and more time-consuming than catching the villains in the first place.

The world he inhabited was filled with an endless succession of nasty people, but few came nastier than the overweight creep whose custody face-on and side profile photographs currently lay in front of him. Carl Venner, a former US Army officer, now residing in the remand wing at Sussex's Category-B prison, Lewes, had made himself a lucrative business out of snuff movies – films of real people being tortured and killed – which he sold on a subscription basis, via the Internet, to wealthy, extremely warped people. Glenn Branson had been shot during the arrest of this creep, which made it even more personal than usual. The trial was looming.

Taking a momentary break, Roy Grace leaned back in his chair and stared out of his window towards the south. The CID headquarters, Sussex House, was in an industrial estate on the outskirts of the city of Brighton and Hove. Directly below him he could see a skeletal tree, planted in the earth and surrounded by an oval-shaped brick wall, and the cracked concrete paving of the building's narrow car park. Beyond was a busy road with a steel barrier, on the far side of which, thinly masked by a row of trees, was the grey slab of an ASDA supermarket, which served as the unofficial canteen for this place. And beyond that, on a clear day, he could see the distant rooftops of Brighton and sometimes the blue of the English Channel. But today there was just a grey haze.

He watched a green ASDA articulated lorry pull out on to the road and begin to crawl up the hill, then he turned back to his screen, tapped the keyboard and brought up the serials, as he did every half-hour or so. This was the log of all reported incidents with their constant updates. Scanning through, he saw nothing new, other than the Portland Road accident, to interest him. Just the usual daily stuff. Road traffic collisions, a noisy-neighbour incident, a missing dog, assaults, burglaries, a van break-in, a stolen car, signings for bail, a broken shop window, a domestic, two bike thefts, suspicious youths spotted by a car, some chocolates stolen from a Tesco garage, a G5 (sudden death) of an elderly lady that was not suspicious – at this stage, anyway.

With the exception of a major rape case, on which Grace had been the Senior Investigating Officer, the first two months of the year had been relatively quiet. But since the start of spring, the whole city seemed to be kicking off. Three of the average twenty murders that Sussex could expect annually had taken place during the past six weeks. In addition there had been an armed robbery on a jewellery shop, resulting in an officer who had given chase being shot in the leg, and four days ago there had been a brutal stranger rape of a nurse walking along Brighton's seafront.

As a consequence, most of the four Major Incident Suites around the county had been in full use, including both the Major Incident Rooms here. Rather than relocate from Sussex House to the Major Crime Suite in Eastbourne, some thirty minutes' drive away, which had available space, Roy Grace had borrowed Jack Skerritt's office, next door to his, for the first briefing of *Operation Violin* – the name the computer had given to the hit-and-run fatality involving the cyclist in Portland Road this morning. The head of HQ CID was away on a course and had a much larger conference table than the small round one in Grace's office.

He planned to keep the inquiry team small and tight. From his study of the evidence so far, and the initial eyewitness reports, it seemed a straightforward case. The van driver could have had any number of reasons for doing what he did – possibly he had stolen the vehicle, or had no insurance, or was worried about being breathalysed, or was carrying something illegal. Grace did not think it would be a hard job to find him. His favoured Deputy Senior Investigating Officer, Lizzie Mantle, was away on leave, so he was using the opportunity to make Glenn his Deputy SIO for this case. It would be a good test of the Detective Sergeant's abilities, he thought – and it would help to distract him from his current marital problems. Further, it would give him an opportunity to really shine before his all-important boards for promotion to inspector, which would be coming up later this year, by showing his ability to manage real-life inquiries.

There was a knock on the door and DC Nick Nicholl entered. He was beanpole tall, wearing a grey suit that looked as if it had been made for someone even taller, and bleary-eyed, courtesy of his young baby. 'You said 5 p.m. for the briefing, guv?'

Grace nodded. He was holding the meeting earlier than his favoured 6.30 for evening briefings, because he was anxious to get back to the hospital and be with Cleo.

'Next door in Detective Chief Superintendent Skerritt's office.'

He followed the DC in there.

'I hear Cleo's in hospital. Is she OK?' Nick Nicholl asked.

'Thanks – yes, so far so good. I seem to remember your wife had problems during her pregnancy, Nick. Is that right?'

'Yeah, internal bleeding twice. First at about twenty-four weeks.'

'Sounds similar. But she was all right?'

'No, not at first.'

'It's a worrying time.'

'Yep, you could say that! You need to see she gets a lot of rest, that's vitally important.'

'Thanks, I will.'

Grace, who managed the police rugby team, was proud of having converted Nick Nicholl from football to rugby, and the young DC was a great wing three-quarter. Except that since the birth of his son some months ago, his focus tended to be elsewhere and he was often zapped of energy.

Nicholl sat down at the long meeting table and was followed a few moments later by Bella Moy. The Detective Sergeant was in her mid-thirties, cheery-faced beneath a tangle of hennaed brown hair and a little carelessly dressed; she carried a box of Maltesers in one hand and a bottle of water in the other. She was stuck in her life beyond work, caring for her elderly mother. Give her a makeover, Grace always thought, and she would be one attractive lady.

Next came DC Emma-Jane Boutwood. A slim girl with an alert face and long fair hair scooped up into a ponytail, the DC had made a miraculous recovery after being nearly killed by a stolen van the previous year.

She was followed by the shambling figure of DS Norman Potting. Because of the pension system in operation for the police, most officers took retirement after thirty years' service. The system worked against them if they stayed on longer. But Potting wasn't motivated by money. He liked being a copper and seemed determined to remain one as long as he possibly could. Thanks to the endless disasters of his private life, Sussex CID was the only family he had – although, with his old-school, politically incorrect attitudes, a lot of people, including the Chief Constable, Grace suspected, would have liked to see the back of him.

However, much though he irritated people at times, Grace couldn't help respecting the man. Norman Potting was a true copper in the golden sense of the word. A Rottweiler in a world increasingly full of politically correct pussycats. Pot-bellied, with a comb-over like a threadbare carpet, dressed in what looked like his father's demob suit from the Second World War, and smelling of pipe tobacco and mothballs, Potting sat down and exhaled loudly, making a sound like a squashed cushion. Bella Moy, who loathed the man, looked at him warily, wondering what he was about to say.

He did not disappoint her. In his gruff rural burr, Potting complained, 'What is it with this city and football? How come Manchester's got Man United, London's got the Gunners, Newcastle's got the Toon Army. What have we got in Brighton? The biggest bloody poofter colony in England!'

Bella Moy rounded on him. 'Have you ever kicked a football in your life?'

'Actually, yes, I have, Bella,' he said. 'You might not believe it, but I used to play for Portsmouth's second team when I was a lad. Centre half, I was. I was planning to be a professional footballer, until I got my kneecap shattered in a game.'

'I didn't know that,' Grace said.

Norman Potting shrugged, then blushed. 'I'm a Winston Churchill fan, chief. Always have been. Know what he said?'

Grace shook his head.

'Success is the ability to go from one failure to another, with no loss of enthusiasm.' He shrugged.

Roy Grace looked at him sympathetically. The Detective Sergeant had three failed marriages behind him and his fourth, to a Thai girl he had found on the Internet, seemed like it was heading in the same direction.

'If anyone would know, you would,' Bella Moy retorted.

Roy Grace looked down at the briefing notes typed out by his assistant as he waited for Glenn Branson, who had just come in, to sit down. Glenn was followed by the cheery uniformed figure of the Road Policing Unit Inspector, James Biggs, who had requested the involvement of the Major Crime Branch in this inquiry.

'OK,' Grace said, placing his agenda and policy book in front of him. 'This is the first briefing of *Operation Violin*, the inquiry into the death of Brighton University student Tony Revere.' He paused to introduce Biggs, a pleasant, no-nonsense-looking man with close-cropped fair hair, to his team. 'James, would you like to start by outlining what happened earlier today?'

The Inspector summarized the morning's tragic events, placing particular focus on the eyewitness reports of the white van which had disappeared from the scene, having gone through a red light and struck the cyclist. So far, he reported, there were two possible sightings of the van from CCTV cameras in the area, but neither was of sufficient quality, even with image enhancement, to provide legible registration numbers.

The first sighting was of a Ford Transit van, matching the description, heading fast in a westerly direction from the scene, less than thirty seconds after the collision. The second, one minute later, showed a van, missing its driver's wing mirror, making a right turn half a mile on. This was significant, Biggs told them, because of pieces of a wing mirror recovered from the scene. Its identity was now being traced from a serial number on the casing. That was all he had to go on so far.

'There's a Home Office post-mortem due to start in about an hour's time,' Grace said, 'which Glenn Branson, temporarily deputizing for me, will attend, along with Tracy Stocker and the Coroner's Officer.' He looked at Glenn, who grimaced.

Then Glenn Branson raised his hand. Grace nodded at him.

'Boss, I've just spoken to the Family Liaison Officer from Traffic who's been assigned to this,' he said. 'He's just had a phone call from an officer in the New York Police Department. The deceased, Tony Revere, was a US citizen, doing a business studies degree at Brighton University. Now, I don't know if this is going to have any significance, but the deceased's mother's maiden name is Giordino.'

All eyes were on him.

'Does that name mean anything to anyone?' Glenn asked, looking at each of the faces.

They all shook their heads.

'Sal Giordino?' he then asked.

There was still no recognition.

'Anyone see *The Godfather*?' Branson went on.

This time they all nodded.

'Marlon Brando, right? The Boss of Bosses? The Godfather, right? *The Man*. The Capo of Capos?'

'Yes,' Grace said.

'Well, that's who her dad is. Sal Giordino is the current New York Godfather.'

21

Standard protocol on receipt of notification of the death of a US citizen overseas was for the NYPD's Interpol office to inform the local police force where the next of kin resided and they would then deliver the death message. In the case of Tony Revere, this would have been Suffolk County Police, which covered the Hamptons.

But anything involving a high-profile family such as the Giordinos was treated differently. There were computer markers on all known Mob family members, even distant cousins, with contact details for the particular police departments and officers that might currently be interested.

Detective Investigator Pat Lanigan, of the Special Investigations Unit of the Office of the District Attorney, was seated at his Brooklyn desk when the call from a detective in the Interpol office came through. Lanigan was online, searching through the affordable end of the Tiffany catalogue, trying to decide on a thirtieth anniversary present for his wife, Francene. But within seconds he picked up his pen and was focusing 100 per cent on the call.

A tall man of Irish descent, with a pockmarked face, a greying brush-cut and a Brooklyn accent, Lanigan had started life in the US Navy, then worked as a stevedore on the Manhattan wharves before joining the NYPD. He had the rugged looks of a movie tough guy and a powerful physique that meant few people were tempted to pick a fight with him.

At fifty-four, he'd had some thirty years' experience of dealing with the *Wise Guys* – the term the NYPD used for the Mafiosi. He knew personally many of the rank and file in all the Mob families, partly helped by his having been born and raised in Brooklyn, where the majority of them – the Gambinos, Genoveses, the Colombos, Lucheses, Bonnanos and Giordinos – lived.

Back in the 1970s, soon after he'd first joined the NYPD, Lanigan had been assigned to the team hunting down the killers of mobster

Joe Gallo, several years on from his death. The mobster had been shot in a retaliation killing during a meal in Umberto's Clam House in Little Italy. But he'd found it hard to feel too much sympathy for the man. *Crazy Joey*, as he had been known, kept a full-grown lion in his basement. He used to starve it for three days, then introduce his debtors to the snarling creature, asking them if they would like to pay up what they owed him or play with his pet.

From that point on, Lanigan had spent most of his career to date on busting the Mafia.

He listened to the information that the Interpol officer relayed. He didn't like the hit-and-run part. Retaliation was a big part of Mob culture. Each of the families had its enemies, the old, historic rivals, as well as new ones created almost daily. He decided that the best way to see if that line of thought had any relevance would be to take a ride to East Hampton and check out the family himself. He liked to visit Wise Guys in their lairs. You got to see a different side of them than you did in a police interview room. And delivering the shock message just might make one of them blurt out a giveaway.

Thirty minutes later, having washed down the chicken pasta salad his wife had made him with a Diet Coke followed by a shot of coffee, he tightened his necktie, pulled on his sports coat and scooped up his regular work buddy, Dennis Bootle. Then they headed out to the parking lot and climbed into an unmarked, sludge-brown Ford Crown Victoria.

Pat Lanigan was an Obama man who spent much of his free time doing charity work for wounded veterans. Dennis Bootle was a diehard Republican who spent most of his free time as an activist for the pro-gun lobby and out hunting. Although two years older than his colleague, Bootle had hair a youthful straw-blond colour, styled in a boyish quiff. Unlike Lanigan, who despite all his dealings with the Mafia had deliberately never once fired his handgun in all his years in service, Bootle had shot three people, on three different occasions, killing two of them. They were chalk and cheese. They argued constantly. Yet they were close.

As Lanigan started the engine and accelerated forward, a twelve-inch square of cardboard printed with the words ON BROOKLYN D.A.

BUSINESS slid off the top of the dash and fell on to Bootle's lap. Bootle stuck it on the rear seat, face down, saying nothing. He was a taciturn man and had moods in which he remained silent, sometimes for hours. But he never missed a thing.

As they headed off, Bootle suddenly said, 'What's this sound like to you?'

Lanigan shrugged. 'Dunno, You?'

Bootle shrugged. 'Sounds to me like a hit. Got *hit* written all over it.'

*

The early-afternoon traffic on Long Island was light and it stayed that way during the next ninety minutes as they approached the Hamptons. In high season, this stretch of road would be slow, the traffic bumper to bumper. Relaxed, Lanigan steered the car along the lush shrub- and grass-lined freeway with one hand, keeping a wary eye on the exit signs, distrustful of the occasional instructions of the satnav he had stuck to the windshield.

Bootle had a new girlfriend who was rich, he told Pat, and had a big spread in Florida. He was planning to retire and move down there with her. The news made Pat sad, because he would miss his buddy. He did not want to think about retirement just yet – he loved his job too much.

The satnav was showing a right turn ahead, as the trees and shrub gave way to the outskirts of East Hampton, with its large houses, set well back from the road, and then a parade of white-painted, expensive-looking shops. They turned right in front of a Mobil Oil garage and headed along a leafy lane with a double yellow line down the middle.

'You know what you can guarantee about the Hamptons?' Bootle said suddenly, in his clipped Bostonian accent, breaking twenty minutes of silence.

'Uh? What's that?' Lanigan always sounded like he was rolling a couple of marbles around in his mouth.

Bootle nodded at a vast colonial-style mansion with a colonnaded portico. 'You ain't going to find any retired NYPD guys living in this area!'

'This isn't ordinary Wise Guy terrain either,' Pat Lanigan retorted.

'This kid's mother, she's married to Lou Revere, right?'

'Uh huh.'

'He's the Mob's banker. You know that? Last election, rumour
has it he gave the Republicans ten million.'

'All the more reason to bust him.'

'Go fuck yourself.'

Pat Lanigan grinned.

The double yellow line ended and the lane narrowed to single-
track. On both sides there were trim hedges.

'Are we right?'

'Yeah.'

The satnav told them they had arrived.

Directly in front of them were closed, tall, grey-painted gates. A
sign below the speaker panel said ARMED RESPONSE.

Pat stopped the car, lowered his window and reached out to
press a button on the panel by the gates. The cyclops eye of a CCTV
camera peered suspiciously down at them.

A voice speaking broken English crackled out: 'Yes, hello,
please?'

'Police,' Pat said, pulling his shield out and holding it up for the
camera to see.

Moments later the gates swung slowly open and they drove
through.

Ahead of them, beyond an expanse of lawn and plants straight
from a tropical rainforest, rose the grey superstructure of an imposing modern mansion, with a circular building to the left that
reminded Pat of the conning tower of a nuclear submarine.

'This a bit like your new lady's pad?' Pat asked.

'Nah. Hers is much bigger than this – this would be like her pool
house.'

Pat grinned as he drove along woodchip, towards a garage large
enough to accommodate an aircraft carrier, and pulled up alongside
a gold Porsche Cayenne. They climbed out and took in the surroundings for a moment. Then, a short distance away, the front
door opened and a uniformed Filipina maid stared out nervously.

They strode over.

'We're looking for Mr and Mrs Revere,' Pat Lanigan said, holding up his shield.

Dennis Bootle flashed his, too.

The maid looked even more nervous now and Pat instantly felt sorry for her. Someone wasn't treating her right. You could always tell that with people.

She mouthed something too quiet for him to hear, then ushered them through into a vast hallway with a grey flagstone floor and a grand circular staircase sweeping up in front of them. The walls were hung with ornately framed mirrors and abstract modern art.

Following her nervy hand signals, they walked after her through into a palatial, high-ceilinged drawing room, with a minstrel's gallery above them. It was like being on the set of a movie about Tudor England, Pat Lanigan thought. There were exposed oak beams and tapestries hanging on the walls, alongside ancestral portraits – none of which he recognized. Bought at auctions rather than inherited, he surmised.

The furniture was all antiques: sofas, chairs, a chaise longue. A large picture window looked out over a lawn, bushes and Long Island Sound beyond. The flagstone floor in here was strewn with rugs and there was a faintly sweet, musky smell that reminded him of museums.

It was a house to die for, and a room to die for, and he was certain of just one thing at this moment. A lot of people had.

Seated in the room was an attractive but hard-looking woman in her mid-forties, with short blonde hair and a made-to-measure nose. She was dressed in a pink tracksuit and bling trainers, holding a pack of Marlboro Lights in one hand and a lighter in the other. As they entered she shook a cigarette out, pushed it between her lips, then clicked the lighter, as if challenging them to stop her.

'Yes?' she said, drawing on the cigarette and exhaling the smoke towards the ceiling.

Lanigan held up his shield. 'Detective Investigator Lanigan and Detective Investigator Bootle. Are you Mrs Fernanda Revere?'

She shook her head, as if she was tossing imaginary long tresses of hair from her face. 'Why do you need to know?'

'Is your husband here?' Lanigan asked patiently.

'He's playing golf.'

The two police officers stared around the room. Both were looking for photographs. There were plenty, over the fireplace, on tables, on shelves. But all of them, so far as Pat Lanigan could ascertain in a quick sweep, were of Lou and Fernanda Revere and their children. Disappointingly, there were no pictures of any of their friends – or *associates*.

'Will your husband be home soon?'

'I don't know,' she said. 'Two hours, maybe three.'

The officers exchanged a glance. Then Lanigan said, 'OK, I'm sorry to have to break this to you, Mrs Revere. You have a son, Tony, is that right?'

She was about to take another drag on her cigarette, but stopped, anxiety lining her face.

'Yes?'

'We've been informed by the police in Brighton, Sussex, in England, that your son died this morning, following a road traffic accident.'

Both men sat down, uninvited, in chairs opposite her.

She stared at them in silence. 'What?'

Pat Lanigan repeated what he had said.

She sat, staring at them like an unexploded bomb. 'You're shitting, right?'

'I'm afraid not,' Pat said. 'I'm very sorry. Do you have someone who could come round until your husband gets home? A neighbour? Friend?'

'You're shitting. Yeah? Tell me you're shitting.'

The cigarette was burning down. She tapped some ash off into a large crystal ashtray.

'I'm very sorry, Mrs Revere. I wish I was.'

Her pupils were dilating. 'You're shitting, aren't you?' she said after a long silence.

Pat saw her hands trembling. Saw her stab the cigarette into the ashtray as if she was knifing someone. Then she grabbed the ashtray and hurled it at the wall. It struck just below a painting, exploding into shards of glass.

'No!' she said, her breathing suddenly getting faster and faster. 'Noooooooooooooooo.'

She picked up the table the ashtray had been on and smashed it down on the floor, breaking the legs.

'Noooooooo!' she screamed. 'Noooooooo! It's not true. Tell me it's not true. Tell me!'

The two officers sat there in silence, watching as she jumped up and grabbed a painting off the wall. She then jerked it down hard over her knees, ripping through the face and body of a Madonna and child.

'Not my Tony. My son. Noooooooooooooo! Not him!'

She picked up a sculpture of a tall, thin man holding dumbbells. Neither officer had any idea who the sculptor was, or of its value. She smashed its head against the floor.

'Get out!' she screamed. 'Get out, get out, get out!'

22

Tyler sat hunched over the pine kitchen table in his grey school trousers, with his white shirt unbuttoned at the neck and his red and grey uniform tie at half-mast. On the wall-mounted television he was watching one of his favourite episodes of *Top Gear*, the one in which the team wrecked a caravan. The sound was up loud.

His straight brown hair fell across his forehead, partially shading his eyes, and with his oval wire-framed glasses several people said he looked like a young Harry Potter. Tyler had no problem with that, it gave him some kudos, but he reminded Carly much more of her late husband, Kes. Tyler was like a miniature version and, as the microwave pinged, she fought back tears. God, how she could have done with Kes now. He'd have known what to do, how best to deal with this mess, how to make her feel a little less terrible than she did at this moment. She removed the plate.

'Elbows off!' she said.

Otis, their black Labrador-something cross, followed her across the tiled floor, ever hopeful. She set the plate down in front of her son, grabbed the remote and muted the sound.

'Meatballs and pasta?' Tyler said, screwing up his face.

'One of your favourites, isn't it?' She put down a bowl of salad beside him.

'I had this for lunch today at school.'

'Lucky you.'

'They make it better than you.'

'Thanks a lot.'

'You told me always to be truthful.'

'I thought I also told you to be tactful.'

He shrugged. 'Whatever.' Then he prodded a meatball suspiciously. 'So, how'm I going to get to school tomorrow?'

'You could walk.'

'Oh great, thanks a lot.' Then he perked up. 'Hey, I could bike!'

The idea sent a chill through her. 'No way. You are so not biking to school. OK? I'll sort out a taxi.'

Otis stared up at Tyler expectantly.

'Otis!' she warned. 'No begging!'

Then she sat down next to her son. 'Look, I've had a shit day, OK?'

'Not as shit as that cyclist, right?'

'What's that meant to mean?'

Tyler suddenly stood up and ran towards the door, yelling, 'I bet he didn't have a drunk for a mother.' He slammed the door behind him.

Carly stared at the door. She half rose from the chair, then sat back down. Moments later she heard the furious pounding of drums upstairs. Otis barked at her, two *woof-woofs* in quick succession. Waiting for a titbit.

'Sorry, Otis, not feeling great, OK? I'll take you for a walk later.'

The smell of the meatballs was making her feel sick. Even sicker than she already felt. She got up, walked over to the door and opened it, ready to shout up the stairs at Tyler, but then thought better of it. She sat back down at the table and lit a cigarette, blankly lip-reading the *Top Gear* characters as she smoked. She felt utterly numb.

The phone rang. Sarah Ellis. Married to a solicitor, Justin, Sarah was not just her closest friend, she was the most sensible person Carly knew. And at this moment, on the day her world had turned into a nightmare – the worst since the day she'd been told that her husband was dead – she badly needed *sensible*.

'How are you, Gorgeous?'

'Not feeling very gorgeous,' Carly replied grimly.

'You were on television – we just saw you on the local news. The accident. The police are looking for a white van. Did they tell you?'

'They didn't tell me much.'

'We're on our way over with a bottle of champagne to cheer you up,' Sarah said. 'We'll be with you as soon as we can.'

'Thanks, I could do with the company – but the last thing I need is a bloody drink.'

23

Cleo was asleep in the hospital bed. The sleeve of her blue hospital gown had slipped up over her elbow and Grace, who had been sitting beside her for the past hour, stared at her face, then at the downy fair hairs of her slender arm, thinking how lovely she looked when she was asleep. Then his eyes fell on the grey plastic tag around her wrist and another coil of fear rose inside him.

Wires taped to her abdomen were feeding a constant flow of information into a computer at the end of the bed, but he did not know what the stuff on the screen meant. All he could hope was that everything was OK. In the weak, stark light and flickering glow of the television she looked so pale and vulnerable, he thought.

He was scared. Sick with fear for her.

He listened to her steady breathing. Then the mournful sound of a siren cut the air as an ambulance approached somewhere below. Cleo was so strong and healthy. She looked after herself, ate the right stuff, worked out and kept fit. Sure, before she had become pregnant she liked a drink in the evening, but the moment she knew she was expecting, she had reduced it right down to just the occasional glass, and during the past few weeks she'd dutifully cut even that out completely.

One of the things he so loved about her was her positive attitude, the way she always saw the good side of people, looked for the best aspects of any situation. He believed she would be a wonderful mother. The possibility that they might lose their baby struck him harder each time he thought about it.

Even worse was the unthinkable idea that, as the consultant had warned, Cleo might die.

On his lap lay a document listing all the files needed for the prosecution case against the snuff-movie creep Carl Venner. For the past hour he'd been trying to concentrate on it – he had to read through it tonight, to check nothing had been omitted, before a meeting with Emily Curtis, a financial investigator, in the morning, to finalize the confiscation documentation – but his mind was all over the place. He reminded himself that he must ask Emily about her dog, Bobby. Besotted with him, she was always talking about Bobby and showing Grace pictures of him.

It was 9.10 p.m. A new crime show was on television, with the volume turned right down. Like most police officers, Grace rarely watched cop shows because the inaccuracies he invariably found drove him to distraction, and he'd given up on the first episode of this one last week, after just fifteen minutes, when the central character, supposedly an experienced detective, trampled all over a murder scene in his ordinary clothes.

His mind returned to the fatal accident this morning. He'd heard summaries of the first accounts from eyewitnesses. The cyclist was on the wrong side of the road, but that was not unusual – idiots did often ride on the wrong side. If it was a planned hit, then the cyclist had given the van the perfect opportunity. But how would the van have known that he was going to be on the wrong side of the road? That theory didn't fit together at all and he wasn't happy with it, even though the van had gone through a red light.

But the New York crime family connection bothered him, for reasons he could not define. He just had a really bad feeling about that.

Plenty of people said that the Italian Mafia, as portrayed in movies like *The Godfather*, was today a busted flush. But Grace knew otherwise. Six years ago he had done a short course at the FBI training centre at Quantico, in Virginia, and become friendly with one particular Brooklyn-based detective whose field of expertise was the Mafia.

Yes, it was a different organization from in its heyday. During Prohibition, the crime families of the US Mafia grew from strength to strength. By the mid-1930s, with command structures modelled on Roman legions, their influence touched almost everyone in America in some way. Many major unions were under their control. They were involved with the garment industry, the construction industry, all rolling stock, the New York docks, cigarettes, gambling, nightclubs, prostitution, extortion through protection rackets of thousands of businesses and premises, and loan-sharking.

Today the traditional established crime families were less visible, but no less wealthy, despite some competition from the growing so-called Russian Mafia. A major portion of their income now came from narcotics, once a taboo area for them, fake designer goods and pirated films, while large inroads had been made into online piracy.

Before leaving the office this evening he had Googled *Sal Giordino* and what he found did not make comfortable reading. Although Sal Giordino was languishing in jail, his extensive crew were highly active. They seemed to be above the law and as ruthless as any crime families before them in eliminating their rivals.

Could their tentacles have reached Brighton?

Drugs were a major factor in this city. For nine years running, Brighton had held the unwelcome title of Injecting Drug Death Capital of the UK. It was big business supplying the local addicts, but recreational drugs like cocaine were an even bigger business. The current police initiative in this sphere, *Operation Reduction*, had been extremely effective in busting several major rings, but no matter how many people were arrested, there were always new players waiting in the wings to step into their shoes. The Force Intelligence Bureau had not to date established links to any US crime families, but could that be about to change?

Suddenly his phone rang.

He stepped out of the room as he answered, not wanting to risk waking Cleo. The consultant had told him she needed all the rest she could get at this moment.

It was Norman Potting, still diligently at work in the Incident Room. Grace knew the sad reason, which was that Potting had such a terrible home life, he preferred to stay late at his desk, in an environment where at least he was wanted.

'Boss, I've just had a phone call from Interpol in New York. The parents of the deceased young cyclist, Tony Revere, are on their way over in a private jet. They are due into Gatwick at 6 a.m. Thought you should know. They've booked a room at the Metropole in Brighton. Road Policing have arranged a Family Liaison Officer to take them to the mortuary a bit later in the morning, but I thought you might want to send someone from Major Crime as well.'

'Smart thinking, Norman,' Grace said, and thanked him.

After he had hung up, he thought hard. He would have liked to meet and assess the parents himself. But he did not want to alert them to any possible police suspicions at this stage and they might just think it odd that an officer of his rank turned up. It wasn't worth the risk, he decided. If there was anything to be gained from meeting the parents, it would be best achieved by keeping things low key. So it would be better to send a more junior policeman – that way it would simply appear to be respect.

He dialled a number and moments later Glenn Branson answered. In the background, Grace could hear a theme tune he recognized from an old Clint Eastwood movie, *The Good, the Bad and the Ugly*. Branson's passion was old movies.

He could picture his friend lounging on the sofa in his – Grace's – house, where he had been lodging for months now since his wife had thrown him out. But not for much longer, as Grace had recently put the place on the market.

'Yo, old-timer!' Branson said, sounding as if he had been drinking.

He'd never been much of a drinker before the collapse of his marriage, but these days Branson was drinking enough to make Grace worry about him.

'How was the post-mortem?'

'It hasn't revealed anything unexpected so far. There was white paint on the boy's anorak on the right shoulder, consistent with abrasions on his skin – probably where the Transit van struck him. Death from multiple internal injuries. Blood and other fluid samples have been sent off for drug testing.'

'All the witness statements say he was on the wrong side of road.'

'He was American. Early morning. Might have been tired and confused. Or just a typical mad cyclist. There's no CCTV of the actual impact.'

Changing the subject, Grace asked, 'Did you remember to feed Marlon?' He had to remind Branson daily to feed his goldfish.

'Yeah, took him to Jamie Oliver's. He had three courses, including dessert.'

Grace grinned.

Then Branson said, 'He looks sad, you know. He needs a mate.'

So do you, badly, Grace thought, before explaining, 'I've tried, but he always bloody eats every mate.'

'Sounds like Ari.'

Ignoring Branson's barb about his wife, he said, 'Hope you weren't planning a lie-in tomorrow?'

'Why's that?'

'I need you back on parade at the mortuary.'

24

At 7.15 a.m., just twelve hours after he had left the place, Glenn Branson parked the unmarked silver Hyundai Getz in the deserted visitors' parking area at the rear of the Brighton and Hove City Mortuary. He switched off the engine, then dug his fingers hard into his temples, trying to relieve the searing pain across the front of his head. His mouth was dry and his throat felt parched, despite having drunk a couple of pints of water, and the two paracetamols he'd taken an hour ago, when he'd woken up, had not yet kicked in. He wasn't feeling confident that they were going to kick in at all.

His hangovers were getting worse. Probably, he reasoned, because his drinking was getting heavier. This time he had a bottle of a special-offer red wine he'd bought in ASDA to thank. He'd only intended to have one glass with his microwaved chicken casserole, in front of the telly, last night, but somehow he'd drained it.

Drowning his anger.

Trying to numb that terrible hurt inside his heart. The constant yearning for his kids, the sharp twist in his guts each time he thought about the new man who was living with his wife, playing with his kids, bathing them, God damn it. Some smarmy personal trainer he was extremely close to killing. And on top of that, all her lies in the divorce papers. They lay beside him, inside the white envelope on the passenger seat.

He had a meeting with his solicitor scheduled for this afternoon to deal with the divorce papers, and to take further advice about the financial repercussions and his contact with the children.

Everything seemed so unfair. While the police busted a gut and risked their lives to prevent crime and to lock up villains, all the moral codes had been thrown out of the window. Your wife didn't have to be faithful. She could go off and shag whoever she wanted, throw you out of the house and move her lover in.

He climbed out despondently into the light drizzle and popped open his umbrella. His clothes weren't helping his mood. He was attired in a navy raincoat over his dark suit, an unusually sombre tie and the plainest pair of black shoes he possessed, polished, like all his footwear, to a mirror shine. One of the few sartorial tips that he had ever been given by Roy Grace, that he actually took notice of, was how to dress respectfully on occasions like this.

With the fresh air reviving him a little, he stared uncomfortably at the closed door of the receiving bay. This place gave him the heebie-jeebies each time he came here, and it was even worse with a hangover.

The building looked greyer, darker. From the front it resembled a long suburban bungalow, with pebbledash walls and opaque windows. At the rear it looked more like a warehouse, with drive-through doors at each end, for the delivery and collection of corpses away from public view. It was situated off the busy Lewes Road gyratory system in the centre of Brighton, shielded from a row of houses next door by a high wall, and had the leafy silence of Woodvale Cemetery rising up the steep hill behind it.

He waited as he heard a car approaching. Moments later Bella Moy drove around the corner in her purple Nissan Micra and parked beside him. She was here at Roy Grace's suggestion because, in addition to being a detective with the Major Crime Branch, she was also a trained and experienced Family Liaison Officer.

Politely, Glenn opened her door and held the umbrella over her as she climbed out.

She thanked him, then gave him a wan smile. 'You OK?'

He grimaced and nodded. 'Thanks, yep. Bearing up.'

He was conscious of her blue eyes looking searchingly at his and wondered if she was noticing they were bloodshot. He was out of shape, that was for sure. It had been a couple of months since he had been to the gym and for the first time in his life his six-pack had been replaced by the slight hint of a belly. Wondering if she could smell alcohol on his breath, he dug his hands into his pocket and pulled out a packet of peppermint gum. He offered it to her, but she shook her head politely. Then he popped a piece in his mouth and began to chew.

He felt sad for his colleague. Bella was a fine detective but a total fashion disaster. She had a nice face, but it was framed by shapeless hair, and she was dressed as messily as usual today, in a bulky red puffa over an old-fashioned bottle-green two-piece and clumsy black ankle boots. Everything about her lacked style, from her dull Swatch with its worn webbing strap down to her choice of wheels – a real old person's car, in his view.

It was as if, at the age of thirty-five, she had resigned herself to a life divided between work and caring for her elderly mother, and didn't give a damn how she looked. If he had the courage to give her a makeover, the way he had modernized Roy Grace, he could transform her into a beautiful woman, he often thought. But how could he say that to her? And besides, in today's politically correct world, you had to walk on eggshells all the time. She might fly back at him and accuse him of being sexist.

Both of them turned at the sound of another car. A blue Ford Mondeo swung into view, pulling up next to them. Branson recognized the driver, PC Dan Pattenden from the Road Policing Unit. Beside him, hunched forward, sat an arrogant-looking man in his early fifties, with slicked-back silver hair and a suspicious expression. As he turned his head, he reminded Branson of a badger. A woman sat behind him.

The badger climbed out and yawned, then peered around, blinking, with a weary, defeated expression. He was wearing an expensive-looking fawn Crombie coat with a velvet collar, a loud orange and brown tie and brown loafers with gold buckles, and he sported an ornate emerald ring on his wedding finger. His skin had the jaundiced pallor of fake tan and a sleepless night.

He'd just lost his son and, regardless of who he might be in the US crime world, Glenn could not help feeling sorry for him at this moment.

The rear door of the car flew open as if it had been kicked. Branson breathed in a sudden snatch of perfume as the woman emerged, swinging her legs out and then launching herself upright. She was a little taller than her husband, with an attractive but hard face that looked tight with grief. Her short blonde hair was fashionably styled and immaculate, and her camel coat, dark brown handbag and matching crocodile boots had a quietly expensive aura.

'Mr and Mrs Revere?' Branson said, stepping forward with his hand outstretched.

The woman looked at him like he was air, like she didn't speak to black people, and tossed her head disdainfully away from him.

The man smiled meekly and gave him an even meeker nod. 'Lou Revere,' he said. 'This is my wife, Fernanda.' He shook Glenn's hand with a much firmer grip than Glenn had expected.

'I'm Detective Sergeant Branson and this is Detective Sergeant Moy. We're here to take care of you and help you in any way we can, along with PC Pattenden. We are very sorry about your son. How was your journey?'

'Fucking awful, if you have to know,' the woman said, still not looking at him. 'They had no ice on the plane. You want to believe that? No ice. And just a bunch of stale sandwiches. Do we have to stand out here in the fucking rain?'

'Not at all. Let's get inside,' Glenn said, and indicated the way forward.

'Honey,' the man said. 'Honey—' He looked apologetically at the two detectives. 'It was a last-minute thing. An associate had just flown in, luckily, and had the plane on the tarmac at La Guardia. So it picked us up from our local airport. Otherwise we wouldn't have been here until much later – if not tomorrow.'

'We paid twenty-five thousand dollars and they didn't have any fucking ice,' she repeated.

Glenn Branson was finding it hard to believe that anyone whose son had just died was going to be worried by something so trivial as lack of ice, but he responded diplomatically. 'Doesn't sound good,' he said, stepping forward and leading the way around to the front of the building. Then he stopped in front of the small blue door, with its frosted glass panel, beneath the gaze of the CCTV camera up above, and rang the bell.

It was opened by Cleo Morey's assistant, Darren Wallace. He was a cheery-looking man in his early twenties, with black hair gelled in spikes, already gowned up in blue scrubs, his trousers tucked inside white gum boots. He greeted them with a pleasant smile and ushered them inside.

The smell hit Glenn Branson immediately, the way it always did, almost making him retch. The sickly sweet reek of Trigene disinfectant could mask, but could never get rid of, the smell of death that permeated the whole place. The smell you always took away with you on your clothes.

They went through into a small office and were introduced to Philip Keay, the Coroner's Officer. A tall, lean man, wearing a sombre dark suit, he had swarthy good looks beneath dark, buzz-cut hair and thick eyebrows, and his manner was courteous and efficient.

The Assistant Anatomical Pathology Technician then led the way along the tiled corridor, past the glass window of the isolation room. He hurried them past the open door of the post-mortem room, where three naked corpses were laid out, and into a small conference room. It had an octagonal table with eight black chairs around it and two blank whiteboards on the wall. A round clock in a stainless-steel frame was fixed to the wall. It read: 7.28.

'Can I offer you any tea or coffee?' Darren Wallace asked, indicating for them to sit down.

Both Americans shook their heads and remained standing.

'I didn't know this was a goddamn Starbucks,' Fernanda Revere said. 'I've flown here to see my son, not to drink fucking coffee.'

'Hon,' her husband said, raising a warning hand.

'Stop saying *Hon*, will you?' she retorted. 'You're like a fucking parrot.'

Darren Wallace exchanged a glance with the police officers, then the Coroner's Officer addressed the Americans, speaking quietly but firmly.

'Thank you for making the journey here. I appreciate it can't be easy for you.'

'Oh really?' Fernanda Revere snapped. 'You do, do you?'

Philip Keay was diplomatically silent for some moments, sitting erect. Then, ignoring the question, he addressed the Reveres again, switching between them as he spoke.

'I'm afraid your son suffered very bad abrasions in the accident. He has been laid on his best side, which might be the way you would like to remember him. I would recommend that you look through the glass of the viewing window.'

'I haven't flown all this way to look at my son through a window,' Fernanda Revere said icily. 'I want to see him, OK? I want to hold him, hug him. He's all cold in there. He needs his mom.'

There was another awkward exchange of glances, then Darren Wallace said, 'Yes, of course. If you'd like to follow me. But please be prepared.'

They all walked through a spartan waiting room, with off-white seats around the walls and a hot-drinks dispenser. The three police officers remained in there, as Darren Wallace led the Reveres and Philip Keay through the far door and into the narrow area that served as a non-denominational chapel and viewing room.

The walls were wood-panelled to shoulder height and painted cream above. There were fake window recesses, in one of which was a display of artificial flowers in a vase, and in place of an altar was an abstract design of gold stars against a black background, set between heavy clouds. Blue boxes of tissues for the convenience of grieving visitors had been placed on shelving on both sides of the room.

In the centre, and dominating the viewing room, was a table on which lay the shape of a human body beneath a cream, silky cover.

Fernanda Revere began making deep, gulping sobs. Her husband put an arm around her.

Darren Wallace delicately pulled back the cover, exposing the young man's head, which was turned to one side. His bereavement training had taught him how to deal with almost any situation at this sensitive moment, but even so he could never predict how anyone was going to react at the sight of a dead loved one. He'd been present many times before when mothers had screamed, but never in his career had he heard anything quite like the howl this woman suddenly let rip.

It was as if she had torn open the very bowels of hell itself.

25

It was over an hour before Fernanda Revere came back out of the viewing room, barely able to walk, supported by her drained-looking husband.

Darren Wallace guided each of them to a chair at the table in the waiting room. Fernanda sat down, pulled a pack of cigarettes out of her handbag and lit one.

Politely Darren Wallace said, 'I'm very sorry, but smoking is not permitted in here. You can go outside.'

She took a deep drag, stared at him, as if he had not said a word, and blew the smoke out, then took another drag.

Branson diplomatically passed his empty coffee cup to her. 'You can use that as an ashtray,' he said, giving a tacit nod to Wallace and then to his colleagues.

Her husband spoke quietly but assertively, with a slight Brooklyn accent, as if suddenly taking command of the situation, looking at each of the police officers in turn.

'My wife and I would like to know exactly what happened. How our son died. Know what I'm saying? We've only heard second-hand. What are you able to tell us?'

Branson and Bella Moy turned to Dan Pattenden.

'I'm afraid we don't have a full picture yet, Mr and Mrs Revere,' the Road Policing Officer said. 'Three vehicles were involved in the accident. From witness reports so far, your son appears to have come out of a side road on to a main road, Portland Road, on the wrong side, directly into the path of an Audi car. The female driver appears to have taken avoiding action, colliding with the wall of a café. She subsequently failed a breathalyser test and was arrested on suspicion of drink driving.'

'Fucking terrific,' Fernanda Revere said, taking another deep drag.

'At this stage we're unclear as to the extent of her involvement in the actual collision,' Pattenden said. He peered down at his notepad on the table. 'A white Ford Transit van behind her appears to have travelled through a red stop light and struck your son, the impact sending him and his bicycle across the road, into the path of an articulated lorry coming in the opposite direction. It was the collision with this vehicle that probably caused the fatal injuries.'

There was a long silence.

'Articulated lorry?' asked Lou Revere. 'What kind of a vehicle is that?'

'I guess it's what you would call a truck in America,' Glenn Branson said helpfully. 'Or maybe a tractor-trailer.'

'Kind of like a Mack truck?' the husband asked.

'A big truck, exactly.'

Dan Pattenden added, 'We have established that the lorry driver was out of hours.'

'Meaning?' Lou Revere asked.

'We have strict laws in the UK governing the number of hours a lorry driver is permitted to drive before he has to take a rest. All journeys are governed by a tachometer fitted to the vehicle. From our examination of the one in the lorry involved in your son's fatal accident, it appears the driver was over his permitted limit.'

Fernanda Revere dropped her cigarette butt into the coffee cup, then pulled another cigarette from her handbag and said, 'This is great. Like, this is so fucking great.' She lit the cigarette contemptuously, before lowering her face, a solitary tear trickling down her cheek.

'So, this white van?' her husband queried. 'What's this guy's story? The driver?'

Pattenden flipped through a few pages of his pad. 'He drove on without stopping and we don't have a description of him at this moment. There is a full alert for the vehicle. But we have no description of the driver to go on. We are hoping that CCTV footage may provide us with something.'

'Let me get this straight,' Fernanda Revere said. 'You have a drunk driver, a truck driver who was over his permitted hours and a van driver who drove away from the scene, like a hit-and-run. I have that right?'

Pattenden looked at her warily. 'Yes. Hopefully more information will emerge as we progress our enquiries.'

'You *hope* that, do you?' she pressed. Her voice was pure vitriol. She pointed through the closed door. 'That's my son in there.' She looked at her husband. '*Our* son. How do you think we feel?'

Pattenden looked at her. 'I can't begin to imagine how you feel, Mrs Revere. All that I, my Road Policing Unit and the Collision Investigation Unit can do is try to establish the facts of the incident as best we can. I'm deeply sorry for you both and for all of your relatives. I'm here to answer any questions you may have and to give you assurances that we will do all we can to establish the facts pertinent to your son's death.' He passed her his card. 'These are my contact details. Please feel free to call me, any time, twenty-four-seven, and I'll give you whatever information I can.'

She left the card lying on the table. 'Tell me something. Have you ever lost a child?'

He stared back at her for some moments. 'No. But I'm a parent, too. I can't imagine what it would be like. I can't imagine what you are going through and it would be presumptuous to even try.'

'Yeah,' she said icily. 'You're right. Don't even try to go there.'

26

Tooth and his associate, Yossarian, sat out on the deck area of the Shark Bite Sports Bar, overlooking the creek at the south end of Turtle Cove Marina, on Providenciales Island. Thirty miles long and five wide, Provo, as it was known to the locals, sat in the Caribbean, south of the Bahamas. It was the main tourist island in the Turks and Caicos archipelago, although it was still mostly undeveloped and that suited Tooth. The day it got too developed, he planned to move on.

The evening air was thirty-six degrees and the humidity was high. Tooth, dressed in denims cut off at the knees, a T-shirt printed with a picture of Jimmy Page and flip-flops, was perspiring. Every few minutes he slapped at the mosquitoes that landed on his bare skin. He was smoking a Lucky Strike and drinking a Maker's Mark bourbon on the rocks. The dog sat beside him, glaring at the world, and occasionally drank from a bowl of water on the wood-planked floor.

It was Happy Hour in the bar and the air-conditioned interior was full of expat Brits, Americans and Canadians who mostly knew each other and regularly got drunk together in this bar. Tooth never talked to any of them. He didn't like talking to anyone. It was his birthday today, and he was content to spend it with his associate.

His birthday present to himself was to have his head shaved and then fuck the black girl called Tia, whom he visited most weeks in Cameos nightclub on Airport Road. She didn't care that it was his birthday and nor did Yossarian. That was fine by him. Tooth didn't do *caring*.

There was a roar of laughter from inside the bar. A couple of weeks ago there had been gunshots. Two Haitians had come in waving semi-automatics, yelling at everyone to hit the deck and hand over their wallets. A drunk, pot-bellied expat English lawyer, dressed in a blazer, white flannels and an old school tie, pulled out a Glock .45 and shot both of them dead. Then he had shouted at the bartender for another pink gin.

It was that kind of a place.

Which was why Tooth chose to live here. No one asked questions and no one gave a damn. They left Tooth and his associate alone and he left them alone. He lived in a ground-floor apartment in a complex on the far side of the creek, with a small garden where his associate could crap to its heart's content. He had a cleaning lady who would feed the dog on the occasions, two or three times a year, when he was away on business.

The Turks and Caicos Islands were a British protectorate that the British did not need and could not afford. But because they sat strategically between Haiti, Jamaica and Florida, they were a favoured stopover for drug runners and illegal Haitian immigrants bound for the USA. The UK made a pretence of policing them and had put in a puppet governor, but mostly they left things to the corrupt local police force. The US Coast Guard had a major presence here, but they were only interested in what happened offshore.

Nobody was interested in Tooth's business.

He drank two more bourbons and smoked four more cigarettes, then headed home along the dark, deserted road with his associate. This might be the last night of his life, or it might not. He'd find that out soon enough. He truly didn't care and it wasn't the drink talking. It was the hard piece of metal in the locked closet at his home that would decide.

Tooth had quit school at fifteen and drifted around for a while. He fetched up in New York City, first doing shift work as a warehouse man, then as a fitter in a Grumman fighter aircraft factory on Long Island. When George Bush Senior invaded Iraq, Tooth enlisted in the US Army. There he discovered that his natural calm gave him one particular talent. He was a very accurate long-range rifle shot.

After two tours in that particular theatre, his commanding lieutenant recommended he apply for the Sniper School. That was the place where Tooth discovered his metier. A range of medals testifying to that hung on one wall of his apartment. Every now and then he would look at them in a detached way, as if he was in a museum looking at the life of some long-dead stranger.

One of the items was a framed certificate for bravery he'd received for pulling a wounded colleague out of the line of fire. Part of the wording read, *A Great American Patriot.*

That drunk English lawyer, in the Shark Bite Sports Bar, who had shot dead the two Haitians, had once insisted on buying him a drink a few years ago. The lawyer had sat there, knocking back a gin, nodding his head, then had asked him if he was a patriot.

Tooth had told him no, he wasn't a patriot, and had moved on.

The lawyer had called out after him, 'Good man. Patriotism is the last refuge of a scoundrel!'

Tooth remembered those words now, as he took one last look at those medals and those framed words, on the night of his forty-second birthday. Then, as he did each year on his birthday, he went out on to his balcony with his associate, and a glass of Maker's Mark.

He sat smoking another cigarette, drinking another whiskey, mentally calculating his finances. He had enough to last him for another five years, at his current cash burn, he figured. He could do with another good contract. He'd accumulated about $2.5 million in his Swiss bank account, which gave him a comfort zone, but hey, he didn't know how much longer he had to live. He had to feed his boat with fuel, his thirty-five-foot motor yacht, *Long Shot*, with its twin Mercedes engines that took him out hunting for his food most days.

His days out on *Long Shot* were his life.

And he never knew how they were numbered.

Each year, his birthday ritual was to play Russian roulette. He would thumb the bullet into one of the six barrels, spin it, listening to the metallic *click-click-click*, then point the gun at his temple and squeeze the trigger, just once. If the hammer clicked on an empty chamber, that was meant to be.

He went back inside, unlocked the cabinet and removed the gun. The same single .38 bullet had been in the chamber for the past ten years. He broke the gun open and tipped it out into the palm of his hand.

Ten years ago he had dum-dummed it himself. Two deep vertical slits in the nose. It meant the bullet would rip open on impact, punching a hole the size of a tennis ball in whatever it hit. He would have no possible chance of survival.

Tooth carefully slid the bullet back into the barrel. Then he spun it, listening to the steady *click-click-click*. Maybe it would end up in the firing chamber, maybe not.

Then he pressed the barrel of the revolver to the side of his head. To the exact part of his temple he knew would have maximum destructive effect.

He pulled the trigger.

27

Grace changed the venue of the morning briefing from Jack Skerritt's office to the conference room, to accommodate the extra people now attending. These included Tracy Stocker, the Crime Scene Manager, James Gartrell, the SOCO photographer, Paul Wood, the sergeant from the Collision Investigation Unit who had attended at the scene yesterday, and his own Crime Scene Manager as well.

Grace had brought in two additions to his own inquiry team. The first was a young PC, Alec Davies, twenty-two, who had previously impressed him when in uniform and whom he had fast-tracked into CID by requesting him for his team now. A quiet, shy-looking man, Davies was to be in charge of the outside inquiry team of PCSOs, who were trawling every business premise within a mile of the accident in the hope of finding more CCTV footage.

The second member was David Howes, a tall, suave DC in his mid-forties. Dressed in a pinstriped grey suit and checked shirt, with neatly brushed ginger hair, he could have passed muster as a stockbroker or a corporate executive. One of his particular skills in the CID was as a trained negotiator. He was also a former Prison Liaison Officer.

This room could hold twenty-five people seated on the hard, red chairs around the open-centred rectangular table and another thirty, if necessary, standing. One of its uses was for press conferences, and it was for these that there stood, at the far end opposite the video screen, a concave, two-tone blue board, six feet high and ten feet wide, boldly carrying the Sussex Police website address and the *Crimestoppers* legend and phone number. All press and media statements were given by officers against this backdrop. Vertical venetian blinds screened off the dismal view of the custody block towering above them.

On the wall beside the video screen was a whiteboard on which

James Biggs had drawn a diagram of the position of the vehicles involved, immediately following the impact with the cyclist.

The white Transit van which had subsequently disappeared was labelled **VEHICLE 1**. The bicycle was labelled **VEHICLE 2**, the lorry **VEHICLE 3** and the Audi car **VEHICLE 4**.

Reading from his prepared notes, Roy Grace said, 'The time is 8.30 a.m., Thursday 22 April. This is the second briefing of *Operation Violin*, the investigation into the death of Brighton University student Anthony Vincent Revere, conducted on day two, following his collision in Portland Road, Hove, with an unidentified van, then a lorry belonging to Aberdeen Ocean Fisheries. Absent from this meeting are DS Branson, PC Pattenden and DS Moy, who are currently attending the viewing of his body with his parents, who have flown over from the United States.'

He turned to Sergeant Wood. 'Paul, I think it would be helpful to start with you.'

Wood stood up. 'We've fed all the information from the initial witness statements, skid marks and debris pattern into the CAD program we are currently using for accident simulation. We have created two perspectives of the accident. The first being from the point of view of the Audi car.'

He picked up a digital remote and pressed it. On the video screen appeared a grey road, approximating the width of Portland Road, but with the pavement and all beyond on either side blanked out in a paler grey. The screen showed the white van tailgating the Audi, the cyclist emerging from a side street ahead and the articulated lorry some way ahead, on the other side of the road, approaching in the distance.

He pressed a button and the animation came to life. On the far side of the road, the lorry began to approach. Suddenly the cyclist began to move, swinging out of the side street, on the wrong side, heading straight for the Audi. At the last minute, the cyclist swerved to the left, towards the centre of the road, and the Audi swerved left on to the pavement. An instant later, the van clipped the cyclist, sending him hurtling across the far side of the road and straight underneath the lorry, between its front wheels and rear wheels. The cyclist spun around the rear wheel arch as the lorry braked to a halt, his right leg then flying out from underneath it.

When the animation stopped, there was a long silence.

Grace finally broke it, turning to the RPU Inspector. 'James, from this simulation it doesn't look as if the Audi driver, Mrs Carly Chase, had any contact with Revere.'

'I would agree with that based on what we have heard so far. But I'm not yet convinced we've heard the full story. It might be that she was unlucky to be breathalysed on a morning-after offence. But it's too early to rule out her culpability at this stage.'

Grace turned to the Major Crime Branch Crime Scene Manager. 'Tracy, do you have anything for us?'

Tracy Stocker, a senior SOCO, a little over five feet tall, was a diminutive power house and one of the most respected Crime Scene Managers in the force. She had a strong, good-looking face framed with straight brown hair and was dressed today in civvies, a navy trouser suit with a grey blouse. A standard police ID card hung from a lanyard around her neck, printed with the words SERVING SUSSEX in blue and white.

'Yes, chief, we have something that may be significant. We have sent the serial number on the part of the wing mirror that was recovered at the scene to Ford. They will be able to tell us if it's from a Ford Transit and the year of manufacture.'

'It's going to be thousands of vans, right?' Nick Nicholl said.

'Yes,' she conceded. But then she added, 'Most of them should have two wing mirrors. Maybe a CCTV camera will give us a shot of a van with one missing. The mirror itself has been shattered, but I've requested fingerprint analysis of the casing. Most people adjust their wing mirrors, so there's a good chance we'll get something off that. It may take a while, though, because the plastic was wet from the rain and it's not good material to get prints off at the best of times.'

'Thanks. Good work, Tracy.'

Grace then turned to Alec Davies. 'Any luck so far from CCTV?'

The young PC shook his head. 'No, sir. We've looked at all the images taken and the angles and distance don't give us enough detail.'

As Davies spoke, Grace's mind began to wander, distracted by his thoughts of Cleo, as he had been every few minutes. He'd spoken to her earlier and she'd sounded a lot better this morning. Hopefully by tomorrow she would be ready to come home.

After a while he realized that Davies was still speaking. He stared blankly at the young PC, then had to say, 'I'm sorry, could you repeat that?'

Once Davies had obliged, Grace gathered his thoughts together and said, 'OK, Alec, I think you should widen the net. If the van is travelling at thirty miles per hour, that's one mile every two minutes. Expand your trawl to a ten-mile radius. Let me know how many people you need to cover that and I'll authorize you.'

Norman Potting raised his hand and Grace signalled to him to speak.

'Boss, in view of the information that came to light yesterday, about the relationship of the deceased to the New York Mafia, should we be concerned that there is more to this than just a traffic accident? I know we have the hit-and-run van to investigate, but could this possibly be a hit in a different sense of the word?'

'It's a good point to raise, Norman,' Grace replied. 'I'm starting to think, from what I've seen so far, that this is unlikely to be some kind of gangland killing. But we need a line of enquiry to ensure that it's not Mafia-related. We need to do some intelligence gathering.' He looked at the crime analyst he had brought into his team, Ellen Zoratti, a bright twenty-eight-year-old. 'Ellen is already in contact with police in New York to try to establish if Tony Revere's family, or his mother's family, are in any kind of dispute with other members of their own family – or other crime families.'

At that moment, Grace's phone rang. Excusing himself, he pressed the answer button. It was his boss, ACC Rigg, saying he needed to see him right away. He did not sound in a happy mood.

Grace told him he would be there in half an hour.

28

Malling House, the headquarters of Sussex Police, was a fifteen-minute drive from Grace's office. It was on the outskirts of Lewes, the county town of East Sussex, and much of the administration and key management needed for the 5,000 officers and employees of the force was handled from this complex of modern and old buildings.

As he pulled the silver Ford Focus up at the security barrier, Roy Grace felt the kind of butterflies in his stomach he used to get when summoned to the headmaster's study at school. He couldn't help it. It was the same each time he came here, even though the new ACC, Peter Rigg, to whom he now reported, was a far more benign character than his predecessor, the acidic and unpredictable Alison Vosper.

He nodded at the security guard, then drove in. He made a sharp right turn, passing the Road Policing Unit's base and driving school, and pulled into a bay in the car park. He tried to call Glenn Branson for an update, but his phone went straight to voicemail. He left a message, then tried Bella Moy's, again without success. Finally, he strode across the complex, head bowed against the steady drizzle.

Peter Rigg's office was on the ground floor at the front of the main building, a handsome Queen Anne mansion. It had a view through a large sash window out on to a gravel driveway and a circular lawn beyond. Like all the rooms, it contained handsome woodwork and a fine stuccoed ceiling, which had been carefully restored after a fire nearly destroyed the building some years back. So far, since the ACC had taken over at the start of this year, Grace knew he had made a good impression. He rather liked the man, but at the same time he always felt he was walking on eggshells in his presence.

Rigg was a dapper, distinguished-looking man in his mid-forties, with a healthy complexion, fair hair neatly and conservatively cut, and a sharp, public school voice. Although several inches shorter than Grace, he had fine posture, giving him a military bearing which made him seem taller than his actual height. He was dressed in a plain navy suit, a gingham shirt and a striped tie. Several motor-racing pictures adorned his walls.

He was on the phone when Grace entered, but waved him cheerily to sit at one of the two leather-covered chairs in front of the huge rosewood desk, then put a hand over the receiver and asked Grace if he would like anything to drink.

'I'd love a coffee – strong with some milk, please, sir.'

Rigg repeated the order down the phone, to either his MSA or his Staff Officer, Grace presumed. Then he hung up and smiled at Grace. The man's manner was pleasant but no-nonsense. Like most of the force's ACCs, he struck Grace clearly as potential Chief Constable material one day. A position he himself never aspired to, because he knew he would not have sufficient self-control to play the required politics. He liked being a hands-on detective; that's what he was best at doing and it was the job he loved.

In many ways he would have preferred to remain a Detective Inspector, as he had been a couple of years ago, involved on the front line in every investigation. Accepting the promotion to his current role as Detective Superintendent, and more recently taking on the responsibility for Major Crime, burdened him with more bureaucracy and politics than he was comfortable with. But at least when he wanted to he still had the option to roll his sleeves up and get involved in cases. No one would stop him. The only deterrent was the ever-growing paper mountain in his office.

'I hear that your girlfriend's in hospital, Roy,' Rigg said.

Grace was surprised that he knew.

'Yes, sir. She has pregnancy complications.'

His eyes fell on two framed photographs on the desk. One showed a confident-looking teenage boy with tousled fair hair, dressed in a rugby shirt, smiling as if he didn't have a care in the world, and the other a girl of about twelve, in a pinafore, with long fair curls and a cheeky grin on her face. He felt a twinge of envy. Maybe, with luck, he'd have photos like that on his desk one day, too.

'Sorry to hear that,' Rigg said. 'If you need any time out, let me know. How many weeks is she?'

'Twenty-six.'

He frowned. 'Well, let's hope all's OK.'

'Thank you, sir. She's coming home tomorrow, so it looks like she's out of immediate danger.'

As the MSA came in with Grace's coffee, the ACC looked down at a sheet of printed paper on his blotter, on which were some handwritten notes. '*Operation Violin*,' he said pensively. Then he looked up with a grin. 'Good to know our computer's got a sense of humour!'

Now it was Grace's turn to frown. 'A sense of humour?'

'Don't you remember that film *Some Like It Hot*? Didn't the mobsters carry their machine guns in violin cases?'

'Ah, yes, right! Of course. I hadn't made the connection.'

Grace grinned. Then he felt a sudden, uncomfortable twinge. It had been Sandy's favourite film of all time. They used to watch it together every Christmas, when it was repeated on television. She could repeat some of the lines perfectly. Particularly the very last line. She'd cock her head, look at him and say, "Well, nobody's perfect!"'

Then the smile slipped from the Assistant Chief Constable's face. 'Roy, I'm concerned about the Mafia connection with this case.'

Grace nodded. 'The parents are over here now, to identify the body.'

'I'm aware of that. What I don't like is that we are not in terrain we're familiar with. I think this has the potential to go pear-shaped.'

'In what sense, sir?'

Immediately, Grace knew he shouldn't have said that, but it was too late to retract it.

Rigg's face darkened. 'We're in the middle of a bloody recession. Businesses in this city are hurting. Tourist trade is down. Brighton's had an unwarranted reputation as the crime capital of the UK for seven decades and we are trying to do something about it, to reassure people this city is as safe as anywhere on the planet to visit. The last thing we need is the bloody American Mafia headlining in the press here.'

'We have a good relationship with the *Argus* so I'm sure we can keep that aspect under control.'

'You are, are you?'

Rigg was starting to look angry. It was the first time Grace had seen this side of him.

'I think if we handle them carefully and give them plenty of information in advance of the national press, yes, we can, sir.'

'So what about this reward?'

The word hit Grace like a sledgehammer. 'Reward?' he asked, surprised.

'Reward. Yes.'

'I'm sorry. I don't know what you mean, sir.'

Rigg waved a hand, summoning Grace round to his side of the desk. He leaned forward and tapped on his keyboard, then pointed at his computer screen.

Grace saw the banner **THE ARGUS** in black letters underlined in red. Beneath were the words: **Latest Headlines. Updated 9.25 a.m.**

MAFIA BOSS'S DAUGHTER OFFERS
$100,000 REWARD FOR SON'S KILLER

His heart sinking, he read on:

> Fernanda Revere, daughter of New York Mafia Capo Sal Giordino, currently serving 11 consecutive life sentences for murder, this morning told *Argus* reporter Kevin Spinella outside the gates of Brighton and Hove City Mortuary, she is offering $100,000 for information leading to the identity of the van driver responsible for the death of her son, Tony Revere. Revere, 21, a student at Brighton University, was killed yesterday after his bicycle was in a multiple-vehicle collision involving an Audi car, a van and a lorry in Portland Road, Hove.
>
> Police are appealing for witnesses. Inspector James Biggs of Hove Road Policing Unit said, 'We are anxious to trace the driver of a white Ford Transit van involved in the collision, which drove off at speed immediately after. It was a callous act.'

'You know what I particularly don't like in this piece, Roy?'

Grace had a pretty good idea. 'The wording of the reward, sir?'

Rigg nodded. '*Identity*,' he said. 'I don't like that word. It worries me. The customary wording is *for information leading to the arrest and conviction.* I'm not happy about this *leading to the identity* wording here. It's vigilante territory.'

'It could just be that the woman was tired – and it wasn't actually what she meant to say.'

Even before he had finished, Grace knew this sounded lame.

Rigg looked back at him reproachfully. 'Last time we spoke, you told me you had this reporter, Spinella, in your pocket.'

At that moment, Grace could happily have killed Spinella with his bare hands. In fact a quick death would be too good for the man.

'Not exactly, sir. I told you that I had forged a good working relationship with him, but I was concerned that he had a mole somewhere inside Sussex Police. I think this proves it.'

'It proves something very different to me, Roy.'

Grace looked at him, feeling very uncomfortable suddenly.

Rigg went on, 'It tells me that my predecessor, Alison Vosper, was right when she said I should keep a careful eye on you.'

29

Grace drove out of the police headquarters and threaded his way around the outskirts of Brighton towards the hospital, seething with anger and feeling totally humiliated.

All the goodwill he'd built up with ACC Rigg on his previous case, the hunt for a serial rapist, was now down the khazi. He had hoped the spectre of Alison Vosper had gone away for good, but now he realized to his dismay that she had left a poisonous legacy after all.

He dialled Kevin Spinella's mobile phone number on his hands-free. The reporter answered almost immediately.

'You've just blown all the goodwill you ever had with me and with HQ CID,' Grace said furiously.

'Detective Superintendent Grace, why – whatever's the matter?' He sounded a tad less cocky than usual.

'You bloody well know what the issue is. Your front-page splash.'

'Oh – ah – right – yeah, that.' Grace could hear a clacking sound, as if the man was chewing gum.

'I can't believe you've been so damned irresponsible.'

'We published it at Mrs Revere's request.'

'Without bothering to speak to anyone on the inquiry team?'

There was a silence for some moments, then, sounding meeker by the moment, Spinella said, 'I didn't think it was necessary.'

'And you didn't think about the consequences? When the police put up a reward it is in the region of five thousand pounds. What do you think you are going to achieve with this? Do you want the streets of Brighton filled with vigilantes driving around in pick-up trucks with gun racks on their roofs? It may be the way Mrs Revere does things in her country, but it's not how we do it here, and you're experienced enough to know that.'

'Sorry if I've upset you, Detective Superintendent.'

'You know what? You don't sound at all sorry. But you will be. This'll come back to bite you, I can promise you that.'

Grace hung up, then returned a missed call from Glenn Branson.

'Yo, old-timer!' the Detective Sergeant said, before Grace had a chance to get a word out. 'Listen, I just realized something. *Operation Violin* – that's well clever! Kind of suitable for something involving the New York Mafia!'

'*Some Like It Hot*?' Grace said.

Branson sounded crestfallen. 'Oh, you're there already.'

'Yep, sorry to ruin your morning.' Grace decided not to spoil his rare moment of one-upmanship on films with his friend by revealing his source. Then rapidly changing the subject, he asked, 'What's happening?'

'We got doorstepped outside the mortuary by that shit Spinella. I imagine there'll be something in the *Argus* tonight.'

'There's already something in the online edition,' Grace said.

Then he told him the gist of the piece, his dressing-down from ACC Rigg and his conversation just now with the reporter.

'I'm afraid I couldn't do anything, boss. He was right outside the mortuary, knew exactly who they were and took them aside.'

'Who tipped him off?'

'Must have been dozens of people who knew the parents were coming over. Not just in CID – could have been someone in the hotel. I'll say one thing about Spinella, he's a grafter.'

Grace did not reply for a moment. Sure, it could easily have been someone at the hotel. A porter getting the occasional bung for tipping off the paper. Perhaps that's all it was. But there was just too much consistency about Spinella always being in the right place at the right time.

It had to be an insider.

'Where are the parents now?'

'They're with Bella Moy and the Coroner's Officer. They're not happy that the body's not being released to them right away – that it's up to the Coroner. The defence may want a second post-mortem.'

'What kind of people are they?' Grace asked.

'The father's creepy but he's pretty sensible. Very shaken. The mother's poison. But, hey, she identified her dead son, right? That's not a good place to judge anyone, so who can tell? But she wears the trousers, for sure, and I'd say she's the bitch queen from hell. I wouldn't want to tangle with either of them.'

Grace was heading west on the A27. Coming up on his right was the campus of Sussex University. He took the left slip, heading to Falmer, passing part of Brighton University on his right, where the dead boy had attended, and the imposing structure of the American Express Community Stadium where the local football team, the Albion, would soon be moving to, a building he was beginning to really like as it took shape, even though he wasn't a football fan.

'The wording Spinella used about the reward. Do you see anything sinister behind that – about paying money for the van driver's identity rather than his arrest and conviction?'

His question was greeted with silence and Grace realized the connection had dropped. He leaned forward and redialled on the hands-free.

When Glenn answered, Grace told him the ACC's concerns.

'What does he mean by *the potential to go pear-shaped*?' Branson queried.

'I don't know,' Grace answered truthfully. 'I think a lot of people get nervous at any mention of the word *Mafia*. The Chief Constable's under pressure to get rid of Brighton's historic image of a crime-ridden resort, so they want to keep the Mafia connection as low key as possible, I'm guessing.'

'I thought the New York Mafia had been pretty much decimated.'

'They're not as powerful as they used to be, but they're still players. We need to find that white van fast and get the driver under arrest. That'll take the heat off everything.'

'You mean get him into protective custody, boss?'

'You've seen too many Mafia movies,' Grace said. 'You're letting your imagination run away with you.'

'One hundred grand,' Glenn Branson replied, putting on an accent mimicking *The Godfather*, sounding as if he had a mouth full of rocks. 'That's gonna be an offer someone can't refuse.'

'Put a sock in it.'

But, Grace thought privately, Branson could well be right.

30

Lou Revere didn't like it when his wife drank heavily, and these past few years, since their three kids had gotten older and left home, Fernanda hit the bottle hard most evenings. It had become the norm for her to be tottering unsteadily around the house by around 8 p.m.

The drunker she was, the more bad-tempered she became, and she would start blaming Lou for almost anything that came into her head that she was not happy about. One moment it was the height at which a television was fixed to the wall, because it hurt her neck to watch. The next might be because she didn't like the way he'd left his golf clothes on the bedroom floor. But the most consistent of her tirades was blaming him for their younger son, Tony, on whom she doted, going to live with that piece of trash in England.

'If you were a *man*,' she would shout at him, 'you'd have put your foot down and made Tony complete his education in America. My father would have never let his son go!'

Lou would shrug his shoulders and say, 'It's different for today's generation. You have to let kids do what they want to do. Tony's a smart boy. He's his own man and he needs his independence. I miss him, too, but it's good to see him do that.'

'Good to see him getting away from our family?' she'd reply. 'You mean, like, *my* family, right?'

He did mean that, but he would never dare say it. Privately, though, he hoped the boy would carve out a life for himself away from the clutches of the Giordinos. Some days he wished he had the courage himself. But it was too late. This was the life he had chosen. It was fine and he should count his blessings. He was rich beyond his wildest dreams. OK, being rich wasn't everything, and the money he handled came in dirty and sometimes bloody. But that was how the world worked.

Despite his wife's behaviour, Lou loved her. He was proud of her looks, proud of the lavish gatherings she hosted, and she could still be wild in bed – on the nights when she didn't fall into a stupor first.

It was true also, of course, that her connections had not exactly done his career any harm.

Lou Revere had started out as an accountant, with a Harvard business degree behind him. Although related to a rival New York crime family, during his early years he'd had no intention of entering the criminal world. That changed the night he met Fernanda at a charity ball. He was lean and handsome then, and she'd particularly liked him because he made her laugh, and something about him reminded her of the deep inner strength of her father.

Sal Giordino had been impressed with Lou's quietly strategic mind and for some time he had wanted to forge links with Lou Revere's own crime family. Wanting the best for his daughter, Sal saw the way to do that was to help the man she intended to marry. And then maybe, in turn, the guy could be of use to him.

Within five years, Lou Revere had become the principal financial adviser to the Giordino crime family, taking charge of laundering the hundreds of millions of dollars' income from their drugs, prostitution and fake designer goods businesses. Over the next twenty years he spread the money through smart investments into legitimate businesses, the most successful of all being their waste disposal empire, which stretched across the United States and up into Canada, and their pornographic film distribution. He also extended the family's property holdings, much of it overseas in emerging countries including China, Romania, Poland and Thailand.

During this period, Lou Revere had cunningly covered his own and his immediate family's backs. When Sal Giordino was initially indicted for tax evasion, Lou was untouched. A close associate of Giordino, faced with the loss of all his money, did a deal with the prosecutors and spent three months giving evidence against the Capo. As a result, what started out as a historic tax investigation ended up with Giordino on trial for multiple counts of conspiracy to murder. He would be dying in jail, and if that bothered the old monster, he was damned well not admitting it. When a newspaper reporter asked him how he felt about never getting out alive, he growled back at the man, 'Gotta die somewhere.'

Fernanda was drunk now. The crew of the Gulfstream jet, chastened by her abuse on the flight over to England, had stocked up with Grey Goose vodka, ice and cranberry juice for the flight back home, as well as an assortment of food which she had not touched. By the end of the seven-hour flight she had finished one bottle and started to make inroads into a second. She was still clutching a glass as the plane touched down at Republic Airport in East Farmingdale at 2.15 p.m. local time.

Lou helped her down the short gangway on to the tarmac. She was barely aware of much of what was happening as they re-entered America through the relaxed immigration control, and fifteen minutes later she was rummaging in the drinks cabinet in the back of the limousine that drove them the short distance home to East Hampton.

'Don't you think you've had enough, hon?' Lou asked her, putting out a restraining hand.

'My father would know what to do,' she slurred in reply. 'You don't know anything, do you?' Clumsily, she thumbed through the *Favourites* address list on her iPhone, squinting at the names and numbers, which were all slightly out of focus. Then she tapped her brother's name.

She was just sober enough to check that the glass partition to the driver's compartment was closed and the intercom was off, as she lifted the phone to her ear, waiting for it to ring.

'Who you calling?' Lou asked.

'Ricky.'

'You already told him the news, right?'

'I'm not calling to give him any news. I need him to do something.' Then she said, 'Shit, got his stupid voicemail. Ricky, it's me. Call me. I need to speak to you urgently,' she said into the phone, then ended the call.

Lou looked at her. 'What's that about?'

Her brother was a sleazebag. Lazy, smug and nasty. He'd inherited his father's ruthless violence, but none of the old man's cunning. Lou tolerated him because he had no choice, but he had never liked him.

'I'll tell you what it's about,' she slurred. 'It's about a drunk woman driver, a goddamn van driver who didn't stop and a truck driver who should not have been on the road. That's what it's about.'

'What do you want Ricky to do?'

'He'll know someone.'

'Someone?'

She turned and glared at him, her eyes glazed, as hard as drill bits.

'My son's dead. I want that drunken bitch, that van driver and that truck driver who killed him, OK? I want them to suffer.'

31

Reading from his prepared notes to the team assembled in the conference room of Sussex House, Roy Grace said, 'The time is 8.30 a.m., Saturday 24 April. This is the sixth briefing of *Operation Violin*, the investigation into the death of Tony Revere, conducted at the start of day four.'

It was of little consequence that it was the weekend. For the first few weeks of any major crime inquiry, the team worked around the clock, though with the current financial cutbacks overtime was controlled much more tightly.

At the previous evening's briefing, PC Alec Davies played CCTV footage he had retrieved from a betting shop a short distance along the road from the scene of the accident. The video was grainy, but it showed that although it had been a near miss, there was no impact between the cyclist and the Audi car. Inspector James Biggs, from the Road Policing Unit, had confirmed that after a second interview with the woman driver, Mrs Carly Chase, and forensic examination of her vehicle, they were satisfied that no contact between the cycle and the Audi had occurred. Moreover they were not intending to charge her with any further offence other than driving while unfit through alcohol.

Carly Chase's mistake, Grace knew, was thinking, like most people, that the alcohol in her blood from the previous night would have all but gone by the following morning. It was something that used to bother him about Cleo. There were times before her pregnancy when she would drink quite heavily after work. He sometimes reckoned he would drink heavily if he did that job, too. He had hoped that she would be coming home yesterday, but at the last minute the consultant decided to keep her in for one more day. Grace was going to pick her up this afternoon.

A major focus of this morning's meeting was on damage limitation concerning the massive reward the dead boy's parents had offered. It had made big headlines in many of the nation's papers, prompting any number of conspiracy theories. These ranged from Tony Revere being murdered by a Brighton crime family in a drugs turf war to this being a revenge killing by a rival crime family or Tony being an undercover agent for the CIA.

Glenn Branson and Bella Moy took the team once more through the reactions of the dead boy's parents. It was agreed that there was no indication from them that their son's death might have been a targeted hit, or that he had any enemies. The only issue with the parents, DS Branson added, had been their anger that they could not take their son's body home with them and that it might be necessary to subject it to a second Home Office post-mortem. Philip Keay, the Coroner's Officer, had explained to them that it could be in their interests. If the van driver was found and brought to trial, his defence counsel would not necessarily be content with the results of the first post-mortem.

In reply, Tony Revere's father had told him, in plain English, that the cause of his son's death did not require *fucking Sherlock Holmes*.

Tracy Stocker, the Crime Scene Manager, raised her hand and Grace indicated for her to go ahead.

'Chief, Philip Keay and I explained to the parents that regardless of whether there needed to be a second PM, the Coroner would not release the body until after the results of the toxicology reports. We could be looking at two weeks minimum for those, maybe more. Tony Revere was on the wrong side of the road and that suggests to me that he might have had drugs or alcohol in his system, possibly from the night before.'

'Are we having a full tox scan, Roy?' asked David Howes.

The Chief Constable, Tom Martinson, was under the cosh from the government to lop £52 million from the annual police budget. CID had been asked to send only what was essential to the labs, as every forensic submission was a big expense. A full toxicology scan, including eye fluids, cost over £2,000.

Ordinarily, Grace would have tried to save this money. The cyclist was clearly in the wrong. The woman in the Audi had been driving while over the limit, but she had not, from what he'd seen, been a contributory factor in the accident. The van driver, however, had gone through a red light and when found would be facing serious charges. The lorry driver, regardless of being over his legal hours, could have done nothing to avoid the collision. The toxicology report was not going to add anything to the facts as they stood, other than to explain the possibility of why the cyclist was on the wrong side. But it could feature in any defence case by the van driver.

Besides, this was not a normal situation. The deceased's parents were demonstrating anger, a natural reaction by any parent, but these people were in a position to do something about their anger. He was pretty sure they would go straight to their lawyers back in New York. Tom Martinson was a belts-and-braces man. If a slew of claims were made by the parents against the woman driver of the Audi, against the missing van driver and against the lorry driver, the insurers would come to the police as their first port of call, wanting to see what they had done to establish the possible culpability of the cyclist. And they would be asking a lot of awkward questions if thorough toxicology tests had not been done.

'Yes, we are, David,' Grace replied. 'I'm afraid it's necessary.' He outlined his reasons to the team, then changed the subject. 'I'm pleased to report a possible breakthrough this morning,' he went on. 'A fingerprint taken from the damaged wing mirror found at the scene, and presumed to have snapped off the door of the Ford Transit van on impact with the cyclist, has been identified. This was from a further fragment discovered during the continued search of the scene yesterday.'

All eyes were on the Detective Superintendent. A sudden and complete silence had fallen in the room. Only to be broken by the *Indiana Jones* ring tone of Norman Potting's mobile phone. He silenced it, murmuring an apology to Grace. Then PC Davies's phone rang, with a stuttering chirrup. He checked the caller display, then quickly silenced that too.

'The print is from Ewan Preece, a thirty-one-year-old convicted drug dealer serving his last three weeks of a six-year sentence in Ford Prison,' Grace said. 'He's on a day-release rehabilitation programme, working on a construction site in Arundel. On Wednesday

21 April, the day of the collision, he failed to return for evening lock-in. I've had a vehicle check run on him at Swansea and the only thing registered in his name is a 1984 Vauxhall Astra which was impounded and destroyed some months ago for no tax or insurance.'

'I know that name,' Norman Potting said. 'Ewan Preece. Little bastard. Nicked him years ago for stealing cars. Used to be one of the Moulsecoomb troublemakers when he was younger.'

'Know anything about him now, Norman?' Grace asked. 'Where he might be? Why would anyone go over the wall with just three weeks left?'

'I know the people to ask, chief.'

Grace made an action note. 'OK, good. If you can follow that up. I spoke to a senior officer at Ford just before this meeting, Lisa Setterington. She told me Preece has been as good as gold in Ford. He's applied himself, learning the plastering trade. She says she knows him well and feels it's out of character for him to have done this.'

'Out of character for a villain like Preece?' Potting snorted. 'I remember him when he was fifteen. I was doing community policing then. He had a formal warning for being mixed up with a bunch of kids who'd been nicked for joyriding. I felt sorry for him and got him lined up for a job at the timber people, Wenban-Smith, but he never turned up for his interview. I stopped him one night a few weeks later, him and two others, and asked why he'd not gone. He gave me a story about his family getting evicted from their council house.' Potting nodded his head. 'It's not easy to be evicted from a council house if you've got young kids – his parents were scumbags. He never had a chance. But I thought maybe he was a decent kid and I felt sorry for him. I bet him a tenner that he'd be in jail by his sixteenth birthday. He took the bet.'

Bella Moy was staring at him incredulously. 'Your own money?'

Potting nodded. 'I knew it was a safe bet. He was banged up six months later for vehicle theft. Doesn't surprise me how he's ended up.' He nodded again, wistfully.

'So did he pay you?' David Howes asked.

'Ha-ha!' Potting replied.

Nick Nicholl suddenly interjected, 'Boss, might it be a good idea to get the word spread around Ford about the reward. It's likely someone in there will know what Preece was up to. All prisoners know each other's business.'

'Good point,' Grace said. 'You should go over there, Norman. See if any of the prisoners will talk to you.'

'I'll do that, chief. I know where to start looking in Brighton as well. A bloke like Ewan Preece isn't capable of hiding for long.'

'Especially,' Grace said, 'when there's a hundred-thousand-dollar price tag on finding him.'

32

Tooth was up at dawn, as he was every morning, before the heat of the sun became too intense. He was running his regular ten-mile circuit up in the arid hills close to his home, dressed in his singlet, shorts and trainers, with his associate loping along at his side.

When he arrived back home, ninety minutes later, he worked out with his weights in the gym in the small, air-conditioned spare room, while Yossarian waited patiently for his breakfast. Then he went through his martial arts routine. Sometimes, when he had been behind enemy lines, using a gun wasn't practical. Tooth was fine with his bare hands. He preferred them to using knives. You could hurt people a lot more with your bare hands, if you knew where to squeeze. You could pop their eardrums, their eyeballs or their testicles. You really could give them a lot of pain before you killed them. And you didn't leave a trail of blood.

He practised his movements in the gym. In particular he worked his hand muscles, slamming the punchbag with his hand weights attached, then worked on his squeezes. He might be small, but he could crush a brick into dust with either his right or his left hand.

When he had finished in the gym, he showered, poured some biscuits into his associate's bowl, opened a tin of dog food and scooped that in, then set it down out on the balcony. A few minutes later he joined Yossarian and had his own breakfast. He drank energy powder mixed with water, staring out at the flat surface of Turtle Bay Cove and the boats moored alongside the pontoon below the Shark Bite Sports Bar, reading today's *New York Times* on his Kindle.

It was a fine day, as it was most days here, and the shipping forecast was good. In a while he and Yossarian would head out to sea on *Long Shot*, switch on the side-scan sonar and start hunting fish. Whatever he caught, he would share with his associate. They were in this shitty life together and they took care of each other.

One time, a few months ago, a local scumbag had gone into his apartment when he'd been out shopping. It wouldn't have been hard, because he left the patio doors open on to the ground-floor terrace and garden in case Yossarian, who liked to lie asleep in the shade indoors, needed to go out to relieve himself. The only way Tooth knew that anyone had been in was from the four severed fingers leaking blood on to the floor tiles, close to the dining table. His associate had done his job.

Before they went fishing, Tooth had a job to do. A ritual, every morning after his birthday. Life was simple: you should take care of the things that took care of you. He took care of his associate and he took care of his Colt revolver.

He removed it from the locked cabinet now, laid it on newspaper and began to dismantle it. He liked the feel of the cold metal. Liked to see the barrel, the trigger, the frame, hammer, sights and trigger guard all laid out in front of him. He liked the knowledge that this inanimate, beautifully engineered machine made the decision for him about when he lived and when he died. It was a good feeling to abdicate all responsibility.

He tipped the can of gun oil on to a piece of rag and wiped along the barrel. He liked the smell of the oil the way some folk, he imagined, liked the smell of a fine wine. He'd seen wine experts on television talk about hints of cedar, cigar, pepper and cinnamon, or about gooseberries, and citrus. This oil had a metallic tang to it, a hint of linseed, copper and rotting apples. It was every bit as fine to him as the finest wine.

He'd spent so much time alone, in enemy territory, with his rifle and his handgun. The smell of the weapons, and of the oil that kept them running smoothly, was more potent to him than the smell of the most beautiful woman on earth. It was the one smell in all the world he could trust.

Suddenly his phone rang.

He looked down at the black Nokia on the table beside him. The number was displayed. A New York State number, but not one he recognized. He killed the call, then waited for some moments, composing his thoughts.

Only one person knew how to contact him. That man had the

number of his current pay-as-you-go phone. Tooth had five such phones in his safe. He would only ever take one call on a phone, then he would destroy it. It was a precaution that had served him well. The man, who was an underboss with a New York crime family, understood Tooth and, in turn, Tooth trusted him.

He removed the SIM card from the phone, then held it in the flame of his cigarette lighter until it had melted beyond recovery. Then he removed another phone from the safe, ensured that it was set to withhold the caller's number and dialled.

'Yep?' said the male voice the other end, answering almost immediately.

'You just called.'

'I'm told you can help me.'

'You know my terms?'

'They're fine. How soon could we meet? Tonight?'

Tooth did a quick calculation of flight times. He knew the flights out of here to Miami and the times of the connecting flights to most capitals that concerned him. And he could always be ready in one hour.

'The guy who gave you this number, he'll give you another number. Call me on that at 6 p.m. and give me the address.' Then Tooth hung up.

He phoned the cleaning lady who took care of Yossarian when he was away. Then he added a few items to his go-bag and ordered a taxi. While he waited for it to arrive he chatted to his associate and gave him an extra big biscuit in the shape of a bone.

Yossarian took it and slunk miserably away to the dark recess within the apartment, where he had his basket. He knew that when he got a big biscuit, his pack leader was going away. That meant no walks. It was like some kind of a punishment, except he didn't know what he had done wrong. He dropped the biscuit in the basket, but didn't start to eat it. He knew he would have plenty of time for that.

A few minutes later he heard a sound he recognized. Departing footsteps. Then a slam.

33

Shortly after 2.30 p.m., Roy Grace left his team at Sussex House, saying he would be back for the 6.30 p.m. briefing, then he drove the few miles down to his house. He wanted to collect his post, check the condition the place was in, as the estate agent had someone coming to view it tomorrow, and make sure that his goldfish, Marlon, had plenty of food in his hopper. He didn't trust Glenn, in his current distracted state over his marriage breakdown, to remember to keep it topped up.

It was a sunny afternoon and the air had warmed up with the first promises of approaching summer. As he made his way down Church Road, passing all the familiar landmarks, he felt a sudden twinge of sadness. A decade ago he used to feel a flutter of excitement each time he drove along the wide residential street, as in a few moments he would be home. Home to the woman he used to adore so much. Sandy.

He waited at the top of the street for an elderly man in a motorized wheelchair to pass in front of him, then drove down towards the seafront. The houses were similar on both sides of the road, three-bedroom mock-Tudor semis, with integral garages, small front gardens and larger plots at the back. Little changed here over the years, just the models of the neighbours' cars and the 'for sale' boards, like the Rand & Co. one outside his house now.

As he slowed and pulled on to the driveway, it felt like a ghost house. He'd made an attempt to remove all the reminders of Sandy during the past few months, even boxing up her clothes and taking them to charity shops, but he could still feel her presence strongly. He halted the Ford in front of the garage door, knowing that on the other side of it was Sandy's ancient black VW Golf, caked in dust, the battery long dead. He wasn't sure why he hadn't sold it, not that it was worth much now. It had been found twenty-four hours after she had disappeared in the short-term car park at Gatwick Airport's

South Terminal. Perhaps he kept it because part of him still wondered if it contained as yet undiscovered forensic clues. Or perhaps just for sentimental reasons.

Whoever had written those words, that the past was another country, was right, he thought. Despite so little having changed around here, this house and this street felt increasingly alien to him each time he came here.

Climbing out of the car, he saw one of the Saturday afternoon constants of this street – a neighbour directly opposite, Noreen Grinstead. A hawk-eyed jumpy woman in her mid-seventies, whose husband had died a couple of years ago from Alzheimer's, she was out there, in her Marigold rubber gloves, polishing her elderly Nissan car as if her very life depended on it. She glanced round, checking him out, and gave him a forlorn wave.

He almost had to pluck up the courage to enter the house these days, the memories becoming increasingly painful. It had been a wreck when they bought it, as an executor sale, and with her great taste and her passion for Zen minimalism Sandy had transformed it into a cool, modern living space. Now, with the house and its Zen garden totally neglected, it was slowly reverting to its former state.

Perhaps some other young couple, full of happiness and dreams, would buy it and make it into their special place. But with the property market in its current long slump, few properties were shifting. The boss of the estate agency, Graham Rand, had suggested he drop the asking price, which he had done. Now it was spring, the market might lift and with luck the house would finally be sold. Then, along with the impending certification of Sandy's death, he would finally be able to move on. He hoped.

To his surprise, his post was in a tidy pile on the hall table, and to his even greater surprise, the hallway looked as if it had been cleaned. So did the living room, which Glenn had turned into a tip these past few months. Grace sprinted upstairs and checked out Glenn's bedroom. That looked immaculate too, the bed beautifully tidy. The place was looking like a show home. Had Glenn done this?

Yet, in a strange way, it made the house seem even more alien. It was as if the ghost of Sandy had returned. She had always kept it almost obsessively tidy.

Marlon's hopper was full and, as far as you could tell with a goldfish, his pet seemed genuinely pleased to see him. It whizzed around the bowl for several laps, before stopping and placing its face close against the glass, opening and shutting its mouth with a mournful expression.

It never ceased to amaze Grace that the creature was still alive. He'd won the fish by target shooting at a fairground, eleven years ago, and he could still remember Sandy's shriek of joy. When he'd later Googled *fairground goldfish*, and posted a request for advice, he'd been told that providing a companion was very important. But Marlon had eaten all the subsequent companions he had bought.

He glanced out of the window and got another shock. The lawn was mown. What, he wondered, was going inside his friend's head? Had the 'for sale' board freaked Glenn out – and did he think by tidying the place up, Grace might relent and take it off the market?

He glanced at his watch. It was coming up to three o'clock and he'd been told he could collect Cleo from the hospital any time after four, when the consultant had done his rounds. He made a cup of tea and sifted through his post, binning the obvious junk mail. The rest was mainly bills, plus a tax disc renewal reminder for his written-off Alfa Romeo. Then he came to one addressed to Mrs Sandy Grace. It was an invitation to a private view at a Brighton art gallery. Modern art had been one of her passions. He binned that, thinking she must be on a very old computer list that was long overdue an update.

*

Twenty minutes later, as he headed off along the seafront towards Kemp Town, he was still puzzling about what had made Glenn Branson tidy the place up so much. Guilt? Then he thought back to the bollocking he'd had from Peter Rigg, which was still hurting him a lot. He could not believe that bitch Alison Vosper had warned the ACC he needed to keep a careful eye on him.

Why? His track record in the past twelve months had been good. Every case he had been on had ended with a result. OK, there had been the deaths of two suspects in a car, and two of his team, Emma-Jane Boutwood and Glenn Branson, had been injured. Perhaps he could have been more careful – but would he have got the results? And even if the ACC did not have total confidence in him, he knew he had the backing of Detective Chief Superintendent Jack Skerritt, the head of HQ CID.

And, shit, he'd already produced one impressive result for the ACC, solving a serial rape case that went back twelve years, hadn't he?

He turned his mind to the current case. Ewan Preece, the driver of the hit-and-run van. First point was they could not be certain he was the driver, even though his fingerprints had been on the mirror. But the fact that he had not returned to Ford Prison that night was a good indicator of guilt. And applying the simple principle of Occam's Razor, which he always interpreted as *the simplest and most obvious is usually the right answer*, he was fairly confident Preece would turn out to be the driver.

He was equally confident the man would be caught quickly. His face was known to half the police in Brighton, both the uniform and CID divisions, and Grace had seen his mugshot on posters of wanted people on police station walls many times. If the police didn't spot him first, someone would grass him up for that reward money, for sure.

With a bit of luck, they'd pot him within a few days – and find out why he did a runner. Probably, Grace speculated, because he should have been working on a construction site near the prison at nine on Wednesday morning and not driving a van in Brighton, twenty-five miles away. Almost certainly with something illegal inside it.

If they could get an explanation out of Preece, he should be able to wrap up the inquiry by the end of next week. And hopefully win some brownie points with Peter Rigg. It all looked pretty straightforward.

Fortunately for Roy Grace's mood at this moment, he didn't know how brutally different things were going to turn out to be.

34

There was a long jam on the approach to the roundabout opposite the Palace Pier – wrongly, in Roy Grace's traditionalist view, renamed *Brighton Pier*. As he sat, slowly crawling forward in the traffic, he watched a couple pushing their stroller along the promenade. He found himself looking at them with intense curiosity. That was something, he realized, that had definitely changed inside him. He'd never, ever, been remotely interested in babies. Yet in recent weeks, wherever in the city he had been, he had suddenly found himself staring at babies in buggies.

A few days ago, buying a sandwich in the ASDA superstore opposite his office, he began making inane comments to the mother and father of a tiny infant in a stroller, as if the three of them were members of a very exclusive club.

Now, as the engine idled, and an old Kinks song played on BBC Radio Sussex, he found himself looking around for more buggies. A few evenings ago, the night before Cleo had gone into hospital, they'd spent a long time studying them on the Internet and had made a shortlist of ones they thought might be suitable.

Cleo was keen on ones he could go jogging with. She thought it would help him to bond with the baby, as his work would preclude them from spending much time together otherwise. One pregnancy book they had been reading together warned of this, that while the mother would be at home, developing her relationship with the baby, the father would be at work, becoming increasingly remote.

Across the road he could see a man about his own age jogging along with a baby in a Mountain Buggy Swift. Then he saw a female jogger with one they favoured, an iCandy Apple Jogger. Moments later he saw another they liked, because of the name, a Graco Cleo. And over on the far side of the promenade he saw a single woman pushing the one that they liked most of all – which was unfortunately one of the most expensive – a Bugaboo Gecko.

DEAD MAN'S GRIP

Money was no object, luckily. Cleo had told him that her parents wanted to buy it for them. Ordinarily Grace would have insisted on paying for everything himself. That was the way he had been brought up. But he had done the sums and the cost of having a baby was terrifying. And seemingly endless. Starting with having to turn the spare room at Cleo's house into the baby's room. They had been advised that it should be painted well in advance, so there was no danger to their baby from paint fumes. Then there were the digital baby monitors Cleo wanted, so they could hear the baby's breathing. The Moses basket for the baby to sleep in during its first few months. Decorations for the room. Clothes – which they could not buy yet as they did not know whether it was a boy or a girl.

It was strange not being able to put a sex to the baby. Just an *it*. Neither he nor Cleo wanted to know. But Cleo had told him on several occasions she believed it would be a boy, because the bump was high up, and because, another old wives' tale, she had been craving savoury rather than sweet things.

He did not mind. All he cared was that the baby was healthy and, more importantly to him, that Cleo was fine. He had read that fathers sometimes, when things went badly wrong, had to make a decision between saving the life of the baby and of the mother. In his mind there was absolutely no question at all. He would save Cleo every time.

A Ziko Herbie stroller went by on the promenade. Followed by a Phil & Teds Dash, a Mountain Buggy and a Mothercare Mychoice. It was sad, he thought, that he had acquired this encyclopedic knowledge of buggies in such a short space of time. Then his phone rang.

It was Norman Potting. 'Boss,' he said. 'I've got good news and – ah – not good news. But I'm running out of battery on my BlackBerry.'

'Tell me?'

All he got in reply was silence.

35

Someone had left the *Münchner Merkur* further along on the wooden trestle table where she sat, alone, beside the Seehaus lake in the Englischer Garten. The *Merkur* was one of Munich's two local papers. On the front page was a photograph of a large silver coach that had rolled on to its side, straddling and buckling an autobahn crash barrier. Emergency service crews in orange suits were standing around it and there was a bleeding victim partially visible on a stretcher.

The headline, which she translated into English in her head as she read, said, SEVEN DIE IN AUTOBAHN COACH CRASH.

Although now fluent in German, she still *thought* in English and, she realized some mornings, still dreamed in English. She wondered if one day that would change. She had German blood. Her grandmother on her mother's side had come from a small town near here and she felt increasingly strongly, with every day that passed, that Bavaria was her true spiritual home. She loved this city.

And this park was her favourite place in it. She came here every Saturday morning that she could. Today the April sunshine was unseasonably hot and she was grateful for the breeze blowing off the lake. Although dressed lightly in a T-shirt, Lycra jogging shorts and trainers, she was perspiring heavily after a ten-kilometre run. Gratefully, she gulped down half the bottle of the cold mineral water she had just bought in one draught.

Then she sat still, breathing in the sweet scents of grass and lake water and wood varnish and pure clean air. Suddenly she caught a waft of cigarette smoke from someone nearby. Instantly, as it did almost every time, that smell brought a twinge of sadness – memories of the man she had once loved so much.

She took another swig of the bottle and reached over to pick up the paper, as no one seemed to be coming back to claim it. Only eleven o'clock and the Englischer Garten was busy already. Dozens of people sat at the beer garden tables, some obviously tourists but many of them locals, enjoying the start to the weekend. Most had a *Maß* of beer in front of them, but some like herself were drinking water or Cokes. Several people were out on the lake in rowing boats and pedalos, and she watched for a moment as a mother duck, following by a string of tiny brown ducklings, rounded the wooded island.

Then suddenly a very determined-looking Nordic walker in her sixties, wearing bright red Lycra, teeth clenched, ski poles clacking on the ground, was heading straight towards her.

Leave me alone, don't invade my space, she thought, planting her elbows on the table and giving the woman a defiant glare.

It worked. The woman clacked off and settled at a table some distance away.

There were times, such as now, when she craved solitude, and there were precious few moments when she was able to find it. That was one of the things she most treasured about her Saturday morning runs. There was always so much to think about and not enough time to focus on it. Her new masters gave her new thoughts to work on every week. This week they had told her, *Before you can seek new horizons, first you have to have the courage to lose sight of the shore.*

Surely she had done that ten years ago?

Then another waft of cigarette smoke set off another sudden pang. She was going through a bad day, a bad week. Doubting everything. Feeling alone and bleak and questioning herself. She was thirty-seven, single, with two failed relationships behind her and what ahead?

Nothing at this moment.

That good old German philosopher Nietzsche said that if you looked long enough into the void, the void would begin to look back into you.

She understood what he meant. To distract herself, she began to read the newspaper report of the coach disaster. All the passengers were members of a Christian fellowship group in Cologne. Seven dead, twenty-three seriously injured. She wondered what they thought of God now. Then she felt bad for letting her mind go there and turned the page.

There was a picture of a cyclist fleeing the police and another road accident, this time a VW Passat that had rolled over. Then on the next page was the story of a factory closure, which did not interest her. Nor did a photograph of a school football team. She turned the page again. Then froze.

She stared at the printed words, unable to believe her eyes, translating each of them into English inside her head.

She read them, then reread them.

Then she just stared at them again, as if she had been turned into a pillar of salt.

It was an advertisement. Not big, just one column wide and six centimetres deep. The wording read:

SANDRA (SANDY) CHRISTINA GRACE

Wife of Roy Jack Grace of Hove, City of Brighton and Hove, East Sussex, England.

Missing, presumed dead, for ten years. Last seen in Hove, East Sussex. She is five feet, seven inches tall (1.70 metres), slim build and had shoulder-length fair hair when last seen.

Unless anyone can provide evidence that she is still alive to Messrs Edwards and Edwards LLP at the address beneath, a declaration will be sought that she is legally dead.

She continued staring, reading it, rereading it, then rereading it again.

And again.

36

'Do you know what I'm really looking forward to?' Cleo asked. 'What I'm absolutely craving?'

'Wild sex?' Roy Grace said hopefully, giving her a sideways grin.

They were in the car, heading home from hospital, and she looked a thousand times better. The colour had returned to her face and she looked radiant. And more beautiful than ever. The rest in hospital had clearly done her good.

She ran a finger suggestively a long way up his thigh. 'Right now?'

He halted the car at traffic lights on Edward Street, almost in view of John Street Police Station – known colloquially as *Brighton nick.*

'Probably not the best place.'

'Wild sex would be good,' she conceded, continuing to stroke the inside of his thigh provocatively. 'But at a risk of denting your ego, there is something I desire even more than your body right now, Detective Superintendent Grace.'

'And what might that be?'

'Something I can't have. A big slice of Brie with a glass of red wine!'

'Terrific! I'm in competition with cheese for your affections?'

'No competition. The cheese wins hands down.'

'Maybe I should take you back to the hospital.'

She leaned across and kissed him on the cheek. Then, as the lights turned green, she pressed her fingers even further into his thigh and said, 'Don't take it badly.'

As he drove forward, he pouted in a mock-sulk and said, 'I'm going to arrest every sodding piece of Brie in this city.'

'Great. Put them in the cooler for after Bump is born and I'll devour them. But I will devour you first, I promise!'

As he turned south into Grand Parade and moved over into the right-hand lane, with the Royal Pavilion ahead of him to the right, Grace was aware of a sudden feeling of euphoria. After all his fears for Cleo and their baby these past few days, everything suddenly seemed good again. Cleo was fine, back to her normal cheery, breezy self. Their baby was fine. The bollocking from ACC Rigg suddenly seemed very small and insignificant in comparison. The two-bit petty crook van driver, Ewan Preece, would be found within days, if not hours, and that would put Rigg back in his box. The only thing that really mattered to him at this moment was sitting beside him.

'I love you so much,' he said.

'You do?'

'Yep.'

'You sure about that? Even with my big tummy and the fact that I prefer cheese to you?'

'I like your big tummy – more to love.'

She suddenly took his left hand and held it to her abdomen. He could feel something moving, something tiny but strong, and he felt a lump of joy in his throat.

'Is that Bump?'

'Kicking away! He's telling us he's happy to be going home!'

'Awwww!'

Cleo released his hand, then pushed her hair back from her forehead. Grace stopped in the right-turn lane, in front of the Pavilion.

'So have you missed me?' she said.

'Every second.'

'Liar.'

'I have.' The lights turned green and he drove across the junction and doubled back around the Old Steine. 'I've kept busy googling buggies and baby names.'

'I've been thinking a lot about names,' she said.

'And?'

'If it's a girl, which I don't think it is, I like Amelie, Tilly or Freya best so far.'

'And if it's a boy?'

'I'd like Jack, after your father.'

'You would?'

She nodded.

Suddenly his phone rang. Raising an apologetic finger, he hit the hands-free button to answer.

It was Norman Potting. 'Sorry about that, chief, my battery is still down. But I thought you should know—'

Then there was silence.

'Know what?' Grace asked.

But he was talking into thin air.

He dialled the Incident Room number to ask if Potting had left any message. But Nick Nicholl, who answered, said no one had heard from him. Grace told him he would be back for the evening briefing, then hung up.

Cleo looked at him provocatively. 'So, this wild sex, then? It'll have to be a quickie?'

'Hard cheese,' he replied.

'It's the soft ones that have listeria.' She kissed him again. 'Hard sounds good.'

37

She did not feel like running any more. She felt in need of alcohol. When the waitress came round, she ordered a *Maß* of beer. One whole litre of the stuff. Then she stared back again at the words in the *Münchner Merkur*.

She could feel blind fury welling inside her. Somehow she had to contain it. It was one of the things she had been learning, anger management. She was much better at it, but she needed to focus hard to do it. Had to spiral back inside her mind to the place she was before she was angry. To the *Münchner Merkur*, lying on the table.

She closed the paper and pushed it away, calming a little. But struggling. A fury inside her was threatening to erupt and she must not let it, she knew. She could not let her anger win. It had already ruled too much of her life and had not ruled it well or wisely.

Extinguish it, she thought. *Extinguish it like the flame of a match in the wind. Just let it blow out. Watch it go.*

Calmer now, she opened the paper again and turned back to the page. She looked at the details at the bottom. There was a mailing address, an email address and a phone number.

Her next reaction was *Why?*

Then, calming a little further, she thought, *Does it matter?*

She'd kept some tabs on him, especially in recent years, now that the local Sussex newspaper, the *Argus*, was available online. As an increasingly prominent police officer it was easy; he was frequently being quoted in the news doing his stuff. Doing what he loved, being a copper. A crap husband, but a great copper. As a wife you'd always be second to that. Some accepted it. Some wives were coppers themselves, so they understood. But it had not been the life she had wanted. Or so she had thought.

But now here, alone, with each passing day she was less certain of the decision she had made. And this announcement was really unsettling her more than she could ever have imagined.

Dead?

Me?

How very convenient for you, Detective Superintendent Roy Grace, now in charge of Major Crime for Sussex. Oh yes, I've been following you. I'm only a few footsteps behind you. The ghost that haunts you. Good for you, with your passion for your career. Your dad only made it to Sergeant. You've already gone higher than your wildest dreams – at least the ones you told me about. How much higher will you go? How high do you want to go? All the way to the very top? The place you told me you didn't actually want to reach?

Are you happy?

Do you remember how we used to discuss happiness? Do you remember that night we got drunk at the bar in Browns and you told me that it was possible to have happy moments in life, but that only an idiot could be happy all of the time?

You were right.

She opened the paper and reread the announcement. Anger was boiling inside her again. A silent rage. A fire she had to put out. It was one of the first things they had taught her about herself. About that anger, which was such a big problem. They gave her a mantra to say to herself. To repeat, over and over.

She remembered the words now. Spoke them silently.

Life is not about waiting for the storms to pass. It is about learning to dance in the rain.

As she repeated them, again and again, slowly she began to calm down once more.

38

Tony Case, the Senior Support Officer at HQ CID, phoned Roy Grace early in the afternoon, to tell him one of the current inquiries at Sussex House had ended in a result sooner than expected and was now winding down, which meant MIR-1 – Major Incident Room One – had become free. Case, with whom Grace got on well, knew that was the place the Detective Superintendent favoured for conducting his inquiries.

As he made his way towards MIR-1 for the 6.30 p.m. briefing, his phone rang. He stopped in the corridor, in front of a diagram on the wall – a white sheet pinned to a red board which was headed CRIME SCENE ASSESSMENT.

It was Kevin Spinella on the line.

'Detective Superintendent, do you have a second for me?'

'Not even a nanosecond, I'm afraid. Nor a picosecond. I don't even have a femtosecond.'

'Ha-ha, very witty. One millionth of one billionth of a second. You can't even spare that?'

'You actually know what that is?' Grace was a little astonished.

'Well, I know that a nanosecond is one billionth of a second and a picosecond is one trillionth of a second. So, yeah, actually, I do know what a femtosecond is.'

Grace could hear him chewing gum, as ever, over the phone. It sounded like a horse trotting through mud.

'Didn't know you were a physicist.'

'Yeah, well, life's full of surprises, isn't it? So, do you have time to talk about *Operation Violin*?'

'I'm just going into a meeting.'

'Your 6.30 p.m. briefing?'

Grace held his temper with difficulty. Was there anything this little shit did not know?

'Yes. You probably know the agenda better than me.'

Ignoring the barb, Spinella said, 'Ewan Preece, your prime suspect . . .'

Grace said nothing for a while. His brain was whirring. How did Spinella know that? How?

But he realized there were dozens of potential sources that could have leaked this name to him, starting with Ford Prison. There was nothing to be gained from going there at this moment.

'We don't have a prime suspect at this stage,' he told the reporter, thinking hard. About how he could make Spinella useful to the investigation. Stalling for time, he said, 'We are interested in interviewing Ewan Preece to eliminate him from our enquiries.'

'And have him back under lock and key at Ford? You must be wondering why someone with only three weeks of his sentence to run would go over the wall, right?'

Grace again thought carefully before replying. It was a question he had been considering in some depth himself. He had tried to put himself in Preece's position. Difficult, because the mindset of a recidivist was unique to his – or her – circumstances. But only an idiot would escape three weeks before the end of a sentence unless there was a pressing reason. Jealousy could be one; a commercial opportunity another.

Perhaps being in the wrong place, at the wrong time was a third? Driving a van in Brighton, when you were meant to be labouring on a construction site in Arundel?

'I'm sure that hundred-thousand-dollar reward is going to help find you the van driver,' Spinella said. 'Presume you've had some calls to the Incident Room?'

There had actually been remarkably few, which had surprised Grace. Normally rewards brought every nutter and chancer out of the woodwork. But this call was an opportunity for more publicity – and especially to put pressure on anyone out there who might know Preece's whereabouts.

'Yes,' he lied. 'We are delighted with the response of the general public and we are urgently following several leads which we believe have come to us directly as result of this massive reward.'

'I can quote you on that?'

'You can.'

Grace ended the call and entered MIR-1. As ever, with a major crime inquiry, some wag had put a humorous picture on the back of the door, making fun of the inquiry name. It was a particularly good one today – a cartoon of a man in a fedora and turned up mackintosh, clutching a violin case and smoking a huge stogie.

The two Major Incident Rooms at Sussex House, MIR-1 and MIR-2, were the nerve centres for major crime inquiries. Despite opaque windows too high to see out of, MIR-1 had an airy feel, good light, good energy. It was his favourite room in the entire head-quarters building. While in other parts of Sussex House he missed the messy buzz of police station incident rooms that he had grown up with, this room felt like a powerhouse.

It was an L-shaped space, divided up by three large workstations, each comprising a long curved desk with room for up to eight people to sit, and several large whiteboards. One, headed OPERATION VIOLIN, had the diagram of the vehicles involved in the accident, which Inspector Biggs from the Road Policing Unit had produced earlier. Another had the start of a family tree of Tony Revere, including the name and immediate family of his girlfriend. On a third was a list of names and contact numbers of principal witnesses.

There was an air of intense concentration, punctuated by the constant warbling of phones, which the members of his expanding team answered haphazardly.

He saw Norman Potting on the phone, making notes as he spoke. He still had not spoken to him since the two attempted calls in his car. He sat down at an empty workstation and placed his notes in front of him.

'Right!' he said, as Potting ended his call, raising his voice to get everyone's attention. 'The time is 6.30 p.m., Saturday 24 April. This is the seventh briefing of *Operation Violin*, the investigation into the death of Tony Revere.' He looked at the Crime Scene Manager. 'Tracy, I understand you have a development?'

There was a sudden blast of house music. Embarrassed, PC Alec Davies quickly silenced his phone.

'Yes, chief,' Stocker replied. 'We've had a positive ID of the van type back from Ford, from their analysis of the serial number on the wing mirror. They've confirmed it was fitted to the '06 model. So, considering the time and location where the mirror-casing fragment was found, I think we can say with reasonable certainty it belonged to our suspect Ford Transit.' She pointed up at the whiteboard. 'Vehicle 1 on the diagram.'

'Do we know how many of these vans were made in that year?' Emma-Jane Boutwood asked.

'Yes,' Stocker answered. 'Fifty-seven thousand, four hundred and thirty-four Ford Transit vans sold in the UK in 2006. Ninety-three per cent of them were white, which means fifty-three thousand, four hundred and thirteen vans fit our description.' She smiled wryly.

Sergeant Paul Wood of the Collision Investigation Unit said, 'One line that would be worth pursuing would be to contact all repair shops and see if anyone's brought a Transit in for wing mirror repair. They get damaged frequently.'

Grace made a note, nodding. 'Yes, I've thought of that. But he'd have to be pretty stupid to take the van in for repairs so quickly. More likely he'd tuck it away in a lock-up.'

'Ewan Preece doesn't sound like the sharpest tool in the shed,' Glenn Branson chipped in. 'I don't think we should rule it out, boss.'

'I'll put it down as an action for the outside inquiry team. Perhaps we can put a couple of PCSOs on it.' Then he turned to Potting. 'Norman, do you have your update from Ford Prison?'

Potting pursed his lips, taking his time before answering. 'I do, chief,' he said finally, in his rich rural burr.

In another era, Grace could have envisaged him as a bloody-minded desk sergeant plod in some remote country town. Potting spoke slowly and methodically, partly from memory and partly referring to his notebook. Every few moments he would squint to decipher his handwriting.

'I interviewed Senior Prison Officer Lisa Setterington, the one you spoke to, chief,' Potting said.

Grace nodded.

'She confirmed that Preece appeared to be a model prisoner, determined to go straight.'

Potting was interrupted by a couple of snorts from officers who'd had previous dealings with the man.

'So if he was a model prisoner,' asked Bella Moy sarcastically, 'how come he was driving a van twenty-five miles away from where he was supposed to be on Wednesday morning?'

'Exactly,' Potting said.

'Model prisoners don't go over the wall either,' she added tartly.

'They don't, Bella, no,' he agreed condescendingly, as if talking to a child.

Grace eyed both of them warily, wondering if they were about to have another of their regular spats.

'Now the good news is,' Potting went on, 'that word of this reward has spread around the prison, as you might imagine. Several inmates who've had contact with Preece have come forward to the Governor, offering suggestions where he might be, and I've got a list of six addresses and contact names for immediate follow-up.'

'Good stuff, Norman,' Grace said.

Potting allowed himself a brief, smug smile and took a swig from his mug of tea before continuing, 'But there's some bad news too. Ewan Preece had a friend in Ford Prison, another inmate – they go back years.' He checked his notes. 'Warren Tulley – had about the same amount of form as Preece. They were thick together inside. The officer had arranged for Tulley to talk to me. Someone went to fetch him to bring him over to the office – and found him dead in his cell. He'd hanged himself.'

There was a momentary silence while the team absorbed this. Grace's first reaction was that this news had not yet reached Spinella.

DC David Howes asked, 'What do we know about his circumstances?'

'He had two months to serve,' Potting said. 'Married with three young kids – all fine with the marriage apparently. Lisa Setterington knew him too. She assured me he was looking forward to getting out and spending time with his kids.'

'Not someone with any obvious reason to top himself?' Howes, who was a former Prison Liaison Officer, probed.

'Doesn't sound like it, no,' Potting replied.

'I'm just speculating, but what it sounds like to me,' Howes went on, 'is that possibly Warren Tulley knew where to find Preece.' He shrugged.

'Which might be why he died?' Grace said. 'Not suicide at all?'

'They're launching a full investigation, working closely with the West Area Major Crime Branch Team,' Potting said. 'Seems a bit coincidental to them.'

'How hard would it be to hang yourself in Ford?' Glenn Branson asked.

'Easier than in a lot of prisons. They've all got private rooms, like motel rooms,' Potting said. 'Being an open prison, they've got much more freedom and are left alone much more than in a higher-category place. If you wanted to hang yourself, you could do so easily.'

'And equally easily hang someone else?' Howes asked.

There was a long, uncomfortable silence.

'One hundred thousand dollars is a lot of folding to someone inside,' Glenn said.

'It's a lot of folding to anyone,' Nick Nicholl replied.

'More than enough to kill for,' Howes said grimly.

PC Alec Davies put up a hand. He spoke quite shyly. 'Sir, I might be stating the obvious, but if Warren Tulley did know where Preece was, then if someone did kill him, he possibly did it for one reason. Because he knows where Preece is too.'

39

Fernanda Revere sat restlessly on the edge of the green sofa. She gripped a glass in one hand and held a cigarette in the other, tapping the end impatiently, every few seconds, into a crystal ashtray. Then, with a sudden snort, she put down her cigarette, snatched up her cellphone and glared at it.

Outside a storm raged. Wind and rain were hurtling in from Long Island Sound, through the dunes and the wild grasses and the shrubbery. She heard the rain lashing against the windows and could feel the icy blast through them.

This huge living room, with its minstrel's gallery, ornate furniture and walls hung with tapestries, felt like a mausoleum tonight. A fire crackled in the grate but she could get no warmth from it. There was a ball game on television, the New York Mets playing some other team, which her brother shouted at intermittently. Fernanda didn't give a shit for baseball. A stupid men's game.

'Why don't those stupid people in England call me back?' she demanded, staring at her phone again, willing it to ring.

'It's the middle of the night there, hon,' her husband replied, checking his watch. 'They're five hours ahead. It's one in the morning.'

'So?' She took another angry drag on her cigarette and puffed the smoke straight back out. 'So this *associate*, where is he? He's going to show up? You sure? You sure about this, Ricky?'

She stared suspiciously at her brother, who was sitting opposite her, cradling a whiskey and sucking on a cigar that looked to her the size of a large dildo.

Lou, in a checked alpaca V-neck over a polo shirt, chinos and boat shoes, looked at Ricky, his face hard suddenly, and said, 'He's going to show, right? He's reliable? You know this guy?'

'He's reliable. One of the best there is. He's in the car – be here any moment.'

Ricky picked up the brown envelope he had prepared, checked its contents once more, then put it down again, satisfied, and turned his focus back to the game.

At forty, Ricky Giordino had the Italian looks of his father, but not the old man's strong face. His face was weak, a tad pudgy, like a baby's, and pockmarked. It shone with an almost permanent shiny patina of grease, from a congenital problem with his sweat glands. His black hair was styled with a quiff and his mouth was slightly misshapen, as if he'd had an operation for a harelip as a child. He was dressed in a thick black cardigan with metal buttons, baggy blue jeans which concealed the handgun permanently strapped to his calf and black Chelsea boots. So far, to their mother's dismay, he had remained single. He had a constant succession of brainless bimbos in tow, but tonight he had come alone, as his particular way of showing respect.

'You done business with this guy before?' Fernanda asked.

'He's recommended.' Ricky gave a self-satisfied smile. 'By an associate of mine. And there's a bonus. He knows this city, Brighton. He did a job there one time. He'll do what you want done.'

'He'd better. I want them to suffer. You told him that, didn't you?'

'He knows.' Ricky puffed on his cigar. 'You spoke to Mamma? How was she?'

'How do you think she was?' Fernanda drained the rest of her Sea Breeze and got up, unsteadily, to walk towards the drinks cabinet.

Ricky turned his attention back to the game. Within moments, he leapt out of his armchair, shaking a hand at the screen and showering cigar ash around him.

'The fuck!' he shouted. 'These guys, the fuck they doing?'

As he sat back down a series of sharp chimes came from the hall.

Ricky was on his feet again. 'He's here.'

'Mannie'll get it,' Lou said.

*

Tooth sat in the back of the Lincoln Town Car, dressed casually but smartly in a sports coat, open-neck shirt, chinos and brown leather

149

loafers, the kind of clothes in which he could go anywhere without raising an eyebrow. His brown holdall lay on the seat beside him.

The driver had wanted to put it in the trunk when he had collected him from Kennedy Airport, but Tooth never let it out of his sight. He never checked it in, it came inside the plane with him on every flight. The bag contained his clean underwear, a spare shirt, pants, shoes, his laptop, four cellphones, three spare passports and an assortment of forged documents all concealed inside three hollowed-out paperback books.

Tooth never travelled with weapons, other than a quantity of the incapacitating agent 3-quinuclidinyl benzilate – BZ – disguised as two deodorant sticks, in his washbag. It wasn't worth the risk. Besides he had his best weapons on the end of his arms. His hands.

In the beam of the headlights he watched the high grey electric gates opening and the rain pelting down. Then they drove on through, until ahead he could see the superstructure of a showy modern mansion.

The driver had said nothing during the journey, which suited Tooth fine. He didn't do conversation with strangers. Now the man spoke for almost the first time since he had checked Tooth's name at the arrivals lobby at the airport.

'We're here.'

Tooth did not reply. He could see that.

The driver opened the rear door and Tooth stepped out into the rain with his bag. As they reached the porch, the front door of the house was opened by a nervous-looking Filipina maid in uniform. Almost immediately, she was joined by a mean-faced, pot-bellied man in a fancy black cardigan, jeans and black boots, holding a big cigar.

Tooth's first reaction was that the cigar was a good sign, meaning he could smoke in here. He stepped inside, into a huge hall with a grey flagstone floor.

A wide circular staircase swept up ahead of him. There were gilded mirrors and huge, bizarre abstract paintings which made no sense to him. Tooth didn't do art.

The man held out a fleshy hand covered in glinting rings, saying,'Mr Tooth? Ricky Giordino. Y'had a good journey?'

Tooth shook the man's clammy hand briefly, then released it as fast as he could, as if it was a decomposing rodent. He didn't like to shake hands. Hands carried germs.

'The journey was fine.'

'Can I fix you a drink? Whiskey? Vodka? Glass of wine? We got just about everything.'

'I don't drink when I'm working.'

Ricky grinned. 'You haven't started yet.'

'I said I don't drink when I'm working.'

The smile slid from Ricky's face, leaving behind an awkward leer. 'OK. Maybe some water?'

'I had water in the car.'

'Great. Terrific.' Ricky checked his cigar, then sucked on it several times, to keep it burning. 'Maybe you want something to eat?'

'I ate on the plane.'

'Not great, that shit they give you on planes, is it?'

'It was fine.'

After five military tours, some of them solo, fending for himself behind enemy lines, eating beetles and rodents and berries sometimes for days on end, anything that came on a plate or in a bowl was fine by Tooth. He wasn't ever going to be a gourmet. He didn't do fine food.

'We're good, then. All set. Do you want to put your bag down?'

'No.'

'OK. Come with me.'

Tooth, still holding his bag, followed him along a corridor furnished with a fancy antique table, on which sat ornate Chinese vases, and past a living room that reminded him of an English baronial hall in a movie he'd seen long ago. A bitch in navy velour was sitting on a sofa, smoking a cigarette, with an ashtray full of butts beside her, and a loser was sitting opposite her, watching a bunch of dumb fuckwits playing baseball.

This is what I risked my life for, gave my all for, so assholes like these could sit in their swell homes, with their fancy phones, watching dickheads playing games on big television screens?

Ricky ducked into the room and reappeared almost immediately carrying a brown envelope. He ushered Tooth back along the corridor to the hall, then led him down the stairs and into the basement. At the bottom was an abstract painting, as tall as Tooth, covered in what looked like photographs with weird faces. His eyes flickered with mild interest.

'That's pretty special,' the man said. 'A Santlofer. One of the up-and-coming great modern American artists. You wanted to buy that now, you'd pay thirty grand. Ten years time, you'll pay a million. The Reveres are great patrons. That's one of the things my sister and my brother-in-law do, they spot rising talents. You gotta support the arts. Y'know? Patrons?'

The painting looked to Tooth like one of those distorting mirrors you saw in fairgrounds. He followed the man through into a huge poolroom, the table itself almost lost against the patterned carpet. There was a bar in one corner, complete with leather stools and a stocked-up wine fridge with a glass door.

The man sucked on his cigar again, until his face was momentarily shrouded in a billowing cloud of dense grey smoke.

'My sister's pretty upset. She lost her youngest son. She doted on the kid. You gotta understand that.'

Tooth said nothing.

'You shoot pool?' the man said.

Tooth shrugged.

'Bowl?'

The man indicated him to follow and walked through into the room beyond. And now Tooth was impressed.

He was staring at a full-size, underground ten-pin bowling alley. It had just one lane, with polished wooden flooring. It was immaculate. Balls were lined up in the chute. All down the wall, beside the lane, was wallpaper that gave the illusion of rows of stacked bookshelves.

'You play this?'

As his reply, Tooth selected a ball and placed his fingers and thumb in the slots. Then he squinted down the length of the lane and could see that all the pins, white and shiny, were in place.

'Go ahead,' the man said. 'Enjoy!'

Tooth wasn't wearing the right shoes, so he made the run-up carefully and sent the ball rolling. In the silence of the basement it rumbled, like distant thunder. It clouted the front pin exactly where he had aimed it, slightly off centre, and it had the desired effect. All ten pins went straight down.

'Great shot! Gotta say, that's not at all bad!'

The man drew again on his cigar, puffing out his cheeks, blowing out the heavy smoke. He hit the reset button and watched the mechanical grab scoop up the pins and start to replace them.

Tooth dug his hand into his pocket, pulled out a pack of Lucky Strikes and lit one. After he had taken the first drag, the man suddenly snatched it out of his hand and crushed it out in an onyx ashtray on a ledge beside him.

'I just lit that,' Tooth said.

'I don't want that fucking cheap thing polluting my Havana. You want a cigar, ask me. OK?'

'I don't smoke cigars.'

'No cigarettes in here!' He glared challengingly at Tooth.

'She was smoking a cigarette upstairs.'

'You're down here with me. You do business my way or you don't do it. I'm not sure I like your attitude, Mr Tooth.'

Tooth considered, very carefully, killing this man. It would be easy, only a few seconds. But the money was attractive. Jobs hadn't exactly been flooding in just recently. Even without seeing this house, he knew about the wealth of this family. This was a good gig. Better not to blow it.

He picked up another ball, rolled it and hit another strike, all ten pins down.

'You're good, aren't you?' the man said, a little grudgingly.

Tooth did not respond.

'You've been to a place in England called Brighton? Like in Brighton Beach here in New York, right?'

'I don't remember.'

'You did a job for my cousin. You took out an Estonian ship captain in the local port who was doing side deals on cargoes of drugs.'

'I don't remember,' he said, again being deliberately vague.

'Six years ago. My cousin said you were good. They never found the body.' Ricky nodded approvingly.

Tooth shrugged.

'So, here's the deal. In this envelope are the names and all we have on them. My sister's prepared to pay one million dollars, half now, half on completion. She wants each of them to suffer, real bad. That's your specialty, right?'

'What kind of suffering?'

'Rumour has it you copied the Iceman's stunt with the rat. That right?'

'I don't copy anyone.'

The Iceman had been paid to make a victim he'd been hired to hit suffer. The client had wanted proof. So he wrapped the man, naked, in duct tape, with just his eyes, lips and genitals exposed. Then he left him in an underground cavern filled with a bunch of rats that had been starved for a week, and a video recorder. Afterwards his client had been able to watch the rats eating him, starting with the exposed areas.

'Good. She'd appreciate you being creative. We have a deal?'

'One hundred per cent cash upfront only,' Tooth said. 'I don't negotiate.'

'You know who you're fucking dealing with?'

Tooth, who was a good six inches shorter, stared him hard in the eye. 'Yes. Do you?' He shook another cigarette out of the pack and stuck it in his mouth. 'Do you have a light?'

Ricky Giordino stared at him. 'You got balls, I tell you that.' He hit the reset button again. 'How can I be sure you'll deliver? That you'll get all three hits?'

Tooth selected another ball from the chute. He lined himself up, ran, then crouched and sent the ball rolling. Yet again all ten pins scattered. He dug his hand in his pocket and pulled out a plastic lighter. Then he held it up provocatively, willing the man to try to stop him.

But Ricky Giordino surprised him by pulling out a gold Dunhill, clicking it open and holding up the flame to his cigarette.

'I think you and I – we're pretty close to understanding each other.'

Tooth accepted the light but did not reply. He didn't do understanding.

40

Self-confident, successful, tender and empa-
thetic man, 46, likes rock & classical music,
Belgian chocolate, bushcraft, integrity and
loyalty. WLTM intelligent and warm female
40–50 to share so many things.

Bushcraft?

Carly was curled up on the sofa with a glass of red Rioja in one
hand and *Top Gear* about to start on the television. The Sunday
supplements were spread all around her. It was her first drink since
the accident and she needed it, as she was feeling very depressed.

The page of the *Sunday Times* she most looked forward to each
week, the Encounters dating column, was open in front of her.
Searching, as ever, not for Mr Right, but for someone to at least go
out with and have fun with.

Bushcraft? What the hell did that mean? She'd learned from long
experience that much of the wording in these ads had a subtext.
How did this bloke get his rocks off? By walking around naked
outside? Going back to nature? Shooting animals with a bow and
arrow? The rest of him sounded fine. But bushcraft? No thanks.

Maybe if he had written *fossils* instead or *archaeology*, subjects
that would appeal to Tyler, she might have given him a whirl. But
she had visions of a bearded weirdo clambering out of an elderly
Land Rover in a Davy Crockett hat and grass underpants. Nothing
would surprise her any more.

It had been a long time since she'd slept with anyone. Over a
year now and that last one had been a disaster. And the one before
that. All the dates had been bloody disasters, with Preston Dave just
the latest in the long line of them.

He'd sent her three more texts this weekend, each of which
she'd deleted.

God, five years on and at times she still missed Kes so much.

155

Often clients told her they felt confident with her because she was so tough. But the truth was, she knew today more than ever, that she wasn't tough at all. That was an act she put on for them. A mask. The *Carly Chase at Work* mask. If she had really been tough, she'd be able to leave her clients behind at the end of each day. But she couldn't, not with a lot of them.

Kes used to tell her sometimes that she cared about her clients too much, to the point where it was getting her down. But she couldn't help that. Good marriages, like theirs had been, gave you a wonderful inner strength and sense of fulfilment in life. Bad marriages, as she encountered every day, in the tears and trembling voices and shakily signed statements of her clients, were a prison.

The *Argus* had been running stories on the accident every day, except today, when, being a Sunday, fortunately it wasn't printed. The front-page headline on Thursday had been the $100,000 reward put up by the dead boy's family for information leading to the van driver's identity. Her photograph had been on the second page: **Brighton Solicitor Arrested At Death Crash.**

She'd been in the paper again on Friday, yesterday too. It had made the national press also, with a big splash in the tabloids, as well as being in the *Sunday Times* today. It was big news that Tony Revere was the grandson of the New York Mafia capo Sal Giordino. She'd even had reporters phoning her at the office, but on the advice of Acott, her colleague and also her solicitor, she had not spoken with them. Although she had badly wanted to – to point out that she had not caused the accident, or even collided with the cyclist.

It seemed that everything that could possibly go wrong, in the house and in her life, was all going wrong at once. A dark gloom swirled inside her. That Monday morning feeling arriving an unwelcome twelve hours early, as it had done for as far back in her life as she could remember, way into early childhood.

Sunday evenings had been worse for her since Kes had died. It had been around this time, five years ago, that two police officers had turned up at her front door. They'd been contacted, via Interpol, by an RCMP officer from Whistler in Canada, asked to inform her that her husband was missing, presumed dead, in an avalanche while heli-skiing. It had been a further four days of anxious waiting, hoping against hope for some miracle, before they had recovered his body.

She often thought of selling the house and moving to a different part of the city. But she wanted to give Tyler some continuity and stability, and several of her friends, and her mother, whom she adored, had advised her in the months immediately following Kes's death not to make any hasty decisions. So she was still here, five years on.

The house wasn't particularly attractive from the outside. It was 1960s red brick, with a double garage beneath it, a clumsy extension, plus ugly secondary double-glazing put in by the previous owners which Carly and Kes had been planning to change. But they had both particularly loved the huge living room, with its patio doors opening on to the large, pretty sloping garden. There were two small ponds, a rockery and a summer house at the top which Kes and Tyler had made into a male domain. Tyler liked to play his drums there, while Kes liked to sit and do his thinking and smoke his cigars.

Kes and Tyler had been close, not just father and son, but proper mates. They went to football together to support the Albion every home match during the season. In the summer they went fishing, or to the cricket, or more often than not to Tyler's favourite place in Brighton, the Booth Museum of Natural History. They were so close that at times she'd found herself almost feeling jealous, thinking that she was being left out of some of their secrets.

After Kes's death, Tyler had moved his drum kit indoors, up to his room, and she had never seen him go to the summer house again. He'd been withdrawn for a long time. She had made a big effort, even taking him to football and to cricket herself, and on a fishing trip on a boat out of Brighton Marina – and she had been violently seasick for her troubles. They'd developed a certain closeness, but there was still a distance between them, a gap she could never quite close. As if the ghost of his father would always be the elephant in the room.

She stared at a spreading brown stain on the wallpaper opposite her. Damp coming in. The house was falling apart around her. She was going to have to get to grips with it, either give it a massive makeover or finally move. But where? And besides, she still liked the place. She liked the feel of Kes's presence. Particularly in this living room.

They'd made it cosy, with two big sofas in front of the television and a modern electric fire with dancing flames. On the mantelpiece above it were invitations to parties and weddings and other social events they'd been planning to go to in the months after Kes got back from his annual boys' skiing trip. She still had not had the heart to remove them. It was like living in a time warp, she knew. One day she would move on. But not yet. She still wasn't ready.

And after the traumas of the past few days, she was less ready than ever.

She looked up at Kes's photograph on the mantelpiece amid the invitations. Standing next to her on the grass outside All Saints' Church, Patcham, on their wedding day, in a black morning coat, striped trousers, holding his top hat in his hand.

Tall and handsome, with slightly unruly jet-black hair, he had a certain air of arrogant insouciance about him. That was if you didn't know him. Behind that façade, which he regularly used with devastating effect in courtroom appearances, was a kind and surprisingly insecure man.

She drank some more wine and batted away a particularly dense and smelly fart from Otis, who was asleep at her feet. Then she increased the volume on the remote. Normally Tyler would come running into the room and curl up on the sofa beside her. This was his favourite programme, and one of the few times they sat and watched anything together. On this particularly gloomy, rain-lashed night, she felt more in need of his company than ever.

'Tyler!' she shouted. '*Top Gear*'s starting!'

Her voice woke up Otis, who jumped to his feet, then suddenly pricked up his ears and ran out of the room, growling.

Jeremy Clarkson, in a louder jacket and even baggier jeans than usual, was talking about a new Ferrari. She grabbed the remote again and froze the image, so that Tyler wouldn't miss anything.

He'd had been in a strange mood these past few days, since her accident. She was not sure why, but it was upsetting her. It was almost as if he was blaming her for what had happened. But as she replayed those moments again, for the thousandth time since Wednesday morning, she still came to the same conclusion: that she was not to blame. Even if she had not been distracted by her phone, and had braked half a second earlier, the cyclist would still have swerved out and then been hit by the van.

Wouldn't he?

Suddenly she heard the clack of the dog flap in the kitchen door, then the sound of Otis barking furiously out in the garden. What at, she wondered? Occasionally they had urban foxes, and she often worried that he might attack one and find he had met his match. She jumped up, but as she entered the kitchen, the dog came running back in, panting.

'Tyler!' she called out again, but still there was no answer from him.

She went upstairs, hoping he wasn't watching the programme on his own in his room. But to her surprise, he was sitting on his chair in front of his desk, going through the contents of his father's memory box.

Tyler had an unusual ambition for a twelve-year-old. He wanted to be a museum curator. Or more specifically the curator of a natural history museum. His ambition showed in his little bedroom, which was itself like a museum, reflecting his changing tastes as he had grown older. Even the colour scheme, which he had chosen himself, of powder-blue walls and pastel-green wood panelling, and the gaily coloured pennants criss-crossing the ceiling, gave the room an ecological feel.

His bookshelves were covered in plastic vegetation and models of reptiles, and crammed with volumes of *Tintin* and *Star Wars* stories, natural history reference books, palaeontology books, and one, so typical of him, called *Really Really Big Questions*.

The walls were covered with carefully selected and mounted photographs, wild life and fossil prints and some cartoon sketches of his own, all divided into sections. One of her favourites of his drawings was headed: *Tyler's Dream*. It depicted himself looking like a mad professor, with a crude skeleton of a prehistoric monster to his left, labelled *Tylersaurus*, and rows of squiggly little objects to his right, labelled *Fossils*. At the bottom of the cartoon he had written,

I want to be a fossil expert at the Natural History Museum . . . Have the biggest fossil collection in the world . . . Discover a dinosaur.

There was also a *Tintin* section, on part of one wall, neatly plastered in cartoons. And his music section, where his drum kit was set up. A guitar hung from the wall, along with a solitary bongo, and his cornet lay on a shelf, with a book beside it entitled *A New Tune a Day.*

'Tyler, *Top Gear*'s on!' she said.

He didn't stir. He was sitting in silence, in his grey cagoule with NEW YORK JETS on the back, with the old shoebox that he had filled with items that reminded him of his dad in the months following Kes's death in front of him. She wasn't sure where he had got the idea of the memory box from, some American TV series he had been watching, she thought, but she had liked it and still did.

He'd moved his computer keyboard and mouse pad aside, and was laying the contents out on the small amount of space not already occupied by his lava lamp, telescope, microscope and slide projector. She saw him take out his father's spotted silk handkerchief, his blue glasses case, fishing permit, a Brighton & Hove Albion season ticket, a box of trout flies and a small cartoon he had drawn, depicting his dad as a winged angel, flying past a signpost directing him up to heaven.

She eased her way carefully around the drum kit and placed her hands on his shoulders.

'What's up?' she said tenderly.

Ignoring her, he removed his father's fishing knife. At that moment there was a dark snarl from Otis. A second later she heard the bang of the dog flap, then Otis was out in the garden again, barking furiously. Puzzled, she walked across to the window and peered down.

It wasn't fully dark and there was some lighting from her windows and those of her neighbours. She looked up the steep lawn, past the ponds, towards the summer house, and saw Otis running around, barking furiously. At what? She could see nothing. But at the same time it unsettled her. This wasn't his normal behaviour. Had there been an intruder? Otis stopped barking and rushed around the lawn again, nose to the ground, as if he had picked up a scent. A fox, she thought. Probably just a fox. She turned back to Tyler and saw to her surprise that he was crying.

She walked the few steps back over to him, knelt and hugged him.

'What is it, darling? Tell me?'

He stared at her, eyes streaming behind his glasses. 'I'm scared,' he said.

'What are you scared of?'

'I'm scared after your crash. You might have another crash, mightn't you?' Then he looked at her solemnly. 'I don't want to have to make another memory box, Mummy. I don't want to have to make one about you.'

Carly put her arms around him and gave him a hug. 'Mummy's not going anywhere, OK? You're stuck with me.' She kissed his cheek.

Out in the garden, Otis suddenly began barking even more ferociously.

Carly got up and moved to the window. She peered out again, feeling a deepening sense of unease.

41

The plane landed hard, hitting the runway like the pilot hadn't realized it was there. All the stuff in the galley rattled and clanked, and one of the locker doors flew open, then slammed back shut. Flying didn't bother Tooth. Since his military days, he considered it a bonus to be landing any place where people weren't shooting at you. He sat impassively, braced against the deceleration, thinking hard.

He'd slept fine, bolt upright in this same position for most of the six-and-a-half-hour flight from Newark. He had gotten used to sleeping this way when he was on sniper missions in the military. He could remain in the same place, in the same position, for days when he needed to, relieving himself into bottles and bags, and he could sleep anywhere, wherever he was and whenever he needed to.

He could have charged the client for a business or first-class seat if he'd wanted, but he preferred the anonymity of coach. Flight crew paid you attention when you travelled up front and he didn't want the possibility of any of them remembering him later. A small precaution. But Tooth always took every small precaution going. For the same reason, he'd flown out of Newark rather than Kennedy Airport. It was a lower-profile place; in his experience it had less heavy security.

Trails of rain slid down the porthole. It was 7.05 a.m. UK time on his watch. The watch had a built-in digital video recorder with the pinhole camera lens concealed in the face. It had its uses for clients who wanted to see his handiwork. Like his current client.

A female voice was making an announcement about passengers in transit which did not concern him. He looked out across the grey sky and concrete, the green grass, the parked planes and signposts and runway lights and slab-like buildings of Gatwick Airport. One civilian airport looked pretty much like another, in his view. Sometimes the colour of the grass differed.

The bespectacled American in the seat next to him was clutching his passport and landing card, which he had filled out.

'Bumpy landing,' he said, 'huh?'

Tooth ignored him. The man had tried to strike up a conversation the moment he'd first sat down last night and Tooth had ignored him then, too.

*

Fifteen minutes later a turbaned immigration officer opened the UK passport up, glanced at the photograph of James John Robertson, brushed it across the scanner and handed it back to the man without a word. Just another British citizen returning home.

Tooth walked through, then followed the signs to the baggage reclaim and exit. No one gave a second glance to the thin, diminutive, shaven-headed man who was dressed in a dark brown sports coat over a grey polo shirt, black jeans and black Cuban-heeled boots. He strode towards the green Customs channel, holding his small bag in one hand and a thick beige anorak folded over his arm.

The Customs hall was empty. He clocked the two-way mirror above the stainless-steel examining benches as he walked through, passing the second-chance duty-free shop and out into the Arrivals Hall, into a sea of eager faces and a wall of placards bearing names. He scanned the faces, out of habit, but saw nothing familiar, no one looking particularly at him, nothing to be concerned about.

He made his way to the Avis car rental desk. The woman checked his reservation.

'You requested a small saloon, automatic, in a dark colour, Mr Robertson?'

'Yes.' He could do a good English accent.

'Would you be interested in an upgrade?'

'If I wanted a better model I'd have ordered one,' he said flatly.

She produced a form for him to sign, wrote down the details of his UK licence, then handed it back to him, along with an envelope with a registration number written on it in large black letters.

'You're all set. Keys are in here. Will you be returning it full?'

Tooth shrugged. If his plans for the days ahead worked out the way he intended, and they usually did, the company would not be seeing the car again. He didn't do rental returns.

42

If there were no developments, the initial energy of any new major crime inquiry could fade fast. Roy Grace had always seen one of his essential duties as the SIO as being to keep his team focused and energized. You *had* to make them feel they were making progress.

And in truth, if you didn't get a quick, early resolution, many major crime inquiries became painstakingly long and drawn out. Too slow-moving for the brass in Malling House, who were always mindful of the press, their obligations to the community and the ever present shadow of crime statistics, as well as far too slow for the families of the victims. Days could quickly become weeks, and weeks would drag into months. And occasionally months could turn into years.

One of his heroes, Arthur Conan Doyle, was once asked why, having trained as a doctor, he had turned to writing detective stories. His reply had been, 'The basis of all good medical diagnosis is the precise and intelligent recognition and appreciation of minor differences. Is this not precisely what is required of a good detective?'

He thought hard now about those words, as he sat with his team in the Monday morning briefing. Day six of the inquiry. 8.30 a.m. A wet, grey morning outside. A sense of frustration inside. It took Norman Potting to say what they were all feeling.

'He's vermin, this Ewan Preece. And he's thick. We're not dealing with someone smart. This is a cretin who lives off the slime at the bottom of the gene pool. My bogies are smarter than he is.'

Bella Moy screwed up her face in disgust. 'Thank you, Norman. So what's your point, exactly?'

'Just what I've said, Bella. That he's not smart enough to hide – not for any length of time. Someone'll shop him, if he isn't spotted by a police officer before then. A reward of a hundred thousand dollars – the bugger doesn't have a prayer.'

'So you're saying we should just wait, not bother with this line of enquiry?' Bella dug into him harder.

Potting pointed at a whiteboard, at the centre of which Ewan Preece's name was written in large red letters and circled, with his prison mugshot pasted beside it. It showed a thin-faced young man. He had short, spiky hair, a scowling mouth that reminded Grace of a braying donkey and a single gold hooped earring. Various lines connected the circle around him to different names: members of his family, friends, known associates, contacts.

'One of that lot, they'll know where Preece is. He's around, here in the city, mark my words.'

Grace nodded. Someone like Preece wouldn't have any contacts outside his small world of petty criminals within Brighton and Hove. This was likely to be the limit of his horizons. Which made it even more irritating that the little toerag had managed to remain at large for five days already without a sighting.

On the typed notes from his MSA he had headings for four of the different lines of enquiry so far.

1. Ewan Preece – family, friends, known associates and contacts
2. Search for the van – local witnesses and CCTV
3. Ford Transit wing mirror
4. Ford Prison – (link to 1.)

He looked up at the whiteboard, at the family tree of Preece's relatives and social network that they were putting together. He stared at the weaselly, scarred face of Preece, so thin he looked almost emaciated. He'd had dealings with him before when he'd done a two-year spell on Response, before he'd joined the CID. Preece was like many in this city, a kid of a single parent from a rough estate, who'd never had guidance from his rubbish mother. Grace remembered going round to see her after Preece, then aged fourteen, had been arrested for joyriding. He could still recall her opening the door with a fag in her mouth, saying, 'What do you expect me to do? I'm on me way to play bingo.'

He turned to PC Davies, who was looking tired. 'Anything to report, Alec?'

'Yes, chief.' He yawned. 'Sorry, been up all night going through

CCTV footage. There were several sightings of what might be our van within the timeline.'

'Did any of the cameras get the index?'

He shook his head. 'No, but several are fairly positive sightings because you can see the wing mirror's missing. In the first of these at the junction of Carlton Terrace and Old Shoreham Road it was heading west. It was still heading west, according to the camera at Benfield Way and Old Shoreham Road. The same at the one sited on Trafalgar Road and on Applesham Way. Then the last sighting was the van heading south towards Southwick.'

'Do any show the driver?' Glenn Branson asked.

Davies nodded. 'Yes, but not clearly enough to identify him. I've given the footage to Chris Heaver in the Imaging Unit to see if he can enhance it for us.'

'Good,' Grace said.

'I think he may have gone to ground somewhere in central Southwick,' Alec Davies said. He stood up and walked uncertainly over to another whiteboard, on which was pinned a large-scale street map of the city. 'My reasoning is this. The vehicle was last sighted here.' He pointed. 'This CCTV camera is outside an off-licence, close to Southwick Green. So far there are no further sightings. I've had officers checking all around that area and there are a number of cameras that would almost certainly have picked up the van if it had gone down to the harbour, or doubled back and along the Old Shoreham Road, or if it had headed on to the A27.' He looked directly at Grace. 'It could be an indication it's still within this area, sir.' Then he circled with his finger around Southwick and Portslade, taking in the northern perimeter of Shoreham Harbour.

'Good work,' Grace said. 'I agree. Map the area out with boundaries and get the Outside Inquiry Team, and local officers who know the area, to do a street-by-street search. Get them to knock on the door of every house that's got an enclosed garage and ask permission to look inside. And see if there are any lock-ups in the area, or anywhere else that a van could be kept concealed. At the same time, get your team to talk to people in the area. Maybe there are witnesses who saw the van driving fast or erratically around that time.'

'Yes, sir.'

'And now I think you need to get some rest.'

Davies grinned. 'I'm tanked on caffeine, sir. I'm fine.'

Grace looked at him hard for a moment, before saying, 'Good lad, but don't exhaust yourself.' He looked down at the next item on his list, then addressed Sergeant Paul Wood from the Collision Investigation Unit. 'Have we got any more information from the van's wing mirror?'

'I wasn't happy, because we hadn't recovered all the parts from the scene, chief,' Wood replied. 'I had the Specialist Search Unit take a look down all the gutters and they found a bit I was missing. Unless there's anything else we haven't found, and I don't think there is, there's a clean break on the arm, which means it's probable the actual mountings for the mirror unit on the van are still intact. Replacing it would be a simple task of buying – or stealing – a replacement wing mirror unit. It could be fitted by anyone in a few minutes with basic tools.'

Grace made a note, thinking that most, if not all, spare parts depots would have been closed yesterday, on a Sunday, then looked up at Norman Potting, who he could always rely on to be thorough. Nick Nicholl was a grafter, too.

'Norman and Nick, I'm tasking you to cover all places where you could obtain a new or second-hand wing mirror for this vehicle. Ford dealers, parts depots, accessories shops like Halfords, breakers' yards – and check to see if there have been any reports of wing mirror thefts off similar vans in the Brighton and Hove area. If you need extra manpower let me know. I want every possibility covered by this evening's briefing, if possible.'

Nicholl nodded like an eager puppy. Potting made a note, his face screwed up in concentration.

'What about eBay? That could be a likely port of call to replace something like this.'

'Good point, Norman. Give that to Ray Packham in the High-Tech Crime Unit. He'll know the most effective way to search it.'

Then he returned to his list. 'OK, the last agenda item is Ford Prison. Glenn and Bella, I want you to go there and see what you can get out of any of the inmates who knew Preece or Warren Tulley.

I spoke to Lisa Setterington, the officer there who was in charge of Preece, and she's lining them up for you. And she's been working with our Prison Liaison Officer. I think your strategy should be to focus on Preece as someone who's gone missing, rather than as a suspect in the hit-and-run, and don't even refer to Tulley. Setterington's an experienced officer. She'll deliver all Preece's associates inside Ford to you. If any of them open up, emphasize the reward ticket. And put the frighteners on them – tell them Preece is going to be shopped by someone, so it might as well be them.'

'Do we have a post-mortem report on Tulley yet, chief?' asked Nick Nicholl.

'I'm waiting for it,' Grace replied. Then he looked back at his notes. 'Preece is a good suspect. All of you speak to any informants you know. Put the word out on the street that we're looking for him – and about the reward. Not everyone reads the papers or listens to the news.'

DC Boutwood raised a hand. 'Chief, I've spoken with an undercover member of *Operation Reduction* who's running a number of informants. He's asked around for me, but none of Preece's regular contacts have heard from him in the past week.'

I don't think I'd talk to my regular contacts with a $100K price tag on my head either, Grace thought, but what he actually said was, 'He's obviously keeping his head down, E-J. But he'll surface somewhere.'

Had he possessed a crystal ball, he might have used a different turn of phrase.

43

When the meeting ended Grace asked Glenn Branson to come and see him in his office in ten minutes' time. Then, as he walked alone along the corridor, he rang Cleo. Despite the consultant's instructions for her to rest, she had insisted on going back to work today, although she had promised Roy she would not do any heavy lifting.

She sounded fine but was too busy to speak for more than a moment. Lots of people died at weekends, falling off ladders doing DIY, born-again bikers going out for fast rides, men pegging out during their solitary bonk of the week and the lonely who found the weekends too much to bear. Her enthusiasm for her grim work never ceased to amaze him. But by the same token, she frequently said the same of him.

He made himself a coffee in the space the size of a small closet, with a kettle, worktop, sink and fridge, that was Sussex House's apology for a canteen and carried it through to his office. He had barely sat down when Glenn entered.

'Yo, old-timer. What's popping?'

Grace grinned at his use of that word. He'd recently circulated to Sussex CID a DVD he'd been sent by a senior detective in Los Angeles, whom he had met last year at the International Homicide Investigators Association annual symposium. It was on the large number of Hispanic gangs prevalent on the streets of LA and in the prisons, giving guidance on how to recognize and interpret their slang, the symbols on their clothing and in their tattoos, and their hand signals, all of which were copied by the less organized but equally nasty UK street gangs.

'Popping?'

'Uh-huh.'

'What's *popping* is that I want you to take this evening's briefing.' Grace grinned, clocking Branson's even sharper than usual suit

– grey with purple chalk stripes. 'That's if you haven't got an appointment with your tailor.'

'Yep, well, I need to make you one, get you some new summer gear.'

'Thanks, you did that last year and cost me two grand.'

'You've got a beautiful young fiancée. You don't want to take her out dressed like an old git.'

'Actually, that's why I need you to take over from me this evening. I'm taking her out tonight. Got tickets for a concert at the O_2 in London.'

Branson's eyes widened. 'Cool. What concert?'

'The Eagles.'

Branson gave him a *sad bastard* stare and shook his head. 'Get real! The Eagles? That's old git's music! She's an Eagles fan?'

Grace tapped his chest. 'No, I am.'

'I know that, old-timer. Seen them in your house. Can't believe how many of their albums you have.'

'"Lyin' Eyes" and "Take It Easy" are two of the best singles of all time.'

Branson shook his head. 'You've probably got Vera Lynn on your iPod, as well.'

Grace blushed. 'Actually I still haven't got an iPod.'

'That figures.' Branson sat down, put his elbows on Grace's desk and stared him hard in the eyes. 'She's just come out of hospital and you're going to inflict the Eagles on her? I can't believe it!'

'I bought the tickets ages ago, for a fortune. Anyhow, it's a quid pro quo.'

'Oh yeah?'

'In exchange, I've promised to take Cleo to a musical.' He gave Glenn a helpless look. 'I don't like musicals. Give and take, right?'

Branson's eyes widened. 'Don't tell me. *The Sound of Music*?'

Grace grinned. 'Don't even go there.'

44

Tooth drove from the Avis section of the car park, made a circuit of the airport and drove in through the entrance marked Long Term Car Park. Instead of following the directions to Today's Parking Area, he headed off, steadily driving up and down the lanes of cars already parked there, looking for other Toyota Yaris models that were of the same year and colour as his own.

Within twenty minutes he had identified five. Three of them were parked in deserted areas, out of sight of any CCTV cameras. Working quickly, he removed each of their front and rear licence plates and put them in the boot of his car. Then, paying the minimum fee, he drove back out of the car park and headed towards the Premier Inn, one of the hotels close to the airport perimeter.

There he requested a second-floor room, one with a view of the hotel parking area and the main entrance. He favoured second-floor rooms. No one outside could see in and should he need to leave in a hurry, via the window, that was a survivable jump, for him. He also told the woman receptionist he was expecting delivery of a FedEx package.

He locked the door, placed his bag on the bed, opened it and took out the brown envelope Ricky Giordino had given him. Then he moved the wooden desk in front of the window, climbed on to it and taped over the smoke detector on the ceiling, before sitting in the purple chair and staring out and down. The hotel had taken trouble over the parking area. Well-trimmed bushes, low ornamental hedges, round wooden tables, a covered smoking shelter. Seventy-two cars, including his small dark grey Toyota, were parked in neat rows. He remembered the make, colour and position of them all. That was something he had learned from his days in the military. You remembered what you could see. When some detail, however small, changed, that was the time to be concerned.

Beyond the far end of the lot was a tall red crane and beyond that the dark hulk of a building rising in the distance with the words GATWICK NORTH TERMINAL near the roofline in large white letters.

He made himself an instant coffee and then studied once more the contents of the envelope.

Three photographs. Three names.

Stuart Ferguson. A stocky man of forty-five with a shaven head and a triple chin, wearing a green polo shirt with the words ABERDEEN OCEAN FISHERIES in yellow. Carly Chase, forty-one, a passably attractive woman, in a chic black jacket over a white blouse. Ewan Preece, thirty-one, spiky-haired scumbag, in a dark cagoule over a grey T-shirt.

He had addresses for the first two, but only a phone number for Preece.

He took out one of his cellphones and inserted the UK pay-as-you-go SIM card he had purchased at Gatwick Airport a short while ago, then dialled the mobile phone number.

It answered on the sixth ring. An edgy-sounding man said, 'Yeah?'

'Ricky said to call you.'

'Oh yeah, right. Hang on.' Tooth heard a scraping sound, then the voice again, quieter, furtive. 'Yeah, with you now. Difficult to talk, you see.'

Tooth didn't see. 'You have an address for me.'

'That's right, yeah. Ricky knows the deal, right?'

He didn't like the way the man sounded. He hung up.

Then he glared up at the smoke detector, feeling in need of a cigarette. Moments later his cellphone rang. The display showed no number. He hit the answer button but said nothing.

After a moment the man he had just spoken to said, 'Is that you?'

'You want to give me the address or you want to go fuck yourself?' Tooth replied.

The man gave him the address. Tooth wrote it down on the hotel notepad, then hung up without thanking him. He removed the SIM card, burned it with his cigarette lighter until it started melting and flushed it down the toilet.

Then he unfolded the street map of the City of Brighton and

Hove he had bought at the WH Smith bookstall and searched for the address. It took him a while to locate it. Then he pulled out another phone he had with him, his Google Android, which was registered in the name of his associate, Yossarian, and entered the address into its satnav.

The device showed him the route and calculated the time. By car it was forty-one minutes from the Premier Inn to this address.

Then on his laptop Tooth opened up Google Earth and entered Carly Chase's address. Some moments later he was zooming in on an aerial view of her house. It looked like there was plenty of secluded garden around it. That was good.

He showered, changed into his fresh underwear and made himself some more coffee. Then, returning to Google Earth, he refreshed his memory of another part of the city, an area he had got to know well the last time he was here, the port to the west of Brighton, Shoreham Harbour. Seven miles of waterfront, it was a labyrinth with a large number of places where no one went. And twenty-four-hour access. He knew it as well as he had known some enemy terrain.

Shortly after 11 a.m., the room phone rang. It was the front desk, telling Tooth that a courier was waiting with a package for him. He went down and collected it, took it up to his room and removed the contents, placing them in his bag. Then he burned the receipt and delivery note, and everything on the packaging that revealed its origins.

He packed everything else back into his bag, too, then picked it up and took it with him. He had already prepaid the room charge for a week, but he didn't yet know when he would return, if he returned at all.

45

Carly did not start the week in a good frame of mind. Her only small and bleak consolation was that, with luck, this week would be marginally less shitty than the previous one. But with the client settling into the chair in front of her now, Monday was not starting on a promising note.

Ken Acott had informed her that the court hearing was set for Wednesday of the following week. He was going to try to get her Audi released from the police pound as soon as possible, but the car was badly damaged and there was no likelihood of it being repaired within the next ten days. She was going to lose her licence for sure, hopefully getting only the minimum of one year's ban.

Clair May, another mother with a son at St Christopher's with whom she was very friendly, had taken Tyler to school this morning and would bring him home this evening. She had told Carly that she was happy to do this for as long as was needed, and Carly was grateful at least for that. It had never occurred to her quite how lost she would be without a car, but today she was determined not to let it get her down. Kes used to tell her to view every negative as a positive. She was damned well going to try.

First thing this morning she had looked into contract taxi prices, Googled bus timetables and had also checked out buying a bike. It was a fair hike to the nearest bus stop from her home and the bus schedule was not that great. A bike would be the best option – at least on days when it wasn't pissing down with rain. But with the memory of the accident scene still vivid in her mind, she could not contemplate cycling with any enthusiasm at this moment.

Her client's file was open in front of her. Mrs Christine Lavinia Goodenough. Aged fifty-two. Whatever figure the woman might once have had was now a shapeless mass and her greying hair appeared to have been styled in a poodle parlour. She laid her fleshy hands on her handbag, which she had placed possessively on her lap, as if she did not trust Carly, and had a look of total affront on her face.

It was rarely the big things that destroyed a marriage, Carly thought. It wasn't so much the husband – or the wife – having an affair. Marriage could often survive problems like that. It was often more the small things, with the tipping point being something really petty. Such as the one the woman in front of her now revealed.

'I've been thinking since last week. Quite apart from his snoring, which he flatly refuses to acknowledge, it's the way he *pees* at night,' she said, grimacing as she said the word. 'He does it deliberately to irritate me.'

Carly widened her eyes. Neither her office nor her desk was grand or swanky in any way. The desk was barely big enough to contain her blotter, the in and out trays, and some pictures of herself and Tyler. The room itself, which had a fine view over the Pavilion – and a less fine constant traffic roar – was so spartan that, despite having been here six years, it looked like she had only just moved in, apart from the stack of overflowing box files on the floor.

'How do you mean, *deliberately*?' she asked.

'He pees straight into the water, making a terrible splashing sound. At precisely two o'clock every morning. Then he does it again at four. If he were considerate, he'd pee against the porcelain, around the sides, wouldn't he?'

Carly thought back to Kes. She couldn't remember him peeing during the night, ever, except perhaps when he had been totally smashed.

'Would he?' she replied. 'Do you really think so?'

Although Carly made her money for the firm in dealing with matrimonial work, she always tried to dissuade her clients from litigation through the court. She got much more satisfaction from helping them negotiate resolutions to their problems.

'Perhaps he's just tired and not able to concentrate on where he is aiming?'

'Tired? He does it deliberately. That's why God gave men willies, isn't it? So they can aim direct where they're pissing.'

Well, God really thought of everything, didn't he?

Though she was tempted to say it, instead Carly advised, 'I think you might find that hard to get across in your hearing.'

'That's coz judges are all blokes with little willies, aren't they?'

Carly stared at the woman, trying to maintain her professional integrity – and neutrality. But she was rapidly coming to the conclusion that if she was this cow's husband, she would long ago have tried to murder her.

Not the right attitude, she knew. But sod it.

46

Tooth wasn't happy as he turned into the residential street and drove over a speed bump. It was wide and exposed, with little tree cover. It was a street you could see a long way down, on both sides, without obstruction. A hard street to hide in. A little parade of shops and mixture of semi-detached houses and bungalows. Some had integral garages, others had had this area converted into an extra front room. Cars were parked along the kerb on both sides, but there were plenty of free spaces. There was a school some way down and that wasn't good news. These days people kept an eye on single men in cars parked near schools.

He saw the house he had come to find, number 209, almost immediately. It was directly opposite the shops and had an attached garage. It was the house where he had been informed that his first target, Ewan Preece, was holed up.

He drove past, continuing along the street for some distance, then meandered along various side roads, before returning to his target street five minutes later. There was an empty space a short distance from the house, between a dilapidated camper van and an original cream Volkswagen Beetle with rusted wings. He reversed into the space.

This was a good position, giving him an almost unobstructed view of the house. It seemed to be in poor repair. The exterior paintwork had once been white but now looked grey. The window-sills were rotten. There were black trash bags in the front garden, along with a rusted washing machine that looked like it had been there for years. People ought to have more self-respect, he thought. You shouldn't leave trash in your front yard. He might mention that to Preece. They'd have plenty of time to chat.

Or rather, Preece would have plenty of time to listen.

He opened his window a little and yawned, then switched the engine off. Although he had slept on the plane, he felt tired now and

PETER JAMES

could use another coffee. He lit a Lucky Strike and sat smoking it, staring at the house, thinking. Working out a series of plans, each contingent on what happened in the coming hours.

He pulled out the photograph of Ewan Preece and studied it yet again. Preece looked an asshole. He'd recognize him if he left – or returned to – the house. Assuming the information was correct and he was still there, in number 209.

There was important stuff he did not know. Starting with who else might be in the house with Preece. Not that it would be a problem. He'd deal with it. The kind of person who would shield a man like Ewan Preece was going to be similar low-life vermin. Never a problem. A few spots of rain fell on the windshield. That was good. Rain would be helpful. Nice heavy rain would frost the glass and make him less visible in here, and keep people off the streets. Fewer witnesses.

Then, suddenly, he stiffened. Two uniformed male police officers came into view around the corner, at the far end of the street. He watched them strut up to the front door of a house and ring the bell. After some moments they rang again, then knocked on the door. One of them pulled out a notebook and wrote something down, before they moved on to the next house, nearer to him, and repeated the procedure.

This time the door opened and he saw an elderly woman. They had a brief conversation on the doorstep, she went back inside, then came out again with a raincoat on, shuffled around to the garage and lifted the up-and-over door.

It didn't take a rocket scientist to figure out what they might be looking for. But their presence here threw him totally. He watched as the two officers nodded, then turned away and walked down to the next house, moving closer still to him. He was thinking fast now.

Driving away was one option. But the police were so close, that might draw attention to him, and he didn't want them taking note of the car. He glanced over the road at the parade of shops. Better to stay here, remain calm. There didn't appear to be any parking restrictions. There was no law against sitting in your car, smoking a cigarette, was there?

He crushed the butt out into the car's ashtray and sat watching them. They got no answer at the next house, had a brief conversation on the pavement, then split, one of them crossing the road, heading up the pavement and entering the first shop in the parade.

His colleague was now knocking on the door of number 209.

Tooth felt in need of another cigarette. He shook one from the pack, put it in his mouth and lit it, watching the windows of the house as the policeman stood on the doorstep, his knock unanswered. Then he glimpsed an upstairs curtain twitch, just a fraction. Such a tiny movement, he wouldn't have noticed it if he hadn't been watching so closely.

It was enough to know there was someone in there. Someone who wasn't going to open the door to a cop. Good.

The officer knocked again, then pressed what Tooth assumed was a bell. After some moments he pushed it again. Then he turned away, but instead of walking to the front door of the next house in the row, he came over to the car.

Tooth remained calm. He took another drag of his cigarette, dropping the photograph of Ewan Preece on the floor between his feet.

The policeman was now bending, tapping on his passenger side window.

Tooth switched on the ignition and powered the window down.

The policeman was in his mid-twenties. He had sharp, observant eyes and a serious, earnest expression.

'Good morning, sir.'

'Morning,' he replied, in his English accent.

'We're looking for a white Ford Transit van that was seen driving erratically in this area last Wednesday. Does that ring any bells?'

Tooth shook his head, keeping his voice quiet. 'No, none.'

'Thank you. Just as a formality, can I check what you are doing here?'

Tooth was ready for the question. 'Waiting for my girlfriend. She's having her hair done.' He pointed at the salon, which was called Jane's.

'Likely to be a long wait, if she's like my missus.'

The officer stared at him for a second, then stood up and walked towards the next house. Tooth powered the window back up, watching him in the mirror. The cop stopped suddenly and turned back to look at his car again. Then he walked up to the front door of the house.

Tooth continued to watch him, and his colleague, working their way along every house, all the way down the street, until they were safely out of sight. Then, in case they returned, he drove off. Besides, there wasn't any point in hanging out in this street in daylight. He would return after dark. In the meantime, he had plenty of work to do.

47

Taking his seat at the workstation in MIR-1, with a coffee in his hand, Roy Grace felt tired and a little despondent. Ewan Preece had gone to ground and there was no telling how long he might remain in hiding. Tomorrow would be a whole week since the collision, without a single reported sighting of the man, despite the reward.

On the plus side was the fact that Preece was not bright, and sooner or later he would make a mistake and be spotted, for sure – if he wasn't shopped first by someone. But in the meantime there was a lot of pressure on him from ACC Rigg, who in turn was under pressure from the Chief Constable, Tom Martinson, to get a fast result.

Sure, it would all die down as time passed, especially when a bigger news story came along, but for the moment *Operation Violin* was making a lot of people uncomfortable. In particular the new Chief Executive of Brighton and Hove City Council, John Barradell, who was doing his best to rid the city of its unwelcome sobriquet Crime Capital of the UK. It was he in turn who was putting the most pressure on the police chiefs.

'The time is 8.30 a.m., Tuesday 27 April,' Grace said at the start of the morning briefing. He looked down at his printed notes. 'We have new information from Ford Prison on the death of Warren Tulley, Ewan Preece's mate.'

He looked at Glenn Branson, then at the rest of his team, which was growing by the day. They had now spilled over into both the other workstations in this large office. The latest addition was DS Duncan Crocker, whom he had brought in as the Intelligence Manager. Crocker, who was forty-seven, had receding wavy hair turning grey at the edges and a constantly jovial demeanour that implied, no matter how grim the work, there would always be a decent drink waiting for him at the end of the day. This belied the man's efficiency. Crocker was a thorough professional, a sharp and astute detective, and a stickler for detail.

Glenn Branson said, 'I have the post-mortem report on Tulley, boss. He was hanging from a steel beam in his cell from a rope made out of strips of bedding sheet. The officer who found him cut him down above the knot and proceeded to perform CPR on him, but he was pronounced dead at the scene twenty minutes later by a paramedic. To summarize the report – ' he held it up to indicate that it was several pages long – 'there are a number of factors to indicate this was not suicide. The ACCT – Assessment, Care in Custody, and Teamwork – report on this prisoner indicates no suicidal tendencies, and, like Ewan Preece, he was due to be released in three weeks' time.'

Norman Potting's mobile phone rang, the *James Bond* theme blaring out. Grunting, he silenced it.

'Have you just changed that from *Indiana Jones*?' Bella Moy said.

'It sort of came with the phone,' he replied evasively.

'That's just so cheesy,' she said.

Branson looked down at his notes. 'There was evidence of a struggle in Tulley's cell and several bruises have been found on his body. The pathologist says that it appears he was asphyxiated by strangling first and then hung. He also found human flesh under some of his fingernails, which has been sent off for DNA analysis. These are all indicative of a struggle.'

'If he was strangled by another prisoner at Ford, that DNA analysis will give us him,' Duncan Crocker said.

'With luck,' Branson said. 'It is being fast-tracked and we should have a result back later today or tomorrow.' He glanced down at his notes again, then looked at Roy Grace as if for reassurance. Grace smiled at him, proud of his protégé. Branson went on. 'According to Officer Setterington, who has spoken with several of the prisoners whom Preece and Tulley hung out with, Tulley was shooting his mouth off about the reward money. They all saw it on television and in the *Argus*. He was boasting he knew where Preece was and was weighing up his loyalty to his friend against the temptation of a hundred thousand dollars.'

'Did he genuinely know?' asked Bella Moy.

Branson raised a finger, then tapped his keypad. 'Every prisoner in a UK jail gets given a PIN code for the prison phone, right? And they have to nominate the numbers they will call – they can have a maximum of ten.'

'I thought they all had mobile phones,' Potting said with a sly grin.

Branson grinned back. It was a standard joke. Mobile phones were strictly forbidden in all prisons – and as a result they were an even more valuable currency than drugs.

'Yeah, well, luckily for us, this fellow didn't. Listen to this recording on the prison phone of a call made by Warren Tulley to Ewan Preece's number.'

He tapped the keypad again, there was a loud crackle, then they heard a brief, hushed conversation, two scuzzy, low-life voices.

'Ewan, where the fuck are you? You didn't come back. What's going on?'

'Yeah, well, had a bit of a problem, you see.'

'What kind of fucking problem? You owe me. It's my money in this deal.'

'Yeah, yeah, yeah, keep yer hair on. I just had a bit of an accident. You on the prison phone?'

'Yeah.'

'Why don't you use a private?'

'Coz I ain't got one, all right?'

'Fuck. Fuck you. I'm lying low for a bit. All right? Don't worry about it. I'll see you right. Now fuck off.'

There was a clank and the call ended.

Branson looked at Roy Grace. 'That was recorded at 6.25 p.m. last Thursday, the day following the accident. I've also checked the timing. Prisoners working on paid resettlement, which is what Preece was doing, are free to leave the prison from 6.30 a.m. and don't have to be back until 10 p.m. That would have given him ample time to be driving in Portland Road around 9 a.m.'

'*Lying low,*' Grace said pensively. 'You need someone you can trust to lie low.' He stood up and went over to the whiteboard where Ewan Preece's family tree was sketched out. Then he turned to Potting. 'Norman, you know a fair bit about him. Any ideas who he was close to?'

'I'll speak to some of the neighbourhood teams, boss.'

'My guess is, since the van seems to have disappeared in Southwick, that he'll be there, with either a girlfriend or a relative.' Grace looked at the names on the whiteboard.

As was typical with the child of a single, low-income parent, Preece had a plethora of half-brothers and sisters as well as step-brothers and sisters, with many of the names well known to the police.

'Chief,' Duncan Crocker said, standing up. 'I've already been doing work on this.' He went over to the whiteboard. 'Preece has three sisters. One, Mandy, emigrated to Perth, Australia, with her husband four years ago. The second, Amy, lives in Saltdean. I don't know where the youngest, Evie, lives, but she and Preece were pretty thick as kids. They got nicked, when Preece was fourteen and she was ten, for breaking into a launderette. She was in his car later when he was done for joyriding. She'd be a good person to look for.'

'And a real bonus if she just happens to be living in Southwick,' Grace replied.

'I know someone who'll be able to tell us,' Crocker said. 'Her probation officer.'

'What's she on probation for?' Branson asked.

'Handling and receiving,' Crocker said. 'For her brother!'

'Phone the probation officer now,' Grace instructed.

Crocker went over to the far side of the room to make the call, while they carried on with the briefing. Two minutes later he returned with a big smile on his face.

'Chief, Evie Preece lives in Southwick!'

Suddenly, from feeling despondent, Grace felt a surge of adrenalin. He thumped the worktop with glee. *Yayyy!*

'Good work, Duncan,' he said. 'You have the actual address?'

'Of course! Two hundred and nine Manor Hall Road.'

The rest of this briefing now seemed redundant.

Grace turned to Nick Nicholl. 'We need a search warrant, PDQ, for two hundred and nine Manor Hall Road, Southwick.'

The DC nodded.

Grace turned back to Branson. 'OK, let's get the Local Support Team mobilized and go pay him a visit.' He looked at his watch.

'With a bit of luck, if the warrant comes through and we get there fast enough, we'll be in time to bring him breakfast in bed!'

'Don't give him indigestion, chief,' Norman Potting said.

'I won't, Norman,' Grace replied. 'I'll tell them to be really gentle with him. Ask him how he likes his eggs and if we should cut the crusts off his toast. Ewan Preece is the kind of man who brings out the best in me. He brings out my inner Good Samaritan.'

48

An hour and a half later, Grace and Branson cruised slowly past 209 Manor Hall Road, Southwick. Branson was behind the wheel and Grace studied the house. Curtains were drawn, a good sign that the occupants were not up yet, or at least were inside. Garage door closed. With luck the van would be parked in there.

Grace radioed to the other vehicles in his team, while Branson stopped at their designated meeting point, one block to the south, and turned the car around. The only further intelligence that had come through on Evie Preece was that she was estranged from her common-law husband and apparently lived alone in the house. She was twenty-seven years old and had police markers going back years, for assault, street drinking, possession of stolen goods and handling drugs. She was currently under an ASBO banning her from entering the centre of Brighton for six months. All three of her children, by three different fathers, had been taken into care on the orders of the Social Services. She and her brother were two peas in a pod, Grace thought. They'd no doubt be getting plenty of lip from her when they went in.

'So, old-timer, tell me, how was the concert last night? What did Cleo think of your sad old git band?'

'She thought the Eagles were great, actually!'

Branson looked at him quizzically. 'Oh yeah?'

'Yeah!'

'You sure she wasn't just humouring you?'

'She said she'd like to see them again. And she bought a CD afterwards.'

Branson tapped his head. 'You know, love does make people go a bit crazy.'

'Very funny!'

'You probably had an old person's nap in the middle of it. The band probably did too.'

'You're so full of shit. You are talking about one of the greatest bands of all time.'

'And you going to London on Friday night to see *Jersey Boys*?' Glenn said.

'Are you going to trash them, too?'

'Frankie Valli and the Four Seasons – they're all right.'

'You actually like their music?'

'Some of it. I don't think *all* white music's rubbish.'

Grace grinned and was about to say something to Glenn, but then he saw in the mirror the dog handler's marked van pulling up behind them. After another few moments the unmarked white minibus, containing eight members of the Local Support Team, halted alongside them, momentarily blocking the road. Two other marked police cars reported they were now in position at the far end of the street.

Jason Hazzard, the Local Neighbourhood Team Inspector, looked in at them and Grace gave him the thumbs up, mouthing, 'Rock 'n' roll.'

Hazzard pulled his visor down and the three vehicles moved forward, accelerating sharply with a sense of urgency now, then braking to a halt outside the house. Everyone bundled out on to the pavement. Thanks to Google Earth they'd had a clear preview of the geography of the place.

Two sets of dog handlers ran up the side to cover the back garden. The members of the Local Support Team, in their blue suits, protective hard plastic knee pads, military-style helmets with visors lowered and heavy-duty black gloves, ran up to the front door. One of them carried a metal cylinder, the size of a large fire extinguisher – the battering ram, known colloquially as the *Big Yellow Door Key*. Two others, bringing up the rear, carried the back-up hydraulic ram and its power supply, in case the front door was reinforced. Two more stood outside the garage to prevent anyone escaping that way.

The first members of the team to reach the door pounded on it with their fists, at the same time yelling, 'POLICE! OPEN UP! POLICE! OPEN UP!' It was a deliberate intimidation tactic.

One officer swung the battering ram and the door splintered open.

All six of them charged in, shouting at the tops of their voices, 'POLICE! POLICE!'

Grace and Branson followed them into a tiny hallway that stank of stale cigarette smoke. Grace's adrenalin was pumping. Like most officers, he'd always loved the thrill of raids, and the fear that went with it. You never knew what you were going to find. Or what missiles or weapons might be used against you. His eyes darted everywhere, warily, ever conscious of the possibility that someone might appear with a weapon, and that both himself and Glenn were less well protected than the members of this team, wearing only stab vests beneath their jackets.

The LST members, all experienced and well trained in this kind of operation, had split up in here. Some were bursting into different downstairs rooms and others at the same time were charging up the stairs, yelling menacingly, 'POLICE! STAY WHERE YOU ARE! DON'T MOVE!'

The two detectives stayed in the narrow, bare hallway and heard doors banging open above them. Heavy footsteps. Then a female member of the team, whom Grace knew and rated as a particularly bright and plucky officer, Vicky Jones, called out to him in a concerned voice, 'Sir, you'd better come in here!'

Followed by Glenn Branson, he walked through the open door-way to his right, into a small and disgustingly cluttered sitting room that reeked of ingrained cigarette smoke and urine. He noticed a wooden-framed settee, bottles of wine and beer littering a manky carpet, along with unwashed clothes, and a massive plasma TV screen on the wall.

Face down, occupying whatever floor space wasn't littered with detritus, was a writhing, moaning woman in a fluffy pink dressing gown, bound hand and foot with grey duct tape, and gagged.

'No one upstairs!' shouted Jason Hazzard.

'Garage is empty!' another voice called out.

Grace ran upstairs very quickly, glanced into the two bedrooms and the bathroom, then went back down and knelt beside the woman, as Vicky Jones and another member of the team worked away the tape over her mouth, then the rest of the bindings.

The woman, in her mid-twenties, had a shock of short, fair hair and a hard face with a flinty complexion. She spoke the moment her mouth was freed.

'Fuckers!' she said. 'What took you so fucking long? What's the fucking time?'

'Five past ten,' Vicky Jones said. 'What's your name?'

'Evie Preece.'

'Are you injured, Evie?' She turned to another officer and said, 'Call an ambulance.'

'I don't need no fucking ambulance. I need a bleedin' drink and a fag.'

Grace looked at her. He had no idea at this stage how long she had been there, but she looked remarkably composed for someone who had been tied and gagged. He wondered if it was a set-up. This was not a woman you could trust with any story.

'Where's your brother?' Roy Grace asked her.

'Which bruvver?'

'Ewan.'

'In prison. Where you pigs put him.'

'So he hasn't been staying here?' he pressed.

'I didn't have no one staying.'

'Someone's been sleeping in your spare bed,' Grace said.

'Must have been the Man in the Moon.'

'Was that who tied you up? The Man in the Moon is into bondage, is he?'

'I want a solicitor.'

'You're not under arrest, Evie. You only get a solicitor if you are charged with something.'

'So charge me.'

'I will do in a minute,' Grace said. 'I'll charge you with obstructing a police officer. Now tell me who slept in your spare room?'

She said nothing.

'The same person who tied you up?'

'No.'

Good, he thought. That was a big step forward.

'We're concerned about your brother,' he said.

'That's bleedin' touching, that is. You been nicking him since he was a kid, but you're suddenly concerned about him? That's rich!'

49

At the evening briefing, Grace brought his team up to speed on the raid. Evie Preece was unable to give any information about her assailant, but the fact that she consented, albeit reluctantly, to a medical examination was an indication to Grace that the attack on her had been real and not a put-up job by herself and her brother, as he had first suspected. The house was such a tip it was hard to gauge whether it had been rifled through, which could have given robbery as a possible motive for the attack.

The police doctor's opinion was that the severe bruising to her neck was indicative of a sharp blow. She added that the side of the neck, just above the collarbone, was the place where someone experienced in martial arts would strike, if they wanted to render their victim instantly unconscious.

This was consistent with Evie's story that around eleven the previous night she had gone out into the garden to let her cat out, and the next thing she had found herself lying, trussed up, on her living-room floor. She was continuing to refute the allegation that her brother had been in the house and she denied vehemently that any vehicle had been in her garage recently, despite evidence to the contrary. The first piece of which was a pool of engine oil on the surface of the garage floor, which looked recent. The second and even more significant was the discovery of male clothing in the spare bedroom. A pair of trainers and jeans that were consistent with Ewan Preece's size, and a T-shirt, also his size, found in her washing machine.

Grace had ordered her to be arrested on suspicion of harbouring a fugitive and obstructing the police, and assigned a trained interview adviser, Bella Moy, to come up with an interview strategy for her while she was being held in police custody.

In addition, he had put a highly experienced POLSA – Police Search Advisor – and a search team under him into the property to see if they could find anything else in the house or garden. So far, in addition to the oil and the clothes, they had come up with what they believed to be signs of a forced entry through kitchen patio doors at the rear of the house. It was very subtly done, with an instrument such as a screwdriver handled by someone with a good knowledge of locks.

To Grace's mind that ruled out the kind of low-life Ewan Preece and his sister dealt with, who might have been after money or drugs. Their scumbag associates would have broken a window or jemmied a lock. Whoever had come in here was skilled. Not just in breaking and entering, but in assault and in bindings. They had found no fingerprints so far, nothing that might yield DNA and no other clues. It was still early days, but it wasn't looking good.

50

Dressed in a heavy fleece jacket, thick jeans, a lined cap and rubber boots, David Harris began his workday at 7.00 a.m. sharp, as he had every day for the past forty-one years, by checking the rows of smokehouses, where the fish had been curing overnight. He was in a cheery frame of mind: business was booming despite the recession and he genuinely loved his work.

He especially loved the sweet scents of the burning wood and the rich, oily tang of the fish. It was a fine, sunny morning, but there was still a crisp chill in the air. The kind of mornings he liked best. He looked at the dew sparkling on the grassy slopes of the South Downs, which towered up behind the smokery, a view which still, after a lifetime of working here, he never tired of looking at.

He might have been less cheery had he known he was being watched and had been since the moment he arrived here this morning.

Springs Smoked Salmon was a household name throughout Europe and the family were proud of the quality. Harris was second-generation, running the company that had been started by his parents. The location, tucked away in a valley in the South Downs, close to Brighton, was an improbable one for a fish company, and the place had an unprepossessing air – the ramshackle collection of single-storey buildings could have belonged to a tumbledown farm rather than containing a business that had become an international legend.

He walked up an incline, past a fork-lift truck and a line of parked delivery vans, between the identical cold-storage sheds. Inside them the rows of headless Scottish salmon and trout, his company's speciality, were being smoked, hung on hooks suspended from overhead racks that stretched back the full hundred-foot length of the shed, or lay packed in white Styrofoam boxes, ready for dispatch to gourmet stores, restaurants and catering companies around the globe. Also stacked on pallets were other fish and seafood products they supplied to their customers, in particular langoustines and scampi, most of which came from Scotland as well as scallops, lobsters and crabs.

He unlocked the padlock on the first door and pulled it open, checking that the temperature was fine. Then he checked each of the next three sheds as well, before moving on to the smokery ovens. These were nearly fifty years old, but still going strong. Huge, grimy, brick and steel walk-in boxes, each with a wood-fired kiln in the base, and the ceiling covered with racks and hooks, on which hung rows of pink and golden-brown fillets of smoking fish.

When he had finished his inspections, and had topped up the burners with oak logs, he entered the shop. This was a long, narrow building with a counter running the entire length of one side, while on the other side shelving was piled with every conceivable canned seafood delicacy, as well as jams, pâtés and preserves. His staff who ran the retail side, all wearing dark blue overalls and white hats, were busy putting out the displays of freshly smoked fish and making up the orders that had come in overnight by phone and email.

Jane, the manageress, flagged up a problem. One of the over-night orders was from a hamper company who were infuriatingly slow payers. They had run up an alarmingly high bill and no payment had been received for nearly three months.

'I think we should tell them we need payment before we dis-patch any more, Mr Harris,' she said.

He nodded. For the next ten minutes they continued to work on the orders, then he sat down and began, on the computer, to check his stock. At that moment the phone rang. As he was the nearest to it, he answered.

An American voice the other end asked, 'How quickly could you supply two thousand, five hundred langoustines?'

'What size and how quickly do you need them, sir?'

After a moment, the American said, 'The biggest available. Before the end of next week. We've been let down by a supplier.'

Harris asked him to hold for a moment, then checked on the computer. 'We are low on stock at the moment, but we do have a delivery coming down overnight from our supplier in Scotland on Tuesday, arriving here early Wednesday morning. If you want that quantity I could get it added to the consignment.'

'When would you need me to confirm?'

'Really as soon as possible, sir. Would you like me to give you the price?'

'That won't be an issue. The consignment would definitely be here? You could guarantee Wednesday morning?'

'We have a delivery from Scotland every Wednesday, sir.'

'Good. I'll come back to you.'

*

In his rental car parked a short distance along the road from the smokery, Tooth ended the call on his cellphone. Then he turned the car round and drove back down the narrow road, passing the sign that said SPRINGS SMOKED SALMON – SHOP OPEN.

He wondered for a moment whether to pull into the customer car park and have a recce inside the shop. Perhaps buy something. But he'd already seen all he wanted and decided there wasn't any point in showing his face. That was just an unnecessary risk.

Besides, he didn't do smoked fish.

51

The week proceeded without any significant progress being made by Roy Grace's team. This was despite the DNA from the flesh found under Preece's fingernails producing a suspect within Ford Prison – a giant of a man called Lee Rogan. Rogan was serving out the final months of a sentence for armed robbery and grievous bodily harm, prior to being released on licence.

Rogan had been arrested on suspicion of murdering Warren Tulley but was claiming in his defence that they'd had a fight over money earlier the same evening Tulley had died. So far the internal investigation had not unearthed any calls made by Rogan using his PIN code, or any mobile phone concealed in his cell. If he had been intending to claim the reward, they had no evidence of it as yet. But with the number of illegal mobile phones that were inside Ford, it was more than possible he had borrowed – or rented – one off another prisoner. Which would be almost impossible to establish. The West Area Major Crime Branch Team were keeping Grace informed of progress.

Thanks to her sharp Legal Aid solicitor, a man called Leighton Lloyd, with whom Grace had had many run-ins previously, Evie Preece had gone *no comment* and had been released on police bail after eighteen hours. Grace had put surveillance on her house, in case her brother returned. It was unlikely, he knew, but at the same time, Preece was stupid enough to do that.

He'd had a conversation with a helpful law enforcement officer in New York, Detective Investigator Pat Lanigan, of the Special Investigations Unit of the Office of the District Attorney, who had given him detailed background on the dead boy's parents, but Lanigan had no specific intelligence on the current situation, other than to tell him of Fernanda Revere's fury when he had broken the news of her son's death to her – which had been confirmed by her actions when she was over in the UK.

Grace always knew it was a bad sign when the reporter from the

Argus stopped phoning him and he had not heard from Spinella for several days now. He decided to call a press conference for the following day, Friday, his hope being to spark some memories in the public, followed by a reconstruction at the collision scene. Apart from other considerations, he needed to show the Revere family that everything possible was being done to find the driver so callously involved in their son's fatal accident.

*

At 11 a.m. the conference room at Sussex House was crammed. The Mafia connection and the $100,000 reward had generated massive media attention – far more even than Roy Grace had anticipated. He appealed to members of the public who might have been in the vicinity of Portland Road on the morning of Wednesday 21 April to cast their minds back and see if they remembered a white Ford Transit van and to attend the reconstruction, which would be held the following day.

Then he appealed specifically to the residents of Southwick, and Manor Hall Road in particular, asking if anyone remembered the van or seeing Ewan Preece – at this point he showed a series of police and prison photographs of the man. Although it stuck in his craw to continue to deal with Spinella, the little shit was now at least being cooperative.

Heading back along the corridors towards his office immediately after the press conference, Grace checked his diary on his Black-Berry. There was an exhibits meeting scheduled for 2 p.m., which he needed to attend.

Glenn Branson caught up with him, saying, 'You know, for an old-timer, you do pretty good at these conferences.'

'Yep, well, that's something you're going to have to learn. We need the press. Love them or loathe them. How do you feel about taking one on your own?'

Branson looked at him. 'Why are you asking?'

'I was thinking I might let you handle the next one.'

'Shit.'

'That's what I say every time, before I start. Another thing, I need you to take this evening's briefing. You OK with that?'

'Yeah, fine. I don't have a life, remember?'

'What's the latest?'

'According to Ari's lawyer, I was bullying and aggressive and made unreasonable sexual demands on her.'

'You did?'

'Yeah, apparently I asked her to sit on me. Goes against her religious principles of the missionary position only.'

'Religious principles?' Grace said.

'In some states in the US it's still illegal to do it any other way than the missionary position. She's now going religious fundamentalist on me. I'm a deviant in God's eyes apparently.'

'Doesn't that make Him a voyeur?'

At that moment Grace's mobile phone rang. Nodding apologetically at Glenn, he answered it.

It was Crime Scene Manager, Tracy Stocker.

'Roy,' she said. 'I'm at Shoreham Harbour. You'd better come down here. I think we might have found Preece.'

52

Grace let Glenn Branson drive. Ever since gaining his green Response and Pursuit driving ticket, Branson was keen to show his friend his prowess. And every time he allowed Branson to take the wheel, Roy Grace quickly regretted it.

They headed down the sweeping dip in the A27, passing the slip road off to the A23 and up the far side, the speedometer needle the wrong side of the 120mph mark, with Glenn, in Grace's view, having a totally misplaced confidence in the blue flashing lights and wailing siren. It didn't take a normal, sane police officer many days of response driving to realize that most members of the public on the road were deaf, blind or stupid, and frequently a combination of all three.

Grace pressed his feet hard against the floor, willing his friend to slow down as they raced past a line of cars, any one of which could have pulled out and sent them hurtling into the central barrier and certain oblivion. It was more by sheer good luck than anything he would want to attribute to driving skill that they finally ended up on the approach road to Shoreham Port, passing Hove Lagoon – a short distance from Grace's home – on their left, with their lives, if not his nerves, still intact.

'What do you think of my driving, old-timer? Getting better, yeah? Think I've nailed that four-wheel-drift thing now!'

Grace was not sure where his vocal cords were. It felt like he had left them several miles back.

'I think you need to be more aware about what other road users might do,' he replied diplomatically. 'You need to work on that.'

They drove straight over a mini-roundabout, narrowly missing a Nissan Micra being driven by a man in a pork-pie hat, and entered an industrial area. There was a tall, brick-walled warehouse to their right, double yellow lines and a blue corrugated metal warehouse to their left. They passed a gap between two buildings, through which

Grace caught a glimpse of the choppy water of Aldrington Basin, the extreme eastern end of the Shoreham Port canal. They passed a van marked D & H Electrical Installations and saw ahead of them a sign above a building advertising pet foods. Then, immediately in front of them was a marked police car, its lights flashing in stationary mode.

As they approached, they saw several parked vehicles, including the Crime Scene Manager's, and a second marked car, turned sideways, between two buildings. It was blocking the entrance to an open gate in the middle of a chain-link fence. Beyond was the quay. A line of crime scene tape ran between the walls of the two buildings and a PCSO scene guard stood in front of it.

They climbed out of the car into the blustery, damp wind, walked up to her and gave their names.

'Need you both to suit up, please, sirs,' she said to Grace, then nodded respectfully at Branson. 'CSM's request.'

The moment a Crime Scene Manager arrived at a potential crime scene, the site became his or her responsibility. One of the key elements was the number of people allowed access, and what they could wear, to minimize their chances of contaminating the scene with such minute items as clothing fibres that could lead to false trails.

They returned to the car and wormed their way into hooded blue paper oversuits. Although he had put one on hundreds of times, Grace found it never became any easier. Your shoes got jammed in them halfway down. Then they seemed to get stuck as you tugged them up over your hips.

When they were finally ready they ducked under the tape and walked down to the quay, passing a grimy sign which read ALL DRIVERS MUST REPORT TO RECEPTION. Grace looked around for CCTV cameras but couldn't see any, to his disappointment. Directly ahead of them was the rear of the large yellow mobile operations truck of the Specialist Search Unit, the prow of a moored fishing boat, a rusty fork-lift truck, a skip piled with rubbish and, on the far side, across the water, the warehouses and piles of lumber of one of the port's major timber depots.

He had always loved this part of the city. He took a deep breath, savouring the tangy smells of salt, oil, tar and rope that reminded him of his childhood, coming down here with his dad to fish off the end of the harbour mole. As a child, he had found Shoreham Harbour a mysterious, exciting place: the tankers and cargo ships along the quay with their international flags, the massive gantries, the trucks, the bollards, the warehouses and the huge power station.

As they rounded the corner, he saw a hive of activity. There were several police officers, all in protective oversuits, and he immediately picked out the short, sturdy figure of the Crime Scene Manager, Tracy Stocker, the tall figure of the SOCO photographer, James Gartrell, and the lean figure of the Coroner's Officer, Philip Keay.

Members of the Specialist Search Unit stood around, dressed in dark blue fleeces, waterproof trousers, rubber boots and black baseball caps with the wording POLICE above the peaks. One of them was standing beside a coil of cable, coloured red, yellow and blue, that ran from a box of apparatus and down over the edge of the quay into the water. Grace realized there was a diver below.

Sitting centre stage on the quay was a dull white, beat-up-looking Ford Transit van, its roof and sides streaked with mud. A steady stream of water poured from its doorsills. Grace could see that the driver's-side wing mirror was missing. Four steel hawsers ran vertically from its wheel arches high above to the pulley on the arm of a mobile crane parked beside it.

But Grace barely gave the crane a second glance. All his focus was on the man clearly visible in the driver's seat, hunched motion-less over the steering wheel.

Tracy Stocker walked up to greet Grace and Branson. She was accompanied by a burly, rugged-looking man in his fifties with a weather-beaten face, wind-blown salt and pepper hair and bare arms sporting nautical tattoos. He wore a fluorescent yellow jacket over a white, short-sleeved shirt, dark workman's trousers and heavy-duty rubber boots and seemed impervious to the biting wind.

'Hi, Roy and Glenn,' she said cheerily. 'This is Keith Wadey, the Assistant Chief Engineer of Shoreham Port. Keith, this is Detective Superintendent Grace, the Senior Investigating Officer, and Detective Sergeant Glenn Branson, the Deputy SIO.'

They shook hands. Grace took an instant liking to Wadey, who exuded a friendly air of confidence and experience.

He turned back to Tracy. 'Have you run a check on the van's index?'

'Yes, chief. False plates. The serial number's been filed off the chassis and engine block, so it's almost certainly nicked, but that's about all we know.'

Grace thanked her, then spoke to Wadey. 'What do we have?' he asked, looking at the figure in the van again.

'Well, sir,' Wadey said, addressing Grace but including Branson. 'We carry out regular side-scan sonar sweeps of the canal, checking for silt levels and for any obstructions. Yesterday afternoon at around 4.30 p.m. we identified what looked like a vehicle about a hundred and twenty feet off the edge of this quay, in twenty-five feet of water. It was upside down, wheels in the air. That tends to happen with motor vehicles that go into deep water – the engine in the front pulls them down and they flip over as they sink.'

Grace nodded.

'There's zero visibility down there. The current caused by the opening and closing of the lock gates churns up the deep layer of mud. I found the vehicle with the aid of a shot line and jackstay, sunk into four feet of mud. I then contacted the police dive team – the Specialist Search Unit – our standard procedure, and we assisted them recovering the vehicle from the water this morning, approximately one hour ago. I'm afraid we found a poor sod in there. Dunno if he's a suicide – we get quite a few of them – because he doesn't seem to have made any effort to get out.'

Grace glanced at their surroundings. A large, rusting warehouse that looked derelict, although the presence of the skip indicated some work was going on.

'What is this place?' he asked.

'It now belongs to Dudman, the aggregates company. They bought it a couple of months ago. It had been empty for several years – a bankruptcy.'

'Anyone working here? Any security guards?'

'No security guards or cameras, sir. There were some workmen here last week, but they've been diverted to do some maintenance on another of the company's buildings.'

This was a secluded spot, Grace thought. Carefully chosen? It wasn't the kind of place you find by accident.

'Is it locked at night?'

'Padlocked with a chain, yes,' Wadey said. 'But it was open when we got here. Either someone unlocked it or picked the lock.'

Grace walked across to the driver's side of the van.

'How long has he been in the water?'

'My guess would be a maximum of three or four days,' the engineer replied. 'You can see the bloating, which starts to happen within twenty-four hours, but he's intact – the fish and crustaceans like to wait for a week or so, until the flesh has started to break down, before they set to work.'

'Thanks.'

Grace peered in through the driver's window, which was down, as was the passenger's, he noted. To help the vehicle sink more quickly, he wondered? The rear doors were open, too. The immediate question in his mind was whether this was an accident, suicide or murder. His experience had taught him never to jump to conclusions.

Even though the body was bloated from gases, the face was still thin, streaked with mud, eyes wide open, staring ahead with a look of shock. In the flesh, he looked even paler than in the photographs, and the gelled hair of the picture was now lifelessly matted to the scalp. But his identity was still clear. Just to double-check, Roy Grace pulled the photograph of Ewan Preece from his pocket and held it up.

And now he was certain. From the knife scar below his right eye, the thin gold chain around his neck and the leather wrist bracelet. Even so, it would take a fingerprint or DNA sample to confirm it beyond doubt. Grace was not inclined to trust a next-of-kin identification by any member of Preece's crooked family. He looked at the dead man's hands.

Preece was gripping the steering wheel as if with grim determination. As if he had thought that somehow, if he kept hold of it, he could steer himself out of trouble.

And that did not make sense.

'Dead man's grip,' said a female voice beside him.

He turned to see the sergeant in charge of the Specialist Search Unit, Lorna Dennison-Wilkins.

'Lorna!' he said. 'How are you?'

She grinned. 'Understaffed, underappreciated and busy as heck. How about you?'

'Couldn't have put it better myself!' He nodded at the dead man and, at the same time, heard a curious metallic scuttling sound from inside the van. 'Dead man's grip?'

'Rigor mortis,' she said. 'It's the suddenness of immersion that brings it on very fast. If someone drowns and they're holding on to something at that moment, it's really hard to prise their fingers off it.'

He stared at Preece's fingers. They were wrapped tightly around the large steering wheel.

'We haven't tried to remove them,' she said. 'In case we damage any forensic evidence.'

As in his past dealing with this woman and her team, Roy Grace was impressed by her understanding of the importance of not contaminating a potential crime scene. But why was Preece holding on to the steering wheel? Had he frozen in stark terror? Grace knew that if he'd just driven off a harbour quay into water, he'd be doing everything he could to get out – not trying to steer.

Had he been knocked unconscious by the impact? That was one possibility. There was no apparent mark on his head, and he was wearing a seat belt, but that was something the pathologist would be able to determine at the post-mortem. What other reason did he have for clinging to the wheel? Trying deliberately to drown? But Ewan Preece seemed an unlikely suicide candidate. From the intelligence he had read about him, and his own prior experience with the man, Preece didn't give a shit about anything in life. He was hardly going to be driven into a state of suicidal grief over the death of a cyclist. And in a short time he would have been out of prison.

Grace snapped on a pair of disposible gloves which he kept in his oversuit pocket, then leaned in through the window and attempted to prise the dead man's right index finger away from the wheel. But it would not move. A tiny crab the size of a fingernail scuttled across the top of the dashboard.

Once more from somewhere in the back of the van he heard the metallic scuttling sound. He tried again to prise the finger off the wheel, conscious of not wanting to risk tearing the flesh and lose the potential for a print, but it would not move.

'Bloody hell!' Keith Wadey said suddenly.

The port engineer ducked in through the rear doors. Moments later he stood up again, holding a large black lobster. It was a good two feet long, with claws the size of a man's hand, and was wriggling furiously.

'This is a nice specimen!' Wadey called out at a group of the SSU, showing them his find.

Immediately he had the attention of everyone on the quay.

'Anyone fancy treating their loved one to lobster thermidor tonight?'

There were no takers. Only looks of disgust and a few exclamations.

He tossed the creature back out into the canal and it disappeared beneath the choppy surface.

53

After a phone discussion with Roy Grace and the Crime Scene Manager, the Home Office pathologist agreed with them that she should definitely see the body in situ, prior to its being taken to the mortuary. But she was finishing a job at a lab in London at the moment, which meant a long wait for the team on the cold harbour front.

The good news was that of the two regular Home Office pathologists for this area, they had been allocated Nadiuska De Sancha, the one whom Grace and everyone else preferred to work with. As an added bonus to the fact that the statuesque, red-haired Spaniard was both good and swift at her job, and extremely helpful with it, she also happened to be very easy on the eye.

In her late forties, Nadiuska De Sancha could easily pass for a decade younger. If people wanted to be bitchy, they might comment that perhaps her plastic-surgeon husband's skills had something to do with her continuing to look so youthful. But because of her warm and open nature, few people were bitchy about her. Far more were envious of her appearance, and half of the males in the Major Crime Branch lusted after her – as well as lusting after Cleo Morey.

A body found in the sea, on its own, would have been taken to the mortuary, where the post-mortem would be carried out the following day by one of the team of local pathologists. But when there were any grounds to give the Coroner suspicion, a full forensic post-mortem would need to be carried out by a trained specialist, of which there were thirty in the UK. A standard post-mortem usually took less than an hour. A Home Office one, depending on the condition of the body and the circumstances, and very much on who was performing it, could take from three to six hours, and sometimes even longer.

As the Senior Investigating Officer, Roy Grace had a duty to attend. And that meant, he realized with dismay, that he did not have a snowball's chance in hell of making it to *Jersey Boys* in London tonight with Cleo. He'd booked a hotel up there, and tomorrow, the start of the May Day holiday weekend, they had tickets to the Army and Navy rugby match at Twickenham – at the invitation of Nobby Hall and his wife, Helen. Nobby was an old friend who had been running the Maritime Police in Cyprus.

At least Cleo would understand – unlike Sandy, he thought, with a sudden twinge of sadness. Although Sandy was fading further from his mind by the week, whenever he did think of her it was like a dark cloud engulfing him and leaving him disoriented. Sandy used to go off at the deep end, regardless of the fact he had carefully explained to her that a murder inquiry meant dropping everything, and the reasons why.

She would tell him she disliked it that she came second to his work. No matter how much he tried to refute this, she was adamant about it, to the point of fixation.

Who would you pick? she had once asked him. *If you had to choose between me and your work, Grace?*

She always called him 'Grace'.

You, he had replied.

Liar! She had grinned.

It's the truth!

I watched your eyes. That movement trick you taught me – if they move one way you are lying, the other you are telling the truth. Yours moved to the right, Grace, that's the side you look to when you are lying!

A gull cried overhead. He glanced at his watch. Almost 12.30 p.m.

A dredger slipped past them in mid-channel, heading towards the lock and then on to the open sea. Nadiuska estimated she would be here by about 2 p.m. She would take a good hour on site at the very minimum, studying and noting the exact position of the body, photographing everything, checking Preece's body for bruises and abrasions that might or might not be consistent with contact with the interior of the van, and searching for clothing fibres, hairs and anything else that might be lost as a result of the body being moved. Although, after several days' immersion in water, Grace doubted there could be much in the way of fibres or hairs on the body, he was constantly surprised at the details good forensic pathologists could find that had eluded hawk-eyed detectives and trained police search officers.

He stared in through the open driver's window. Preece's lean, sharply delineated features from his photographs were unaltered, but his skin now had a ghostly, almost translucent sheen. At least no visible nibbles had been taken from him by any scavengers. Preece was wearing a white, mud-spattered T-shirt and black jeans, and was barefoot. Odd to be driving barefoot, Grace thought, and cast his mind back to the pair of trainers that had been found in the spare bedroom of his sister's house. Had Preece left in too much of a hurry to put them on?

An undignified end to a short, sad and squandered life, he thought. At least Preece had been saved from the crustaceans. Or perhaps, with this particular specimen of human trash, it was the other way around.

54

Grace phoned the Incident Room to tell them to call off the search for Ewan Preece and the Ford Transit and instead to concentrate on the immediate neighbours of Preece's sister, to see if anyone had seen or heard anything during the night of Monday 26 April or early morning of Tuesday the 27th. He also wondered whether the dead man's sister might be sufficiently shocked into telling the truth about what had happened that night – if she genuinely knew.

An hour later, Grace completed a careful inspection of the surrounding area. He was looking in particular for any CCTV cameras that might have the approaches to this quay in view, but without success. Freezing cold, he gratefully accepted the offer of coffee inside the Specialist Search Unit truck, where there was a snug seating area around a table.

He clambered up the steps, followed by Branson, both of them rubbing some warmth back into their hands. A PCSO had been dispatched to a nearby supermarket to get some sandwiches. They were joined moments later by the tall figure of Philip Keay, the Coroner's Officer, and Tracy Stocker, who announced that Nadiuska De Sancha had phoned to say she was only a few minutes away. Two members of the SSU, one a burly man nicknamed Juice by his colleagues and the other, slightly built with fair hair, who was nicknamed WAFI, which stood for Water Assisted Fucking Idiot, moved over to make room.

Grace tried to call Cleo, but both her mobile phone and the mortuary phone went to voicemail. He felt a prick of anxiety. What if she was alone in the place and had collapsed? Most of the time, when no post-mortems were being carried out, there were only three people – Cleo, Darren and Walter – in the building. If Darren and Walter went out to recover a body, she could have been left on her own. If anything happened to her, she could lie undiscovered for a couple of hours.

He had often worried in the past about her being in that place on her own, but now he felt it even more acutely. He rang her house, but there was no answer there either. He was seriously considering driving to the mortuary to make sure she was OK, when suddenly, to his surprise, he heard her voice.

'Oi! Call this working?' she called out cheekily, standing at the door of the truck.

Grace stood up. Not many people make blue paper oversuits look like a designer garment, he thought, but Cleo did. With the trousers tucked into her boots, her hair clipped up and the bump in her stomach, she looked like someone who had just arrived in a spaceship from a planet where everyone was much more beautiful than here on earth. A new world that he still could not totally believe he was now a part of. His heart flipped with joy, the same way it did each time he saw her.

Juice and WAFI both wolf-whistled at her.

With some colour back in her face now, Cleo looked more radiant than ever, he thought, going down the steps to greet her with a light peck on the cheek.

'What are you doing here?' he asked, wanting to hug her, but not in front of a bunch of cynical colleagues who would rib him at the slightest opportunity.

'Well, I figured the musical was off, so I thought I'd take a trip to the seaside instead. Gather you've got a particularly interesting species of underwater creature.'

He grinned. 'You are under strict doctor's orders not to do any lifting, OK?'

She jerked her head, pointing. 'It's OK. I'll use that fork-lift truck!' Then she smiled. 'Don't worry, Darren's here with me. Walter's off sick today.'

A voice came through Grace's radio. It was the scene guard at the entrance. 'Sir, there's someone here to see you – says you're expecting him. Kevin Spinella?'

Grace was expecting him, the way he would expect to see blowflies around a decomposing cadaver. He walked around the corner and up to the barrier. Spinella stood there, short and thin, collar of his beige mackintosh turned up in the clichéd fashion of a movie gumshoe, chewing a piece of gum with his ratty teeth, his gelled spiky hair untouched by the wind.

'Good morning, Detective Superintendent!' he said.

Grace tapped his watch. 'It's afternoon, actually.' He gave the reporter a reproachful glance. 'Unlike you to be behind the times.'

'Ha-ha,' Spinella said.

Grace stared at him quizzically but said nothing.

'Hear you've got a body in a van,' the reporter said.

'Surprised it took you so long,' Grace replied. 'I've been here for hours.'

Spinella looked nonplussed. 'Yeah, right. So, what can you tell me about it?'

'Probably not as much as you can tell me,' he retorted.

'Don't suppose it could be Ewan Preece, could it?'

An educated guess, Grace wondered? Or had one of the team here phoned Spinella?

'There is a body in a van, but the body has not been identified at this stage,' Grace replied.

'Could it be the van you are looking for?'

He saw Nadiuska De Sancha, gowned up in an oversuit and white boots, walking towards them, carrying her large black bag.

'Too early to tell.'

Spinella made a note on his pad.

'It's ten days since the accident. Do you feel you are making progress with your enquiries regarding the van and its driver, Detective Superintendent?'

'We are very pleased with the level of response from the public,' Grace lied. 'But we would like to appeal to anyone in the Southwick area who saw a white van between the hours of 6 p.m. Monday 26 April and 8 a.m. Tuesday 27 April to contact us on our Incident Room number, or to call *Crimestoppers* anonymously. Do you want the numbers?'

'I've got them,' Spinella said.

'That's all I have for now,' Grace said, nodding a silent greeting at the pathologist and signalling he would be with her in a moment. 'Perhaps you'll be kind enough to let me know when you've identified the body and confirmed what the van is?'

'Very funny.'

Nadiuska signed the scene guard's log, then ducked under the tape which Grace lifted for her.

'Home Office pathologist?' Spinella said. 'Looks to me like you could have a murder inquiry going on.'

Grace turned and eyeballed him. 'Makes a change, does it, being the last to know?'

He turned, with great satisfaction, and escorted Nadiuska De Sancha towards the quay and across to the right, out of the reporter's line of sight. Then, knowing that she liked to work alone, in her own time, he left the pathologist and went to join Cleo and the rest of the team inside the warmth of the SSU truck.

*

Half an hour later Nadiuska De Sancha came up the steps and said, 'Roy, I need to show you something.'

Worming himself into his anorak, Grace followed her outside and around to the white van. The pathologist stopped by the driver's door, which was open.

'I think we can safely rule out accidental death, Roy, and I'm fairly confident we can rule out suicide, too,' she said.

He looked at her quizzically.

She pointed up at a small cylindrical object Grace had not taken in before, clipped to the driver's-side sun visor. 'See that? It's a digital underwater camera – and transmitter. And it's switched on, although the battery's dead.'

Grace frowned and at the same time felt annoyed that he had not spotted it. How the hell had he missed it? About an inch in diameter and three inches long, with a dark blue metal casing and a fish-eye lens. What was it there for? Had Preece been filming himself?

Then, interrupting his thoughts, she pointed at the man's hands and gave him a bemused look.

'Dead man's grip is caused by rigor mortis, right?'

Grace nodded.

She reached in with a blue, latex-gloved hand and raised one of Preece's fleshy, alabaster-white fingers. The skin of the tip remained

211

adhered to the steering wheel. It looked like a blister with tendrils attached.

'I'll need to do some lab tests to confirm it, but there's some kind of adhesive that's been applied here. Looks to me, as an educated guess, that the poor man's hands have been superglued to the steering wheel.'

55

Tooth sat at the desk in his room at the Premier Inn, in front of his laptop, sipping a mug of coffee and editing the video of Ewan Preece's last few minutes. The smoke detector in the ceiling was still taped up and a pack of cigarettes and a plastic lighter lay beside the saucer that he was using as an ashtray.

He had used three cameras: the one on his wrist, the one he had fitted to the interior of the van and one he had balanced on the edge of the skip. The film, still in rough-cut stage, which he would refine, began with an establishing exterior shot of the van at night, at the edge of the quay. There was a bollard to its right. A time and date print at the top right of the frame showed it was 2 a.m., Tuesday 27 April. Preece could be seen at the wheel, apparently unconscious, with duct tape over his mouth.

Then it cut to the interior. There was a wide-angle shot of Preece, buckled into his seat, in a grubby white T-shirt. He was opening his eyes as if awaking from sleep, seemingly confused and disoriented. Then he peered down at his hands, which were on the steering wheel, clearly puzzled as to why he could not move them.

He began to struggle, trying to free his hands. His eyes bulged in fear as he started to realize something was wrong. A hand appeared in frame and ripped the duct tape from his mouth. Preece yelped in pain, then turned his head towards the door, speaking to a person out of shot. His voice was insolent but tinged with fear.

'Who are you? What are you doing? What the fuck are you doing?'

The driver's door slammed shut.

The camera angle changed to an exterior shot. It showed the whole driver's side of the van and a short distance behind it. A figure, wearing a hoodie, his face invisible, drove a fork-lift truck into view, steered it right up to the rear of the van, rammed it a few inches forward and began to push it steadily towards the edge of the quay.

Then the van suddenly lurched downwards, as the front wheels went over and the bottom of the chassis grounded on the stonework, with a metallic grating sound.

The film cut back to the interior of the van. Ewan Preece was bug-eyed now and screaming, 'No, no! What do you want? Tell me what you want? Please tell me! Fucker, tell me!' Then he visibly lurched forward, held by the seat belt, and his mouth opened in a long, silent scream, as if, in his terror, he could not get any more words out.

The film cut back to the exterior again. The fork-lift truck gave a final shove and the rear of the van disappeared over the edge of the quay and momentarily out of sight. There was a hollow splash.

Now there was a new exterior angle. It was the van floating, rocking in the waves, a short distance away from the quay. It was looking distinctly nose-heavy, and sinking slowly but steadily, bubbles erupting around it

The viewpoint returned to the camera inside the van. Preece's face was a mask of terror. He was fighting to free his hands – frantically pumping his body backwards and forwards as much as he could against the seat belt, jigging his arms and shoulders, his mouth contorted, yammering in terror. 'Please . . . Please . . . Please . . . Help me! Help me! Someone help me!'

There was now a long exterior shot, with the van conveniently rotated broadside on to the quay. Preece could be seen gyrating like a contortionist through the open window as the nose sank lower, the whole van now starting to tip forward, water pouring over the sills of the open windows.

The viewpoint returned to the interior again. There was a loud, muffled roaring sound. Dark water with white, foaming bubbles was flooding in. The level was rising rapidly, increasingly covering more of Preece's thrashing chest. He was rocking himself backwards and forwards, sharp, violent jerks of desperation, trying to free himself, whimpering now, a steady low 'No . . . No . . . No . . . No . . .'

The water now covered his neck to just below his chin, then the bottom of his earring, and it was rising rapidly. In seconds it was over his chin. Some went into his mouth and he spat it out. Then his mouth was submerged. In desperation he threw his head back, his chin breaking free from the water. He was crying pitifully now: 'Help me, please. Someone help me.'

The water rose relentlessly, swallowing up his exposed neck until it reached his chin again. He thrashed his head from side to side.

Tooth took a sip of his coffee, then lit a fresh cigarette, watching dispassionately. He listened to the man breathing, taking deep gulps of air, as if frantically trying to stock up with the stuff.

Then the water reached the ceiling of the van. Preece's head was twitching, his eyes still wide open. The image became very blurred. A stream of bubbles jetted from his mouth. The twitching slowed, then stopped, and his head moved more gently now, rocking with the current.

The last shot in the sequence was another exterior one. It showed the rear section of the van now, the doors open, slipping beneath the surface of the choppy, inky water. There were some bubbles, then the waves closed over it, like curtains.

56

The post-mortem room at the Brighton and Hove City Mortuary had recently been doubled in size. The work had been necessary both to increase the number of bodies that could be prepared for post-mortem at the same time and to replace the existing fridges with a new, wider generation able to cope with the growing trend for obesity in society.

Roy Grace had always found the previous room claustrophobic, especially when it was occupied by the considerable numbers required for a Home Office post-mortem. Now at least there was more space for them. Although this place, with its tiled walls and stark, cold lighting, still gave him the creeps just as much as ever.

When he had been at the police training college, learning to be a detective, an instructor had read out the FBI moral code on murder investigation, written by its first director, J. Edgar Hoover:

> No greater honor will ever be bestowed on an officer or a more profound duty imposed on him than when he is entrusted with the investigation of the death of a human being.

Grace always remembered those words, and the burden on him as the Senior Investigating Officer, on every case. Yet at the same time as feeling that weight of responsibility, he would feel other emotions in this room, too. Always a tinge of sadness for the loss of a life – even the life of a scumbag like Ewan Preece. Who knew what kind of a person Preece might have been under different circumstances, if life had dealt him a less hopeless hand?

In spite of his sense of responsibility, Grace also at times felt like an intruder in this room. To be a corpse, opened up and splayed out here was the ultimate loss of privacy. Yet neither the dead nor their loved ones had any say in the matter. If you died under suspicious circumstances, the Coroner would require a post-mortem.

At this moment, Ewan Preece was a surreal sight, lying on his back, in his jeans and T-shirt, on the stainless-steel PM table, his hands still gripping the black steering wheel, which Nadiuska De Sancha had requested be detached from the vehicle and brought with him to the mortuary. He looked, in death, as if he was driving some spectral vehicle.

At a PM table on the other side of the archway, the bloody internal organs of another corpse were laid out for a student, who was receiving instructions from one of Brighton's consultant pathologists, and Grace's stomach was heaving, as ever, from the stench of disinfectant, blood and decaying human innards. He glanced over, clocked the brains, liver, heart and kidneys sitting there, and the electronic weighing scales on a shelf just beyond. Beside them, on another table, lay the corpse from which they had been removed – an elderly woman the colour of alabaster, her mouth gaping, her midriff wide open, the yellow fatty tissue of the insides of her breasts facing upwards, her sternum laid across her pubis as if in some attempt by the pathologist to protect her modesty.

He shuddered and took a few steps closer to Preece, his green gown rustling as he walked. Nadiuska was plucking delicately at the skin of one of the fingers with tweezers. James Gartrell, the SOCO photographer, was steadily working his way around the body. Glenn Branson was in a corner, surreptitiously talking on his phone. To his wife, Ari? Grace wondered. Or his solicitor? The Coroner's Officer, Philip Keay, was standing in a green gown, blue mask hanging from its tapes just below his chin, dictating into a machine with a worried frown.

Cleo and her assistant, Darren, stood by, ready to assist the pathologist, but at the moment they had nothing to do but watch. Occasionally she would look in Grace's direction and give him a surreptitious smile.

The Detective Superintendent was thinking hard. Preece's hands glued to the wheel confirmed, beyond any doubt in his mind, that the man had been murdered. And the presence of that camera in the vehicle was bothering him a lot. Put there by the killer? Some sadistic bounty-hunter associate of Preece who had known where he had been hiding?

Or was there an even darker aspect to this? The Mafia connection was weighing heavily on his mind. Could this have been a sadistic revenge hit?

The body had not yet been formally identified. That would be done later by his mother or sister. Nadiuska said she would be able to dissolve the glue with acetone, leaving Grace's team able to get fingerprints which would further confirm his identity, and as backup they would be able to get a DNA sample. But from the tattoos on his body and the scar on his face, Ford Prison had already confirmed his identity beyond much doubt.

With Kevin Spinella from the *Argus* and the rest of the press having been kept well away from the crime scene, only the immediate team at the quay, and those here in the mortuary, knew that the man's hands had been glued to the steering wheel. Grace intended to keep this information quiet for the moment. If it made the press during the next few hours, he would know where to look for the leak.

He stepped out of the PM room and made a call to MIR-1, instructing Norman Potting to organize a group within the inquiry team to find out all they could about the camera, in particular where such a device was available for sale, in Brighton or beyond, and any recent purchases that had been made.

Next he made a phone call to Detective Investigator Pat Lanigan, who was their liaison officer with the Revere family in America, to ask him whether in his experience the dead boy's parents were the kind of people who might be sufficiently aggrieved to go for a revenge killing.

Lanigan informed him that they had the money, the power and the connections – and that with people like this a whole different set of rules applied. He said that he would see what intelligence he could come up with. Sometimes, when a contract was put out, they would get to hear of it. He promised to come back to Grace as soon he found out anything.

Grace hung up with a heavy heart. Suddenly he found himself hoping that whoever had killed Preece was just a local chancer. The notion of a Mafia-backed killing in the heart of Brighton was not something that would sit well with anyone – not the council, not the tourist board, not his boss, ACC Rigg, and not with himself, either.

He sat on a sofa in the small front office of the mortuary, poured himself a stewed coffee from the jug that was sitting on the hotplate and felt a sudden grim determination. Lanigan had said *a whole different set of rules applied.*

Well, not in his beloved city, they didn't.

57

'The time is 8.30 a.m. Saturday 1 May,' Roy Grace announced to his team in MIR-1. 'This is the eighteenth briefing of *Operation Violin*. The first thing I have to report is the positive identification of Ewan Preece.'

'Shame to have lost such an upstanding member of Brighton society, chief,' said Norman Potting. 'And such a tacky way to die.'

There was a titter of laughter. Grace gave him a reproachful look.

'Thank you, Norman. Let's hold the humour. We have some serious issues on our hands.'

Bella Moy rattled her Malteser box, extracted a chocolate and popped it into her mouth, biting into it with a crunch. Grace looked back down at his notes.

'It will be some days before we get the toxicology reports, but I have significant findings from the PM. The first is that there was bruising to the side of Preece's neck very similar to the bruising that was found on his sister, Evie, who is claiming to have remembered nothing after going outside on Monday night to let her cat out. According to Nadiuska De Sancha, this is consistent with a martial arts blow with the side of a hand to cause instant loss of consciousness. This could be the way Preece was overpowered by his assailant.'

Grace looked down again. 'The seawater present in Preece's lungs indicates that he was alive at the time the van went into the water and he died from drowning. The fact that his hands were glued to the steering wheel makes this extremely unlikely to have been suicide. Does anyone have a different view?'

'If he was unconscious, sir,' said Nick Nicholl, 'how did the van actually get into the water? It would have been difficult for someone to physically push it, because when the front wheels went over the edge of the quay, surely the bottom of the chassis would have grounded on it. Wouldn't it have needed to be driven at some speed?'

'That's a good point,' Grace said. 'Dudman, who own that particular section of the wharf, say that their fork-lift truck had been moved. It could have been used to push the van in.'

'Wouldn't that have required someone with an ignition key?' asked Bella Moy.

'I'm told that particular kind of fork-lift has a universal ignition key,' Grace replied. 'One key operates all of those vehicles in the UK. And anyone with a basic knowledge could have started it with a screwdriver.'

'Has the kind of glue been established?' asked DS Duncan Crocker.

'It has been sent for lab analysis. We don't have that information yet.'

'There was no tube of glue found in the vehicle?' Crocker asked.

'No,' Grace replied. 'The Specialist Search Unit did an extensive dive search around the area where the van was recovered, but so far they have found nothing. There is almost zero visibility down there, which is not helpful. They are continuing searching today and doing a fingertip search of the quay areas. But my sense is that they are not going to find anything helpful.'

'Why do you think that, chief?' Glenn Branson asked.

'Because this smells to me like the work of a professional. It has all the hallmarks,' Grace said. Then he looked around at his team. 'I did not like the mention of the hundred-thousand-dollar reward from the get-go. It wasn't put up, as is usual, for information leading to the arrest and conviction, but just for the driver's identity. I think we could be looking at an underworld hit here.'

'Does that change anything in this inquiry, sir?' Emma-Jane Boutwood asked.

'In the 1930s this city got the sobriquet Murder Capital of Europe,' Grace retorted. 'I don't intend to let anyone think they can come here, kill someone for a bounty and get away with it. And that's what we could be dealing with right now.'

'If it's a professional Mafia hit,' Nick Nicholl said, 'whoever did this could already be back in America. Or wherever he came from.'

'Evie Preece does not have an internal door into her garage,' Grace replied. 'If our man knocked Preece out, he would have had to carry him out of the house and into the garage – on a street in a densely populated neighbourhood. When he got to Shoreham Harbour, he would have had to leave him in the van while he opened the gates. Then he would have had to glue his hands to the wheel, start the fork-lift truck and use it to push the van into the water. OK, I'm speculating. But Evie Preece had a whole bunch of neighbours. Also, there are houses all around Shoreham Harbour. It's possible Preece's killer got lucky and no one saw a thing. But I want to ramp up those house-to-house enquiries in her street and around the harbour. Someone might have been out walking their dog or whatever. Someone must have seen *something*, and we have to find them.'

He looked down at his notes again, then turned to DC Howes. 'David, do you have anything to report from Ford?'

'Not so far, boss,' he replied. 'It's the usual prison situation, with everyone closing ranks. No one saw anything. They're still working on it – going through all the recorded phone conversations around the time in question, but that could take several days.'

Grace then turned to DC Boutwood and DC Nicholl, to whom he had delegated the line of enquiry regarding the camera found in the van.

'Do you have anything to report?'

E-J shook her head. 'Not so far, sir. The camera is a Canon model widely on sale here, at a price of around a grand, and overseas. There are seventeen retail outlets in Brighton that stock it, as well as numerous online stores, including Amazon. In the US there are thousands of retail outlets, Radio Shack, a national chain, being among the major discounters.'

'Great. So we're looking for a needle in a haystack, is that what you're saying?'

'That's about it, sir.'

'OK,' Grace replied, staring her back, hard, in the eye. 'That's one of the things we do best. Finding needles in haystacks.'

'We'll try our hardest, sir!'

He made another note, then sat in silent thought for some

moments. He could not put a finger on it, but he had a bad feeling. *Copper's nose*, they used to call it. Gut feelings. Instinct.

Whatever.

The little shit Kevin Spinella was pushing him to hold another press conference. But he wasn't ready for that yet and he would stall for time. All the reporter knew at this stage – unless he had something from his inside source – was that a dead body in a van had been recovered from Shoreham Harbour. The fact that the story merited only a handful of lines in today's paper, both in its print and online editions, indicated to him that, so far at least, the reporter was in the dark.

And that was good.

Except, Grace thought, he was in the dark too. And that was not a good place to be at all.

58

Tooth was also in the dark. And that was exactly where he wanted to be. Dressed all in black, with a black baseball cap pulled low over his face, he knew he would be almost invisible outside.

Tuesday night: 11.23 p.m. It was dry and the motorway was dark and busy. Just tail lights, headlights and occasional flashing indicators. He concentrated as he drove, thinking, working out his next steps, covering alternatives, best- and worst-case scenarios.

At long last the lorry he had been following from Aberdeen was pulling into a service station. The driver had been going steadily for nearly five hours since he had stopped for a break on the A74M, just south of Lockerbie, and Tooth needed to urinate. The need had been getting so pressing he had been close to using the expandable flask he kept in the car for such purposes. The same kind he used to take with him behind enemy lines so he didn't leave any traces for them to track him.

He followed the tail lights of the truck along the slip road and up a slight incline. They passed signs with symbols for fuel, food, accommodation and another one for the goods vehicles' parking area.

Conveniently, as if obeying Tooth's silent wishes, the driver headed the articulated refrigeration lorry along past rows of parked lorries, then pulled into a bay several spaces beyond the last one, in a particularly dark area of the car park.

Tooth switched off his lights. He had already, some miles earlier, disabled the Toyota's interior light. He halted the car, jumped out and ran, crouching low, invisible. There were no signs of activity around him. He couldn't see CCTV cameras in this area. The lorry nearest to his target had its blinds pulled. The driver was either asleep or watching television or having sex with a motorway hooker. Despite his desperate need to pee, he held off, waiting and watching.

*

Inside the cab of his sixteen-wheel, twenty-four-ton Renault fridge-box artic, Stuart Ferguson reached down for the parking brake, then remembered it was in a different position from the one in the Volvo he normally drove. That vehicle was currently in a Sussex Police vehicle pound, where, apparently, it would remain until the inquest on the young man the vehicle had run over and killed – a fortnight ago tomorrow – was complete.

He switched off the engine and killed the lights, and the voice of Stevie Wonder on the CD player fell silent with them.

He was still badly shaken and had been having nightmares. Several times during these past two weeks, sweet Jessie had woken him gently, telling him he was crying and shouting out. He kept seeing that poor laddie tumbling across the road towards him, coming straight at him, still gripping the handlebars of his bike. Then the severed leg, in his rear-view mirror, some yards behind the vehicle when he had stopped.

On top of that, he had been worrying this could be the end of his trucking career. Because he was over his allotted hours, he'd had the threat of a Death by Dangerous Driving charge hanging over him, and it had been a relief to hear the police were only going to prosecute him for the relatively minor and straightforward hours offence. Despite the accident, he loved this job, and besides, with his ex-wife, Maddie, pretty much cleaning him out, he needed to earn a substantial wage just to pay her maintenance and to make sure the kids had everything they needed.

At least it felt OK being back behind the wheel again. In fact it felt much better than he had thought it would. He'd missed his regular journey to Sussex last Tuesday because the company did not have a spare vehicle available and his boss had given him the week off. In fact, all things considered, the company was being very supportive to him, despite his pending prosecution. Driving out of hours was not something they could ever sanction officially, but everyone knew it went on. Hell, they were in a recession, everyone needed business.

If there had been one silver lining to the cloud of horrors, Jessie, four months pregnant with their child, had been so incredibly caring. He'd seen yet another lovely side to her. More than ever he longed to get his cargo of frozen fish and seafood offloaded and head back home to her. If there were no hitches, he could be climbing into bed with her, slipping his arms around her warm, naked body, in the early hours of Thursday morning. He so much looked forward to that and was tempted to call her one more time this evening. But it was now half-past eleven. Too late.

He looked forward also, at this moment, to a strong coffee and a sugar hit. A doughnut or a custard Danish would go down a treat, and a chocolate bar as well, to sustain him for the last leg to Sussex. When he was a few miles north of Brighton, he would pull into a lay-by and have a few hours' kip.

He climbed down on to the footplate, and closed and locked the door. Then, as his right foot touched the tarmac, he felt a blow on his neck and his head filled with dazzling white streaks, followed by a shower of electric sparks. Like a psychedelic light show, he thought, in the fraction of a second before he blacked out.

*

Tooth knelt, holding the limp body of the short, sturdy man in his arms, and looked around him. He heard the hum of traffic on the motorway a short way away. The rattle of a diesel engine firing up. Strains of music, very faint, from a parked lorry somewhere nearby.

He dragged the man the short distance to his car, the lorry driver's heavy-duty Totectors scraping noisily along the tarmac, but Tooth was confident no one was around to hear them. He hauled him on to the rear seat, closed the doors, then drove a short way across the car park and pulled up in an area of total darkness, away from all the vehicles.

Next he tugged the man's polo shirt out of his trousers. With his thumbs he felt up the man's spine before carefully counting down again from the top to C4. Then, using a movement he had been taught in the military for disabling or killing the enemy silently, with bare hands, he swung him out of the car, lifted him up, then dropped him down hard, backwards, across his knees, hearing the snap. This location on the spine he had chosen would not kill the lorry driver. It would just stop him from running away.

He manoeuvred him back into the car and set to work, binding the man's mouth and arms with duct tape. Then he jammed him down into the gap between the front and rear seats and covered him with a rug he had bought for the purpose, just in case he got stopped later by the police for any reason, then locked up.

He had one more job to do, which involved a screwdriver. It took him only fifteen minutes. Afterwards, he sauntered across to the service station cafeteria, pulling the baseball cap even lower over his face and turning the collar of his jacket up as he spotted the CCTV camera. He walked past, facing away, as he entered the building.

Tooth finally used the restroom, then bought himself a large black coffee and a custard Danish. He chose a table in a quiet section, ate his pastry and sipped some scalding coffee. Then he carried the cup outside, leaned against a wall, lit a cigarette and drank some more. The cigarette tasted particularly good. He felt good. His plan was coming together, the way his plans always came together.

He didn't do abortive missions.

59

Stuart Ferguson woke feeling confused. For an instant he thought he was home with his ex-wife, Maddie. But the room felt unfamiliar. Jessie? Was he with Jessie? Swirling darkness all around him, like a void. His head was throbbing. He heard a noise, a hum, a faint whine like tyres on tarmac. His head was jigging, vibrating, rocking slightly, as if it was floating in space.

Was he asleep in his cab?

He tried to think clearly. He had pulled into the service station to get something to eat and to have a rest. Had he gone to sleep in his bunk? He tried to reach out for the light switch, but nothing seemed to be happening – it was as if he had forgotten how to move his arm. He tried again. Still nothing. Was he lying on it? But he could not feel any of his limbs at all, he realized.

His head became hot, suddenly, with panic. Beads of sweat trickled down his face. He listened to the hum. The whine. He tried to speak, then realized he could not move his mouth.

He was face down. Was he trussed up? Why couldn't he feel anything? Had he had an accident? Was he being taken to hospital?

Sweat was in his eyes now. He blinked, the salt stinging them. His left cheek itched. What had happened? Shit. He concentrated on listening for a moment. He was definitely in a moving vehicle. He was conscious of lights. Headlights. But he could see nothing of where he was. Just dark fibres. There was a smell of dusty carpet in his nostrils.

Something was very wrong. Panic and fear swirled through his head. He wanted Jessie. Wanted to be in her arms. Wanted to hear her voice. He grunted, tried to turn his head. He could hear a clicking sound now. Steady, every few seconds, *click-click-click.* The vehicle was decelerating. His fear accelerated.

He thought about Jessie. Sweet Jessie. He so desperately wanted to be with her. He cried out to her, but no sound came through his taped mouth.

60

David Harris, dressed as usual in his heavy fleece, thick jeans, cap and rubber boots, looked up at the sky as he made his morning inspection of the smokery. The solid cloud cover of earlier this morning seemed to be breaking up, with shards of glassy blue sky appearing in the gaps. The air felt a little bit warmer today, too. Spring was late but perhaps it was finally starting.

He glanced at his watch: 7.45. The delivery driver from Aberdeen Ocean Fisheries was usually here at 7.30 a.m. every Wednesday, on the nail. A cheery little Scot called Stuart Ferguson. The man was always quick and businesslike. He would unload, help Harris and his staff into the sheds with the cargo, getting the items checked and ticked on his docket, then have it signed and be on his way. He always seemed in a hurry to get off.

Last week was one of the few times in all the years Harris could remember when there'd been no delivery from Aberdeen. The previous week the lorry had been involved in that bad accident that had been all over the news. Some big New York crime family's son had been killed. Ferguson had been named as the lorry driver – and Harris had worked out that the accident must have happened only a short while after the driver had made his delivery here.

He wondered if it would be Ferguson again today or whether they would have put a different driver on. He hoped it would be Ferguson, because it would be interesting to find out from him what had actually happened. But perhaps the man had lost his job over this. Or was suspended. He looked at his watch again and listened for a moment, to see if he could hear the sound of an approaching lorry. But all he could hear was the faint, insistent bleating of sheep up on the Downs above him. Must be a new driver, he thought, either with a different schedule or perhaps lost – not hard on the narrow, winding roads to this place.

He walked up the incline between two low buildings, passing a row of his parked delivery vans, then, to his surprise, he noticed the padlock on the first of the smokehouse doors, which one of his staff always locked last thing at night, was hanging loose and open. He felt a sudden twist of unease inside him. Each of the brick and steel smokehouses contained many thousands of pounds' worth of fish, and so far, in the company's history, they'd never been burgled. Which was why he'd never thought it necessary to invest in expensive security systems such as alarms or CCTV. Perhaps he might have to now, he thought.

Hurrying over, he pulled the door open and stepped inside. The strong, familar fug that he loved, of smoke and fish, enveloped him. Inside the dim interior, everything looked fine, the fish – all wild Scottish salmon in this kiln – hung in dense, packed rows on hooks from the ceiling. He was about to leave, when he decided to do a quick check, and cranked the handle that moved the fish along the ceiling rail, so they could be rotated for inspection purposes. At the halfway point, he suddenly saw four large fish had fallen from their hooks and lay on the draining tray beneath.

How the hell could they have fallen, he wondered?

Had there been a problem with this kiln during the night? One of the pieces of high-tech they had invested in was a temperature alarm system. If the temperature in one of the kilns dropped too low, or the temperature in one of the cold-storage sheds rose too high his engineer, Tom White, would get a call on his mobile phone and have to come straight over. Had Tom needed to do some work on this kiln? But even if he had, Tom was a careful man; he wouldn't leave four expensive salmon lying in the draining tray.

He called the engineer's mobile – the man would probably be in his workshop at the far end of the smokery at this time of day. White answered immediately, but it wasn't the reply David Harris had hoped for. There hadn't been any problems overnight. No call-out.

As he hung up, he wondered if there been an attempted burglary. Hurriedly, he hooked the salmon back up, then checked each of the next four kilns, but everything was fine. Then he walked along to the cold-store sheds and stared, in growing bewilderment and unease, at the sight of the padlock on the first shed door, also hanging loose and open.

Shit!

He strode over and yanked the heavy, sealed sliding door open, fully expecting to find the entire contents of the shed missing. Instead he stared, in momentary disbelief, as the blast of refrigerated air greeted him. Everything looked normal, fine, undisturbed. Rows of smoked salmon hung from hooks from ceiling rails on the motorized pulley system. Six rows, with not enough space to walk between them, forming an almost solid wall. He slid the door shut again, relieved.

It wasn't until much later in the day, when his staff began to package the fish for dispatch to customers, that they would discover what he had missed in this shed.

61

'The time is 8.30 a.m. Wednesday 5 May,' Roy Grace read from his notes to his team in MIR-1. 'This is the twenty-sixth briefing of *Operation Violin.' And we're not making any sodding progress*, he felt like adding, but he refrained. There were flat spots like this in almost every inquiry.

He was in a bad and worried mood. His biggest worry was Cleo. She had almost fainted stepping out of the shower this morning. She insisted it was purely because the water had been too hot, but he had wanted to take her straight to hospital. She'd refused, saying that she felt fine, right as rain; they were short-handed at the mortuary and she needed to be there.

He was worried about this case, too. This was a full-on murder inquiry, yet he sensed a spark was missing. Although he had most of his trusted regulars in his team, there didn't seem to be the air of commitment and focus that he was used to feeling. He knew the reason. It was the wrong reason, but it was human nature. It was because the murder victim was Ewan Preece.

Despite the horrific nature of his death, no one from Sussex Police was going to be shedding a tear at Preece's funeral – although he would send a couple of undercover officers along, to keep an eye on who turned up, or lurked nearby.

But regardless of however undesirable a character Preece was, he had been murdered. And Grace's job was not to be judgemental, but to find the killer and lock him up. To do that, he needed to get his team better motivated.

'Before we go through your individual reports,' he said, 'I want to recap on our lines of enquiry.' He stood up and pointed to the whiteboard, on which there were three numbered headings, each written in caps in red. 'In the first, we look into the possibility that there is no link between Preece's killing and the death of cyclist Tony Revere, clear? Preece was a man who made enemies naturally.

We could be looking at a drugs turf war or something like a double-crossing. He could have just screwed the wrong person.'

Duncan Crocker put up his hand. 'The camera's the thing that bothers me with that line of enquiry, chief. Why wouldn't they just kill him? Why chuck away an expensive camera like that?'

'There are plenty of sadists out there,' Grace replied. 'But I agree with your point about the camera. We'll come back to that. OK, right, the second line of enquiry is that Preece was killed by someone who was after the reward money.'

'Doesn't the same apply with the camera, boss?' asked Bella Moy. 'If they're after the reward, why chuck away a camera of that value?'

'It would be a good idea to remind ourselves of the wording of the reward, Bella,' Grace replied. 'It's not the usual, *for information leading to the arrest and conviction.*' He looked down at his notes for a moment and searched through a few pages. Then he read, 'This reward is for information leading to *the identity* of the van driver responsible for the death of her son.' He looked up. 'That's a big difference.'

'Do you think something might have gone wrong, Roy?' Nick Nicholl asked. 'Perhaps the killer was planning to get Preece to fess up into the camera and it didn't happen.'

'Maybe it did happen,' Glenn Branson said. 'The camera transmits – we don't know what was said or transmitted to whom.'

'He probably didn't say too much underwater,' Norman Potting butted in, and chortled.

Several of the others stifled grins.

'I can't speculate on whether anything went wrong, Nick,' Grace replied to DC Nicholl. Then he pointed at the whiteboard again. 'Our third line of enquiry is whether, bearing in mind Revere's family's connection with organized crime, this was a professional revenge killing – a hit. So far, from initial enquiries I've made to connections I have in the US, there is no intelligence of any contract of any kind that's been put out regarding this, but we need to look at the US more closely.' He turned to Crocker. 'Duncan, I'm tasking you with getting further and better information on the Revere family and their connections.'

'Yes, boss,' the DS said, and made a note.

'I have a 3.30 p.m. meeting with the ACC. I need to take him something to show that we're not all sodding asleep here.'

At that moment his phone rang. Raising a hand apologetically, Roy Grace answered it. Kevin Spinella was on the other end and what the reporter from the *Argus* told him suddenly made his bad mood a whole lot worse.

62

This Wednesday was not promising to be one of the best days of Carly's life. She was due to meet her solicitor and colleague, Ken Acott, outside Brighton Magistrates' Court at 9.15 a.m., and have a coffee with him before her scheduled court appearance.

Quite unnecessarily in her view, Ken had warned her not to drive, as she was certain to lose her licence and the ban would be effective instantly. As her smashed Audi was still currently in the police pound, driving had not been an option in any event and she had come by taxi.

She was wearing a simple navy two-piece, a white blouse and a conservative Cornelia James silk square, with plain navy court shoes. Ken had advised her to look neat and respectable, not to power-dress and not to be dripping with bling.

As if she ever was!

Then, as she stepped out of the taxi, her right heel broke, shearing almost clean off.

No, no, no! Don't do this to me!

There was no sign of Acott. A couple of teenagers and an angry-looking, scrawny middle-aged woman were standing nearby. One youth, in a tracksuit and baseball cap, had a pathetic, stooping posture, while the other, in a hoodie, was more assertive-looking. All three of them were smoking and not talking. The woman was the mother of one or both of them, she presumed. The boys looked rough and hard, as if they were already seasoned offenders.

Carly felt the warmth of the sun, but the promise of a fine day did little to relieve the dark chill inside her. She was nervous as hell. Acott had already warned her that a lot depended on which trio of magistrates she came in front of this morning. In the best-case scenario she would get a one-year driving ban – the minimum possible for drink-driving in the UK – and a hefty fine. But if she got a bad call, it could be a lot worse. The magistrates might decide that even if the police were not going to prosecute her for death by careless or dangerous driving, they would come up with a punishment to fit the circumstances and throw the book at her. That could mean a three-year ban, or even longer, and a fine running into thousands.

Fortunately, money had not been a problem for her so far, since Kes's death, but provincial law firms did not pay highly and next year Tyler would move on to his public school, where the fees would be treble what she was currently paying at St Christopher's. She was going to be stretched. So the prospect of a three-year driving ban and all the costs of taxis involved, and a huge fine as well, quite apart from the fact that her conviction was bound to be splashed over the local news, was not leaving her in the best frame of mind.

And now her sodding heel had broken. How great an impression was that going to make, hobbling into court?

She leaned against a wall, catching a tantalizing whiff of cigarette smoke, and tugged her shoe off. A gull circled overhead, cawing, as if it was laughing at her.

'Fuck off, gull,' she said sullenly.

The heel was hanging by a strip of leather. Two tiny, bent nails protruded from the top of it. She looked at her watch: 9.07. She wondered if she had enough time to hobble to a heel bar and get it fixed, but where was the nearest one? She'd noticed one quite recently, not far from here. But where?

Her iPhone pinged with an incoming text. She took it out of her handbag and checked the display. It was Ken Acott, saying he'd be there in two minutes.

Then she flicked across the phone's apps screen to Friend Mapper, to check that her friend Clair May had safely delivered Tyler to school. His mood was upsetting her. She'd always been close to him – and Kes's death had created a special bond between them – but now he'd put a wall around himself and was even resenting putting Friend Mapper on each day.

'Don't you want to be able to see where I am?' she had asked him yesterday.

'Why?' He'd shrugged.

For the past two years they had used this GPS app daily. A

small blue dot marked her precise position on a street map and a purple one – his choice of colour – marked his. Each time either of them logged on they could see where the other was. It was like a game to Tyler and he'd always enjoyed following her, sending her the occasional text when she was away from the office, saying: **I can c u** ☺

To her relief the purple dot was where it should be, near the corner of New Church Road and Westbourne Gardens, where St Christopher's School was located. She put the phone back in her bag.

At that moment Ken Acott came around the corner, looking sharp in a dark grey suit and a green tie, swinging his massive attaché case. He was smiling.

'Sorry I'm late, Carly. Had to deal with an urgent custody hearing, but I've got some good news!'

From the expression in his face it looked as if he was going to tell her that the case had been dropped.

'I've just had a quick conversation with the clerk of the court. We've got Juliet Smith in the chair. She's very experienced and very fair.'

'Great,' Carly said, greeting the news with the same level of enthusiasm someone under a death sentence might have shown on being told that the execution chamber had recently been redecorated.

63

Tooth was tired but he had to keep going, keep up the pace. Speed was vital. Cut the police some slack and they could catch up with you very fast. He needed to keep two jumps ahead of them. Equally, it was when you were tired that you risked making a mistake.

He was running on adrenalin and catnaps, the way he used to in the military, when he was behind enemy lines. Five minutes' shut-eye and he was good to go again. That had been part of his sniper school training. He could function for days like that. Weeks if he had to. But those catnaps were vital. Deprive a cat of sleep and it would die in two weeks. Deprive a human and he would become psychotic.

He would sleep later, when the job was complete, then he could do so for as long as he wanted, until that day the Russian roulette finally came good. Not that he had ever slept for more than four hours at a stretch in his life. He wasn't comfortable sleeping – didn't like the idea that stuff could happen around you while you weren't aware of it.

He peered out at the neighbourhood as he drove. It didn't take a rocket scientist to figure that people had to be well off to live around here. Detached houses, nice lawns, smart cars. Money bought you isolation. Better air to breathe. Privacy. These houses had big gardens. Gardens were urban jungles. He was good at urban jungles.

There was a big park on his left as he drove around the wide, curved road. Tennis courts. An enclosed playground with kids in it and their mothers watching. Tooth scowled. He didn't like children. He saw a woman picking up her dog's shit in a plastic bag. Saw a game going on between soccer posts. This was the kind of safe neighbourhood that five centuries of winning wars against invaders bought you. Here you didn't have to worry any more about marauding soldiers killing the menfolk and raping the women and children

– unlike some places in the world that he had seen, where that went on.

The comfort zone of civilization.

The comfort zone Carly Chase inhabited, or so she thought.

He turned into her street. Hove Park Avenue. He'd already paid a visit here earlier on his way back from Springs Smoked Salmon.

This was going to be easy. His client would like it, a lot. He was certain.

64

Grace was still seething at the thought of his conversation with Kevin Spinella as he entered Peter Rigg's office punctually at 3.30 p.m. The ACC, looking dapper in a chalk-striped blue suit and brightly coloured polka-dot tie, offered him tea as he sat down, which he accepted gratefully. He hoped some biscuits might come along with it, as he'd had no lunch. He'd been working through the day, trying to gather some positive scraps of information to give his boss about *Operation Violin*, but he had precious little. In his hand he held a brown envelope containing the latest exhibits list, which he had taken away from the exhibits meeting an hour earlier.

'So how are we doing, Roy?' Rigg asked chirpily.

Grace brought him up to speed on his team's three current lines of enquiry, as well as their growing involvement in the investigation into the murder of Warren Tulley at Ford Prison. Then he handed him a copy of the exhibits list and ran through the key points of that with him.

'I don't like the camera, Roy,' the ACC said. 'It doesn't chime.'

'With what, sir?'

Rigg's MSA brought in a china cup and saucer on a tray, with a separate bowl of sugar and, to Grace's delight, a plate of assorted biscuits. A bonus he never had in the days of the previous ACC. Rigg gestured for him to help himself and he gulped down a round one with jam in the centre, then eyed a chocolate bourbon. To his dismay his boss leaned across the table and grabbed that one himself.

Speaking as he munched it, Rigg said, 'We've seen plenty of instances of low-life filming their violent acts on mobile phone cameras, *happy slapping*, all that. But this is too sophisticated. Why would someone go to that trouble – and, more significantly, that expense?'

'Those are my thoughts too, sir.'

'So what are your conclusions?'

'I'm keeping an open mind. But I think it has to have been done by someone after that reward. Which brings me on to something I want to raise. We have a real problem with the crime reporter from the *Argus*, Kevin Spinella.'

'Oh?'

Rigg reached forward and grabbed another biscuit Grace had been eyeing, a custard cream.

'I had a call from him earlier. Despite all our efforts at keeping from the press, at this time, that Ewan Preece's hands were glued to the steering wheel of the van, Spinella has found out.'

Grace filled him in on the history of leaks to the reporter during the past year.

'Do you have any view on who it might be?'

'No, I don't at this stage.'

'So is the *Argus* going to print with the superglue story?'

'No. I've managed to persuade him to hold it.'

'Good man.'

Grace's phone rang. Apologizing, he answered.

It was Tracy Stocker, the Crime Scene Manager, and what she had to say was not good news.

Grace asked her a few brief questions, then ended the call and looked back at his boss, who was studying the exhibits list intently. He eyed once more a chocolate digestive on the plate, but all of a sudden he'd lost his appetite. Rigg put down the list and looked back at him quizzically.

'I'm afraid we have another body, sir,' Grace said.

He left the office, then hurried across the Police HQ complex to his car.

65

One of the many things Roy Grace loved about Brighton was the clear delineation to its north between the city limits and stunning open countryside. There was no urban sprawl, just a clean dividing line made by the sweep of the A27 dual carriageway between the city and the start of the Downs.

The part of that countryside he was driving towards now, the Devil's Dyke, was an area that never ceased to awe him, no matter how often he came here and no matter his purpose, even this afternoon, when he knew it was going to be grim.

The Devil's Dyke was the beauty spot where he used to bring Sandy in their courting days and they often hiked here at weekends after they were married. They would drive up to the car park at the top and walk across the fields, with their spectacular views across the rolling hills in one direction and towards the sea in another. They would take the path past the old, derelict and slightly creepy fort that he used to love coming to as a child with his parents. He and his sister would play games of cowboys and Indians, and cops and robbers in and around its crumbling walls – always being careful to avoid treading in one of the numerous cowpats that were its major hazard.

If it was too blustery on the top, he and Sandy used to walk down the steep banks into the valley below. Legend had it that the Devil had dug out a vast trench – in reality a beautiful, natural valley – to allow the sea to come inland and flood all the churches in Sussex. It was one of the least true of the myths about his city's dark heritage.

In those first few years after Sandy had vanished, he often came up here alone and either just sat in his car, staring through the windscreen, or got out and walked around. There was always the dim hope in his mind that she might just turn up here. It was one of the beliefs he had clung to that she might have lost her memory. A neurologist he had consulted told him that sometimes people with this condition regain fragments of their memory and might go to places familiar to them.

But sometimes in those lonely years he came here just to feel close to her, to feel her spirit in the wind.

He had never done any of these walks with Cleo. He didn't want the memories casting clouds over their relationship. Didn't want Cleo meeting his ghosts. They'd made other parts of the city and its environs their own special places.

He drove as fast as he dared along the high top road, on blue lights and wailing siren. Open land stretched away on both sides, shimmering beneath the almost cloudless afternoon sky. A mile or so to the south, the fields gave way to the houses of the residential area of Hangleton and, even further to the south, Shoreham and its harbour. Taking his eyes off the empty road ahead for a fleeting second, he caught a glimpse of the tall smokestack of the power station, a landmark for the city and for sailors.

As he swept the silver Ford Focus around a long right-hander, he saw a car some distance off about to pull out of the car park of the Waterhall Golf Club into his path and he jabbed the button on the panel in the centre of the dash to change the pitch of the siren to a stentorian *honk-whup-honk-whup* bellow. It did the trick and the car, to his relief, halted sharply.

Each time he headed towards a crime scene, Roy Grace went through a series of mental checks. Reminding himself of all the key elements in the detective's bible, the *Murder Investigation Manual*. A summary sheet, with its headings and flow-chart diagrams, was prominently pinned to the wall in the main corridor of the Major Crime Branch. Every detective who worked there would walk past it several times a week. No matter how many times you ran an investigation, you had to remind yourself to start with the basics. Never get complacent. One of the qualities of a good detective was to be methodical and painstakingly anal.

Grace felt the burden of responsibility just as strongly every time. He'd felt it last week on the quay, with Ewan Preece, and he was feeling it now. The first stage was always the crime scene assessment. Five big headings were ingrained in his mind: LOCATION. VICTIM. OFFENDER. SCENE FORENSICS. POST-MORTEM.

This first, crucial stage of an investigation, literally the hour immediately following the discovery of a murder victim, was known as the *golden hour*. It was the best chance of getting forensic evidence before the crime scene became contaminated by increasing numbers of people, albeit in protective clothing, and before weather, such as rain or strong wind, might change things.

He drove flat out through the picture-postcard village of Poynings, then the even prettier village of Fulking, taking the sharp right-hand bend past the Shepherd and Dog pub, where he had brought Sandy for a drink and a meal on one of their first dates. Then he accelerated along the road at the bottom of the Downs.

Springs Smoked Salmon was a Sussex institution with a world-wide reputation. He'd eaten in many restaurants which boasted their smoked fish as a hallmark of quality, and he'd always wondered about their choice of location, here in the middle of, effectively, nowhere. Maybe they had selected this place originally because there were no neighbours to offend with the fishy smells.

He passed a cluster of farm buildings and dwellings, then slowed as he went down a sharp dip. Rounding the next bend he saw the flashing lights of a halted police car. Several more vehicles, some marked police cars, the Crime Scene Investigator's estate car and a SOCO van were pulled tightly into the bushy side of the road.

He drew up behind the last car, switched off his engine, pressed the button on the dash-mounted panel marked STATIONARY LIGHTS and climbed out. As he wormed himself into his paper oversuit, he could smell wood smoke and the sharper, heavier tang of fish mixed with the fresh, grassy countryside smells.

There was a line of blue and white police tape across the entrance to the smokery and a young constable, acting as a scene guard, whom he did not recognize.

Grace showed his ID.

'Good afternoon, sir,' he said, a little nervously.

Grace pulled on a pair of gloves and ducked under the tape. The constable directed him to walk up a steep incline, between two rows of sheds. Grace only had to go a short distance before he saw a cluster of people similarly attired in oversuits. One of them was Tracy Stocker.

'We can't go on meeting like this, Roy!' she said chirpily.

He grinned. He liked Tracy a lot. She was brilliant at her work, a true professional, but – compared to some of her colleagues, or at least one in particular – she had managed to avoid becoming cynical. As an SIO you soon learned that an efficient Crime Scene Manager could make a big difference to the start of your investigation.

'So what do we have?'

'Not the prettiest picture I've ever seen.'

She turned and led the way. Grace nodded at a couple of detectives he knew. They would have been called here immediately by the response officers to assess the situation. He followed her across to the first of a row of grey, single-storey sheds, each of which had a thick asphalt roof and sliding white door. The door of the building was open.

He suddenly caught a whiff of vomit. Never a good sign. Then Tracy stepped aside, gesturing with her arm for him to enter. He felt a blast of icy air on his face and became aware of a very strong, almost overpowering, reek of smoked fish. Straight ahead he saw a solid wall of large, headless, dark pink fish, hanging in rows, suspended by sturdy hooks to a ceiling rack. There were four rows of them, with narrow aisles between them, hardly wide enough for a person to walk through.

Almost instantly his eyes were drawn to the front of the third row. He saw what at first looked like a huge, plump animal, its flesh all blackened, hanging among the fish. A pig, he thought, fleetingly.

Then, as his brain began to make sense of the image, he realized what it actually was.

66

She loved her view of the Isar, the pretty river that bisected Munich, running almost entirely through parkland. She liked to sit up here at the window, in her fourth-floor apartment above the busy main road of Widenmayerstrasse, and watch people walking their dogs, or jogging, or pushing infants in their strollers along the banks. But most of all she liked to look at the water.

It was for the same reason she liked to go to the Englischer Garten and sit near the lake. Being close to water was like a drug to her. She missed the sea so much. That was what she missed most of all about Brighton. She loved everything else about this city but some days she pined for the sea. And there were other days when she pined for something else, too – the solitude she used to have. Sure, she had resented it at times, that enforced solitude, when work would summon her husband and their plans would be cancelled at the drop of a hat, and she'd find herself alone for an entire weekend, and the following weekends too.

The Italian author Gian Vincenzo Gravina wrote that *a bore is a person who deprives you of solitude without providing you with company.*

This was how it was starting to feel now in her new life. He was so damned demanding. Her new life totally revolved around him. She checked her watch. He would be back soon. This was what it was like now. Every hour of her new life accounted for.

On the screen of her computer on her desk was the online edition of the Sussex newspaper the *Argus*. Since seeing the announcement in the local Munich paper that Roy Grace had placed, about having her declared legally dead, she now scanned the pages of the *Argus* daily.

If he wanted to have her declared dead, after all this time, there had to be a reason. And there was only one reason that she could think of.

She took a deep breath, then she reminded herself of the mantra to control her anger. *Life is not about waiting for the storms to pass. It is about learning to dance in the rain.*

She said it aloud. Then again. And again.

Finally she felt calm enough to turn to the Forthcoming Marriages section of the newspaper. She scanned the column. His name was not there.

She logged off with the same feeling of relief she had every day.

67

Over the years Roy Grace had seen a lot of horrific sights. Mostly, as he had grown more experienced, he was able to leave them behind, but every now and then, like most police officers, he would come across something that he took home with him. When that happened he would lie in bed, unable to sleep, unpacking it over and over again in his mind. Or wake up screaming from the nightmare it was giving him.

One of his worst experiences was as a young uniformed officer, when a five-year-old boy had been crushed under the wheels of a skip lorry. He'd been first on the scene. The boy's head had been distorted and, with his spiky blonde hair, the poor little mite reminded Grace absurdly and horrifically of Bart Simpson. He'd had a nightmare about the boy two or three times a month for several years. Even today he had difficulty watching Bart Simpson on television because of the memory the character triggered.

He was going to take this one in front of him home too, he knew. It was horrific, but he couldn't stop looking, couldn't stop thinking about the suffering during this man's last moments. He hoped they were quick, but he had a feeling they probably weren't.

The man was short and stocky, with a buzz cut and a triple chin, and tattoos on the backs of his hands. He was naked, with his clothes on the ground, as if he had taken them off to have a bath or a swim. His blue overalls, socks and a green polo shirt that was printed with the words ABERDEEN OCEAN FISHERIES sat, neatly folded, next to his heavy-duty boots. Patches of his skin were smoke-blackened and there were some tiny crystals of frost on his head and around his face and hands. He was hung from one of the heavy-duty hooks, the sharp point of which had been pushed up through the roof of his wide-open jaw and was protruding just below his left eye, like a foul-hooked fish.

It was the expression of shock on the man's face – his bulging, terrified eyes – that was the worst thing of all.

The icy air continued to pump out. It carried the strong smell of smoked fish, but also those of urine and excrement. The poor man had both wet and crapped himself. Hardly surprising, Grace thought, continuing to stare at him, thinking through the first pieces of information he had been given. One of the smokehouses had been broken into as well. Had the poor sod been put in there first, and then in here to be finished off by the cold?

The mix of smells was making him feel dangerously close to retching. He began, as a pathologist had once advised him, to breathe only through his mouth.

'You're not going to like what I have to tell you, Roy,' Tracy Stocker said breezily, seemingly totally unaffected.

'I'm not actually liking what I'm looking at that much either. Do we know who he is?'

'Yes, the boss here knows him. He's a lorry driver. Makes a regular weekly delivery here from Aberdeen. Has done for years.'

Grace continued to stare back at the body, fixated. 'Has he been certified?'

'Not yet. A paramedic's on the way.'

However dead a victim might appear, there was a legal requirement that a paramedic attend and actually make the formal certification. In the old days it would have been a police surgeon. Not that Grace had any doubt about the man's condition at this moment. The only people who looked more dead than this, he thought cynically, were piles of ash in crematorium urns.

'Have we got a pathologist coming?'

She nodded. 'I'm not sure who.'

'Nadiuska, with any luck.' He looked back at the corpse. 'Hope you'll excuse me if I step out of the room when they remove the hook.'

'I think I'll be stepping out with you,' she said.

He smiled grimly.

'There's something that could be very significant, Roy,' she said.

'What's that?'

PETER JAMES

'According to Mr Harris, the guv'nor here, this is the driver involved in our fatal in Portland Road. Stuart Ferguson.'

Grace looked at her. Before the ramifications of this had fully sunk in, the Crime Scene Manager was speaking again.

'I think we ought to get a bit closer, Roy. There's something you need to see.'

She took a few steps forward and Grace followed. Then she turned and pointed to the interior wall, a foot above the top of the door.

'Does that look familiar?'

Grace stared at the cylindrical object with the shiny glass lens.

And now he knew for sure that his worst fears were confirmed.

It was another camera.

250

68

Carly greeted the woman who entered her office with a smile as she ushered her into a seat. The appointment was late, at 4.45, because her whole day was out of kilter. At least it was her last client, she thought with relief.

The woman's name was Angelina Goldsmith. A mother of three teenagers, she had recently discovered that her architect husband had been leading a double life for twenty years and had a second family in Chichester, thirty miles away. He hadn't actually married this woman, so he wasn't legally a bigamist, but he sure as hell was morally. The poor woman was understandably devastated.

And she deserved a solicitor who was able to focus a damned sight better than Carly was capable of doing at the moment, Carly thought.

Angelina Goldsmith was one of those trusting, decent people who was shocked to the core when her husband dumped her and went off with another woman. The woman had a gentle nature, she was a nice-looking brunette with a good figure, and had given up her career as a geologist for her family. Her confidence was shattered and she needed advice urgently.

Carly gave her sympathy and discussed her options. She gave her advice that she hoped would enable her to see a future for herself and her children.

After the client had left, Carly dictated some notes to her secretary, Suzanne. Then she checked her voicemail, listening to a string of messages from clients, the final one from her friend, Clair May, who had driven Tyler to school and back home again. Clair said that Tyler had been crying all the way home, but would not tell her why.

At least her mother was there to look after him, until she got home. He liked his gran, so hopefully he'd cheer up. But his behaviour was really troubling her. She'd try and have a long chat with him as soon as she got home. She rang for a taxi, then left the office.

*

In the taxi on the way home, Carly sat immersed in her thoughts. The driver, a neatly dressed man in a suit, seemed a chatty fellow and he kept trying to make conversation, but she did not respond. She wasn't in the mood for conversation.

Ken Acott had been right about the magistrate. She'd got a one-year ban and a £1,000 fine, which Ken Acott said afterwards was about as lenient as it could get. She'd also accepted the court's offer for her to go on a driver-education course which would reduce her ban to nine months.

She'd felt an idiot, hobbling up to the dock on her uneven shoes and out again. Then, just when she was looking forward to lunch with Sarah Ellis, to cheer her up, Sarah had phoned with the news that her elderly father, who lived alone, had had a fall, and a suspected broken wrist, and she was on her way to hospital with him.

So Carly had thought, sod it, and instead of going to find a shoe repair place, she stumbled along to a store in Duke's Lane for a spot of retail therapy. She was wearing the result now, a pair of reassuringly expensive and absurdly high-heeled Christian Louboutins in black patent leather with twin ankle straps and red soles. They were the only thing today that had made her feel good.

She looked out of the window. They were moving steadily in the heavy rush-hour traffic along the Old Shoreham Road. She texted Tyler to say she'd be home in ten minutes and signed it with a smile and a row of kisses.

'You're towards the Goldstone Crescent end, aren't you, with your number?'

'Yes. Well done.'

'Uh-huh.'

The driver's radio briefly burst into life, then was silent. After a few moments he said, 'Do you have a low-flush or high-flush toilet in your house?'

'A high-flush or low-flush toilet, did you say?'

'Uh-huh.'

'I've no idea,' she replied.

She got a text back from Tyler: **U haven't got Mapper on** ☹

She replied: **Sorry. Horrible day. Love you XXXX**

'High flush, you'd have a chain. Low flush, a handle.'

'We have handles. So low flush, I guess.'

'Why?'

The man's voice was chirpy and intrusive. If he didn't shut up about toilets he wasn't going to get a damned tip.

Mercifully he remained silent until they had halted outside her house. The meter showed £9. She gave him £10 and told him to keep the change. Then, as she stepped out on to the pavement, he called out, 'Nice shoes! Christian Louboutin? Size six? Uh-huh?'

'Good guess,' she said, smiling despite herself.

He didn't smile back. He just nodded and unscrewed the cap of a Thermos flask.

Creepy guy. She was minded to tell the taxi company that she didn't want that driver again. But maybe she was being mean; he was just trying to be friendly.

As she climbed up the steps to her front door, she did not look back. She entered the porch and fumbled in her bag for her key.

On the other side of the road, Tooth, in his dark grey rental Toyota that was in need of a wash, made a note on his electronic pad: **Boy 4.45 p.m. home. Mother 6 p.m. home.**

Then he yawned. It had been a very long day. He started the car and pulled out into the street. As he drove off, he saw a police car heading down slowly, in the opposite direction. He tugged his baseball cap lower over his face as they crossed, then he watched in his rear-view mirror. He saw its brake lights come on.

69

Carly could hear the clatter of dishes in the kitchen, which sounded like her mother clearing up Tyler's supper. There was a smell of cooked food. Lasagne. Sunlight was streaking in through the window. Summer was coming, Carly thought, entering the house with a heavy heart. Normally her spirits lifted this time of year, after the clocks had gone forward and the days were noticeably longer. She liked the early-morning light, and the dawn chorus, too. In those first terrible years after Kes died, the winters had been the worst. Somehow, coping with her grief had been a little easier in the summer.

But what the hell was *normally* any more?

Normally Tyler would come running out of the school gates to greet her. Normally he would come rushing to the front door to hug her if she had been out. But now she stood alone in the hallway, staring at the Victorian coat stand that still had Kes's panama hat slung on a hook, and the fedora he'd once bought on a whim, and his silver duck-handled umbrella in its rack. He'd liked cartoons and there was a big framed Edwardian one of people skating on the old Brighton rink in West Street hanging on the wall, next to a print of the long-gone Brighton chain pier.

The realization was hitting her that everything was going to be a hassle this summer with no driving licence. But, sod it, she thought. She was determined to think positively. She owed it to Tyler – and herself – not to let this get her down. After her father died, four years ago, her mother told her, in the usual philosophical way she had of coping with everything, that life was like a series of chapters in a book and now she was embarking on a new chapter in her life.

So that's what this was, she decided. The *Carly Has No Licence* chapter. She would just have to get to grips with bus and train timetables, like thousands of other people. And as one bonus, how *green* would that be? She was going to use her holidays to give Tyler exactly the same kind of summer he always had. Days on the beach.

Treat days to zoos and amusement parks like Thorpe Park and to the museums in London, particularly the Natural History Museum, which he loved best of all. Maybe she'd get to like travelling that way so much she wouldn't bother with a car again.

Maybe the skies would be filled with flying pigs.

As she walked into the kitchen, her mother, wearing an apron printed with the words TRUST ME, I'M A LAWYER over a black roll-neck and jeans, came up and gave her a hug and a kiss.

'You poor darling, what an ordeal.'

Her mother had been there for her throughout her life. In her mid-sixties, with short, auburn hair, she was a handsome, if slightly sad-looking woman. She had been a midwife, then a district nurse, and these days kept herself busy with a number of charities, including working part-time at the local Brighton hospice, the Martlets.

'At least the worst part's over,' Carly replied. Then she saw the *Argus* lying on the kitchen table. It looked well thumbed through. She hadn't bought a copy because she hadn't had the courage to open it. 'Am I in it?'

'Just a small mention. Page five.'

The main story on the front page was about a serial killer called Lee Coherney, who had once lived in Brighton. The police were digging up the gardens of two of his former residences. The story was on the news on the small flat-screen TV mounted on the wall above the kitchen table. A good-looking police officer was giving a statement about their progress. The caption at the bottom of the screen gave his name as Detective Chief Inspector Nick Sloan of Sussex CID.

She riffled through the pages until she found her tiny mention and felt momentarily grateful to this monster, Coherney, for burying her own story.

'How's Tyler?' she asked.

'He's fine. Upstairs, playing with that lovely little friend of his, Harrison, who just came over.'

'I'll go and say hi. Do you need to get off?'

'I'll stay and make you some supper. What do you feel like? There is some lasagne and salad left.'

'I feel like a sodding big glass of wine!'

'I'll join you!'

The doorbell rang.

Carly looked at her mother quizzically, then glanced at her watch. It was 6.15 p.m.

'Tyler said another friend might be joining them. They're playing some computer battle game tonight.'

Carly walked into the hall and across to the front door. She looked at the safety chain dangling loose, but it was early evening and she didn't feel the need to engage it. She opened the door and saw a tall, bald black man in his mid-thirties, dressed in a sharp suit and snazzy tie, accompanied by a staid-looking woman of a similar age. She had a tangle of hennaed brown hair that fell short of her shoulders and wore a grey trouser suit over a blouse with the top button done up, giving her a slightly prim air.

The man held up a small black wallet with a document inside it bearing the Sussex Police coat of arms and his photograph.

'Mrs Carly Chase?'

'Yes,' she answered, a tad hesitantly, thinking she really did not want to have to answer a whole load more questions about the accident tonight.

His manner was friendly but he seemed uneasy. 'Detective Sergeant Branson and this is Detective Sergeant Moy from Sussex CID. May we come in? We need to speak to you urgently.'

He threw a wary glance over his shoulder. His colleague was looking up and down the street.

Carly stepped back and ushered them in, unsettled by something she could not put a finger on. She saw her mother peering anxiously out of the kitchen door.

'We need to speak to you in private, please,' DS Branson said.

Carly led them into the living room, signalling to her mother that all was fine. She followed them in and pointed to one of the two sofas, then shut the door, casting an embarrassed glance at the spreading brown stain on the wallpaper, which now covered almost entirely one wall. Then she sat down on the sofa opposite them, staring at them defiantly, wondering what they were going to throw at her now.

'How can I help you?' she asked eventually.

'Mrs Chase, we have reason to believe your life may be in immediate danger,' Glenn Branson said.

Carly blinked hard. 'Pardon?'

Then she noticed for the first time that he had a large brown envelope in his hand. He was holding it in a strangely delicate way for such a big man, the way he might have held a fragile vase.

'It's concerning the road traffic collision two weeks ago today, which resulted in the death of a young student at Brighton University, Tony Revere,' he said.

'What do you mean exactly by *immediate danger*?'

'There were two other vehicles involved, Mrs Chase – a Ford Transit van and a Volvo refrigerated lorry.'

'They were the ones that actually struck the poor cyclist, yes.' She caught the eye of the female DS, who smiled at her in a sympathetic way that irritated her.

'Are you aware of who the cyclist was?' he asked.

'I've read the papers. Yes, I am. It's very sad – and very distressing to have been involved.'

'You're aware that his mother is the daughter of a man purported to be the head of the New York Mafia?'

'I've read that. And the reward she offered. I didn't even know they existed any more. I thought that the Mafia was something from the past, sort of out of *The Godfather*.'

The DS exchanged a glance with his colleague, who then spoke. 'Mrs Chase, I'm a Family Liaison Officer. I think as a solicitor you may be familiar with this term?'

'I don't do criminal law, but yes.'

'I'm here to help you through the next steps you choose. You know the Ford Transit van that was just mentioned?'

'The one that was right behind me?'

'Yes. You need to know that the driver of this van is dead. His body was found in the van on Friday, in Shoreham Harbour.'

'I read in the *Argus* that a body had been found in a van in the harbour.'

'Yes,' Bella Moy said. 'What you won't have read is that he was the driver we believe was involved in the collision. You also won't have read that he was murdered.'

Carly frowned. 'Murdered?'

'Yes. I can't give you details, but please trust us, he was. The reason we are here is that just a few hours ago the driver of the Volvo lorry involved in the death of Tony Revere was also found murdered.'

Carly felt a cold ripple of fear. The room seemed to be swaying and there was a sudden, terrible, intense silence. Then it seemed as if she wasn't really inside her body any more, that she had left it behind and was drifting in a black, freezing, muted void. She tried to speak but nothing came out. The two officers drifted in and out of focus. Then her forehead was burning. The floor seemed to be rising beneath her, then sinking away, as if she was on a ship. She put her right hand on the arm of the sofa, to hold on.

'I—' she began. 'I – I – I thought the reward that – that the mother – that the mother had put up – was for the identification of the van driver.'

'It was,' Bella Moy said.

'So – so why would they be murdered?' A vortex of fear was swirling inside her.

'We don't know, Mrs Chase,' Glenn Branson replied. 'This could just be an extraordinary coincidence. But the police have a duty of care. The inquiry team have made a threat assessment and we believe your life may be in danger.'

This could not be happening, Carly thought. This was a sick joke. There was going to be a punchline. There was some kind of subtle entrapment going on. Her lawyer's mind was kicking in. They'd come in order to scare her into some kind of confession about the accident.

Then Glenn Branson said, 'Mrs Chase, there is a range of things we can do to try to protect you. One of them would be to move you away from here to a safe place somewhere in the city. How would you feel about that?'

She stared at him, her fear deepening. 'What do you mean?'

Bella Moy said, 'It would be similar to a witness being taken into protective custody, Mrs Chase – can I call you Carly?'

Carly nodded bleakly, trying to absorb what she had just been told. 'Move me away?'

'Carly, we'd move you and your family under escort to another house, as a temporary measure. Then, if we feel the threat level is going to be ongoing, we could look at moving you to a different part of England, change your name and give you a completely new identity.'

Carly stared at them, bewildered, like a hunted animal. 'Change my name? A new identity? Move to somewhere else in Brighton? You mean right now?'

'Right now,' Glenn Branson said. 'We'll stay here with you while you pack and then arrange a police escort.'

Carly raised her hands in the air. 'Wait a second. This is insane. My life is in this city. I have a son at school here. My mother lives here. I can't just up sticks and move to another house. No way. Certainly not tonight. And as for moving to another part of England, that's crazy.' Her voice was trembling. 'Listen, I wasn't part of this accident. OK, I know, I've been convicted of driving over the limit – but I didn't hit the poor guy, for Christ's sake! I can't be blamed for his death, surely? The traffic police have already said so. It was said in court today, as well.'

'Carly,' Bella Moy said, 'we know that. The dead boy's parents have been given all the information about the accident. But as my colleague has said, Sussex Police have a legal duty of care to you.'

Carly wrung her hands, trying to think clearly. She couldn't. 'Let's clarify this,' she said. 'The driver behind me, in the white van, you say he is dead – that he's been murdered?'

Glenn Branson looked very solemn. 'There's not any question about it, Mrs Chase. Yes, he has been murdered.'

'And the lorry driver?'

'Not any question about his death either. We've carried out intelligence as best we can on the dead boy's family and, unfortunately, they are fully capable of revenge killings such as this. Dare I say it, these things are part of their culture. It's a different world they inhabit.'

'That's fucking great, isn't it?' Carly said, her fear turning to anger. She suddenly felt badly in need of a drink and a cigarette. 'Can I get either of you something to drink?'

Both officers shook their heads.

She sat still for a moment, thinking hard, but it was difficult to focus her mind. 'Are you saying there's a hit man, or whatever they're called, hired by this family?'

'It's a possibility, Carly,' Bella Moy said gently.

'Oh, right. So what are the other possibilities? Coincidence? It would be a big, bloody coincidence, right?'

'One hundred thousand dollars is a lot of money, Mrs Chase,' DS Branson said. 'It is indicative of the parents' anger.'

'So you're saying my son and I might need to move away from here? Get a new identity? That you'll protect us for the rest of our lives? How's that going to work?'

The two detectives looked at each other. Then DS Moy spoke. 'I don't think any police force has the resources to provide that level of protection, Mrs Chase, unfortunately. But we can help you change identity.'

'This is my home. This is our life here. Our friends are here. Tyler's already lost his dad. Now you want him to lose all his friends? You seriously want me to go into hiding, with my son, tonight? To consider quitting my job? And what if we do move house – and then county? If these people are for real, don't you think they're going to be able to find us? I'm going to spend the rest of my life in fear of a knock on the door, or a creak in the house, or the crack of a twig out in the garden?'

'We're not forcing you to move out, Carly,' Bella Moy said. 'We're just saying that would be the best option in our view.'

'If your decision is to stay we will give you protection,' Glenn Branson said. 'We'll provide CCTV and a Close Protection Unit, but it will be for a limited period of two weeks.'

'Two weeks?' Carly retorted. 'Why's that – because of your budget?'

Branson raised his hands expansively. 'These are really your best two options.' Then he picked up the envelope and removed a document from it. 'I need you to read and sign this, please.'

Carly looked down at it. Seeing it in print sent an even deeper chill swirling through her.

70

APPENDIX F – SUSSEX POLICE

'Osman' Warning

Notice of Threat to Personal Safety

Mrs Carly Chase
37 Hove Park Avenue
Hove
BN3 6LN
East Sussex

Dear Mrs Chase

I am in receipt of the following information, which suggests that your personal safety is now in danger.

I stress that I will not under any circumstances disclose to you the identity of the source of this information and whilst I cannot comment on the reliability or otherwise of the source or the content of this information, I have no reason to disbelieve the account as provided. I am not in receipt of any other information in relation to this matter nor do I have any direct involvement in this case.

I have reason to believe, following the deaths of Ewan Preece, the driver of the van which collided with cyclist Tony Revere, and Stuart Ferguson, driver of the lorry which also collided with Tony Revere, that your own life is in immediate and present danger from revenge killings ordered by person or persons unknown and carried out by person or persons currently unknown.

Although Sussex Police will take what steps it can to minimize the risk, the Police cannot protect you from this threat on a day-by-day, hour-by-hour basis.

I also stress that the passing of this information by me in no way authorizes you to take any action which would place you in contravention of the law (e.g. carrying weapons for defence, assault on others, breaches of public order) and should you be found to be so committing you will be dealt with accordingly.

I therefore suggest that you take such action as you see fit to increase your own safety measures (e.g. house burglar alarms, change of daily routines etc.). It may even be that you decide that it is more appropriate for you to leave the area for the foreseeable future. That is a matter for you to decide.

If you wish to provide me with full details of the address at which you will be resident I will ensure that the necessary surveys can be undertaken by police staff to advise you regarding the above safety measures.

I would also ask that you contact the Police regarding any suspicious incidents associated with this threat.

Signed   Detective Superintendent Roy Grace

Time/Date   5.35 p.m. Wednesday 5 May

I .... acknowledge that at ...... hrs on .... 20 ...

the above notice was read out to me by ....

of Sussex Police

Signed ....

Signed by Officer reading notice to ....

Time/Date ....

Signed by Officer witnessing reading ....

Time/Date ....

Carly read it through. When she had finished she looked up at the two officers.

'Let me understand something. Are you saying that if I don't agree to move, that's it, I'm on my own?'

Bella Moy shook her head. 'No, Carly. As DS Branson explained, we would provide you with a round-the-clock police guard for a period of time – two weeks. And we would put in CCTV surveillance for you. But we cannot guarantee your safety, Carly. We can just do our best.'

'You want me to sign?'

Bella nodded.

'This isn't for me, is it, this signature? It's to protect your backsides. If I get killed, you can show you did your best – is that about the size of it?'

'Look, you're an intelligent person,' Glenn Branson said. 'All of us at Sussex Police will do what we can to protect you. But if you don't want to move away, and I can understand that, and I imagine you don't want to be locked away in a secure panic room, then what we can do is limited. We'll have to try to work together.' He placed his card in front of Carly on a coffee table. 'Detective Sergeant Moy will be your immediate contact, but feel free to call me twenty-four-seven.'

Carly picked up her pen. 'Great,' she said, as she signed it, sick with fear, trying hard to think straight.

71

Roy Grace lay in bed beside Cleo, tossing and turning, wide awake, totally wired. He'd been at the mortuary until 2 a.m., when the post-mortem on the lorry driver was finally completed. At least he'd managed to persuade Cleo to go home early, so she'd left shortly before midnight. He now lived in constant fear that Cleo would have another bleed at any moment. Potentially a life-threatening one, for herself and for their baby.

Nadiuska De Sancha had been unavailable and they'd been saddled with the pedantic Home Office pathologist Dr Frazer Theobald for the post-mortem. But although slow, Theobald was thorough, and he had provided some good, immediate information regarding the unfortunate victim's death.

The bright blue dial on the clock radio, inches from Grace's eyes, flicked from 3.58 a.m. to 3.59 a.m., then after what seemed an interminable time to 4.00 a.m.

Shit.

He faced a long, hard day in front of him, during which he would need to be on peak form to manage his expanding inquiry team, to cope with the inevitable quizzing from Peter Rigg and to make important decisions on a revised press strategy. But most importantly of all, the absolute number one priority, he had to safeguard a woman who could be in imminent life-threatening danger.

He looked at the clock radio again: 4.01.

The first streaks of dawn were breaking over the city. But there was a deepening darkness inside him. How the hell could you fully protect someone, short of locking them away in a cell, or walling them up in a panic room? She wasn't willing to leave her home, which would have been the best option, and he could understand her reasons. But the buck stopped with him to make sure she was safe.

He thought again about the sight of Ewan Preece in the van. And the grisly spectre of Stuart Ferguson on the hook. But it was those cameras he was thinking about most. Particularly the second one.

The transmission range was only a few hundred yards. Which meant that the killer had to have been waiting nearby with a receiving device – almost certainly in a vehicle. Grace could understand it would have been difficult to retrieve the camera in the van, but surely he could have gone back for the second one? The two cameras, waterproof and with night vision, were worth a good thousand pounds each. A lot of money to throw away.

Who was this killer? He was clever, cunning and organized. In all of his career, Grace had never come across anything quite like this.

The filming reminded him of a case he had worked on the previous summer, involving a sick, snuff-movie ring, and it had crossed his mind he could be in the same terrain here, but he doubted it. This was about revenge for Tony Revere's death. The driver with his lorryload of frozen seafood being executed in the smokery left little room for doubt.

The pathologist estimated that Ferguson would have been dead in under two hours in the cold store and probably less than that. If the killer had been waiting nearby and picking up the transmission, and presumably waiting until the lorry driver was dead, why had he not retrieved the camera?

Because he hadn't wanted to take the risk? Had he been disturbed by someone arriving there? Or a passing police patrol car perhaps? Or was it to leave a message – a sign – for someone? Just a cynical message for the next victim? *This is what is going to happen to you and money is no object . . .*

Had the killer sat in his car, watching the transmitted images of Ferguson wriggling, shivering and steadily freezing to death for two hours? Frazer Theobald said that the man's skin was partially burned and he had smoke inhalation in his lungs, but not sufficient to have asphyxiated him. The hook through his jaw and out beneath his eye would have been agonizing but not life-threatening. His death in the cold store would have been excruciating.

What might this sadist be planning for Carly Chase?

Detective Investigator Lanigan's team were interviewing the Revere family, as well as Fernanda Revere's brother, who had assumed the position as official head of this crime family following his father's incarceration, but Lanigan was not optimistic about getting anywhere with them.

Grace sipped some water, then as gently as he could turned his pillows over, trying to freshen them up.

Cleo was not sleeping well either, finding it hard lying on her left, with a pillow tucked under her arm, as she had been instructed, as well as needing to go to the loo almost every hour. She was asleep now, breathing heavily. He wondered if reading for a few minutes might calm him down enough to get to sleep. On the floor, a short distance from the bed, their puppy, Humphrey, a Labrador and Border Collie cross, was snoring intermittently.

Moving slowly, trying not to disturb Cleo, he switched on the dimmest setting of his reading light and peered at the small pile of books on his bedside table, half of them bought on his colleague Nick Nicholl's recommendation.

Fatherhood. From Lad to Dad. The New Contented Little Baby Book. Secrets of the Baby Whisperer.

He picked up the top one, *Fatherhood*, and continued reading from the place he'd marked. But after a few pages, instead of calming down, he became increasingly concerned about the burden of responsibility of fatherhood. There was so much to take on board. And all that on top of his police workload.

From the moment Cleo had first given him the news that she was pregnant, he had determined that he would be an involved and committed parent. But now, reading through these books, the time and responsibilities required of him seemed daunting. He wanted to commit that time and he wanted those responsibilities, but how was it all going to be possible?

At 5.30 he finally quit trying to sleep, slipped out of bed, went into the bathroom and splashed some cold water on his face. His eyes felt like he'd been rubbing them with sandpaper. He wondered whether a short run would perk him up, but he felt just too tired. Instead, pulling on his tracksuit, he decided on a walk around the block, focusing his thoughts on the day ahead, and taking Humphrey, who had insisted on joining him, on his lead. Then he dosed himself up on coffee, showered and dressed, and drove to the office.

He arrived there just before 7 a.m., drank a Red Bull and made a phone call to the senior officer of the Close Protection Team that was concealed outside Carly Chase's house. To his relief, all had been quiet.

For this past night, at any rate.

72

'I want you all to know,' said Roy Grace at the start of the 8.30 a.m. briefing in MIR-1, 'that I am not a happy sodding bunny.'

Everyone in the room was already up to speed on the murder of the lorry driver. Major developments in an inquiry of this scale were passed around instantly.

Taking a sip of his coffee and looking down at his notes, he went on, 'Item One on my agenda is the ongoing series of leaks coming from someone to our friend Kevin Spinella at the *Argus*. OK?'

He looked up at thirty-five solemn faces. Yesterday afternoon's horrific discovery had shaken even the most hardened of this bunch. 'I'm not accusing any of you, but someone has leaked to him about Preece's hands being superglued to the steering wheel of his van. It is either a member of this inquiry team, or the Specialist Search Unit, or an employee at Shoreham Harbour, or one of the team in the mortuary. At some point I'm going to find that person and, when I do, I'm going to hang them out to dry on something even more painful than a meat hook. Do I make myself clear?'

Everyone nodded. All those who worked with Roy Grace knew him to be even-tempered and placid, someone who rarely lost his head. It startled them to see him in a temper.

He took another sip of his coffee. 'Our media strategy could be vitally important. We believe a professional contract killer is here in Brighton, in all probability hired by the Revere family in New York to avenge their son's death. We need to manage the media extremely carefully, both to try to get assistance from the public in finding this killer before he strikes again and to avoid any possible impact on the community.'

'Sir,' said DC Stacey Horobin, a bright-looking young woman in her early thirties, with fashionable straggly brown hair, who had been newly drafted into the inquiry team, 'what exactly are your concerns on community impact?'

Nick Nicholl's phone rang. Under Grace's withering glare, he hastily silenced it. There was a brief moment when Grace looked as if he would explode, but his response was calm. 'I think we can assure the public, if it comes to it, that there is no general risk to them,' he replied. 'But I do not want our force to appear incapable of protecting an innocent member of the public.'

'Was the Osman served on Mrs Chase, chief?' asked Duncan Crocker.

'Yes,' Glenn Branson replied on Grace's behalf. 'Bella and I served it yesterday evening just after 6 p.m. Mrs Chase was offered the opportunity to be moved away, out of the area, but she refused for family and business reasons. Frankly, I think she's unwise. DS Moy spent the night in her house, pending the installation of CCTV equipment this morning, and a Close Protection Team unit have been in place outside her residence since 9 p.m. last night. So far without incident.'

'Is there any protection on her commute to work?' asked Norman Potting. 'And while she's in her workplace?'

'I've spoken to Inspector Hazzard at the Hove Neighbourhood Policing Team,' Grace said. 'Today and tomorrow, and for the first part of next week, she will be driven to and from work in a marked police car. And I'm putting a PCSO in reception at her office. I want to send a clear signal to this killer, if he's out there and targeting this woman, that we are on to him.'

'What about Revere's family in New York, chief?' said Nick Nicholl. 'Is anyone speaking to them?'

'I updated our NYPD contact on the situation and they're on the case. He told me that the killings sound similar to the style of a former Mafia hitman, a charmer called Richard Kuklinski who was known as the Iceman. He used cold stores, and one of his specialities was tying up victims and putting them in a cave, then leaving a camera in there to record them steadily being eaten alive by rats.'

Bella, who had been about to pluck a Malteser from the box in front of her, withdrew her hand, wrinkling her face in disgust.

'He sounds our man, chief!' Norman Potting said animatedly.

'He does, Norman,' Grace replied. 'There's just one problem with Kuklinski.'

Potting waited apprehensively.

'He died in prison four years ago.'

'Yes, well, I suppose that might rather tend to eliminate him,' Potting retorted. He looked around with a grin, but no one smiled back. 'Fishy business, this cold store, yesterday,' he added, and again looked around, without success, for any smiles. All he got was a withering glare from Bella Moy.

'Thank you Norman,' Grace said curtly. 'Detective Investigator Lanigan was going to go and see Mr and Mrs Revere last night and report back to me. But frankly I'm not expecting anything from them. And one thing Lanigan told me, which is not good news for us, is that their intelligence on contract killers is very limited.'

'Chief, did this Kuklinski character paralyse his victims first?'

'Not from what I've learned so far from the post-mortem, Nick, no. Our man didn't paralyse Preece – only Ferguson.'

'Why do you think he did that?'

Grace shrugged. 'Maybe sadism. Or perhaps to make him easier to handle. Hopefully,' he said, raising his eyebrows, 'we'll get the chance to ask him that.'

'Boss, what information are you releasing to the press about the death of the lorry driver?' DC Emma-Jane Boutwood asked.

'For now, no more than a man was found dead in a cold store at Springs Smoked Salmon,' Grace said. 'I don't want speculation. Let people think for the moment that it might have been an industrial accident.'

He glanced down at his mobile phone, which was lying next to his printed notes on the work surface in front of him, as if waiting for the inevitable call from Spinella. But it remained, for the moment, silent. 'I haven't yet decided what we should release beyond that. But I've no doubt someone will make that decision for me.'

He gave a challenging stare to his team, without looking at any specific individual. Then he glanced down at his notes again. 'OK, according to his employers, Stuart Ferguson left the depot in the fridge-box lorry shortly after 2 p.m. on Tuesday. We need to find this lorry.' He looked at DC Horobin. 'Stacey, I'm giving you an action which is to try to plot the lorry's route and sightings from the time it left the depot in Aberdeen to wherever it currently is. We need to find it. You should be able to plot much of its journey fairly easily from an ANPR search.'

Automatic Number Plate Recognition cameras were positioned along many of the UK's motorways and key arterial roads. They filmed the registration plates of all passing vehicles and fed them into a database.

'Yes, sir,' she said.

Grace then read out a summary of the post-mortem findings so far. After he dealt with several questions on that, he drained the last of his coffee and moved on to the next item on his list.

'OK, an update on lines of enquiry. The murder of Preece's friend Warren Tulley at Ford Prison is still ongoing.' He looked at DS Crocker. 'Duncan, do you have anything there for us?'

'Nothing new, chief. Still the same wall of silence from the other inmates. The interviewing team is talking to each of the prisoners, but so far we have no breakthrough.'

Grace thanked him, then turned to DC Nick Nicholl. 'The superglue on Ewan Preece's hands. Nick, anything to report?'

'The Outside Inquiry Team are continuing to visit every retail outlet in the Brighton and Hove area that sells superglue. It's a massive task, chief, and we're really understaffed for it. Every news-agent, every DIY and hardware shop, every supermarket.'

'Keep them on it,' Grace said. Then he turned to Norman Potting. 'Anything to report with the camera?'

'We've covered every retailer that sells this equipment, chief, including the Cash Converters stores that sell 'em second-hand. One of them was good enough to check the serial number on the one in the van. He reckons it's not a model sold in the UK – it can only be bought in the USA. I haven't had a chance to start checking the one found in the cold store at Springs yet, but it looks identical.'

As the meeting ended, Glenn Branson received a call on his radio. It was from one of the security officers, Duncan Steele, on the front desk.

He thanked him, then turned to Roy Grace. 'Mrs Chase is down-stairs.'

Grace frowned. 'Here, in this building?'

'Yep. She says she needs to see me urgently.'

'Maybe she's come to her senses.'

73

Tooth sat at the desk in his room at the Premier Inn, with his laptop open in front of him. Through the window he kept an eye on the parking area. He could see the North Terminal building of Gatwick Airport in the distance beyond it and the blue sky above it. It would not be long before he was on an airplane in that blue sky, heading home, to the almost constant blue sky of the Turks and Caicos. He liked heat. Liked it when he had been in the military in hot places. From his experience of English weather, it rained most of the time.

He didn't do rain.

A Lucky Strike dangled between his lips. He stared at the screen, doing some blue-sky thinking, clicking through the images. Photographs of Hove Park Avenue, where Carly Chase lived. Photographs of the front, back and sides of her house.

Early in the morning after he had finished at Springs smokery he had driven down this street, memorizing the cars. Then he'd paid a brief visit to her property. A dog had started barking inside the house and an upstairs interior light came on as he was leaving. Last night he'd taken another drive down there and had spotted the parked dark-coloured Audi, with a shadowy figure behind the wheel. The Audi had not been there previously.

The police weren't stupid. He'd learned over the years never to underestimate the enemy. You stayed alive that way. Out of jail that way. In the US, police surveillance operated in teams of eight, on eight-hour shifts, twenty-four officers covering a twenty-four-hour watch. He had little doubt there were others out there in that area he hadn't spotted. Some on foot, probably in the back garden or down the sides of the house.

He had already listened to the conversation inside the house that the minute directional microphones he had concealed in her garden, pointed at her windows, had picked up when the police had visited her yesterday evening. When she had told them she did not want to leave.

He looked down at his notes. The kid had been picked up in his school uniform at 8.25 a.m. today by a woman in a black Range Rover, with two other kids in it. At 8.35 Carly Chase had left home in the back of a marked police car.

At 9.05 he made a phone call to her office, masquerading as a client, saying he needed to speak to her urgently. He was told she had not yet arrived. A second phone call told him she had still not arrived at 9.30.

Where was she?

74

Carly Chase sat down beside Glenn Branson at the small round conference table in Roy Grace's office. Grace joined them.

'Nice to meet you, Mrs Chase,' he said, sitting down. 'I'm sorry it's not under better circumstances. Would you like something to drink?'

She felt too sick with fear to swallow anything. 'I'm – I'm OK, thank you.'

She was conscious of her right foot jigging and she couldn't stop it. Both the policemen were staring at her intently and that was making her even more nervous.

'I wanted to talk to you,' she stammered, glancing at Glenn Branson, then looking back at the Detective Superintendent. 'Detective Sergeant Branson and his colleague explained the situation to me yesterday evening. I've been thinking about it overnight. I'm not sure if you know, but I'm a solicitor specializing in divorce.'

Grace nodded. 'I know a fair bit about you.'

She wrung her hands, then swallowed to try to stop her ears popping. Her eyes darted from a collection of old cigarette lighters on a shelf to framed certificates on the wall, then to a stuffed trout in a display case and back to Grace.

'I'm a great believer in compromise rather than confrontation,' she said. 'I try to save marriages, rather than destroy them – that's always been my philosophy.'

Grace nodded again. 'A very noble sentiment.'

She gave him a sideways look, unsure if he was taking the mickey, then realized she knew nothing about his own private life.

'In my experience, dialogue is so often missing,' she said, and shrugged, her foot jigging even harder.

Grace stared at her. He had no idea what point she was leading up to.

'I lost my husband five years ago in a skiing accident. He was buried in an avalanche in Canada. My first reaction was that I wanted to get on a plane to Canada, find the guide who had taken him on that mountain – and who survived – and kill him with my bare hands. OK?'

Grace glanced at Branson, who gave him a helpless shrug back. 'Everyone has to deal with grief in their own way,' he replied.

'Exactly,' Carly replied. 'That's why I'm here.' She turned to Glenn Branson. 'You told me last night that my life is in danger from a revenge killing arranged by the parents of the poor boy who died on his bike. But I wasn't a guilty part of that. OK, I know I've been prosecuted for drink driving, but it wouldn't have made a damned bit of difference if I'd been stone cold sober – your traffic police have confirmed that. It wasn't the van driver's fault either, even if he did do a hit-and-run, and it sure as hell wasn't the lorry driver's fault. The whole thing was caused by the poor kid himself, cycling on the wrong side of the road!'

Branson was about to reply, but Grace cut in on him. 'Mrs Chase, we're aware of that. But, as my colleague has explained, we are not dealing with normal, rational people. The Reveres, from what we understand, come from a culture where differences are settled not in court, but by physical brutality. They have been informed that you did not collide with their son, and it may be that they've now finished with their terrible revenge – if that's what these two killings are about. But I'm responsible for your safety and I have a duty of care to you.'

'I can't live my life in fear, Mr Grace – sorry – Detective Superintendent. There's always a way through a problem and I think I have found a way through this one.'

Both police officers looked hard at her.

'You do?' Glenn Branson said.

'Yes. I – I didn't sleep a wink last night, trying to figure out what to do. I've decided I'm going to go and see them. I'm going to New York to talk woman to woman to Mrs Revere. She's lost her son. I lost my husband. Both of us would like to try to blame other people to try to find some sense in our losses. I think constantly about that stupid ski guide who should never have taken my husband on that slope in those weather conditions. But nothing vengeful is going to bring Kes back or ease the pain of my loss. I have to find ways to move forward in life. She and her husband are going to have to do the same.'

'I know a little bit about loss too,' Roy Grace said gently. 'I've been there. I have a sense of where you are coming from. But from what I know about this family, I don't think going to see them is a good idea – and it's certainly not something Sussex Police could sanction.'

'Why not?' She glared at Grace with a sudden ferocity that startled him.

'Because we're responsible for your safety. I can protect you here in Brighton, but I couldn't look after you in New York.'

She turned to Glenn Branson. 'You told me last night that you could only guard me for a fortnight. Right?'

Branson nodded, then said, 'Well, we would review the situation before the end of that period.'

'But you can't protect me for the rest of my life. And that's what I would be scared of. I can't spend the next fifty years looking over my shoulder. I have to deal with this now.' She was silent for a moment, then she spoke again. 'Are you saying you'd stop me from going?'

Grace opened his arms expansively. 'I have no powers to stop you. But I cannot guarantee your safety if you go. I could send an officer with you, but frankly he wouldn't be able to do a lot out of his jurisdiction—'

'I'm going alone,' she said determinedly. 'I can look after myself. I can deal with it. I deal with difficult people all the time.'

Glenn Branson admired her determination, secretly wishing he'd hired this terrified but feisty woman to act for him in his divorce, instead of the rather wishy-washy solicitor he had.

'Mrs Chase,' Roy Grace said, 'we have some intelligence on the Revere family. Do you want to hear it before you make your final decision?'

'Anything you can tell me would be helpful.'

'OK. Until recently they owned a club in Brooklyn called the Concubine. They would invite their enemies there for a drink and when they arrived, as special guests of honour, these unfortunates would be invited downstairs to the VIP lounge. When they entered they would be greeted by three men, one of whom was a tall American-Italian charmer nicknamed Dracula, because he looked like Bella Lugosi. A fourth man, whom they would never see, would shoot them in the back of the head with a silenced handgun. Dracula would drain their blood into a bathtub. Another guy, who had started out as a butcher, would dismember their cadavers into six pieces. The fourth guy would package up each limb, the torso and the head, and dispose of them in various waste dumps around New York and in the Hudson River. It is estimated they murdered over one hundred people. Sal Giordino, Tony Revere's grandfather, is currently serving eleven consecutive life sentences for this, with a minimum of eighty-seven years in jail. Do you understand the people you would be dealing with?'

'I've been Googling them,' she said. 'There's a lot of stuff about Sal Giordino, but I've not found anything about his daughter. But from what you've told me about their world, isn't this all the more reason for me to go there and try to talk reason to them?' she said.

'These people don't reason,' Grace said.

'At least give me the chance to try. Do you have their address? The home address?'

'What about emailing or phoning Mrs Revere first, to see what reaction you get?' Grace asked her.

'No, it's got to be face to face, mother to mother,' Carly replied.

The two detectives looked at each other.

'I can find the address out for you on one condition,' Roy Grace said.

'Which is?'

'You allow us to arrange an escort for you in New York.'

After a long silence she said, 'Could – could I make that decision?'

'No,' he answered.

75

At 10.17 an alert pinged on Tooth's laptop. A voice file was recording. Which meant someone was speaking inside Carly Chase's house.

He clicked and listened in. She was on the phone to a woman called Claire, asking about flights to New York today and confirming she had a valid visa waiver, from a trip last year. It sounded like Claire was a travel agent. She reeled off a list of flight times. After some moments of checking availability, she booked Carly Chase on a 14.55 British Airways flight from London to Kennedy Airport, New York, this afternoon. Then they discussed hotels. The travel agent made a reservation for her at the Sheraton at Kennedy Airport.

Tooth glanced at his watch, double-checking the time and smiling. She was making this very easy for him. She had no idea!

Next he heard Carly Chase speak to a taxi company called Streamline. She booked a car to Terminal 5 at Heathrow Airport, to collect her at 11.30 a.m. – just over an hour's time. Then she made a further call.

It was to someone called Sarah. The woman sounded like a friend. Carly Chase explained to her that Tyler had a dental appointment at 11.30 a.m. the following morning to have an adjustment made to his tooth brace, which was hurting him. Ordinarily his gran could have taken him, but her doctor had booked her in for a scan on something he wasn't happy about in her tummy and Carly did not want her to miss that. She explained she had been planning to take Tyler herself, but something urgent had come up – would it be possible for Sarah to take him?

Sarah could not, because of her father, whose wrist was indeed broken, but she said that Justin had taken the week off to do some work on their new house and she was sure he could pick Tyler up. She said she would call back in a few minutes.

Tooth made himself another coffee and smoked another ciga-rette. Then his laptop pinged again and he listened to Sarah telling Carly Chase that everything was fine. Justin, who was presumably her husband, would pick Tyler up from school at 11.15 tomorrow. Carly Chase gave her the address and thanked her.

Tooth stared down at his notepad, on which he had written Carly Chase's flight details. She'd only booked one way, on an open ticket. He speculated about where she was going, and had a good idea. He wondered what she was like at ten-pin bowling.

Except he did not think she would get as far as the Reveres' bowling alley.

He just hoped they wouldn't kill her, because that would spoil all his plans.

76

'We can't let her do this,' Roy Grace said, placing his hands on the workstation top in MIR-1 and leaning over towards Glenn Branson.

'We don't have any legal power to stop her,' Branson replied. 'And she's terrified out of her wits.'

'I know. I could see that. I would be, too, in her situation.'

It was an hour since Carly Chase had left his office. Grace had a ton of urgent stuff to deal with, one of the most important of which was organizing a press conference. A lesson he had learned a long time back was that you got much better cooperation from the media by telling them about a murder, rather than waiting for them to tell you. Particularly in the case of Kevin Spinella.

But he hadn't been able to focus on any of that. He was desperately worried for this woman's safety. It was 5.30 a.m. in New York and Detective Inspector Pat Lanigan's phone went straight to voicemail. It was probably switched off. Sensible man, Grace thought. And lucky. Since he became Head of Major Crime he no longer had the luxury of being able to turn his phone off at night.

Branson's mobile phone was ringing. The DS raised a hand to his boss, answered it, then said curtly, 'Can't speak now. Bell you back.' He killed the call. Then, looking down at the phone, said, 'Bitch.' He shook his head. 'I don't get it. Why does she hate me so much? I could understand if I'd had an affair, but I didn't, ever. I never looked at another woman. Ari encouraged me to better myself, then it's like – like she resented it. Said I put my career before her and my family.' He shrugged. 'Did you ever figure out what goes on inside a woman's head?'

'I'd like to figure out what's going on inside this mad woman's head,' Grace replied.

'That's easy. I can tell you that, without a two hundred and fifty quid per hour bill from a shrink. Fear. All right, old-timer? She's sodding terrified. And I don't blame her. I would be, too.'

Grace nodded. Then his phone rang. It was one of his colleagues asking him if he would be joining their regular Thursday poker game tonight. For the second week running Grace apologized, but no, he wouldn't be. The game had been going for years and fortunately they were all police officers, so they understood about work commitments.

'Got to be a shit situation when someone feels we can't protect them. Right?' Branson said, as Grace hung up.

'We *can* protect them – but only if they want to be protected,' the Detective Superintendent replied. 'If they're willing to move and change their identity, we can make them reasonably safe. But I can understand where she's coming from. I wouldn't want to leave my home, my job and take my kid out of school. But people do it all the time – they up sticks and move – and not just because they're being hunted.'

'We're just going to let her go to New York alone? Shouldn't we send someone with her? Bella?'

'Aside from the cost, we don't have any jurisdiction there. Our best hope for her safety is to get the New York police guarding her. We'll keep a watch on her house – with her mother and her son on their own in it – and as a precaution, we should put a tail on the school run. Our contact in New York, Detective Investigator Lanigan, sounds a good guy. He'll know what to do far better than anyone we can send over.' Then Grace grimaced at his friend. 'So, no change with Ari?'

'Oh, she's changed all right. She's grown fucking horns out of the sides of her head.'

77

Carly stood in a long, snaking queue in the crowded Immigration Hall at Kennedy airport. Every few minutes she looked anxiously at her watch, which she had set back five hours to New York time, then she checked and rechecked the white Customs form she had filled in on the plane.

Her nerves were jangling. She'd never felt less sure of herself in her life.

The flight had been almost two hours delayed and she hoped the limousine she had ordered online was waiting. It was 10.30 p.m. in England, which meant it was 5.30 p.m. here. But it seemed like the middle of the night. Maybe that Bloody Mary, followed by a couple of glasses of Chardonnay on the plane, had not been such a good idea. She'd thought they might calm her and help her to sleep for a few hours, but now she had a blinding headache and a parched mouth, and was feeling decidedly spaced out.

It was strange, she thought. She'd brought Tyler to New York as a pre-Xmas treat last December. They'd both felt so excited in this queue then.

She dialled home, anxious to check on him. But just as her mother answered an angry-looking man in a uniform was in her face, pointing at a sign banning the use of mobile phones. Apologetically, Carly hung up.

Finally, after another twenty minutes, she reached a yellow line and was next. The immigration officer, a cheery-looking plump black woman, chatted interminably with the spindly man carrying a backpack who was in front of her. Then he moved on and Carly was summoned forward. She handed over her passport. She was asked to look into a camera lens. Then she was told to press her fingers on the electronic pad.

The woman might have smiled and joked with the previous person, but she was in no laughing mood now.

'Press harder,' she dictated.

Carly pressed harder.

'I'm not getting any reading.'

Carly pressed harder still and finally the red lights changed to green.

'Now your right thumb.'

As she pressed down hard with her right thumb, the woman frowned at her screen.

'Left thumb.'

Carly obeyed.

Then the woman suddenly said, 'OK, I need you to come with me.'

Bewildered, Carly followed her behind the line of immigration desks and through a door at the far end of the room. She saw several armed immigration officers standing chatting and several weary-looking people, from a mix of ethnic backgrounds, seated around the room, most of them staring vacantly ahead.

'Mrs Carly Chase from the United Kingdom,' the woman announced loudly, seemingly to no one in particular.

A tall man in a checked sports jacket, plain white shirt and brown tie, ambled over to her. He spoke with a Brooklyn accent.

'Mrs Chase?'

'Yes.'

'I'm Detective Investigator Lanigan from the Brooklyn District Attorney's Office. I've been asked by your police department in Sussex, England, to take care of you while you're over here.'

She stared back at him. In his fifties, she guessed, he had a powerful physique, a pockmarked face beneath a greying brush-cut and a concerned but friendly expression.

'I understand you have the home address of Mr and Mrs Revere for me?' she said.

'Yes. I'm going to take you there.'

She shook her head. 'I have a car booked. I need to go alone.'

'I can't allow you to do that, Mrs Chase. That's not going to happen.'

The firm way he spoke made her realize that the decision had been taken and was not going to be reversed.

Carly thought hard for a moment. 'Look, OK, follow me to their place, but at least let me go in alone. I can handle myself. Can I please do that?'

He stared at her for some moments.

'It's about a two-and-a-half-hour drive from here. We'll go in convoy. I'll wait outside, but here's what we're going to do. You're going to text me every fifteen minutes so I know you're OK. If I don't get a text I'm coming in. Understand what I'm saying?'

'Do I have any option?'

'Sure, you do. I can have Immigration put you on the first available flight back to London.'

'Thanks,' she said.

'You're welcome, lady.'

78

In the back of the Lincoln Town Car it was dark and silent. Carly sat immersed in her thoughts, occasionally sipping water from one of the small bottles in the rack in the central armrest. Maybe she should have said yes to the New York detective and let Immigration put her on a flight back to England. She felt a lump in her throat and a chill of fear running through her, worsened by the cold air-conditioning in the car.

The black leather seats and blacked-out windows made the interior feel as gloomy as her mood. The driver seemed in a bad mood, too, and had barely said two words to her since leaving the airport. Every few minutes his phone rang. He would gabble a few angry words in a language she didn't know and hang up.

Each time it irritated her more. She needed silence. Needed to think. She'd phoned home again as soon as she'd got into the car and her mother told her all was fine. She reminded her about Tyler's dental appointment in the morning and wished her good luck with the scan.

Her grandmother had died of colon cancer and now there was something in her mother's tummy her doctor did not like the look of. Since Kes had died, her mother had been the total and utter rock in her life. And if anything happened to Carly, her mother would become Tyler's rock too. The thought that she could get sick and die was too much for Carly to bear at this moment. She just fervently hoped and prayed the scan wouldn't show anything.

Then she turned her thoughts back to what she was going to say when she arrived at the Revere family's front door. If they even let her in.

From time to time she turned her head and looked out of the rear window. The dark grey sedan which Detective Investigator Lanigan was driving remained steadily on their tail. She felt inhibited by his presence and her instinct was that she had to be seen to be alone if she was going to have any chance with Fernanda Revere.

Most of the time she stared out at a dull landscape of seemingly endless straight road, bordered by green verge and low trees. The sun was setting behind them and dusk was falling rapidly. In another hour it would be dark. In her mind, the meeting with the Reveres was going to have taken place in daylight. She looked at her watch. It was 7.30. She asked the driver what time he expected to arrive.

The surly reply came back, 'Nine or thereabouts. Lucky this isn't summer. Be 'bout eleven then. Traffic no good in summer.'

Her headache was worsening by the minute. As were her doubts. All the confidence she'd had earlier today was deserting her. She felt a growing slick of fear inside her. She tried in her mind to reverse the roles. How would she feel in this woman's situation?

She simply did not know. She felt tempted, suddenly, to ask the driver to turn around and go to the hotel she had booked and forget all about this.

But what then?

Maybe nothing. Maybe those two killings had been coincidental? Maybe they'd been all the revenge the family wanted? But then, thinking more lucidly, she wondered how she would ever know that. How would she stop living in fear?

And she knew that she could not, ever, without resolving this.

Her determination became even stronger. She had the truth on her side. All she had to do was tell the woman the truth.

Suddenly, it seemed only minutes later, they were arriving in a town.

'East Hampton,' the driver said in a more friendly tone, as if he'd woken up to the fact that he was close to blowing his chances of a tip.

Carly looked at her watch. It was 8.55 p.m., which meant it was 1.55 a.m. in the UK. Her stomach tightened. Her nerves were in tatters.

Her fear deepened as the car made a right turn in front of a Mobil Oil garage and headed down a leafy lane with a double yellow line in the middle. All her clear thinking suddenly turned into a fog of panic. She was breathing deeper, perspiring, close to hyperventilating. She turned and through the rear window she saw the headlights of Detective Investigator Lanigan's car following, and now, instead of feeling irritated, she was comforted by his presence.

She felt a lump in her throat and a tightening knot in her stomach. Her hands were shaking. She took a few deep breaths to calm down. She tried to organize her thoughts, to rehearse that crucial way she would introduce herself. The driver's phone rang again, but as if sensing her mood he killed the call without answering it.

The double yellow line ended and the lane narrowed to single track. In the glare of the headlights Carly saw trim hedges on both sides of them.

The car slowed, then halted. Directly in front of them were tall, closed gates, painted grey, with spikes along the top. There was a speaker panel and a warning sign beside that which said ARMED RESPONSE.

'Want me to ring?' the driver asked.

She turned and peered through the rear window and saw that the detective was getting out of his car. Carly climbed out too.

'Good luck, lady,' Lanigan said. 'Let's see if they let you in. If they do, I'll be waiting here. I'll be waiting for that first text in fifteen minutes' time. You don't forget that, right?'

She tried to reply, but nothing came out. Her mouth was parched and it felt like there was an iron band around her throat. She nodded.

He entered his number on Carly's phone and tapped in 'OK'. 'That's what you're gonna text me, every fifteen minutes.'

The air was still and mild. Carly had dressed casually but conservatively, wearing a lightweight beige mackintosh over a dark grey jacket, plain white blouse, black jeans and black leather boots. Every shred of her confidence seemed to have deserted her and, despite the adrenalin pumping, she felt even more spaced out now. She tried to block from her mind the fact it was past 2 a.m., body time.

She pressed the square metal button. Instantly a light shone in her face. Above it she could see a CCTV camera pointing down at her.

A voice speaking in broken English crackled. 'Yes, who is this?'

Carly stared straight back at the camera and forced a smile. 'I've come from England to see Mr and Mrs Revere. My name is Carly Chase.'

'They expect you?'

'No. I think they know who I am. I was in the accident involving their son, Tony.'

'You wait, please.'

The light went off. Carly waited, clutching her iPhone, her finger on the *Send* button. She turned and saw Detective Investigator Lanigan leaning against his car, smoking a cigar. He gave her a good-luck shrug. She caught a whiff of the rich smoke and it reminded her for an instant of Kes.

A minute later, the gates began to swing open, in almost total oiled silence. There was just a faint electric whirr. Feeling sick with fear, she climbed back into the car.

79

Carly stepped out into the silence of the night. Above her loomed the façade of a huge modern mansion. It looked dark and unwelcoming, with barely any lights showing. She turned back to look at the limousine, having second thoughts. It was parked a few yards away on the woodchip-covered drive, close to a Porsche Cayenne sports utility vehicle. Floodlights printed stark shadows of shrubs and trees across an immaculate lawn. Her nerves shorting out, she sensed faces peering from the darkened windows down at her. She swallowed, then swallowed again, and stared at the front door, which was set beneath an imposing portico with square, modern pilasters.

Christ, am I up to this?

The silence was pressing in all around her. She heard the faint, distant, restless sound of the sea. She breathed in tangy, salty air and the scent of freshly mown grass. The normality of that scared her. These people, their life going on as normal. Their son was dead, but they still mowed the lawn. Something about that spooked her. She had not mown the lawn after Kes died. She'd let the garden go wild and the house turn into a tip around her. It was only for Tyler's sake she eventually pulled herself together.

Before she had a chance to change her mind, the front door opened and a woman emerged, unsteadily, dressed in a turquoise tracksuit and sparkly trainers. She had short, blonde hair, an attractive but hard face, and held a martini glass tilted at an angle in one hand and a cigarette in the other. Her whole demeanour was hostile.

Carly took a few, faltering steps towards her. 'Mrs Revere?' She tried to put on the smile she had been practising, but it didn't feel like it was working. 'Fernanda Revere?'

The woman stared at her with eyes as cold and hard as ice. Carly felt as if she was staring right through her soul.

'You got fucking balls coming here.' The words were slightly slurred and bitter. 'You're not welcome in my home. Get back in your car.'

The woman scared her, but Carly stood her ground. She had been preparing herself for a whole range of different responses and this was one of them, although she had not factored in that Fernanda Revere might be smashed.

'I've flown from England to talk to you,' she said. 'I just want a few minutes of your time. I'm not going to begin to pretend I understand what you must be going through – but you and I have something in common.'

'We do? We're alive, that's about all I can see we have in common. I don't believe we have much else.'

Carly had known all along this was not going to be easy. But she had nurtured the hope that perhaps she could get a dialogue going with this woman and find some common ground.

'May I come in? I'll leave the moment you want me to. But please let's talk for a few minutes.'

Fernanda Revere drew on her cigarette, snorted out smoke through her mouth and nose, then tossed the butt away with a contemptuous flick of her jewelled hand. It landed on the drive in a shower of sparks. With her drink slopping over the rim of her glass, she tottered back and gestured for Carly to enter, glowering hatred, only faintly diluted with curiosity, at her.

Carly hesitated. This woman looked dangerously unpredictable and she had no idea how her husband was going to react. Glad now that Detective Investigator Lanigan was sitting outside the gates in his car, she surreptitiously glanced at her watch. Thirteen minutes left before her first text.

She entered a grand hallway with a flagstone floor and a circular staircase, and followed the woman, who bumped against the wall several times, along a corridor furnished with antiques. Then they entered a palatial drawing room, with a minstrel's gallery. It had oak beams and tapestries hanging from the walls, alongside fine-looking oil paintings. Almost all of the furniture was antique, except for one item.

Seated, with his legs up in an incongruously modern leather recliner armchair, was a man in his fifties, with slicked-back grey hair and dense black eyebrows, watching a ball game on television. He held a can of beer in one hand and a large cigar in the other.

The woman walked towards him, picked up the TV remote from the antique wooden table beside him, peered at it for some moments as if she had never seen one of these before in her life, then muted the sound and dropped the remote back down with a clatter.

'Hey, what the—' the man protested.

'We have a visitor, Lou.' Fernanda pointed at Carly. 'She's come all the way from England. How nice is that?' she said icily.

Lou Revere gave Carly a weak smile and an abstracted wave of his hand. Then, keeping his eyes on the silent players on the screen, he turned to his wife and reached out for the remote.

'This is kind of an important moment in the game.'

'Yeah, right,' Fernanda said. 'Well, this is kind of an important moment, too.' She reached down, picked up a pack of Marlboro Lights and shook out a cigarette. Then she gave Carly a crushing glare.

Carly stood awkwardly, eyes darting between the two of them, thinking, trying desperately to remember her script.

'Know who this bitch is?' Fernanda said to her husband.

Lou Revere grabbed the remote and unmuted the sound.

'No. Listen, I need some quiet here.' Then he added, 'Get this lady a drink.' He glanced disinterestedly at Carly. 'You wanna drink?'

Carly felt in desperate need of a drink. And the sweet rich smell of the smoke was tantalizing. She craved a cigarette.

'I'll die before I give this fucking bitch anything,' Fernanda Revere said, staggering over to an antique drinks cabinet, the doors of which were already open, and clumsily refilling her glass from a silver cocktail shaker, slopping the contents over the side. Then she drank some, put the glass down, tottered back over to her husband, grabbed the remote and switched the television completely off.

'Hey!' he said.

She dropped the remote on to the rug and stamped hard on it. There was the sound of splintering plastic.

Carly's fear deepened. This woman was crazy and totally unpredictable. She looked at the man again, then back at the woman, before sneaking a glance at her watch. Three minutes had passed. What the hell was the woman going to do next? Somehow she had to bring her out of her anger.

'Jesus Christ!' Her husband put down his beer and ejected himself from his chair. Turning to his wife, he said, 'Do you know how important this goddamn game is? Do you? Do you care?'

He strode towards the door. Grabbing him by the arm and dropping her glass, which broke on the floor, Fernanda screamed at him, 'Do you fucking know or care who this bitch is?'

'Right now, I care about the New York Yankees winning this game. You know how bad it would be if they lost?'

'And you fucking think they care that you're watching? You want to just focus a second? This is the bitch who killed our son. You hear what I'm saying?'

Carly watched him, her eyes swinging between them. She was trying to keep calm, but her nerves were in meltdown. The man stopped in his tracks and turned towards her. He glanced for a moment back at his wife and said, 'What do you mean, hon?' Then he turned back to Carly, his whole demeanour changing.

'This is the bitch who was arrested at the scene for drunk driving. She killed our son, now she's fucking standing here in front of us.'

Fernanda Revere made her way over to the bar, taking measured steps across the floor as if it were an obstacle course. There was sudden menace in Lou Revere's voice as he spoke now. Gone was the mildly angry guy of a few seconds ago.

'Just what the hell do you think you are doing? Turning up at our home like this? Not satisfied you've caused us enough pain, is that what it is?'

'It's not that at all, Mr Revere,' Carly replied, her voice quavering. 'I'd just appreciate the opportunity to talk to you and Mrs Revere and explain what happened.'

'We know what happened,' he said.

'You were drunk and our son died,' his wife added bitterly. Then she staggered back over towards them, slopping more of her drink over the rim of her fresh glass.

Carly drew on all her reserves. 'I'm desperately sorry for you both. I'm desperately sorry for your loss. But there are things about this accident that you need to know, that I would want to know if it was my child. Could we please sit down, the three of us, and talk this through? I'll leave when you want me to, but please let me tell you how it actually happened.'

'We know how it happened,' Fernanda Revere said. Then she turned to her husband. 'Get rid of this bitch. She's killed Tony and now she's polluting our home.'

'Hon, let's just hear her out,' he said, without taking his glare off Carly.

'I can't believe I married someone who fell out of a fucking tree!' she shouted. 'If you don't tell her to go, I'm leaving. I'm not staying in this building with her. So tell her!'

'Hon, let's talk to her.'

'GET HER THE FUCK OUT OF HERE!'

With that Fernanda stormed out of the room and some moments later a door slammed.

Carly found herself facing Lou Revere, feeling very awkward. 'Mr Revere, maybe I should go . . . I'll come back . . . I can come back in the morning if that's—'

He jabbed a finger at her. 'You came to talk, so talk.'

Carly stared at him in silence, trying to think of the best way to calm him down.

'What's the matter? You gone dumb or something?' he said.

'No, I . . . look, I – I can't begin to understand how you must be feeling.'

'Can't you?' he said, with a bitterness that startled her.

'I have a young son,' she replied.

'*Have?*' he replied. 'Well you're a lucky lady, then, aren't you? My wife and I *had* a young son, too, before a drunk driver killed him.'

'It didn't happen like that.'

Outside, through the window, Carly heard a faint clunk, like a car door.

'Oh, it didn't happen like that?' Lou Revere looked, at this moment, as if he was about to strangle her with his bare hands. He raised them in the air, clenching and then opening them.

And suddenly Carly realized what it was that the two detectives in Brighton had meant when they'd tried to explain the nature of these people to her. That they were different. Their whole culture was different. She wavered for an instant about hitting the *Send* button on her phone, but she had to stand her ground. Had to find a way through to this man.

He was, she realized, her only chance.

80

Pat Lanigan, standing by his car and smoking his cigar, heard an automobile engine fire up, then saw the gates opening. Was the crazy English woman coming out already? She'd only been there five minutes. He glanced at his watch again, double-checking.

It was a positive, he thought, that at least she *was* coming out. Although if she had only lasted in there for five minutes, then for sure it had not gone well. Maybe she'd had some sense knocked into her reckless little head.

Then, to his surprise, instead of seeing the limousine, he saw a Porsche Cayenne, with the silhouette of a woman at the wheel, come at a reckless speed through the gates, then accelerate past him like a bat out of hell.

He turned, clocked the licence plate and watched the tail lights disappear round a bend in the lane. This did not feel good. He glanced down at the display of his phone. There was no text, no missed call. He didn't like this at all.

He flicked through his stored numbers and dialled the Suffolk County Police duty office, explained who he was and asked them to put an alert out for the Cayenne. He wanted to know where it was headed.

*

Fernanda Revere braked to a halt at the T-junction by the gas station, pulled a cigarette pack out of her purse, shook out a Marlboro Light and jammed it between her lips. Then she stabbed the cigar lighter, made a left and accelerated down the highway. Everything was a blur in her drunken fury. She overtook a slow-moving cab, her speed increasing: 70 . . . 80 . . . 90. She flashed past a whole line of tail lights, lit her cigarette and tried to replace the lighter, but it fell into the footwell.

She was shaking with rage. The road snaked away into the distance. Steering with one hand, smoke from the cigarette curling into her eyes, she rummaged in her purse and pulled out her diamanté-encrusted Vertu phone, then squinted through the smoke at the display. It was a blur. She brought it closer to her face, scrolled to her brother's number and hit the dial button.

She overtook a tractor-trailer, still steering with one hand. Had to get away. Just had to get away from the bitch polluting her home. After six rings, it went to voicemail.

'Where the fuck are you, Ricky?' she shouted. 'What the fuck's going on? The English bitch came to the house. She's there now. Do you hear me? The bitch who killed Tony is in my house. Why isn't she dead? I paid you this money, so why isn't she dead? What's going on here? You gotta deal with this, Ricky. Call me. Goddamn call me!'

She ended the call and tossed the phone down beside her on the passenger seat. She did not know where she was heading. Just away from the house and into the rushing darkness. The further the better. Lou could get rid of the bitch. She'd go back when Lou phoned her, when he told her the bitch was gone, out of their home, out of their lives.

She overtook another car. The night was hurtling past. Oncoming lights were a brief, blurred flash, then gone.

Tony was gone. Dead. He'd nearly died as a baby. That first year of his life he'd been in hospital on a ventilator for most of the time. Much of it inside a perspex isolation dome. She'd sat there day and night, while Lou had been working or kissing her father's ass or out on the golf course. Tony'd come through that, but he was always a sickly child, too, a chronic asthmatic. At the age of eight he'd spent the best part of a year bedridden with a lung virus. She'd spoonfed him. Mopped his brow. Got him through it. Nurtured him until slowly he'd grown stronger. By the time he reached his teens he was just like any other kid. Then, last year, he'd fallen for that stupid English girl.

She'd begged Lou to stop him going, but had he? Never. All he'd done was give her a whole bunch of crap about letting kids live their own lives. Maybe some kids would be fine in a foreign land. But Tony had been dependent on her. He needed her. And this proved it.

Three scumbags had taken his life away. Some asshole in a van. Some asshole in a truck. And this drunken bitch who had the nerve to come to their home with her whiny little voice. *I'd just appreciate the opportunity to talk to you and Mrs Revere and explain what happened.*

Yeah, well, I'll tell you what happened, Mrs Whining Bitch. You got drunk and you killed my son, that's what happened. Any part of that you don't understand?

The speedometer needle was hovering on 110mph. Or maybe it was 120, she could barely see it. A light began flashing on the passenger seat. Her phone was ringing, she realized. She grabbed it and held it up in front of her. The name was blurry but she could just about read it. Her brother.

She answered it, hurtling past another car, still steering with one hand into a tight left curve. The cigarette between her lips was burned right down to the butt and tears were streaming from her eyes and on to her cheeks.

'Ricky, I thought you were dealing with this?' she said. 'How do you let this stupid bitch come to the house? How?'

'Listen, it's all cool!'

'Cool? She came to my house – that's cool? You wanna tell me what's cool about that?'

'We have a plan!'

She steered the car through the curve, then there was another curve to the right, even sharper. She was going into it too fast, she realized. She stamped on the brake pedal and suddenly the car began snaking left, then right, then even more violently left again.

'Shit.'

She dropped the phone. The cigarette butt fell between her legs. There were bright lights coming in the opposite direction, getting brighter and more dazzling by the second. She heard the blare of a horn. She jerked the wheel. The Cayenne began a lumbering pirouette. The steering wheel suddenly turned with such force it tore free of her hands, spinning like it had taken on a mind of its own.

The lights got brighter. The horn was blaring, deafening her. The lights were straight at her eye level. Blinding her. She was spinning too now, like the wheel. Backwards for a second. Then sideways again. Sucking those blinding lights towards her as if she were a magnet.

Closer.

The horn even louder, shaking her eardrums.

Lights burning into her retinas.

Then a jarring impact. A clanging metallic boom like two giant oil drums swinging into each other.

In the silence that followed, Ricky's voice came through her phone. 'Hey, babe? Fernanda? Sis? Babe? Listen, you OK? Babe? Babe? Listen, we're cool. Listen, babe!'

But she could no longer hear him.

81

'You've really upset my wife,' Lou Revere said. 'She's pretty distressed already and so am I. I don't know what you thought you'd achieve by coming, but we don't want you here. You're not welcome in our house.' He stabbed his cigar at her. 'I'm gonna show you out.'

'Please just give me a chance,' Carly said, her desperation making her sound on the verge of tears.

'You had your chance, lady, when you were deciding whether to get into your automobile drunk or not. That's more chance than my son had.'

'It wasn't like that, Mr Revere. Please believe me. It wasn't like that.'

He stopped and for a moment Carly thought he was going to relent. Then he stabbed his cigar in even greater fury. 'Sure it wasn't like that, lady. We've had the toxicology report on our son from your police. He had nothing in him. Not one drop of alcohol, not one trace of any drug.' He lowered his head like a bull about to charge. 'How was your toxicology report? Huh? You wanna tell me how your toxicology report read? Tell me. I'm listening. You got my full attention.'

They faced each other in silence. Carly was trying desperately to find a way through to him. But he scared her. It was as if beneath his skin there was something venomous and feral. Outwardly he might be playing the role of a grieving father, but there was something truly chilling about him. She had met difficult people in her time, she'd had to deal with deep dislike, but she had never encountered anyone like Lou Revere. It felt as if she was in the presence of total, inhuman evil.

'I'm listening,' he repeated. 'I'm not hearing anything, but I'm listening.'

'I think maybe I should come back tomorrow,' she replied. 'Can I do that?'

He took another step towards her, quivering. 'You come back,' he said. 'You come back – if you dare come within one hundred miles of my home, I'll tear you apart with these.' He held up his trembling hands. 'You understand what I'm saying?'

Carly nodded, her mouth dry.

He pointed. 'That's the way out.'

Moments after she stepped out into the night, the front door slammed behind her.

82

It seemed only moments after he had fallen asleep that Roy Grace was woken by the sound of his phone ringing and vibrating.

He rolled over, reaching out for the flashing display in the darkness. The clock beside it said 1.37 a.m.

'It's OK. I'm awake,' said Cleo, a tad grumpily.

He switched on his bedside light, grabbed the phone and hit the green button. 'Yurrr?'

It was Duncan Crocker. 'You awake, boss?'

It was a dumb question, Grace thought. Did Detective Sergeant Crocker know many people who were capable of answering a phone in their sleep? He slid out of bed and tripped over Humphrey, who responded with a startled yelp. He dropped the phone and grabbed the side of the bed, just managing to stop himself falling flat on his face on the floor. He retrieved the phone.

'Hang on, Duncan.'

Wearing only the T-shirt he'd been sleeping in, he padded out of the room, accompanied by the dog, which jumped up excitedly, its sharp claws digging painfully into his leg.

'Down, boy!' he hissed, closing the door behind him.

Humphrey raced down the staircase, barking, then ran back up and launched himself at Grace's crotch.

Crocking the phone under his ear and protecting himself with his hands, he said, 'Be with you in a sec, Duncan. Down! Humphrey, off, off!'

He went downstairs, followed by a madly barking Humphrey, switched the lights on, moved a copy of *Sussex Life* that was open at the property pages – Cleo had suddenly gone into house-hunting mode – and sat on a sofa. Humphrey jumped on to the cushion beside him. Stroking him, trying to keep the dog quiet, Grace said, 'Sorry about that. What's up?'

'You asked me to let you know as soon as we found the lorry, boss.'

'You've found it? You're still at work?'

'Yes.'

'Thanks for staying so late. So, tell me?'

'Just had a call from Thames Valley Road Policing Unit. It's in a parking area at Newport Pagnell Services on the M1.'

'How did they find it?' Grace was doing his best to think clearly through his tiredness.

'It was logged by an ANPR camera as it entered Bucks on the M1 on Tuesday night, boss. There were no further logs, so we asked the local police to check likely pull-ins.'

'Good stuff. What CCTV do they have at the service station?'

'They've got cameras on the private vehicle and truckers' entrances.'

'OK, we need those, to see if Ferguson went inside. How long are you planning on staying up?'

'As long as you need me.'

'Ask them for copies of the videos from the time the ANPR clocked him to now and get them down to us as quickly as possible. If it helps them, we can send someone up there.'

'Will do.'

Grace stroked the dog again. He knew he wasn't thinking as clearly as he needed to at this moment.

'Sorry, one other important thing – Ferguson's lorry. I want it protected as a crime scene. Get on to Thames Valley Police to secure it. They need to cordon off a good twenty-foot radius around it. If the driver was attacked, it's likely to have happened close to the vehicle. We need a search team on to it at first light. What's the weather up there at the moment?'

'Dry, light wind – it's been the same since Tuesday night. Forecast the same for the morning.'

That was a relief to Grace. Rain could wash away forensic evidence very rapidly.

'I'll sort out the search team, Duncan. If you deal with the CCTV, please. Then go home and get some sleep. You've done well.'

'Thanks, boss.'

Grace let Humphrey out on to the patio and watched him pee. Then he went into the kitchen and put the kettle on. Upstairs he heard the sound of the loo flushing and wondered, for a moment, if Cleo was going to come down and join him. But instead he heard the bedroom door slam – a little too loudly.

Sandy used to slam the bedroom door when she was angry about a late-night phone call that had disturbed her. Cleo was a lot more tolerant, but he could sense her pregnancy getting to her. It was getting to both of them. Most of the time it was a shared joy, or a shared anxiety, but just occasionally it seemed like a growing wedge between them and she had been in a really grumpy mood last night.

He made a phone call, apologetically waking Crime Scene Manager Tracy Stocker and bringing her up to speed. He asked her to send a SOCO team up to Newport Pagnell – about a two-and-a-half-hour drive from Brighton – to be there ready to start at dawn. At the same time, in light of the latest development, he discussed the joint strategy she would need with the POLSA – the Police Search Advisor – and search team.

Then he spooned instant coffee into a mug, poured boiling water on to it, stirred it and carried it out into the living room. He felt chilly, but he could not be bothered to put on any more clothes.

He sat down on the sofa with his laptop, bleary-eyed, stirring the coffee again and staring at the laptop as it powered up. Humphrey found a chew and started a life or death tussle with it on the floor. Grace smiled at him, envying him his uncomplicated life. Maybe if he got the chance to choose, when he died he'd come back as a dog. So long as he got to pick his owners.

He Googled *Newport Pagnell Services*. Moments later he had a full listing of what was there, but that did not help him. He opened Google Earth and again he entered *Newport Pagnell Services*.

When the globe appeared, he zoomed in. Within moments he saw a close-up of the M1 motorway and the surrounding area. He stared at it, sipping his hot coffee and thinking hard.

Ferguson must have continued on down to Sussex in another vehicle. His assailant's? So how had he met his assailant?

Was it someone he knew and had arranged to rendezvous with

in the car park? Possible, he thought. But to his mind, it was more probable that the assailant had been following him, looking for a suitable opportunity. And if this assumption was right, it meant that the assailant could not have been more than a few vehicles behind Ferguson's lorry.

He put his coffee down and started suddenly, pacing around the room. Humphrey jumped up at him again, wanting to play.

'Down!' he hissed, and then he dialled MIR-1, relieved when DS Crocker answered almost immediately. 'Sorry, another task for you, Duncan. We need the indexes of the vehicles either side of Ferguson's lorry on the motorway immediately before Newport Pagnell Services,' he said. 'Get everything up to five vehicles in front and twenty back. I want to know every one of the vehicles that went into the services at the same time as him and where they went when they left afterwards. It's very likely that Ferguson was in one of those. Willingly or otherwise. I think it is highly likely to be a rental car, so we're looking, primarily, for late-model small to medium saloons.'

'I'll get what I can, but it may take me a while to check out every vehicle. Is the morning briefing meeting soon enough?'

No, it wasn't soon enough, Grace thought. But he needed to be realistic and Crocker sounded exhausted.

'Yes, that's fine. Do what you can, then get some sleep.'

Deciding to follow his own advice, he climbed back upstairs, followed by Humphrey, and went back to bed, trying not to disturb Cleo. At midday he was holding a press conference to announce that the police were treating the death of Stuart Ferguson as murder now. But although he had discussed it at length with ACC Rigg and the whole of the Sussex Police media team, he had not decided on the way he wanted to slant the conference. He wanted to make it clear that the police knew the two murders were linked, and the direction in which they were looking, but above all he needed witnesses to come forward. However, if he played up the Mafia link and the hit-man hypothesis, that might, he worried, actually do more harm than good, by scaring people into silence.

The only small positive was that Spinella seemed to have been as duped as the rest of the press into believing, to date, that

Ferguson's death was an industrial accident. That gave him some small satisfaction.

Finally, he fell into a troubled sleep, to be woken an hour later by Cleo going to the loo.

83

Carly sat in the back of the limousine as they drove through the gates of the Revere home. A few yards on she could see Detective Investigator Lanigan standing by his car and told her driver to stop.

'So?' he asked with an inquisitive but sympathetic stare.

'You were right,' she said, and gave a helpless shrug. She was still in shock from the way Lou Revere had spoken to her.

'It didn't go like you planned it?'

'No.'

'What's with Mrs Revere driving off like that? She was pissed at you?'

Carly fumbled in her handbag, pulled out a pack of cigarettes and lit one, inhaling deeply.

'She was drunk. She wasn't in a rational state of mind. I have to try again,' she said. 'Maybe I could come back in the morning when she's sobered up.'

He dragged on his cigar and blew the smoke out pensively. 'Lady, you've got guts, I'll give you that.' He smiled. 'You look like you could use a drink.'

Carly nodded. Then she said, 'What's your advice? What do you think I should do – you know – how can I deal with these people? There must some way – there always is.'

'Let's get you to your hotel. We'll have a drink and you can talk me through what happened in there. Before we leave, is there any point in me trying to speak to Mr Revere?'

'I don't think so,' she said. 'Not tonight. No.'

'OK. Your driver knows where to go?'

'The Sheraton JFK Airport Hotel.'

'I'll follow you. I'll be right behind.'

She took two more rapid drags on her cigarette, crushed it, then got back into the limousine and gave the driver her instructions.

She sat perched on the edge of her seat, replaying the events of the past ten minutes in her mind, as they drove away down the lane, then made a left turn, heading away from the town. Inside she was jangling, with nerves and tiredness. The bad dream just seemed to keep getting worse.

She closed her eyes and prayed, a short silent prayer. She asked the God she had not spoken to in years to give her some strength and a clear mind. Then she rummaged in her bag for her handkerchief and dabbed away the tears that were streaming down her cheeks.

Darkness slid by on either side of the car. For several minutes it did not occur to her that it was strange that no headlights were coming in the opposite direction. She looked at her watch: 9.25 p.m. New York time, 2.25 a.m. in England. Too late to call Detective Sergeant Branson and give him an update. She would do that in the morning. Hopefully after she had made a revised plan with Detective Investigator Lanigan later this evening.

She yawned. Ahead, through the windscreen, she saw red flashing lights and the bright tail lights of traffic braking and backing up. Moments later the limousine slowed, braking increasingly sharply, and they came to a halt behind a line of stationary vehicles.

The driver ended yet another of the constant calls he was on and turned his head towards her. 'Looks like an accident up ahead.'

She nodded silently. Then she heard a rap on her window and saw Detective Investigator Lanigan standing there. She pressed the button and lowered the window.

'You want to come with me? Sounds like Mrs Revere's involved in a wreck up ahead. They've closed the road.'

'An accident? Fernanda Revere?'

'Yup,' he said grimly, and opened the door for her.

The words flooded her with dread. She climbed out shakily and the night air suddenly seemed a lot chillier than ten minutes ago. She pulled her mackintosh tightly around her as she followed the detective past a line of cars towards a stationary police car that was angled across the road, its roof spinners hurling shards of red light in every direction. A row of traffic cones was spread across the road behind it.

An accident. The woman would be blaming her. Everyone would be blaming her.

A cacophony of sirens was closing in on them. Just beyond the patrol car now, she could see the mangled wreckage of a car partially embedded in the front of a halted white truck. Carly stopped. This wasn't just a minor bump, this was major. Massive. Horrific. She turned away, towards Lanigan.

'Is she OK?' Carly asked. 'Have you heard if she's OK? Is she injured?'

The sirens got louder.

He strode on, through the cones, saying nothing. Carly hurried after him, feeling like a thousand different knots were being tightened inside her all at the same time. She tried to look away from the accident, but at the same time she was mesmerized by it, kept looking, looking, staring.

A cop was standing in their way, blocking their path. A young plump man wearing glasses and a cap that was too big for him. He looked about eighteen years old and waiting to grow into his uniform.

'Stay back, please, folks.'

Lanigan held up his police shield.

'Ah, right. OK. OK, sir.' Then he pointed questioningly at Carly.

'She's with me,' the Detective Investigator said.

He waved them past, then turned in confusion as an ambulance and fire tender screamed to a halt.

Over to her right, Carly saw a man in a boiler suit walking around unsteadily, as if he were disoriented. He was in shock, she realized. Ahead of her, Lanigan had pulled out a torch and switched it on. In the beam she saw what might have been a grim tableau in a museum of modern art.

The front wheels of the truck had been pushed back several feet by the impact, so that they were right underneath the cab. The side of the gold Porsche facing them had been so badly buckled that the front and rear of the car were almost at right angles to each other. The destroyed vehicle resembled a crudely sculpted artistic impression of a snow plough, as if it was actually part of the front of the truck.

Carly smelled the stench of vomit, then heard a retching sound. There was a smell of petrol, too, and of oil, but another deeply unpleasant, coppery smell mixed in.

'Jesus!' Lanigan exclaimed. 'Oh shit!'

He stepped back and put out an arm to prevent Carly from seeing the same sight. But he was too late.

In the torch beam Carly saw a pair of legs, covered from the knees down by turquoise tracksuit bottoms, but the top part was naked. A mess of crimson, black, dark red and bright red was splayed out around the crotch. Out of the middle of it rose, for about eighteen inches, what looked like a giant white fish bone.

Part of the woman's spine, she realized, clutching the detective's arm involuntarily, her stomach rising up into her throat. Fernanda Revere had been cut in two.

Carly turned away, quaking in horror and shock. She staggered a few yards, then fell to her knees and threw up, her eyes blinded by tears.

84

A large whiskey at the hotel bar, followed by two glasses of Pinot Noir, helped calm Carly down a little, but she was still in shock. Detective Investigator Lanigan drank a small beer. He looked fine – as if he saw stuff like that accident all the time and was immune to it. Yet he seemed such a caring man. She wondered how anyone could ever get used to something as horrific as that.

Despite the woman's rudeness to her, she felt a desperate sadness for Fernanda Revere. Lanigan told her she didn't need to feel any pity, because this was a woman with blood on her hands, and from a brutal family living high off the spoils of violence. But Carly could not help it. Whatever her background had been, Fernanda Revere was still a human being. A mother capable of intense love for her son. No one deserved to end up the way she had.

And Carly had caused it.

The Detective Investigator told her she should not think that way. Fernanda Revere had no business getting into a vehicle in the state she was in. She didn't have to drive away, that was her choice. She could, and should, have simply told Carly to leave. Driving away – and doing so drunk – was not a rational act.

But Carly still blamed herself. She could not help thinking, over and over, that she had caused it. That if she had not gone to the house, Fernanda Revere would still be alive. Part of her wanted to drive straight back out to the Hamptons and try to apologize to Lou Revere. Pat Lanigan nixed that one fast and hard.

They stood outside for a long time while he smoked another cigar and she smoked her way through half a pack of cigarettes. The question neither of them could answer was *What happens next*?

She felt utterly bewildered. How was Fernanda Revere's husband going to react? The other members of the woman's family? When she had boarded the plane to come here, she knew she had a difficult task ahead of her. But she had never, remotely, thought of a consequence like this. She lit another cigarette with a trembling hand.

'I think now, Carly, you're going to have to think pretty seriously and quickly about entering a witness protection scheme,' Pat Lanigan said. 'I'm going to see that you have someone guarding you all the time you're here, but people like the Reveres have long memories and a long reach.'

'Do you really think I'd ever be truly safe in a witness protection scheme?'

'You can never say one hundred per cent, but it would give you your best chance.'

'You know what it means? To move to another part of the country, just you and your child, and never see any of your family or friends again, ever. How would you like to do that?'

He shrugged. 'I wouldn't like it too much. But if I figured I didn't have any option, then I guess it would be better than the alternative.'

'What – what alternative?'

He gave Carly a hard stare. 'Exactly.'

85

The air-conditioning was too cold and too loud, but nothing Carly did to the controls in her hotel bedroom seemed to make any difference. She couldn't find any extra bedding either, so had ended up almost fully clothed, under the sheets, tossing and turning, a tsunami of dark thoughts crashing through her mind.

Shortly after 6 a.m. and wide awake, she slipped out of bed, walked across to the window and opened the blinds. Light flooded in from a cloudless dark blue sky. She watched a jet plane climb into it, then dropped her gaze on to a sprawling mess of industrial buildings and a busy road, thirty floors below.

Her head was pounding. She felt queasy and very afraid. God, how she desperately wished Kes was here now, more than ever. Just to talk this through with him. He was bigger than any shit the world could throw at him. Except that damned white stuff that had encased and suffocated him.

Shit happens, he was fond of saying. He was right. His death was shit. Her accident was shit. Fernanda Revere's death was shit. Everything was shit.

But most of all, the idea of walking away from her life and going into hiding, forever, was total and utter shit. It wasn't going to happen. There had to be a better solution.

Had to be.

Suddenly her mobile phone rang. She hurried across and picked it off her bedside table, staring at the display. It simply said, *International*.

'Hello?' she answered.

'Hi, Carly?' It was Justin Ellis and his voice was sounding strange.

'Yes. You all right?' Carly replied, conscious her voice was strained. She needed paracetamol and a cup of tea, badly.

'Well – not really,' Justin replied. 'I think there's been some mix-up over Tyler.'

'How do you mean? His dentist appointment? Have I screwed up?' She looked at the clock radio, doing a mental calculation. She always got the time differences wrong. England was five hours ahead. Coming up to 11.15 a.m. there. Tyler's appointment was for 11.30, wasn't it?

'What's the problem, Justin?'

'Well, you asked me to take him to the dentist. I'm at the school now to collect him, but they're telling me you arranged a taxi to take him there.'

Carly sat down on the side of the bed. 'A taxi? I didn't arrange any—'

A terrible, dark dread began to seep through her.

'A taxi collected him half an hour ago,' Justin said, sounding a little pissed off. 'Did you forget?'

'Oh, God,' Carly said. 'Justin! Oh, my God. Tell me it's not true?'

'What do you mean?'

'This can't have happened. They must have made a mistake. Tyler has to be in the school somewhere. Have they checked? Have they looked everywhere?' Her voice was trembling with rising panic. 'Please get them to check. Tell them to check. Tell them they *have* to check.'

'Carly, what's the matter? What is it?'

'Please let him be there. Please, Justin, you have to find him. Please go in there and find him. Please! Oh, my God, please.' She stood up, hyperventilating now, walking around the room blindly. 'Please, Justin!'

'I don't understand, Carly. I spoke to Mrs Rich. She walked him to the gate and watched until he was safely in the taxi.'

'It's not possible! It's not possible, Justin. Please don't tell me he's not there.' She was sobbing and shouting in her desperation. 'Please tell me he's still there!'

There was a brief moment of silence, then Justin said, 'What's the matter, Carly. Calm down! Tell me – what's the matter?'

'Justin, call the police. I did not order a taxi.'

86

The traffic jam along the seafront was irritating Tooth. This had not been part of his plan. On his schedule he'd allowed a maximum of ten minutes for this section of the journey, but it had already taken twenty-two. And they were still barely moving in stop-start traffic that was being coned into a single lane by roadworks ahead.

The noise behind him was irritating him too, but it was keeping the kid distracted while he drove, so that was a good thing. He watched him in the mirror. The boy, in his red school blazer and wire-framed glasses, was concentrating hard on some electronic game.

Click. Beeehhh . . . gleeep . . . uhuhuhurrr . . . gleep . . . grawww- wwp . . . biff, heh, heh, heh-warrrup, haha . . .

Suddenly the kid looked up. 'Where are we going? I thought we were going to the Drive? This isn't the right way.'

Tooth spoke in his English accent. 'I had a message that the address got changed. Your dentist is working at his other clinic today in a different part of the city, over in Regency Square.'

'OK.'

Click. Beeehhh . . . gleeep . . . uhuhuhurrr . . . gleep . . . grawww- wwp . . . biff, heh, heh, heh-warrrup, haha . . .

The taxi's radio crackled, then a voice said, 'Pick up for Withdean Crescent. Anyone close to Withdean Crescent?'

From behind Tooth came, *Twang . . . heh, heh, heh, graww- wwpppp . . .*

They were getting closer now. In a few moments he would make a left turn.

Twang . . . eeeeeekkkk . . . greeeep . . . heh, heh, heh . . .

'What game are you playing?' Tooth asked, wanting the kid to feel OK, relaxed, normal, at least for the next couple of minutes.

'It's called Angry Birds. It's ace. Have you played it?'

Concentrating now, Tooth did not reply. The Skoda taxi made a sharp left turn off the seafront into Regency Square. As it did so, Tooth sneezed, loudly, then sneezed again.

'Bless you,' Tyler said politely.

Tooth grunted. He drove up the square of terraced Regency houses, all painted white and in different stages of dilapidation, some divided into apartments and some converted into hotels. At the top he made a right, following the road around the grassy park in the middle of the square and then back down towards the seafront. He swung right into the entrance to the underground car park and partway down the ramp, had another fit of sneezing. He halted the car, sneezing again and pulling a handkerchief out of his pocket. He sneezed once more into it.

'Bless you,' Tyler said again.

The driver turned. Tyler thought the man was going to thank him, but instead he saw something black in the man's hand that looked like the trigger of a gun, but without the rest of the weapon. Then he felt a hard jet of air on his face, accompanied by a sharp hiss. Suddenly he found it hard to breathe, and he took a deep gulp, while the air still jetted at him from the capsule.

Tooth watched the boy's eyes closing, then turned and continued down the ramp, lowering his window, then removing the handkerchief from his face. He carried on winding down to the car park's lowest level, which was deserted apart from one vehicle. His rental Toyota, with new licence plates.

He reversed into the bay alongside it.

87

At 11.25 a.m. Roy Grace was seated at his desk, making some last-minute adjustments to his press statement, which he was due to read out at midday.

So far nothing seemed to be going his way in this investigation, and to make matters even more complicated, the trial of snuff-movie merchant Carl Venner was starting in just over two weeks' time. But for now he had no time to think about anything other than *Operation Violin*.

There had been no progress reported on any of the lines of enquiry at this morning's briefing meeting. The Outside Inquiry Team had not found anyone who had sold the cameras that had filmed Preece's and Ferguson's demise. No one so far had witnessed anything unusual outside Evie Preece's house. The West Area Major Crime Branch Team had had no breakthrough yet in their investigation into Warren Tulley's murder in Ford Prison.

So many people had bought tubes of superglue in shops around the city during the past week that it made any follow-up a resourcing nightmare. Despite that, the team members had collected all available CCTV footage from inside and outside each of the premises that was covered by it. If – and when – they were able to put a face to the suspect, then they'd begin a trawl through these hundreds of hours of video.

His phone rang. It was his Crime Scene Manager, Tracy Stocker, calling from Newport Pagnell Services.

'Roy, we've found one item of possible interest so far. The stub of a Lucky Strike cigarette. I can't tell you if it is significant, but it's a relatively unusual brand for the UK.'

As a smoker, albeit an occasional one, Grace knew a bit about cigarette brands. Lucky Strikes were American. If, as he surmised, the killings of Preece and Ferguson were the work of a professional, it was a distinct possibility that a hit man known to the Reveres and trusted by them had been employed. He could be an American, sent over here. He felt a beat of excitement, as if this small item did have the potential to be interesting – although he knew, equally, its presence could have a totally innocent explanation.

'Did you manage to get a print from it, Tracy?' he asked.

Getting fingerprints from cigarette butts was difficult and depended to some extent on how they had been held.

'No. We can send it for chemical analysis, but we may have more luck with DNA. Do you want me to fast-track it?'

Grace thought for a moment. Fast-tracking could produce a result within one to two days. Otherwise it would take a working week or longer. The process was expensive, at a time when they were meant to be keeping costs down, but money was less of an issue on murder inquiries.

'Yes, fast-track definitely,' he said. 'Good work, Tracy. Well done.'

'I'll ping you the photos of it,' she said.

'Any luck with shoe prints or tyre prints?'

'Not so far. Unfortunately the ground's dry. But if there is anything, we'll find it.'

He smiled, because he knew that if anyone could, she would. He asked her to keep him updated. Then, as he hung up, his phone rang again. It was Duncan Crocker, sounding as if he had been up all night.

'Boss, we've had two possible hits on cars at Newport Pagnell that arrived at the same time as Stuart Ferguson. One is a Vauxhall Astra and the other is a Toyota Yaris – both of them common rental vehicles,' the Detective Sergeant said. 'We've eliminated the Astra, which was being driven by a sales rep for a screen-printing company. But the Yaris is more interesting.'

'Yes?'

'You were right, sir. It's a rental car – from Avis at Gatwick Airport. I put a marker on it and it pinged an ANPR camera on the M11 near Brentwood at 8 a.m. this morning. A local traffic unit stopped it. It was a twenty-seven-year-old female driver who lives in Brentwood, on her way to work.'

Grace frowned. Was Crocker being dim?

'It doesn't sound like you got either of the right vehicles, Duncan.'

'I think it may do when you hear this, sir. When the young lady got out of the car, she realized it wasn't her licence plates on the car. Someone had taken hers and replaced them with these.'

'While she was in the Newport Pagnell Services?'

'She can't swear that, sir – she can't remember the last time she noticed her number plates. To be honest, a lot of us probably don't.'

Grace thought for a moment.

'So it may be that our suspect has switched plates with hers. Have you put a marker out on her plates?'

'I have, sir, yes. So far nothing.'

'Good work. Let me know the instant anyone sees that car.'

'Of course, sir.'

'Have you sent someone down to Avis at Gatwick?'

'I've sent Sara Papesch and Emma-Jane Boutwood.'

Grace frowned. 'Who's Sara Papesch?'

'She's just joined the team. Bright girl – a Kiwi detective, over here on a secondment.'

'OK, good.'

Grace liked to know everyone on his team personally. It worried him when an inquiry started getting so big that his team members began taking on new members without his sanction. He was feeling, for one of the rare moments in his career, that things were getting on top of him. He needed to calm down, take things steady.

He looked at the round wooden clock on his wall. It had been a prop in the fictitious police station in the TV police series *The Bill.* Sandy had bought it for his twenty-sixth birthday. Beneath it was a stuffed seven pound, six ounce brown trout Sandy had also bought him, from an antiques stall in Portobello Road, early in their marriage. He kept it beneath the clock to give him a joke he could crack to detectives working under him, about patience and big fish.

It was also there as a reminder to himself. To always be patient. Every murder investigation was a puzzle. A gazillion tiny pieces to find and fit together. Your bosses and the local media were always breathing down your neck, but you had to remain calm, somehow. Panic would get you nowhere, other than leading you to make wrong, uninformed decisions.

His door opened and Glenn Branson came in, looking as he did most of the time these days, as if he was carrying the weight of the world on his shoulders. Grace waited for him to begin regaling him with the latest saga in his marriage break-up, but instead the DS placed his massive hands on the back of one of the two chairs in front of his desk and leaned forward. 'We have a development, old-timer, and it's not a good one. I've just had a call from Carly Chase in New York.'

Now he had Grace's full attention. 'Her mission isn't going well, as predicted, right?'

'You could say that, boss. Tony Revere's mother was killed in a car smash last night.'

Grace stared at him in stunned silence. He could feel the blood draining from every artery in his body.

'Killed?'

'Yes.'

For some moments, the Detective Superintendent was too shell-shocked to even think straight. Then he asked, 'What information do you have? How? I mean, what happened?'

'I'll come back to it – that's the least of our problems. We have a much bigger one. Carly Chase's twelve-year-old son has gone missing.'

'Missing? What do you mean?'

'It sounds like he's been abducted.'

Grace stared into Branson's big, round eyes. He felt as if a bolus of cold water had been injected into his stomach. 'When – when did this happen?'

'A friend of Carly, called Justin Ellis, should have picked her son up from St Christopher's School at 11.15 a.m. to take him to a dental appointment – he was having a brace adjusted. Ellis got there at ten past, to discover the boy had been collected twenty minutes earlier by a taxi. But Carly Chase is absolutely adamant she didn't order a taxi.'

Grace stared at him, absorbing the information, trying to square it with the news he had just had about the licence plates from Duncan Crocker.

'She seemed in a pretty ramped-up state yesterday. Are you sure she didn't forget she'd ordered one?'

'I just came off the phone to her. She didn't order it, she's one hundred per cent sure.'

Branson sat down in front of him, folded his arms and went on, 'One of his teachers at the school got a call that the taxi was outside. She knew he was being picked up, because his mum had already told them that was going to happen. She didn't think to query it.'

'Did she see the driver?'

'Not really, no. He was wearing a baseball cap. But she wasn't really focused on him. Her concern was that Tyler got into the car safely – and she watched him do that from the school gates.'

'So they just let their pupils get into taxis without checking with anyone?' Grace quizzed.

'They have strict procedures,' Branson replied. 'The parents have to have given prior sanction, which Carly Chase had, on a blanket basis. Apparently Tyler was regularly dropped off and picked up by taxis, so no one had any reason to question it today.'

Grace sat in silence for some moments, thinking hard and fast. He looked at his watch. 'The appointment is for 11.30 a.m.?'

'Yes.'

'Has anyone checked with the dentist to see if he's turned up?'

'Someone's on that now. He hadn't as of a couple of minutes ago.'

'Where's the dentist?'

'In Wilbury Road.'

'St Christopher's is a private school, right? On New Church Road?'

Branson nodded.

'That's a five-minute drive. Ten, max. He was picked up just before 11 a.m.?'

'That's right.'

'Are you on to the taxi companies?'

'All of them. I've got Norman Potting, Nick Nicholl, Bella Moy and Stacey Horobin making calls right now.'

Grace thumped his desk in anger and frustration. 'Shit, shit, shit! Why wasn't I told about this dental appointment?'

Branson gave him a helpless look. 'We guarded her house with the boy and her mother – the boys' gran – in it all night. And we had a friend of Carly Chase, who was doing the school run, tailed – to make sure he got there safely. We were going to do the same this afternoon when he came out of school. No one said anything about him having an appointment.'

Grace shook his head. 'She was vulnerable. That meant anyone close to her was vulnerable, too. We should have had someone at the school today.'

'Hindsight's easy. Most people wouldn't get out of bed in the morning if they knew what was going to happen.'

Grace stared at him bleakly. 'Knowing what was going to happen would make this job a damned sight easier.' He picked up a pen and began making notes on his pad, his brain going into overdrive. 'OK, do we have a photograph of this boy?'

'No. I have a description of him. He's five foot tall, looks a little like a young Harry Potter – floppy brown hair, oval wire-framed glasses, wearing a school uniform of red blazer, white shirt, red and grey tie, and grey trousers.'

'Good, that's fairly distinctive,' Grace said. 'We need a photo PDQ.'

'We're on to that.'

'Has anyone spoken to the gran?'

'She's at a doctor's appointment at the Sussex County. I have someone on their way there.'

'Do we have the make of the taxi? Was it a saloon or an estate car or a people carrier?'

'I don't have that yet.'

'Why not?'

'Because I haven't had time. I wanted you to know right away.'

Grace looked up at a map of East and West Sussex on his wall, then at his bookshelf, where he could see a copy of the official *Kidnap Manual*, which contained all the procedures and protocols for kidnap and abduction. He knew a lot of them by heart, but he would check carefully through it. Before that he had some urgent fast-time actions to carry out. He grabbed the phone off his desk and, as he dialled, he said, 'Glenn, we need to plot an arc around the school – how far away someone could be in any direction now and in thirty minutes' time. We've got to get the make of vehicle. Is someone going to see the teacher?'

'Two officers from the Outside Inquiry Team should be at the school now.'

'We need more officers down at that school immediately, talking to everyone around it, in houses, walking their dogs, cats, goldfish.'

Grace dialled the number for Ops-1 – the Duty Inspector in the Force Control Room, Becky Newman. He gave her a quick summary and asked her who the Force Gold was today. The Gold Commander was normally a Superintendent or Chief Superintendent who would take control of any Critical Incident that happened on his watch.

He was pleased to hear it was Chief Superintendent Graham Barrington, the current Commander of Brighton and Hove, an exceptionally able and intelligent officer. Moments later he was on the line. Grace quickly brought him up to speed. Barrington said he wanted a Detective as Silver and suggested Chief Inspector Trevor Barnes. He quickly reeled off the Bronzes to complete his command team: one a POLSA for searches, then one for Intelligence, one for Investigations and one for Media. In all child abductions or kidnaps, the way the media was handled was crucial.

'I think because of the gravity we should have an ACC handle the media. ACC Rigg is on call today.'

Grace smirked. He liked the idea of the very slightly arrogant Peter Rigg being given a role down the pecking order, beneath the Chief Superintendent.

'I think we should make your deputy SIO the Investigations Bronze, as he'll be up to speed. Who is that?"

'Glenn Branson.'

'He's a DS?'

'Yes, but he's good,' Grace said, turning to his colleague and winking.

'OK.'

'I think our very first priority, Graham, is road checks.'

'Yes, we'll get them on all major routes. What do you think? Forty-five minutes' or one hour's drive away?'

Grace looked at his watch, doing a calculation. It would take time to get cars in place.

'An hour's drive, to be safe. Can we scramble Hotel 900.'

Hotel 900 was the call sign for the police helicopter.

'Right away. Get me a description of the taxi as quickly as possible to give to them. What about utilizing *Child Rescue Alert*?'

'Yes, definitely. I'm about to do that,' Grace said, although he was aware of the deluge of calls his team would receive from this, most of which would be false alarms.

Child Rescue Alert was a recent police initiative, modelled on the US's *Amber Alert*, for getting descriptions of missing or abducted children circulated fast, nationwide. It included mobile messaging, social-networking sites, news bulletins and posting descriptions on motorway signs. Its use always generated thousands of responses, each of which would have to be checked out. But it was a valuable resource and ideal for this current situation.

'We need an all-ports alert out, too,' Grace said. 'No one's leaving this country with a young boy until we've cleared them. We need to throw everything we have at this. We need to find this bastard and we're going to have to find him fast, before he has a chance to hurt the kid.'

Grace hung up, leaving the Chief Superintendent to get started, and turned back to Branson.

'OK, you're Investigations Bronze. Chief Superintendent Barrington will brief you shortly, but there are three urgent things you need to do.'

'Yes?'

'The first is to get the boy's computer – I assume he must have one – down to the High-Tech Crime Unit for analysis. Find out who he's been talking to and engaging with on Facebook, chat lines, email.'

Branson nodded. 'I'll access that via his gran.'

'The second is to get every inch of his house and garden

searched, and his immediate neighbours', and the homes of all his friends. You may be able to draft in some locals as volunteers to help search his entire home area.'

'Yep.'

'The third is to keep checking with the dentist and the school. I don't want egg all over my face if this kid turns up safe and sound because his mum forgot to tell you something.'

'Understood, but that's not going to happen. Not from what she's told me.'

'It had better not.' Then Grace shrugged. 'Although I wish it would, if you know what I mean.'

Branson nodded, getting up to leave. He knew exactly what Roy meant.

As the door closed, Grace grabbed the *Kidnap Manual* off the shelf and laid it on his desk, but before he opened it he scribbled down several more actions on his pad as they came into his head, then sat in silence for some moments, thinking. His phone rang. It was his MSA, Eleanor Hodgson, asking if he had the amended draft of his press statement ready for retyping.

In the panic of the last few minutes he'd forgotten all about it, he realized. He told her he was going to have to rewrite it totally because of the latest development and that the press conference might need to be delayed by half an hour.

He felt very afraid for this young boy. This man who had killed Preece and Ferguson was a cruel sadist. There was no telling what he had in mind for Tyler Chase, and all Grace's focus now was on how to get the boy safely out of his clutches. Thirty minutes had elapsed so far. They could be in a lot of different places in thirty minutes. But a taxi was distinctive. A man and a young boy were distinctive – particularly if Tyler was still in his school uniform.

He felt a deep, dark dread inside him. This was not his fault, but he still had overall responsibility for providing the protection Carly and her family needed, and he was angry with himself for letting this happen.

At least the timing of the press conference could hardly be better. Within the next hour, combining *Child Rescue Alert*, the press and the media, he could have nationwide blanket coverage on the missing boy.

Then he picked up his phone and made the call that he was not looking forward to.

Assistant Chief Constable Peter Rigg answered on the first ring.

88

Carly walked around her hotel room in a black vortex of terror, tears streaming down her face, desperately wanting to get back to England. Her brain was jumping around all over the place and she was feeling physically sick.

How could she have been so damned stupid leaving him at home, unprotected like this? Why, oh why, hadn't she thought everything through more carefully before making this dumb decision to come here?

Was she forgetting something? A simple explanation for the taxi? Was there something she had overlooked in the chaos of the past weeks? She regularly ordered taxis to take him places when she was tied up at work. Had she double-booked Tyler for another appointment somewhere else? With whom? Had she perhaps ordered this taxi weeks ago for that and forgotten all about it? Perhaps the taxi had picked up the wrong boy? That could be it, a mix-up at the school!

She felt a fleeting moment of relief.

Clutching at straws, she knew.

She tried to shut the images of Fernanda Revere in the wreckage of her car from her mind. Some of them were intertwined, horrifically, with Tyler's face. She shivered and thought about getting into a hot shower, but she did not want to risk missing a call. She had to get home. Someone helpful down at the front desk was looking into flights to England for her. She had to get back today, somehow had to, had to. She looked at her watch but could hardly read the dial. Her eyes felt as if they weren't working properly. Everything she looked at seemed out of focus.

She had to think straight. Had to think clearly. But the only thing that came to her mind was the image of Tyler getting into a taxi.

Driven by a monster.

She walked over to the window and looked out again. It had

been a blue sky a few minutes ago. Now it was grey. The landscape was all washed out. She watched a man on a dumper truck. *Has your son been kidnapped?* She saw a woman get out of a small car. Starting her day. Just a day like any other, for her. *Has your son been kidnapped?*

She went into the bathroom to brush her teeth, but her hands were shaking so much the toothpaste fell into the sink each time she tried to squeeze some on to her brush. A coiled spring felt as if it was being wound tighter and tighter inside her. She filled the kettle, but then could not find the switch on the damned thing. All the time she kept her phone beside her, willing Tyler to ring. Desperately praying he would ring.

And suddenly it began ringing. The display said, BLOCKED.

'Yes-hi-hello,' she blurted.

'Carly? It's DS Branson.'

'Yes?' she said, trying to mask her disappointment. But maybe he had news? *Please, please have news.*

'I need to ask you some questions, Carly.'

Her heart sinking, she rushed on, 'I was thinking – I don't know – is it possible there was a mix-up at the school and the taxi was for another boy? Have they checked he's not somewhere at the school. He likes science, history, stuff like that. He often just goes into the labs and works on his own. He can be a loner. Did they check? Did they?'

'They're searching the school now. The taxi was definitely there to collect your son, Tyler.'

'Did he turn up at the dentist? Do you have any news at all?'

'So far not, but we'll find him, don't worry. But I need your help.'

'DON'T WORRY? YOU'RE TELLING ME NOT TO WORRY?' she shouted.

'We're doing everything we possibly can, Carly.'

'I'm going to get the first flight home. Maybe I can get a daytime one and be home this evening.'

'I think you should get back as fast as you can. Let me know your flight details when you can and we'll meet you at the airport. We've heard about Mrs Revere.'

'This is just a nightmare,' she said. 'Please help me. Please find my son. Oh, God, please help me.'

'One thing that could be significant. Can you tell me who might have known about Tyler's dental appointment?'

'Who? Only – only his school – and my friends, Sarah and Justin Ellis. He – Justin – was going to take him. I – I can't think of anyone else.'

'Our High-Tech Unit's done some searches. Tyler's on a number of social networking sites, which I presume you know,' Branson said.

'Well – some.'

'Did he Tweet it? He had put that he was going to the dentist up on Facebook, making a joke of it. Did he talk to you about any of the responses he had?'

'No,' she said. 'These past two weeks since my accident he's been in a really strange mood. I – I—' She was fighting off tears. 'Tyler's a – he's a very special child. He's incredibly resourceful. He wouldn't get into a car with a stranger. You may wonder how I know that for sure, but I do, I can promise you. He's streetwise. Have you checked he didn't go home?'

'We're keeping a round-the-clock watch on your home. There doesn't appear to be anyone in. But he definitely went off from his school in a taxi.'

'Please find him,' she said. 'Please find him.'

'We are going to find him, I promise you. The whole nation's looking for him.'

Tears were stinging her eyes and everything was a blur. The detective's kind voice was making her weepy.

'The Revere family,' she sobbed. 'They can do anything they want to me. I don't care. Tell them that. Tell them they can kill me. Tell them to give me my son back and then kill me.'

He promised to call her back the moment he had any news. As she hung up, she crossed back over to the window and stared out at the drab landscape. Christ, the world was a big place. How could you find someone? Where did you start looking? Way down below her on the ground she watched a man walking along, phone to his ear. And suddenly she had a thought.

Wiping away tears, she stared down at the screen of her iPhone, fingered through the apps, sliding them across, until she reached the one she was looking for. Then she tapped it hard.

Moments later she felt a sudden flicker of hope. She stared at it harder, brought it closer to her face.

'Oh yes! Oh, you good boy, Tyler! Oh, you clever boy!'

89

Grace came out of the press conference at 12.50 p.m., pleased with the solid performance ACC Rigg had delivered, and very relieved. He found all press conferences to be minefields. One wrong answer and you could be made to look a total idiot. Rigg had been sensible, keeping it tight and focused, and brief.

He was tailed by Kevin Spinella, as ever wanting one more question answered. But the Detective Superintendent was in no mood to talk to him. As he reached the security door at the start of the corridor, he turned to face the reporter.

'I don't have anything to add. If you want more information you need to speak to ACC Rigg, who is now responsible for press liaison on *Operation Violin*.'

'I know you're still angry with me over writing about the reward,' Spinella said. 'But you seem to forget sometimes, Detective Superintendent, that you and I both have a job to do and it's not the same job. You solve crimes, I have to help sell newspapers. You need to understand that.'

Grace stared at him incredulously. A child's life was at stake, he was right in the middle of the fast-time stage of one of the most serious critical incidents of his career, and this young reporter had decided now was the moment to start lecturing him about the newspaper business.

'What part of that do you think I don't understand, Kevin?' Grace said, turning back to the door and holding up his security card to the pad.

'You have to realize that I'm not your puppet. I want to help you, but my first loyalty will always be to my editor.'

'Why don't you save your breath right now, hurry back to your office and file a story that might help save Tyler Chase's life?'

'Coz I don't need to. I can use this,' Spinella said. Then he fished out his BlackBerry and held it up, with a smug grin.

Grace slammed the door behind him. He was about to call the Gold Commander for an update, when his phone rang. It was Glenn Branson.

'You out of the conference, boss?'

'Yes.'

'We're cooking with gas! We have a development with Tyler.'

'Where are you?'

'MIR-1.'

'I'll be right there.'

Grace threw himself down a few steps, sprinted along the corridor and entered the packed Incident Room. In contrast to the corridor, which had a permanent smell of fresh paint, MIR-1 at lunchtime always smelled like a canteen. Today an aroma of hot soup and microwaved Veg Pots was mixed with a tinge of curry.

There was that quiet buzz of energy in here that Grace loved so much. A sense of purpose. Some members of the team at their workstations – on the phone or reading or typing – and some standing, making adjustments to the family tree or photograph displays on the whiteboards. There was a constant muted ringing of landline phones, plus the louder cacophony of mobile phones and the rattle of keyboards.

Some of the team were eating as they worked. Norman Potting was hunched over a printout, munching a huge Cornish pasty, oblivious to the crumbs falling like sleet down his tie and bulging shirt.

Glenn Branson was seated in the far corner of the room, close to a water dispenser. Grace hurried across to him, ignoring Nick Nicholl and David Howes, who both tried to get his attention. He glanced at his watch, then at the clock on the wall, as if to double-check. It was something he often did and could not help. Every second of every minute in this current situation was crucial.

'Boss, have you used an iPhone?'

'No. Why?' Grace frowned.

'There's an app called Friend Mapper. It operates on GPS, just like a satnav. You and someone you know with an iPhone can both be permanently logged on to it. So, for instance, if you and I are logged on to it, provided you've got the app running, I'd be able to see where you are, anywhere in the world, and ditto you'd be able to see me, to within about fifty yards.'

Grace suddenly had a feeling he knew where this was going.

'Carly Chase and her son?'

'Yes!'

'And? Tell me.'

'That apparently was the deal when Carly Chase got her son an iPhone, that he had to keep Friend Mapper on all the time he was out of her sight.'

'And it's on now?'

We had a call from her twenty minutes ago. 'It's not moving, but there was a signal coming from Regency Square. We don't know whether it's been switched off or the battery's dead – or he could, as I suspect, just be in a bad reception area.'

'How old is this signal?'

'She can't tell, because she's only just checked. But she doesn't understand why it's where it is. Regency Square's a couple of miles east of the school and nowhere near where his dental appointment is. She says Tyler would not have had any reason to be there. She's magnified the map as much as she can. She says it looks like it's very near the entrance to the underground car park.'

Grace suddenly felt himself sharing Branson's excitement. 'If he's in the car park that could explain the lack of a signal!'

Branson smiled. 'Gold's got every unit in Brighton down there now. They're ring-fencing it, covering every exit, searching the place and any vehicle that leaves.'

'Let's go!' Grace said.

90

With his memory of Glenn Branson's driving still too close for comfort, Grace took the wheel. As they blitzed through Brighton's lunchtime traffic, the Detective Sergeant said, 'Carly Chase is booked on a BA flight that leaves at 8.40 a.m. New York time – 1.40 p.m. UK time – less than an hour. She'll get back to Heathrow at 8.35 p.m.'

'OK.'

Grace's phone rang. 'Could you answer it, Glenn?'

Branson took the call while Grace overtook a line of traffic waiting at a red light at the junction of Dyke Road and the Old Shoreham Road, blazing down the wrong side of the road. He checked that everyone had seen him, changed the tone of his siren, then accelerated over the junction.

When Branson ended the call he turned to Grace. 'That was E-J, reporting back from Avis. That Toyota Yaris was rented Monday morning of last week to a man called James John Robertson, according to his licence. The address he had given was fictitious and the information received back from the High-Tech Crime Unit was that the Visa credit card he had paid with was a sophisticated clone. Avis gave a description of the renter, but it wasn't much to go on. A short, thin man with an English accent, wearing a baseball cap and dark glasses. He'd been offered an upgrade which he had declined.'

'Interesting to decline an upgrade,' Grace said. 'Wonder why?'

Branson nodded. 'You know, it would be brilliant if we could take Carly Chase's son to the airport to greet her,' he said.

'It would.'

'And with a bit of luck, that's going to happen.'

Roy Grace shared his friend's hope, but not his optimism. After enough years in this job, your optimism gradually got eroded by experience. So much so that if you weren't careful, one day you'd wake up the cynical bastard you'd always promised yourself you would never become.

Driving normally, the journey to Regency Square from Sussex House would have taken around twenty minutes. Grace did it in eight. He turned off the seafront, ignoring the No Entry sign, and pulled up behind two marked cars and two police transit vans that were halted either side of the car park entry ramp. They were both out of the Ford almost before the wheels had stopped turning.

The entire historic, but in parts dilapidated, square was teeming with uniformed police officers, and the statuesque figure of the Brighton and Hove Duty Inspector, Sue Carpenter, was heading over to greet them. In her early forties, she stood a good six feet tall and the hat riding high on her head, with her long dark hair pushed up inside it, made her look even taller. Grace remembered her from some years back, when she was a sergeant, and had been impressed by her competence.

'Good afternoon, sir,' she said, greeting him with nervous formality, and then giving Glenn Branson a quick smile.

'How are you doing?' Grace asked.

'We've just found a taxi parked on the third level – the lowest. The vehicle is locked, sir. It's a bit unusual to find a taxi in a city multi-storey car park. We've radioed Streamline, which it's registered with, to see if we can get any information.'

'Let's take a look,' Grace said.

As a precaution, never knowing when he might need them, he took out a pair of blue gloves from his go-bag in the boot of the car, and a couple of small, plastic evidence bags. Then he glanced quickly around the grassy centre of the square. Across the far side, where the exit was, he saw a halted Jaguar surrounded by police, with its boot open.

'Presumably there's CCTV on the entrance and exit?'

'There are cameras, sir, and some inside. Every single one of them was vandalized last night.'

'All of them?'

'Yes, they're being replaced later today, but that doesn't help us, I'm afraid.'

'Shit, shit, shit,' he said, banging his knuckles together. He shook his head. 'Seems a little coincidental, the timing.'

'This car park is quite a hot spot for trouble, sir – in fact this

whole area is,' she reminded him, and pointed across the road at
the ruin of the West Pier – one of Brighton's biggest landmarks,
which had been burned down some years before in one of the city's
biggest ever acts of vandalism.

Grace and Branson followed Inspector Carpenter past a PCSO
who was guarding the entrance and down a smelly concrete stair-
well. Then they walked along the bottom level of the car park, which
was almost deserted and smelled of dry dust and engine oil. The
old, tired-looking concrete floor, white stanchions and red piping
stretched away into the distance, gridded by parking-bay markings.

Over to the right, partially obscured by a concrete abutment, he
saw a Skoda saloon taxi that had been reversed into a bay and
backed up tight against the rear wall. Two young officers stood
beside it.

As they approached, Grace noticed a few fragments of black
plastic on the ground close to the car. He fished the gloves from his
pocket and snapped them on. Then he knelt, picked the fragments
up and put them in an evidence bag, just in case.

At that moment a controller's voice came through Inspector
Carpenter's radio. Grace and Branson could both hear it clearly.
Apparently the Streamline operator was concerned, as she'd not
been able to get a response from the driver since just after midnight
last night.

'Do we have a name?' Carpenter asked.

'Mike Howard,' the voice crackled back.

'Ask if she has a mobile phone number for him,' Grace said.

He peered into the front, then the rear of the car before trying
each of the doors in turn, but they were all locked.

Sue Carpenter radioed the request. A few moments later the
operator came back with the number. Grace scribbled it down on
his notebook, then immediately dialled it.

A few moments later they heard a muted ringtone from inside
the rear of the taxi. Grace ended the call, turned to one of the PCs
and asked him for his baton. Looking apprehensive, the young
officer produced it and handed it to him.

'Stand back!' Grace said, as he swung the baton hard at the
driver's door window.

It cracked, with a loud bang, but remained intact. He hit it again, harder, and this time the glass broke. He smashed away some of the jagged edges with the baton, then slipped his arm in, found the handle and tugged it. He pulled the door open, leaned in and released the handbrake.

'Give me a hand,' he said to the officers, and began trying to push the car.

For an instant it resisted, then slowly, silently, it inched forward. Grace kept going until it was a few feet out from the wall, then jerked the brake back on. He leaned in, staring at the unfamiliar controls, saw the driver's ID on the windscreen, which showed a photograph of a burly-looking man in his forties with thinning brown hair and a startled expression. The name *Mike Howard* was printed beneath. Grace looked around hard, wondering if there was an internal boot release. Moments later he found it and the boot lid popped open.

Glenn Branson reached the rear of the car first.

Then, as he stared in, his face dropped.

'Oh shit,' he said.

91

Carly, seated in the busy waiting area by boarding gate 47, looked at her watch. Then she stared for a moment at the two British Airways women standing and chatting behind the desk. Occasionally there was a *bong*, then a brief announcement. Final call for boarding for some other flight. She looked at her watch again. Twenty-two minutes past eight. The flight was due to depart in less than twenty minutes and they hadn't even started boarding yet. What was going on?

She gripped her handbag and kept her holdall right in front of her. No checked luggage, she did not want any risk of delay at the other end. Her legs kept knocking together. She badly needed a cup of tea and something to eat, but she did not feel able to swallow anything.

She called her mother. She was almost in a worse state than Carly was, blaming herself for having her medical appointment and not picking Tyler up. Then Carly just sat, shaking, raw-eyed, staring around the room at her fellow passengers, and occasionally looking through the emails that were pouring into her iPhone. Mostly work stuff. Questions or information she had requested from clients. Emails from her colleagues. Jokes from a couple of friends who hadn't yet heard about Tyler. She did not read any of them. All she was interested in was looking to see if, by chance, an email had come in from her son.

Two middle-aged couples sat near her, Americans in a jovial mood, heading to the UK for a golfing holiday. They were talking about golf courses. Hotels. Restaurants. The normality was irritating her. These people were in earnest discussion. Her son had been kidnapped and they were chatting away about long carries and fast greens and some water hazard they'd all had a problem with on their visit last year.

She stood up and moved away, walked up to the desk and asked if the flight was going to be leaving on time. She was told they would be starting boarding in a couple of minutes.

That gave her some small relief. But not much.

She checked Friend Mapper on her phone for the hundredth time since leaving the hotel. But Tyler's purple dot remained stubbornly in that same place, close to the entrance to Regency Square car park.

Why there? Why are you there?

The screen blurred with her tears. It had been over an hour since she'd spoken to DS Branson. She wondered if she should call him one more time before she got on the plane.

But he had already promised to call the moment he had any news and she was sure he would; he seemed a good communicator. But what if he had been calling and was unable to get through? The flight was about seven hours long. How the hell was she going to be able to sit there for seven hours without news?

She dialled to check her messages, but there were no new ones. Nothing from DS Branson. So she called his mobile number and, to her relief, he answered almost immediately.

'It's Carly,' she said. 'I'm at Kennedy Airport, about to board. Just thought I'd check in with you.'

'Right, yeah. You OK?'

'Just about.'

'We've got your flight times and one of us will be at the gate to meet you when you land.'

His voice sounded strange, as if he was hiding something from her. And he sounded in a hurry.

'So – no – no news?'

'Not yet, but we hope to have some for you later. We have just about every police officer in the county looking for Tyler. We're going to find him.'

'I had a thought – if there is – you know – any news while I'm up in the air, can you get a message to me via the pilot?'

'Yes, we can. We can get you an ACARS text message via the cockpit, and most long-haul planes have satellite phones in the cockpit. The moment there's any news I'll get it relayed straight to you. OK?'

She thanked him and hung up. As she did so, she heard the boarding announcement. She towed her overnight bag over towards the rear of the rapidly lengthening queue, her insides a solid knot that was getting tighter by the second.

Seven hours.

Seven hours of waiting.

Carly handed over her passport and boarding card for inspection, then walked on in a silent haze, more alone and scared than she'd ever felt in her life.

Suddenly, as she stood in the crush in the aisle of the plane, her phone pinged with an incoming text. Her heart flipped with sudden hope and she looked down eagerly. But to her disappointment it was from the phone company, O2, warning her she was close to her 50 MB overseas data limit.

She deleted it, then found her seat. Or at least the part of it which wasn't already occupied by the damp, overflowing girth of a perspiring bald man who looked like he weighed uncomfortably north of 500 pounds.

If her day wasn't already bad enough, the journey from hell had now got even worse. She sat, squashed, her elbows tucked uncomfortably in against her chest, her whole body trembling with fear.

Fear that she might never see her son alive again.

92

In the total darkness, Tyler's head hurt. He couldn't see anything, couldn't move his arms or legs. He was frightened and confused and knew this was not a game, that something bad was happening.

They were travelling, he could sense that. Motion. There were strong smells of carpet and plastic, new-car smells. He'd been in a friend's mother's brand-new Hyundai recently and it had smelled like this. He thought he could detect rubber, too. Could hear a hum. He must be in the boot of a car, he reckoned. The taxi? Braking and accelerating. All he could move were his knees – he could bend and flex them just a little. He tried to wedge them against something solid, to get a grip, but moments later he was thrown away back-wards and felt himself rolling over, until he hit something hard.

He tried to shout to the driver, to ask him who he was, where they were going, but he could not move his mouth and his voice sounded all muffled.

After the two police officers had come to their house and his friends had left, his mum had sat down in his bedroom and told him there were bad things happening. Bad people. They had to be careful. They needed to keep a watch for strangers near the house. He must call the police if he saw anyone.

Was this one of the bad people driving him now?

At least he had his iPhone in his jacket and it was switched on. Friend Mapper would be logging him and his mum would know that. She'd know exactly where he was and she would tell the police. He didn't really need to be afraid. They would find him.

He just hoped they would find him soon, because he had an IT class this afternoon that he really did not want to miss. And because he did not like this darkness, and not being able to move, and his arms were hurting, too.

But it was going to be all right.

93

Grace dashed around to the rear of the taxi, just as Glenn Branson leaned into the boot.

The man inside looked terrified and there was a sour reek of urine. His fleshy face was pale and clammy. Duct tape was wound around his arms, legs and mouth, the same kind of tape that Evie Preece had been bound with, Grace clocked, as he fished out his warrant card and held it up to give the man reassurance.

'Police,' he said. 'Don't worry, you're safe. We'll get you out of there.'

He turned to Branson and to Inspector Sue Carpenter, who had joined them.

'Let's get the tape off his mouth first. Sue, call for a paramedic and POLSA and a search team, and get someone to bring some water, or tea if you can. And I want this level of the car park closed, as well as all the stairwells, in case they left by foot.'

'Yes, sir.'

Then he leaned in and, as gently as he could, got his fingertips in the join in the tape. It would have been easier without his gloves, he knew, but he kept them on and finally managed to start peeling it off, mindful that although it would be extremely painful for the man, at the same time he needed to preserve it as best he could for forensic analysis.

As he peeled it away from his mouth, the man shouted out in pain.

'Sorry,' Grace murmured.

The tape went all the way around the back of the man's head and he didn't want to hurt him any more.

'Mike Howard?' he asked.

'Yes! Jesus, that hurt,' the man said, then smiled.

Grace folded the tape back on itself. 'I'm sorry. We're going to lift you out. Are you injured? In pain?'

He shook his head. 'Just get me out.'

Mike Howard was a big, heavy man. With considerable difficulty, between himself and Glenn Branson they managed to manoeuvre him forward to the edge of the boot. They freed his arms and legs, and tried as best they could to remove the rest of the tape around his head. Then they stood him up and walked him around a little, supporting him until the circulation was back in his legs and he was steadier. But he was wheezing, close to hyperventilating, so they sat him down on the Skoda's rear bumper.

'Can you tell us what happened?' Grace asked him gently.

'I'm sorry,' he said. 'I pissed. I couldn't help it. I couldn't keep it in any more.'

'It's OK, don't worry. Are you able to tell me what happened?'

'What time is it?'

'Half past one,' Glenn Branson said.

'What day?'

'Friday.'

The man frowned. 'Friday? Friday morning?'

'It's afternoon, lunchtime.'

'Holy shit.'

'How long have you been there?' Grace asked.

Mike Howard took several deep breaths. 'I was working nights. I was just heading home – about 1 a.m. – and this man hailed me along the seafront.'

'Where exactly?'

'Just near the Peace Statue. He got in the back and told me to take him to Shoreham Airport – said he was working a night shift there. I remember turning into the perimeter road – and that's the last thing.'

Grace knew that road. It had no street lighting.

'The last thing you remember?'

'I woke up being shaken about. I could smell diesel and fumes. I figured out I was in the boot of my cab. I was terrified. I didn't know what was going to happen.'

'Can you remember what this guy looked like?' Grace asked.

'He was wearing a baseball cap pulled low. I tried to get a look at his face – you always do in this game when you pick someone up late at night off the street. But I couldn't see it.'

Grace was relieved that the taxi driver seemed to be cheering up a little.

'What about his accent?'

'He didn't say much. Sounded English to me. Do you have any water?'

'There's some on its way. Do you need anything to eat?'

'Sugar. I'm diabetic.'

'An ambulance will be here any minute – they'll have something for you. Will you be all right for a few minutes?'

Mike Howard nodded.

Grace continued his questioning. 'We think the man who did this to you has kidnapped a child and we need to find him urgently. I know you've had a horrendous ordeal, but anything you can tell us, anything at all that you can remember, would be valuable.'

Mike Howard eased himself forward and stood up. 'Agggghhh,' he said. 'I've got the most terrible cramp.' He stamped his foot, then stamped it again. 'I'm trying to think. He was short. A short, thin little fellow, like a weasel. Promise me something?'

'What?' Grace asked.

'If you find him, can I get him to pay me what he owes me, then thump him one, really hard, where it hurts?'

For the first time in what felt a long while, Grace smiled. 'You'll have to beat me to it,' he said.

'I will, mate, don't you worry.'

Glenn Branson then said to the driver, 'Is there someone you'd like us to contact and tell that you're safe?'

Grace looked at his watch pensively. Almost two and a half hours since Tyler Chase had been picked up. Why was he brought here? His assumption was that the abductor had a car parked here, with luck the rental Toyota Yaris, choosing this as a good location to attack and disable the boy, then switch vehicles. Even more ideal with its CCTV cameras out of action. Inspector Carpenter might think it was scummy Brighton vandals, but he didn't. He had a feeling he was starting to recognize the killer's handwriting.

He did a calculation in his head. There were roadworks along the seafront clogging up the traffic, badly. The journey from the school would have been in the region of fifteen to twenty minutes, assuming they came straight here. The pervert seemed to like to film his victims dying. Grace was able to make another assumption, that he had not done that here. From the image he was building of the man, this wasn't his style of location. He was going to take the boy somewhere he could film him dying. And he sensed it would be somewhere dramatic. But where?

Where in this whole damned city – or beyond?

He studied his watch again. If he'd brought the boy in here around 11.20 a.m., it was likely he'd not hung around. He would have left again within a few minutes. Certainly within half an hour.

Two paramedics, accompanied by a uniformed officer, were running towards them. Grace edged Glenn Branson to one side to make way for them, then he said the DS, 'We're out of here.'

'Where to?'

'I'll tell you in the car.'

94

assuming Tooth came straight back. He parked, squeezed to the side, and his arms shaking. Grey sea-mist made visibility somewhat... that he had not had their lights from the road above. It beginning of the year, in December, when the sea was going to freeze, any sense where he would be driving. And he guessed it could be some short distance, but even so.

Tooth, keeping rigidly to the 30mph speed limit, drove the Toyota west along the main road above Shoreham Harbour. He was looking at the flat water of the basin, down to his left, where Ewan Preece had taken his last drive, and almost did not notice a roadworks traffic light turning red in front of him.

He braked hard. Behind him in the boot of the car he heard a thud and further back a scream of locked tyres. For an anxious moment he thought the car behind was going to rear-end him.

Then the sudden wail of a siren gave him a new concern. Moments later, blue lights flashing, a police car tore past from the opposite direction. He kept a careful watch in his mirrors, but it kept on going, either not noticing or not interested in him. Relieved, he drove on for some distance, passing a number of industrial buildings to his left, until he saw his landmark, the blue low-rise office block of the Shoreham Port Authority building.

He turned right into a narrow street opposite it, passing a modern kitchen appliances showroom on the corner. He drove a short way up the street, which rapidly became shabbier and went under a railway bridge up ahead. But before then he turned off it into a messy area that was part industrial estate and part low-rent apartment blocks. He remembered it all well and it seemed un-changed.

He passed a massive, grimy printing works on his left and various cars, some of which were parked on the road, while others had been left haphazardly in front of and around different buildings. It was the kind of area where no one would notice you, or take any interest in you if they did.

He turned right again, into the place he had discovered six years ago. He drove along the side of a shabby ten-storey apartment block, passing cars and vans parked outside, and came into a wide, half-empty parking area at the rear of the building, bounded by a crumbling wall on two sides, a wooden fence on a third and the rear of the apartment block.

He reversed the car in, backing it tight up against the wall, then sat and ate the chicken sandwich he had bought earlier at a petrol station, drank a cranberry juice, got out and locked up. With his cap pulled down low and his sunglasses on, he peered up at the grimy windows for any sign of an inquisitive face, but all he saw was laundry flapping from a couple of balconies. He stood by the car, pretending to be checking a rear tyre, listening to make sure that his passenger was silent.

He heard a thud.

Angrily he opened the boot and saw the boy's frightened eyes behind his glasses. It didn't matter how tightly he bound him, there was nothing to anchor him to in here. He wondered if it would be wisest to break his back and paralyse him – but that would mean lifting him out first and he didn't want to take that risk.

Instead he said, 'Make another sound and you're dead. Understand what I'm saying?'

The boy nodded, looking even more frightened.

Tooth slammed down the lid.

95

Tyler was terrified by the man in the black baseball cap and the dark glasses, but he was angry, too. His wrists were hurting from the bindings and he had cramp in his right foot. He listened, hard, could hear footsteps crunching, getting fainter.

He'd felt the car move when the man got out, but it hadn't moved again, which meant he hadn't got back in. He must have gone somewhere.

Tyler tried to work out what time it was, or where he might be. He'd just seen daylight when the boot lid rose up. And the wall of a building, a crummy-looking wall, and a couple of windows, but it could have been anywhere in the city, anywhere he had ever been to. But the fresh air that had come in, momentarily, smelled familiar. A tang of salt, but mixed with timber and burnt gas and other industrial smells. They were close to a harbour, he thought. Almost certainly Shoreham Harbour. He'd been kayaking here with his school, several times.

The daylight wasn't bright, but it didn't feel like it was evening, more just overcast as if it was going to rain.

They would find him soon. His mother would know where he was from Friend Mapper. She might even ring him – not that he would be able to answer it.

Defiantly, he threw himself against the side of the car, kicking out as hard as he could. Then again. And again.

He kicked until he had tired himself out. It didn't sound as if anyone had heard him.

But surely they would find him soon?

96

Grace, followed by Branson, sprinted up three floors at Brighton's John Street Police Station, hurried along a corridor and went into the CCTV Control Room, which was manned around the clock.

It was a large space, with blue carpet and dark blue chairs, and three separate workstations, each comprising a bank of CCTV monitors on which was a kaleidoscope of moving images of parts of the city of Brighton and Hove and other Sussex locations, keyboards, computer terminals and telephones. Every police CCTV camera in the county could be viewed from here.

Two of the workstations were currently occupied by controllers, both hunched over them with headsets on. One of them looked busy, engaged in a police operation, but the other turned as they came in and nodded a greeting. He was a fresh-faced man in his late thirties with neat brown hair, wearing a lightweight black jacket. His badge gave his name as Jon Pumfrey. Moments later they were joined in the room by Chief Superintendent Graham Barrington, the Gold Commander.

Barrington, in his mid-forties, was a tall, slim man with short, fair hair, and the athletic air of a regular marathon runner. He wore a short-sleeved white uniform shirt with epaulettes, black trousers and shoes, held a radio in his hand and had a phone clipped to his belt.

'Jon,' the Chief Superintendent said, 'which are the nearest cameras to the Regency Square car park?'

'There's a police one right opposite boss,' Pumfrey said, 'but it's hopeless – there's some constant interference with it.'

He tapped the keyboard and a moment later they saw successive waves rippling up and down one of the screens directly in front of him.

'How long's it been like that?' Roy Grace asked suspiciously.

'At least a year. I keep asking them to do something about it.'

He shrugged. 'There are also cameras to the east and west – which direction do you want?'

'We've just done a quick recce,' Grace said. 'If you exit in a vehicle from the Regency Square car park, you have to turn left on the seafront, on Kings Road – unless you go around up to Western Road, but that's complicated.'

Part of that road was buses and taxis only. Grace did not think the abductor would take the risk of getting stopped there.

'I've set some parameters,' he said. 'What we need to see is the video footage showing all vehicles in motion close to the car park, travelling east or west on King's Road between 11.15 a.m. and 11.45 a.m. today. We're looking particularly for a dark-coloured Toyota Yaris saloon, with a single male driving, either accompanied by a twelve-year-old boy or solo.'

Graham Barrington said, 'All right, you guys, I'll leave you to it. Anything you want, just shout.'

Grace thanked him, and the two detectives then stood behind Pumfrey and began to watch intently.

'The Yaris is a popular car, sir,' Pumfrey said. 'Must be thousands on the roads. We're likely to see a few.'

'We'll put markers on the first five we see, to start with,' Grace said. 'If they're turning left, they're heading east, but that might be only for a short distance, before they make a U-turn and head west. Let's check east first.'

Almost as he spoke they saw a dark-coloured Yaris heading east, past the bottom of West Street. The camera was on the south side of the road.

'Freeze that!' Branson said. 'Can you zoom in?'

Jon Pumfrey tapped the keyboard and the camera zoomed in, jerkily but quickly, on the driver's door and window. It was a grainy zoom, but they could see clearly enough that it was two elderly ladies.

'Let's move on,' Grace said.

They watched the fast-forwarding images, cars darting by in flickering movements.

Then Grace called out, 'Stop! Go back.'

They watched the tape rewind.

'OK! That one.' They were looking at a dark grey Yaris with what appeared to be a single occupant, a male, driving. The time said 11.38.

'Now zoom in, please.'

The image was again grainy, but this time it looked like a male, most of his face obscured by a baseball cap and dark glasses.

'It's not that bright out there. Why's he wearing dark glasses?' Pumfrey queried.

Grace turned to Branson. 'That was the description by the school teacher – the taxi driver was wearing a baseball cap. And so was the man who rented the car from Avis!' Suddenly he felt his adrenalin pumping. Turning back to Pumfrey, he asked, 'Is that the best image you can get?'

'I can send it for enhancement, but that would take a while.'

'OK, run forward. Can we get the registration?'

Pumfrey inched the car forward frame by frame.

'Golf Victor Zero Eight Whisky Delta X-Ray,' Branson read out, as Grace wrote it down.

'Right. Can you run an ANPR check from here?' he asked Pumfrey.

'Yes, sir.'

They continued watching. Then, to Grace's excitement, the car reappeared, this time travelling west.

'It's gone round the roundabout at the Palace Pier, doing a U-turn!' he said. 'Where's the next camera?'

'Other than the dud one opposite the Regency Square car park, the next is a mile to the west, on Brunswick Lawns.'

'Let's look at that one,' Grace said.

Five minutes later, which indicated the vehicle was sticking rigidly to the speed limit, and allowing for a couple of traffic-light stops and the roadworks delay, the car appeared, still travelling west.

'Where's the next?' Grace asked.

'That's the last of the city's CCTV cameras in this direction, sir,' Pumfrey said.

'OK. Now let's see if this vehicle has triggered any ANPR camera since 11.15 a.m. What's the first one west of this position?'

Pumfrey turned to a different computer and entered the data.

Grace noticed his partially eaten lunch on the wooden table beside him. An empty plastic lunchbox, a coil of orange peel and an unopened yoghurt. Healthy, he thought, depending of course on what had been in the sandwich.

'Here we are: 11.54 a.m. This is the ANPR camera at the bottom of Boundary Road, Hove, at the junction with the end of the Kingsway.'

Suddenly a photograph of the front of a dark grey Yaris appeared on the screen, its number plate clearly visible, but the occupant hard to make out through an almost opaque screen. By looking very closely it was possible to distinguish what might have been someone in a baseball cap and dark glasses, but without any certainty.

'Can't we get a better image of the face?' Branson asked.

'Depends how the light hits the windscreen,' Pumfrey replied. 'These particular cameras are designed to read number plates, I'm afraid, not faces. I can send it for enhancement if you want?'

'Yes, both of those images, please,' Grace said. 'Is that the only ANPR it's triggered?'

'The only one showing today.'

Grace did a mental calculation. If the driver avoided breaking the law, and with a kidnapped child on board he would not want to risk getting stopped . . . The exit from the car park on to King's Road was a left turn only . . . That meant he would have driven east to the end of King's Road and then gone round the roundabout, by the Palace Pier, and then come back on himself. Allowing for the distance and hold-ups at traffic lights, that would put the car there at the right time from its sighting on King's Road. Excitement was growing inside him.

The car's location was alongside Shoreham Harbour, close to Southwick. He was certain that the sadist knew this area. A lot of villains perpetrated their crimes in the places they knew, their comfort zones. He made a note of a new line of enquiry, to have Duncan Crocker do a search on all previous violent crimes in this area. But first, still staring at the frozen image of the front of the Yaris and the faint silhouette of its driver, on the monitor, he called for a PNC check on the car.

The information came back almost immediately that the owner

was a male, Barry Simons, who lived in Worthing, West Sussex, some fifteen miles to the west of Brighton. Grace's excitement waned at this news. That fitted with the car's occupant and position, heading in the direction where he lived. The only thing that kept him hopeful was the fact that the Yaris appeared to have stopped somewhere in Shoreham or Southwick. He was about to call Gold to ask him to get the helicopter over there and block off the area when his phone rang.

It was Duncan Crocker. 'Roy, we've found a car, a Toyota Yaris, driving on those switched plates taken from the service station at Newport Pagnell – the plates from the woman's car – that twenty-seven-year-old who was stopped on the M11 near Brentwood. It's just pinged an ANPR camera, heading north from Brighton on the A23.'

97

Tyler tried kicking again. He could hear the hollow metallic *boom-boom-boom* echo around him.

What if the man did not come back?

There was a story he had read – he was trying to remember the book – in which someone was locked in the boot of a car and nearly suffocated. How long could you stay in one? How long had he already been here? Was there any sharp edge he could rub against? He tried rolling over, exploring the space as best he could, but it was tiny and seemed to be completely carpeted.

His watch was luminous but he couldn't see the face. He had lost all track of time. He didn't know how long the man had been gone, whether it was still day out there or if night had fallen. If the man did not come back, how long would it be, he wondered, before someone wondered about a strange car?

Then he had a sudden panic about Friend Mapper. Had his mother remembered to log on? She made him keep it on all the time, but she often forgot herself. And she was crap with technology.

Maybe he should keep kicking, in case someone passed by and heard him. But he was scared. If the man came back and heard him he might get really angry. He had just made the decision to wait a little longer when he heard footsteps approaching – quick, sharp crunches. Then he felt the car tilt slightly.

Someone had got in.

98

In the CCTV room, Grace stared at the frontal photograph of a dark grey Toyota Yaris on a familiar stretch of the A23, just north of Brighton. But to his dismay the windscreen was even more opaque than the car by Shoreham Harbour in the previous photograph. He could see nothing at all inside, no shadows or silhouettes, no clue as to how many people might be in it.

Branson immediately informed Gold, then listened intently to his radio.

Grace ordered Jon Pumfrey to put out a *high-act* nationwide marker on the car. He did not intend to take any risks. Then he sat for a moment, clenching his fists. Maybe, finally, this was it.

'What CCTV units do you have on the A23?' he asked the controller.

'The only fixed ones are ANPRs on the motorway. The next one, if he keeps heading north, is Gatwick.'

Grace was feeling excitement but, at the same time, frustration. He would have liked to be out there, on the road, present when they stopped the car. Pumfrey pulled up a road map on to one of the monitors, showing the position of the two ANPR cameras. There were plenty of opportunities for the suspect to turn off the motorway. But with luck the helicopter would have him in sight imminently.

He turned back to the bank of monitors and looked at the car that had been photographed heading east along the seafront, owned, according to its registration document, by Barry Simons. Just as a precaution, he phoned the Incident Room. Nick Nicholl answered. Grace tasked him with finding Barry Simons and establishing for certain that he had been driving his car along Brighton seafront this morning.

From the suspect's current position on the A23, it would take him about twenty-five minutes, Grace estimated, to ping that next

ANPR camera at Gatwick. On the radio he could follow the developments. This was a true fast-time operation. The helicopter, which was also fitted with ANPR, would be over the M23 in ninety seconds. One unmarked car was already on the motorway, approximately two miles behind the target, and two more were only minutes away. It was policy in kidnap pursuits to use unmarked cars wherever possible. That way, the perpetrator would not panic as he might at the sight of a marked car passing him, with the risk of involving his victim in a high-speed chase. If they could get unmarked cars in front of and behind the suspect, a minimum of three vehicles, and preferably four, they could box him in – TPAC him – before he realized what was happening.

'I need to get back to Sussex House,' Glenn said.

'Me too.'

'I can patch any images you want through to you in the Incident Room,' Pumfrey said.

Grace thanked him and the two detectives left. As they walked out of the rear of the building into the car park, Grace's phone rang. It was Inspector Sue Carpenter at the Regency Square car park.

'Sir,' she said, 'I don't know if this is significant, but I understand that the Regency Square car park was identified by an application on the missing boy's iPhone.'

'Yes,' Grace replied, his hopes rising. 'An application called Friend Mapper. We're hoping he keeps it on – that it could lead us to him if we can't find him before.'

'I'm afraid, sir, one of the search team has found a smashed iPhone in a bin in the car park – close to the taxi.'

99

As he climbed into his car, Grace instructed Sue Carpenter to get the phone checked immediately for finger- and footprints, then get it straight to the High-Tech Crime Unit. He told her he wanted it in their hands, having been dusted for prints, within the next thirty minutes. Getting the contents of the phone analysed was more important to him at this stage than getting forensic evidence from it.

Then, as he drove out and turned left down the steep hill, he said to Branson, who was listening to the Ops-1 instructions on his radio, 'I'm still struggling to get my head around the motive here. Did the perp take this boy as a substitute because his mother was unavailable?'

'Because she'd unexpectedly gone to New York, so the boy was the next best thing? Is that what you're saying?'

'Yes,' Grace replied. 'Or was taking the boy his plan all along?'

'What's your sense?'

'I think he plans everything. He's not someone who takes chance opportunities. My view is that probably, by going to the States, Carly Chase made seizing the boy a little easier for him.'

Branson nodded and looked at his watch. 'Just over six hours until she lands.'

'Maybe we'll be able to greet her with good news.'

'I promised I'd get a message to her on the plane as soon as we have any.'

'With a bit of luck, that could be any minute now.'

Grace gave Branson a wistful smile, then glanced at the car clock. It was half past two. He should eat something, he knew, but he didn't have any appetite, and he didn't want to waste valuable time stopping anywhere. He fished in his suit jacket pocket and produced a Mars bar in a very crumpled wrapper that had been there for some days.

'Haven't had any lunch. You hungry?' he said to Branson. 'Want to share this?'

'Boy, you know how to give someone a good time!' Branson said, peeling off the wrapper. 'A slap-up, no-expenses-spared lunch with Roy Grace. Half an old Mars bar. This been in your pocket since you were at school?'

'Sod off!'

Branson tore the chocolate bar in two and held out the slightly larger portion to Grace, who popped it in his mouth. 'You ever see that film about—'

Grace's phone rang. As he wasn't driving at high speed, he stuck it into the hands-free cradle and answered. Both of them heard the voice of Chief Inspector Trevor Barnes, the newly appointed Silver Commander. An experienced and methodical Senior Investigating Officer, Barnes, like Roy Grace, had handled many major crime investigations.

'Roy,' he said, 'we've just stopped the Toyota Yaris on the M23, four miles south of the Crawley interchange.'

Grace, his mouth full of chewy chocolate and toffee, thumped the steering wheel with glee.

'Brilliant!' Branson replied.

'That you, Glenn?' Barnes asked.

'Yeah, we're in the car. What's the situation?'

'Well,' Barnes said, his voice somewhat lacking in enthusiasm, although he always spoke in a considered, deadpan tone, 'I'm not sure that we have the right person.'

'What description can you give us, Trevor?' Grace asked, the Silver's words now making him uneasy.

He halted the car at a traffic light.

'Well, I'm assuming your hit man is not eighty-four years old.'

'What do you mean?' Grace had a sinking feeling.

'Toyota Yaris, index Yankee Delta Five Eight Victor Juliet Kilo? Is that the correct one?'

Grace pulled out his notebook and flipped to the right page. 'Yes. Those are the plates that were taken from a car at Newport Pagnell that we believe our suspect is using.'

'The driver of this Yaris is eighty-four years old and has his wife who is eighty-three with him. It's their car, but it's not their registration number.'

'Not their registration?' Grace echoed.

The lights changed and he drove on.

'The licence plates on the car aren't theirs, Roy. The driver may be old, but he has all his marbles, I'm told. Knew his registration number off by heart. Sounds like someone's nicked his plates and replaced them with different ones.'

'Where's he come from?' Grace asked, but he had a feeling he already knew the answer.

'They've been in Brighton. They enjoy the sea air, apparently. Like to take their dog for a walk between the piers. It's their regular constitutional. They have fish and chips at some place on the front.'

'Yep, and let me guess where they parked. The Regency Square car park?'

'Very good, Roy. Ever thought of going on *Mastermind*?'

'Once, when I had a brain that worked. So, give us their index that's been stolen.'

Branson wrote it down.

Grace drove in silence for some moments, thinking about the killer with grudging admiration. *Whoever you are, you are a smart bastard. What's more, you clearly have a sense of humour. And just in case you don't know, right at this moment I have a major sense-of-humour failure.*

His phone rang again. This time it was Nick Nicholl in MIR-1, sounding perplexed.

'Chief, I'm coming back to you on the vehicle owner check you asked me to do, on Barry Simons.'

'Thanks. What do you have, Nick?'

'I've just spoken to him. I sent someone round to his house and they asked a neighbour who knew where he worked – and I got his mobile phone number from his company.'

'Well done.'

The Detective Constable sounded hesitant. 'You asked me to check if it was him driving his car first east on King's Road, then west past the junction between Kingsway and Boundary Road this morning? Index Golf Victor Zero Eight Whisky Delta X-Ray?'

'Yes.'

'Well, he's a bit baffled, chief. He and his wife are lying on a beach in Limassol in Cyprus at the moment. They've been there for nearly two weeks.'

'Could anyone they know be driving this car while they're away?'

'No,' Nick Nicholl said. 'They left it at the long-term car park at Gatwick Airport.'

Grace pulled over to the side of the road and stopped sharply.

'Nick, put a high-act marker on that index. Get on to the Divisional Intelligence Unit – I want to know every ANPR sighting from the day Barry Simons's car arrived at Gatwick to now.'

'To double-check, chief, index Golf Victor Zero Eight Whisky Delta X-Ray.'

'Correct.'

Grace switched on the car's lights and siren, then turned to Glenn Branson.

'We're taking a ride to Shoreham.'

'Want me to drive?' Branson asked.

Grace shook his head. 'Thanks for the offer, but I think I'll be of more help to Tyler Chase alive.'

100

Tooth sat in the Yaris in the parking lot behind the apartment block. The same cars were still here that had been here when he left to do his reconnaissance an hour ago. It was still the middle of the afternoon and maybe the lot would fill up when people came back from work. But it hadn't filled up last time, six years ago. The windows of the apartment block didn't look like they had been cleaned since then either. Maybe it was full of old people. Maybe they were all dead.

He stared at the text that had come in and which had prompted his early return to the car. It said just one word: **call.**

He removed the SIM card and, as he always did, burned it with his lighter until it was melted. He would throw it away later. Then he took one of the phones he had not yet used from his bag and dialled the number.

Ricky Giordino answered on the first ring. 'Yeah?'

'You texted me to call.'

'What the fuck took you so long, Mr Tooth?'

Tooth did not reply.

'You still there? Hello, Mr Tooth?'

'Yes.'

'Listen to me. We've had another tragedy in our family and that woman, Mrs Chase, she's the cause of it. My sister's dead. I'm your client now, understand me? You're doing this for me now. I want that woman's pain to be so bad. I want pain she's never going to forget, you with me?'

'I'm doing what I can,' Tooth replied.

'Listen up, I didn't pay you a million bucks to do what you can do. Understand? I paid you that money to do something more than that. Something different, right? Creative. Give me a big surprise. Blow me away. Show me you got balls!'

'Balls,' Tooth commented.

'Yeah, you heard, balls. You're going to bring those videos to me, right? Soon as you're done?'

'Tomorrow,' Tooth said.

He ended the call, again burned the SIM card, then lit a cigarette. He did not like this man.

He didn't do rudeness.

101

Roy Grace turned the siren and lights off as they passed Hove Lagoon, two shallow man-made recreational lakes beside a children's playground. Up on the promenade beyond there was a long row of beach huts facing the beach and the sea.

The Lagoon ended at Aldrington Basin, the eastern extremity of Shoreham Harbour, and from this point onwards, until Shoreham town, a few miles further on, the buildings and landscape along this road became mostly industrial and docklands. He slowed as they approached the junction with Boundary Road and pointed up through the windscreen.

'There's the ANPR camera that Barry Simons pinged this morning.'

Then Nick Nicholl radioed through. 'Chief, I've got the information you requested on the Toyota Yaris index Golf Victor Zero Eight Whisky Delta X-Ray. It's rather strange, so I went back an extra two weeks and I now have all sightings for the past month. For the first two weeks it pinged cameras during weekdays that are consistent with a regular morning and evening commute from Worthing to central Brighton and back. Then on Sunday morning, just under two weeks ago, it travelled from Worthing to Gatwick.'

'Consistent with what Simons told you,' Branson said, butting in, 'that they drove to Gatwick Airport long-term parking before their flight to Cyprus.'

'Yes,' Nicholl said. 'Now here's the bit that doesn't make sense. The next sighting was the one this morning, when it pinged the CCTV camera on the seafront at the bottom of West Street, travelling east. There's nothing to show how the car got from Gatwick Airport down to Kingsway. Even if it drove directly from the airport down to Brighton, with the marker on the vehicle it should have been picked up by the A23 camera at Gatwick, and by another on the approach to Brighton, and I would have thought by others in Brighton.'

'Unless it commenced its journey from the Regency Square car park,' Grace said thoughtfully. 'Then it would have exited the car park on King's Road and had to make a left turn along the seafront, which would explain why it passed the CCTV camera at the bottom of West Street twice – first going east and then, a few minutes later, west. Followed by the one on Brunswick Lawns, a mile further west, and then this one.'

'You've lost me, sir,' Nicholl said. 'That doesn't explain how the car got from Gatwick Airport to that car park in the first place.'

'It didn't, Nick,' Grace said. 'Our suspect has already demonstrated he is rather cute with number plates. We believe he rented this Toyota from Avis at Gatwick. I'm prepared to put money on Mr and Mrs Simons returning from their Cyprus holiday to find their number plates are missing. Good work. What about subsequent sightings since Boundary Road?'

'None, sir.'

Which would indicate, Grace thought, that either the car was parked up somewhere or the killer had changed number plates yet again.

He ended the conversation and immediately called Graham Barrington to update him.

'My hunch is that he's in the Shoreham area,' Grace said. 'But we can't rely on that. I think you need to get every dark-coloured Toyota Yaris within a three-hour drive of Brighton stopped and searched.'

'That's already happening.'

'And we need to throw everything we have at Shoreham Harbour and its immediate vicinity.'

'The problem is, Roy, it's a massive area.'

'I know. We also need to search every ship leaving and every plane at Shoreham Airport. We need to check the tides. The harbour has a shallow entrance, so there's a lot of shipping can't come in or leave for a period of time either side of low water, from what I remember as a sailor.'

'I'll get that information. Where are you now?'

'At the bottom of Boundary Road with DS Branson – the position of the last sighting of our suspect. I think we should set an initial search parameter of a half-mile radius west of this camera.'

'Harbour and inland?'

'Yes. We need house-to-house, all outbuildings, garages, sheds, industrial estates, ships, boats. We're beyond the range of the Brighton and Hove CCTV network, so we need to focus on commercial premises that have CCTV. A car doesn't disappear into thin air. Someone's seen it. Some camera's picked it up.'

'Just to be clear, Roy, the last sighting of the vehicle is at the bottom of Boundary Road, the junction with Kingsway, and it was heading west?'

'Correct, Graham.'

'Leave it with me.'

Grace knew that the Gold Commander, who happened, fortunately, to be one of the officers he most respected in the entire force, would leave no stone unturned. He should let Barrington get on with it and return to Sussex House, first to MIR-1 to show support to his team, and then prepare for this evening's briefing. With the Chief Constable, Tom Martinson, and the Assistant Chief Constable, Peter Rigg, both due to attend, it was vital he was well prepared. But he was reluctant to leave the chase.

The killer was in Shoreham somewhere, he was certain of it. If anyone had asked him why, his only answer would have been a shrug of his shoulders and the lame response, *copper's nose*. But Glenn Branson understood. That was why, one day, his mate would get to the very top of their profession, so long as he was able to survive his marriage wreckage.

Grace made a call to the Incident Room and Nick Nicholl answered.

'Nick, I want you to get everyone in MIR-1 to stop doing what they're doing for two minutes and have a hard think about this, right? If you'd abducted a child, where in Shoreham might be a good place to hide him? Somewhere no one goes. Maybe somewhere no one even knows about. This whole city is riddled with secret passages going back to smuggling days. Have a quick brainstorm with the team, OK?'

'Yes, chief, right away.'

'We're dealing with someone smart and cunning. He'll choose a smart place.'

'I'm on to it now.'

Grace thanked him and drove on, turning right at the next opportunity. He drove slowly through a network of streets, a mixture of terraced houses and industrial buildings. Looking for a needle in a haystack, he knew. And remembering, as a mantra, the words that his father, who had been a policeman too, had once told him. *No one ever made a greater mistake than the man who did nothing because he could only do a little.*

102

Tyler felt the car rock suddenly. Then he heard a loud boom, like a door slamming. Followed by scrunching footsteps.

He waited until he could not hear them any more, then he threw himself around again, kicking as hard as he could, drumming with his feet and with his right shoulder and his head, breaking out into a sweat, drumming and drumming until he had exhausted himself.

Then he lay still again, thinking.

Why hadn't they found him yet?

Come on, Mum, Mapper! Remember Mapper!

Where was his phone? It had to be in here somewhere. If he could somehow get whatever was covering his mouth off, then he could shout. He rolled himself over on to his stomach, moved his face around, but all he could feel was the fuzz of carpet. There had to be a sharp edge somewhere in here. He wormed forward, raised his head up. Soft new carpet, like rubbing against a brush.

What would his heroes have done? What would Harry Potter have done? Or Alex Rider? Or Amy and Dan Cahill in *The 39 Clues*? They all got out of difficult situations. They'd have known. So what was he missing?

Suddenly he heard a scrunching sound. A vehicle! He started kicking out wildly, as hard as he could again. *Here! In here! In here!*

He heard doors slam. More footsteps.

Fading away.

103

Carly did not hear a word from Sussex Police throughout the flight. Every time a member of the cabin crew walked down the aisle in her direction, she hoped it would be with a message. It was now 8.45 p.m., UK time. Tyler had been missing for almost ten hours.

Feeling sicker by the minute, she had eaten nothing, just sipped a little water, that was all, on the flight-from-hell, squashed in the tiny part of her seat that the sweating fat man next to her, who stank of BO and drank non-stop vodka and Cokes, hadn't overflowed into.

She replayed her decision to go to New York over and over. If she had not gone, she'd have collected Tyler herself from school and he would be safe. He'd be up in his room now, on his computer, alone or with a friend, or doing something with his fossil collection, or practising his cornet.

Fernanda Revere, who could have stopped all this, was dead.

Lou Revere scared her. There was something feral and evil about him. Woman to woman, she might have had a chance with Fernanda Revere, when she was sober. But not with the husband. No chance. Especially not now.

The plane came to a halt. There was a *bing-bong*, followed by the sound of seat belts being unclipped and overhead lockers popping open. People were standing up and she joined them, relieved to get away from the stinking fat blob. She pulled her bag and coat down, then quickly called her mother to say they had landed, and in the hope she had some news. But there was none.

A couple of minutes later she nodded to the two cabin crew standing by the exit, then followed the passengers in front of her out through the plane's door and on to the covered bridge. Instantly she saw, waiting for her, the tall figure of Glenn Branson, accompanied by a younger male officer in uniform, whom she did not recognize, and DS Bella Moy.

'Do you have any news?' Carly blurted.

Branson took her bag for her and steered her to one side, away from the crush of emerging passengers. She looked at him, then at DS Moy, then at the stranger who was in uniform, desperate to read something positive in their eyes, but she could see nothing.

'I'm afraid not yet, Carly,' Bella Moy said. 'Presumably you've heard nothing?'

'I rang all his friends – the parents – before I got on the plane. No one's seen him.'

'They're certain he's not anywhere in their house or their garden or garage?'

'They've all searched thoroughly,' she said forlornly.

'How was the flight?' Glenn Branson asked.

'Horrendous.'

'One positive thing, Carly,' Branson went on, 'is we are fairly sure that Tyler is still within the Brighton and Hove area. We believe he may be in Shoreham or Southwick or Portslade. Do you have any friends or relatives over there that he might go to if he runs away?'

'From his captor, you mean?'

'Yes.'

'I have some friends on Shoreham Beach,' she said. 'But I don't think Tyler knows where they live.'

'We'll get you home as quickly as we can,' Bella said, 'and we'll keep you constantly updated.' Then she gestured to the uniformed officer. 'This is PC Jackson from the Metropolitan Police – we're in his jurisdiction here at Heathrow. He's very kindly going to fast-track you through the Immigration process.'

Carly thanked him.

Fifteen minutes later she was in the back of a police car, heading through the airport tunnel. Glenn Branson drove and Bella Moy sat in the front passenger seat. Moy turned to face her.

'We have a number of questions we need to ask you about Tyler, Carly. Are you happy to talk in the car or would you rather wait until we get you home?'

'Please, now,' Carly said. 'Anything I can give you that might be helpful.'

'You've already given us the names and addresses of his friends. We're looking to see who he's been in contact with, outside of his immediate circle, on his computer and iPhone. They're being examined by the High-Tech Crime Unit.'

'His iPhone?' Carly said. 'You have his phone?'

DS Moy's face froze. She glanced at Branson, then awkwardly back at Carly. 'I'm sorry – didn't anyone tell you?'

'Tell me what?' Carly began shivering and perspiring at the same time. She leaned forward. 'Tell me what?' she said again. 'What do you mean?'

'His iPhone was found in that underground car park – the one you alerted us to on his Friend Mapper.'

'Found? How do you mean *found*?'

Bella Moy hesitated, unsure how much to tell the woman. But she had a right to know the truth.

'There were broken fragments on the ground – then it was discovered in a waste bin in the car park.'

'No,' Carly said, her voice quavering. 'No. Please, no.'

'He may have dropped it, Carly,' Glenn Branson said, trying to put a positive slant on the situation, trying to give her some cause for optimism – to give them all some cause for optimism. 'He might have dropped it while running away. That's our best hope at the moment, that he's hiding somewhere.'

In utter desperation, and shaking with terror, Carly said, 'Please don't tell me you found his phone. Tyler's bright. I thought he was going to keep Friend Mapper on. I thought that would take us to him. I really, really felt that was our best hope.'

She began to sob uncontrollably.

104

By 9.30 p.m. it was dark, the wind had risen and rain was falling. Tooth returned to Shoreham in a Toyota Camry he had rented from Sixt in Boundary Road, Brighton, just a short distance away, using a different ID. He drove around the side of the apartment block and into the pitch-dark parking area at the rear. The space next to the Toyota Yaris was free. He reversed into it, then switched off the engine and lights.

He was in a bad mood. No matter how well you planned things, shit happened. There was always something you hadn't accounted for. On this particular job now, it was tides. It just had not occurred to him. Now in the rucksack he had bought, lying beside him on the passenger seat, he had a tide chart which he'd printed out at an Internet café half an hour ago. He'd study it carefully in a few minutes and get his head around it. Meanwhile he was anxious to move the boy on. The area was crawling with police and it looked as if a massive systematic search was in progress. A quarter of a mile further up the road there was a roadblock, but the only vehicles they seemed interested in were Toyota Yaris saloons.

Too much heat on those vehicles. Too much danger of his being found. The search line still had a while to go before they reached this locality, he worked out, an hour and a half, maybe two hours. He would make sure they didn't find anything.

He climbed out of the car, popped open the boot, then swiftly walked across to the rear of the Yaris.

*

Tyler, clenched up, fighting an urgent need to pee that was getting worse and worse, and craving water for his parched mouth and throat, had heard the sound of a car moving close by, then stopping. He was about to start kicking again when suddenly there was a sharp, metallic *clunk* and the boot opened. He felt a blast of fresh, damp air, but could not see any daylight now, just darkness with an orange streetlighting tinge to it.

Then he saw the dazzling beam of a torch and the shadowy shape of a baseball cap and dark glasses beyond. He was truly scared. If he could just speak, maybe the man would get him some water and something to eat?

Suddenly he felt himself being lifted. He was swung through the air, feeling spots of rain on his face, then dropped, painfully, inside another space that smelled similar, but different. Maybe even newer?

There was a thud and he was entombed once more in pitch darkness. He listened for footsteps but instead heard the car starting up. From the bumping motion, he could tell they were moving.

The car accelerated harshly, sending him rolling backwards and cracking his head painfully on something sharp. He let out a muffled cry of pain. Then the car braked sharply and he tumbled forward a couple of feet.

Whatever he had hit had definitely been sharp. He wormed his way back, as the car accelerated again, then felt with his face, rubbing his nose up against what he thought must be the rear of the boot. Then he found something that was protruding. He didn't know what it was – perhaps the back of one of the rear light housings. He tried to press his mouth up against it and rub, but the car was swaying too much and he was finding it hard to keep steady.

Then he felt the car brake sharply and turn, and keep on turning. He was rolled, helplessly, on his side. There was a massive bump and he cracked his head again on the boot lid, then the car halted, throwing him forward.

*

Tooth looked carefully as he pulled off the side of the road above the harbour, bumping over the kerb and on to the grass, driving far enough away so that the car was almost invisible from the road. The lights of traffic flashed past above him and he could see the glow from the houses across the road, most of them with curtains or blinds drawn.

He halted beside a small, derelict-looking building, the size of a bus shelter, directly opposite the massive edifice of Shoreham Power

Station, across the black water of the harbour. The little building was constructed in brick, with a tiled roof, and had a rusting metal door with a large, rusted padlock on it. It was the padlock he had put on last time he was here, six years ago. Clearly no one had been in, which was good. Not that anyone had any reason to go in there. The place was condemned, highly dangerous, toxic and in imminent danger of collapsing. A large yellow and black sign on the wall displayed an electricity symbol and the words KEEP OUT – DANGER OF DEATH.

In the distance he could hear a helicopter. It had been flying around, on and off, for most of the afternoon and evening. From his rucksack, with his gloved hands, he pulled out a head-mounted flashlight, strapped it around his baseball cap and removed the bolt cutters he had acquired in a hardware store. He switched on the flashlight, then snapped the padlock on the door of the brick building and switched the light off again. He checked the windows of the houses once more before lifting the boy out of the car and carrying him inside the building, along with his rucksack. He pulled the door closed with an echoing clang.

Then he switched on his flashlight once more. Directly in front of him was a short, narrow flight of concrete steps going down, between two brick walls. A pair of tiny red eyes appeared momentarily in the darkness at the bottom of the steps, then darted away.

Tooth put the boy down on his feet, still holding him to stop him falling over.

'You need to take a piss, kid?'

The boy nodded. Tooth helped him and zipped him back up. Then he carried the boy down the steps, brushing past several spider webs. At the bottom was a gridded metal platform, with a handrail, and a whole cluster of pipes, some overhead, some on the walls, most of them bare, exposed metal, rusting badly and covered in what looked like fraying asbestos. It was as silent as a tomb in here.

On the other side of the handrail was a shaft, with a steel ladder, that dropped 190 feet. Tooth looked at the boy, ignoring the pleading in his eyes, then tilted him over the handrail and, shining his flashlight beam down, to enable the boy to see the vertical drop. The boy's eyes bulged in terror.

Tooth pulled a length of blue, high-tensile rope from his ruck-sack and tied it carefully around the boy's ankles. Then he lowered the boy, who was struggling now, thrashing in terror and making a whining, yammering sound through the duct tape across his mouth, a short distance down the shaft and tied the rope around the guard rail.

'I'll be back in a while, kid,' Tooth said. 'Don't struggle too much. You wouldn't want your ankles coming loose.'

105

Tyler's glasses were falling up his nose. He was scared that at any moment they would drop into the void below. But worse, he could feel the rope slipping, especially down his left ankle. He was swaying and starting to feel giddy and totally disoriented.

Something tiny was crawling over his nose. A cold draught blew on his face, the air dank, musty and carrying the fainter, noxious odour of something rotting.

The rope slipped a little more.

Was the man going to come back?

Where was his phone? Was it in the car? How would anyone find him here without Mapper?

He began to panic, then felt the rope slip further. His glasses fell further, too. He froze, stiffening his legs and feet, pushing them against the bindings to keep them as tight as he could. The creature was climbing over his lips now, tickling his nose. He could feel the rush of blood in his head. Suddenly, something touched his right shoulder.

He screamed, the sound trapped inside him.

Then he realized he had just swung into the side of the shaft.

The walls had looked rough, he thought, in the brief moment he had seen them in the beam of the torch. The edges of the ladder would be rough, or at least sharp. As gently as he could, he tried to swing himself around, swaying, bumping into the shaft again, and again, then painfully against the ladder.

Yes!

If he could rub the bindings around his arms up and down against the rough edge, maybe he could saw through them.

His glasses moved further up his forehead. The insect was now crawling over his eyelid.

The rope slipped further down his ankles.

106

This place had worked well for him last week, Tooth reasoned. It was dark, no one overlooked it and there were no cameras. Aside from the power station, there were only timber warehouses, closed and dark for the night, on the far wharf. And the water was deep.

Someone had replaced the padlock on the chain-link fence. He cut through it with his bolt cutters and pushed the gates open. The southerly wind, which seemed to be rising by the minute and was coming straight off the choppy water of the harbour basin ahead, instantly pushed one gate shut. He opened it again and hauled an old oil drum, lying on its side nearby, in front of it.

Then he jumped into the Yaris and drove it forward on to the quay, passing the skip crammed with rubbish that had been there last week and the old fork-lift truck that had been conveniently left for his use. Not that he would need it now.

He got out of the car and took a careful look around. He could hear the lapping of water, the distant *clack-clack-clack* of yacht rigging in the wind. He could also, in the distance, hear the clatter of a helicopter again. Then, with the aid of his flashlight, he did a final check on the interior of the vehicle, pulling out the ashtray, taking the contents to the water's edge and throwing the butts and melted SIM cards into the dark, choppy water. Satisfied he had left nothing else in the car, he prepared himself by taking several deep breaths.

Then he backed the car up a short distance, opened all the windows and doors and popped the boot lid. He slid back behind the steering wheel and, keeping the driver's door open, he put the car into gear and accelerated hard at the edge of the quay. At the very last minute, he threw himself sideways and rolled as he hit the hard surface. Beyond him he heard a deep splash.

Tooth scrambled to his feet and saw the car floating, submerged up to its sills, pitch-poling backwards and forwards in the chop. He was about to snap on his flashlight, to get a better view, when to his dismay he heard an engine. It sounded as if it was approaching. A boat coming down the basin.

He froze.

Bubbles rose all around the car, making a steady *bloop-bloop-bloop* sound. The car was sinking. The engine compartment was almost underwater. The sound of the engine was getting louder.

Sink. Sink, damn you. Sink!

He could see a light, faint but getting brighter, approaching from the right.

Sink!

Water lapped and bubbled, up to the windshield now.

Sink!

The engine sound was louder now. Powerful twin diesels. The light was getting rapidly brighter.

Sink!

The roof was going under now. It was sinking. The rear window was disappearing. Now the boot.

It was gone.

Moments later, navigation lights on and search lights blazing, a Port Authority launch came into view, with two police officers standing on the deck.

Tooth ducked down behind the skip. The boat carried on past. For an instant, above the throb of its engines and the thrash of its bow wave, he heard the crackle of a two-way radio. But the sound of the vessel was already fading, its lights getting dimmer again.

He breathed out.

107

Tyler heard a loud, metallic *clang*. Then a sound like footsteps. For an instant his hopes rose.

Footsteps getting nearer. Then the smell of cigarette smoke. He heard a familiar voice.

'Enjoying the view, kid?'

*

Tooth switched on the flashlight, untied the rope from the balcony and began lowering the boy further, carefully paying the rope through his gloved hands. He could feel the boy bumping into the sides, then the rope went slack.

Good. The boy had landed on the first of the three rest platforms, spaced at fifty-foot intervals.

With his rucksack on his back and the light on, Tooth began to descend the ladder, using just one hand and taking up the slack of the rope as he went with the other. When he reached the platform, he repeated the procedure, then again, until the boy landed face down on the floor of the shaft. Tooth clambered down the last flight and joined him, then pulled a small lamp from his rucksack, switched it on and set it down.

Ahead was a tunnel that went beneath the harbour. Tooth had discovered it from an archive search during the planning for his previous visit. Before it had been replaced because of its dangerous condition, this tunnel carried the electricity lines from the old power station. The tunnel had been replaced, and decommissioned, at the same time as the new power station had been built and a new tunnel bored.

It was like looking along the insides of a rusted, never-ending steel barrel that faded away into darkness. The tunnel was lined on both sides with large metal asbestos-covered pipes, containing the old cables. The flooring was a rotted-looking wooden walkway, with pools of water along it. Massive livid blotches of rust coated the insides of the riveted plates, and all along were spiky cream-coloured stalactites and stalagmites, like partially melted candles.

But it was something else entirely that Tooth was staring at. The human skull, a short distance along the tunnel, greeting him with its rictus grin. Tooth stared back at it with some satisfaction. The twelve rats he had bought from pet shops around Sussex, then starved for five days, had done a good job.

The Estonian Merchant Navy captain's uniform and his peaked, braided cap had gone, along with all of his flesh and almost all of the sinews and his hair. They'd even had a go at his sea boots. Most of his bones had fallen in on each other, or on to the floor, except for one set of arm bones and an intact skeletal hand, which hung from a metal pipe above him, held in place by a padlocked chain. Tooth hadn't wanted to risk the rats eating through his bindings and allowing the man to escape.

Tooth turned and helped the boy to sit upright, with his back propped against the wall, and a view ahead of him along the tunnel and of the bones and the skull. The boy was blinking and something looked different about him. Then Tooth realized what that was. His glasses were missing. He shone his flashlight around, saw them and replaced them on the boy's face.

The boy stared at him. Then flinched at the skeletal remains, his eyes registering horror and deepening fear as Tooth held the beam on it.

Tooth knelt and ripped the duct tape from the boy's mouth.

'You all right, kid?'

'Not really. Actually, no. I want to go home. I want my mum. I'm so thirsty. Who are you? What do you want?'

'You're very demanding,' Tooth said.

Tyler looked at the sight.

'He doesn't look too healthy to me. What do you think, kid?'

'Male, between fifty and sixty years old. Eastern European.'

Tooth frowned. 'You want to tell me how you know that?'

'I study archaeology and anthropology. Can I have some water now please – and I'm hungry.'

'You're a goddamn smartass, right?'

'I'm just thirsty,' Tyler said. 'Why have you brought me here? Who are you?'

'That guy,' Tooth said, pointing at the skeleton, 'he's been here for six years. No one knows about this place. No one's been here in six years. How would you feel about spending six years down here?'

'I wouldn't feel good about that,' Tyler said.

'I bet you wouldn't. I mean, who would, right?'

Tyler nodded in agreement. This guy seemed a little crazy, he thought. Crazy but maybe OK. Not a lot crazier than some of his teachers.

'What had that man done?'

'He ripped someone off,' Tooth said. 'OK?'

Tyler shrugged. 'OK,' he said, his voice coming out as a parched, frightened croak.

'I'll get you sorted, kid. You have to hang on. You and me, we have a big problem. It's to do with the tides, right?'

Tyler stared at him. Then he stared at the remains, shaking. Was this going to be him in six years?

'Tides?' he said.

The man pulled a folded sheet of printout from his rucksack, then opened it up.

'You understand these things, kid?'

He held the paper in front of Tyler's face, keeping his flashlight trained on it. The boy looked at it, then shot a glance at the man's wristwatch.

'Big ships can't come into this harbour two hours either side of low tide,' Tooth said.

He stared at the boxes, each of which had a time written inside it, below the letters LW or HW. Alongside was written *Predicted heights are in metres above Chart Datum.*

'This is not easy to figure out. Seems like low tide was 11.31 p.m. here, but I'm not sure I've got that right. That would mean ships start coming in and out again after 1.31 a.m.'

'You're not looking at today's date,' Tyler said. 'Today it will be 2.06 a.m. Are you taking me on a boat?'

Tooth did not reply.

108

The phones in MIR-1 had been ringing off the hook ever since the *Child Rescue Alert* had been triggered, and the abduction of Tyler Chase was front-page news in most of the papers, as well as headline news on radio and television. It was coming up to 12.30 a.m. During the nearly fourteen hours since his abduction just about everyone in the nation who didn't live under a rock knew his name and a good many of them had seen his photograph.

The room was as busy now as it was in the middle of the day and the air was thick with the continuous ringing of landline and mobile phones. Roy Grace sat, jacket off, sleeves rolled up, tie slackened, reading through a list that had been emailed over by Detective Investigator Lanigan of the methods of operation of all known currently active contract killers. Not wanting to restrict their search to the US, police forces around Europe had also been contacted and their information was starting to come in.

But nothing matching their man so far.

Or his car.

In view of the frequency with which the suspect appeared to go about changing number plates, Grace had sent out requests to every police force in the UK to stop and search every dark-coloured Yaris, regardless of whether it was grey or not. He wanted to eliminate any possible risk of the suspect slipping through the net, including a mistake being made by someone who might be colour blind.

It was possible the boy was already abroad, despite the watch that had been put on all airports, seaports and the Channel Tunnel. There were private aircraft and private boats that could easily have slipped the net. But he was fairly certain that the Toyota Yaris belonging to Barry Simons was the one Tyler Chase had been driven in from the Regency Square car park. And if that was the case, Grace did not think he had left the Shoreham area.

Checks had been carried out with the Harbour Master, the Port

Authority and the Coast Guard. All vessels that had sailed from Shoreham Harbour today had been accounted for. No cargo ship had passed through the lock after eight o'clock this evening. A few fishing boats had gone out, but that was all.

Suddenly Stacey Horobin came over to him and said, 'Sir, I have a Lynn Sebbage on the phone, from a firm of chartered surveyors called BLB. She's asking to speak to Norman Potting – said she's tried his mobile but he's not picking up. She says she's been working through the night to look for the information he asked her for, urgently, and she thinks she's found it.'

Grace frowned. 'Chartered surveyors?'

'Yes, called BLB.'

'You mean chartered surveyors as in *structural engineers*?'

Horobin nodded. 'Yes, sir, that area.'

'What do they want at this hour of the morning?'

'I don't know.'

'Where is DS Potting?'

'DS Moy says she thinks he may have gone out to get something to eat, sir.'

'OK, let me speak to the woman. Did you say Sebbage?'

'Lynn Sebbage.'

He picked up the phone and moments later she was put through. 'Detective Superintendent Grace,' he said. 'Can I help you?'

'Yes,' she said. She sounded as fresh as if it was the middle of her normal working day. 'I'm a partner in BLB. We're very old-established chartered surveyors in Brighton. We had a visit from Detective Sergeant Potting late this afternoon, regarding the little boy who's been abducted, saying he was looking for places around Shoreham Harbour where someone might be concealed. The Chief Engineer told him that he knew my firm, BLB, has done a lot of work at the harbour over the past century, particularly in the construction of the original coal-fired power station. He said he thought there was a tunnel bored then that's been disused for decades.'

'What kind of a tunnel?' Grace asked.

'Well, I've been hunting through our archives all night – they go back over a hundred years – and I think I've found what he was referring to. It's a tunnel that was built for the old power station, Shoreham B, about seventy years ago, to carry the electricity cables under the harbour, and it was decommissioned when the new power station was built twenty years ago.'

'How would someone other than a harbour worker know about it?'

'Anyone studying the history of the area could find it easily. It's probably on Google if people look hard enough.'

She then explained where the access to it was.

A couple of minutes later, just as he thanked her and hung up, Glenn Branson walked in carrying two steaming mugs.

'Brought you a coffee.'

'Thanks. Want to come and take a ride? We could both do with a quick change of scenery.'

'Where to?'

'Somewhere in Brighton you and I have never been before.'

'Thanks for the offer, boss man, but being a tourist at 1 a.m. doesn't float my boat.'

'Don't worry. We're not going boating – we're going to go underwater.'

'Terrific. This is getting better every second. Scuba-diving?'

'No. Tunnelling.'

'Tunnelling? Now? At this hour? You're not serious?'

Grace stood up. 'Get your coat and a torch.'

'I'm claustrophobic.'

'So am I. We can hold hands.'

109

'What do you think the chances are?' Glenn Branson said, as Grace drove slowly along the road, peering to the left, looking for the building Lynn Sebbage had described. A strong wind buffeted the car and big spots of rain spattered on the windscreen.

'One in a million? One in a billion? One in a trillion that he's in this tunnel?'

'You're not trying to think like the perpetrator,' Grace said.

'Yeah, and that's just as well, coz I'd be hanging you on a meat hook and filming you right now if I did.'

Grace smiled. 'I don't think so. You'd be trying to outsmart us. How many times has he changed number plates? Those cameras he left behind, like giving us two fingers. This is a very smart guy.'

'You sound like you admire him.'

'I do admire him – for his professionalism. Everything else about him I loathe beyond words, but I admire his cunning. If he's holed up anywhere with that kid, it's not going to be some garden shed full of mushrooms. It's going to be somewhere he knows that we haven't thought of. So I don't think we're looking at one in a million. I think we're looking at very good odds and we need to eliminate this place.'

'You could have sent a couple of uniforms along,' Branson said grumpily. 'Or Norman Potting.'

'And spoiled our fun?' Grace said, pulling over on the kerb. 'This looks like it.'

Moments later, in the beam of his torch, Grace saw the broken padlock lying on the ground. He knelt and peered at it closely.

'It's been cut through,' he said.

Then he pulled the door open and led the way down the concrete steps. At the bottom they stepped on to a gridded metal platform with a handrail. A network of old metal pipes spread out all around them.

Branson sniffed. 'Someone's managed to use this place as a toilet,' he said.

Grace peered over the handrail, then shone his torch beam down the vertical shaft.

'Shit,' he said under his breath. It looked a long, long way down. Then he shouted, as loudly as he could, 'POLICE! Is anyone down there?'

His voice echoed. Then he repeated his question again.

Only the echo, falling into silence, came back at them.

The two officers looked at each other.

'Someone's been here,' Glenn Branson said.

'And might still be here,' Grace replied, peering down the shaft again, and then looking at the ladder. 'And I'm sodding terrified of heights.'

'Me too,' Branson said.

'Heights and claustrophobia? Anything you're not scared of?' Grace quizzed him with a grin.

'Not much.'

'Shine the torch for me. I can see a rest platform about fifty feet down. I'll wait for you there.'

'What about Health and Safety?' Branson asked.

Grace tapped his chest. 'You're looking at him. You fall, I'll catch you.'

He climbed over the safety rail, decided he was not going to look down, gripped both sides of the rail, found the first rung and slowly, carefully, began to descend.

It took them several minutes to get to the bottom.

'That was seriously not fun,' Glenn Branson said, and flashed his torch around. The beam struck the tunnel. 'Holy fucking shit!' He was staring at the skeletal remains.

Both men took a few steps towards them.

'Looks like a new cold case to add to your workload, boss,' Branson said.

But Grace wasn't looking at the skull and bones any more. He was looking at a screwed-up ball of paper on the ground. He pulled on a pair of gloves, knelt, picked it up and opened it out. Then he frowned.

'What is it?' Branson said.

Grace held it up. 'A tide chart.'

'Shit! How long do you reckon that's been down here?'

'Not long,' Grace replied. 'It's current. This week's – seven days' tides for Shoreham, starting yesterday.'

'Why would someone want a tide chart?'

'The entrance to the harbour mouth is only six feet deep at low tide. There's not enough draught for big ships two hours either side of low water.'

'You think this is connected with Tyler?'

Grace almost failed to spot the tiny object lying beneath a section of rusted piping. He knelt again and picked it up, carefully, between his gloved forefinger and thumb, then held it up.

'I do now, for sure,' he said. 'A Lucky Strike cigarette.' He pressed the burnt end to his check. 'You know what? That's still warm.'

Pulling on gloves himself, Glenn Branson took the tide chart and studied it for a moment. Then he checked his watch.

'The harbour mouth opens, if that's what they call it, at 2.06 a.m. That's fifty-six minutes' time. Shit! We have to stop any ship from leaving.'

This time, all his fear of heights forgotten, the Detective Sergeant threw himself up the first rungs of the ladder, with Grace inches behind.

110

Tyler, utterly terrified, was whimpering with fear and quaking, yet at the same time he did not dare struggle too much. Choppy, ink-black water splashed at him like some wild, angry creature just inches below his feet. Rain lashed down on him. He was hung by his arms, which were agonizingly outstretched like in a crucifixion.

He had thought he was being thrown into the water but then he had been jerked tight just above it. He kept trying to cry out, but there was tape over his mouth again and all his cries just echoed around and around inside his skull.

He was crying, sobbing, pleading for his mother.

There was a strong stench of seaweed. The blindfold the man had put around his head after he had climbed back up from the tunnel had been taken off only at the last minute before he had been dropped.

Above the sound of the water he heard the *chop-chop-chop* of a helicopter approaching. A dazzling beam of light passed over him, briefly, then darkness again.

Come over here! Come over here! I'm here! Come over here!

Please help me. Please help me. Mum, please help me, please.

111

It wasn't until they reached the top of the ladder that Grace and Branson were able to get any radio or phone signal. Grace immediately called Trevor Barnes, the Silver Commander, who was at his desk in Sussex House.

The two detectives sprinted up the stone steps and out into the fresh wind and rain, sweating profusely, grateful for the cooling air. Above them they heard the clatter of the helicopter swooping low over the harbour basin, the dazzling bright pool of its searchlight illuminating a wide radius of the choppy water.

Moments later Barnes radioed back that he'd checked with the Harbour Master and the only vessel scheduled to leave the harbour, via the large lock, was the dredger the *Arco Dee*. It had already left its berth and was heading along the canal towards the lock.

'I've been on that ship,' Grace shouted at Branson, above the noise of the helicopter and the howling of the wind. 'There's any number of ways he could kill that kid on it.' Then he radioed to the Silver Commander. 'Trevor, get it boarded and searched while it's in the lock.'

For some moments Grace stood still, following the beam of light as it crossed the massive superstructure of Shoreham Power Station. The building had a dog-leg construction, with the first section, which had a flat roof, about sixty feet high, and then the main section about 100 feet high. At the western end was the solitary chimney stack, rising 200 feet into the sky. Suddenly, as the beam traversed it, he thought he saw something move on the flat roof.

Instantly he radioed the Controller. 'Patch me through to Hotel 900.'

Moments later, through a crackling connection, he was speaking to the helicopter spotter. 'Go back round. Light up the power station roof again,' he shouted.

Both detectives waited as the helicopter turned in a wide arc.

The beam struck the chimney first and the ladder that went all the way up it. Then the flat roof of the first section. They could see a figure scurrying across it, then ducking down behind a vent.

'Keep circling,' he instructed. 'There's someone up there!' He turned to Branson. 'I know the quick way there!'

They ran over to the car and jumped in. Grace switched on the blues and twos and raced out into the road.

'Call Silver,' he said. 'Get all available units to the power station.'

A quarter of a mile on he braked hard and swung left, in front of the Port Authority building, then sped down the slip road beside it, until they reached a barrier of tall steel spikes. The sign ahead of them, fixed to the spikes, read:

SHOREHAM PORT AUTHORITY
NO UNAUTHORIZED ACCESS
PUBLIC ROUTE ACROSS LOCKS

Abandoning the car, they ran along the walkway, which was bounded on each side by a high railing. Grace flashed his torch beam ahead of them. To their right now he could see, brightly illuminated by a bank of floodlights on a tower, the harbour's two locks, a small one for fishing boats and yachts, the other, much larger, for tankers, dredgers and container ships.

A long quay separated the locks, in the middle of which was a substantial building housing the control room. On its wall, beneath the windows, was a vertical traffic light, with three red signals showing.

He briefly clocked a warning sign on the entrance gate to this quay, forbidding unauthorized people to enter. The gate had no lock on it, he observed, but his focus was to his left, to the massive superstructure of the power station, partially lit by the helicopter's beam. He ran on, followed by a puffing Branson, stepping over metal slats and then past more red warning lights at the start of the curved walkway over the main lock gates. A sign cautioned against entering when the red lights were flashing and the siren was sounding.

When he reached the join in the middle, between the two halves of the ancient, massive wooden lock gates, he turned and looked at the power station again. What the hell was he doing up there, if it was the suspect? For sure it would be a terrific vantage point, but for what? Did he have the boy up there with him?

They ran on, around the curve of the other half of the lock gates and on to the quay, then sprinted towards the power station. Ahead Grace saw a stack of pallets against the tall spikes of the power station's perimeter fence.

'Wait here,' he said to Branson, then scrambled up the pallets.

Having clambered over the top of the spikes, he dropped down ten feet or so to the other side. He landed with a painful jolt and allowed himself to fall forward, trying to roll to break his fall, but instead hit the ground chest first and lay there winded.

Above, the helicopter clattered, the beam passing momentarily over him, illuminating the steel ladder up the side of the power station superstructure.

He ran to it and began to clamber up, as fast as he could, the wind pulling at him as he climbed higher and higher. This is sodding crazy, he thought. But he climbed on, gripping each rung tightly, clinging to it, the rain lashing him while the wind pulled at him harder and harder, as if it was on a mission to dislodge him. Suddenly he heard a terrible, pitiful crying sound, like a woman in distress, and a huge black shape swooped out of the darkness at him.

He turned his head instinctively and saw the lights of the harbour, and the city beyond, miles beneath him. The wind ripped at him even harder. The black creature was swooping, flapping, crying again. The peregrine falcons, he suddenly remembered, that were in a nesting box on the power station wall – some damned ecological deal that had been made when the place was built.

The bird swooped again.

Great! I've survived twenty years as a copper and now I'm going to be killed by a sodding protected bird.

He clung to the rung, vertigo suddenly hitting him.

Don't let go. Hang on. Hang on. Remember rule one of ladders. Always keep three limbs on and you can't fall off.

With his fourth limb, his right arm, he swiped at the air, not caring at this moment how much damage he did to a protected bird of prey. Then he climbed on, the wind stronger still.

The bird seemed to have taken the hint and vanished back into the night.

Finally, he was at the top. He hauled himself over, on to the asphalt roof, and crawled forward on his knees until he was safely away from the edge. He then stopped and crouched down, trying to get his breath back. His heart felt like it was about to explode as he looked around in the darkness. Moments later he heard the sound of the helicopter and the beam momentarily turned the entire roof, and the wall of the next stage of the superstructure, into daylight.

Then he saw the camera.

It was directly in front of him, on a squat metal tripod, the telephoto lens aimed down.

He looked beyond it, for a brief instant, for the figure he had seen earlier, but there was no sign of the man. As the helicopter beam moved away, he ran to the camera, a complex-looking affair, found the viewfinder and squinted through it.

Oh shit. Oh no. Oh no.

In eerie green night vision, in a tight close-up, he could see Tyler Chase. The boy was suspended across the middle of the lock gates, several feet below the top, his feet inches above the surface of the water. His arms were outstretched, his hands strapped to the left and right gates. A tiny flashing light indicated the camera was running in recording or transmitting mode.

And now to his horror he realized what that tide chart had been all about.

He tried to raise Glenn on his radio but the channel was busy. Frustrated, he tried again. At the third attempt, with the helicopter right overhead, he heard his colleague's voice.

'Glenn!' he shouted. 'Stop the lock gates from opening! For Christ's sake stop them! They're going to kill the boy! They're going to tear him in half!'

The din of the helicopter and wind and the rain, which was now pelting down, was deafening.

'Say that again?' Branson said. 'Can't hear you, boss.'

'STOP THE FUCKING LOCK GATES FROM OPENING!' Grace screamed.

Then a blow on the back of his head sent him crashing to the ground.

He dimly heard a crackle, then a voice from his radio saying, 'Did you say stop the lock gates?'

He tried to stand up, and fell over, sideways. He lay there, feeling like he was going to throw up. Ahead, he saw a figure scramble over the lip of the roof and disappear. In the light beam of the helicopter hovering overhead again, he stared at the camera. In fury he rolled over towards it, into the base of the tripod, and sent it crashing over. He tried to stand again, but his legs gave way. In desperation he hauled himself on to his hands and knees, looking around for his radio, but it had vanished.

He tried to stand again, but this time the wind blew him over. *No, no, no.* He got up again, virtually oblivious to the splitting pain in his head, and staggered across the roof. He grabbed the top rung of the ladder, then made the mistake of looking down.

The whole world spun 360 degrees.

He had to do it. Had to. Had to. Gripping the top ladder posts, he swung his legs over the roof. The wind tried to push him over, backwards.

Don't look down.

He thought for an instant of Cleo. Of their unborn child. Of their life ahead. And of how, in the next few moments, he might plunge to his death. Was this worth it?

Then he thought of the image of the boy, suspended by his arms from the lock gates. Anything that might save his life was worth it.

Half climbing, half sliding, he descended as fast as he could. Looking ahead all the time, never down. He still had his gloves on, he realized, and they protected his hands for a few seconds until the ladder cut through them, burning into his hands as he slid.

Then his feet hit the bottom and he tumbled over on to his back. He scrambled to his feet. Over to his right he could see the light on the bow of the *Arco Dee* dredger slipping steadily past the end of the power station. He saw red lights on the lock ahead, starting to flash.

No. No. No.

He ran to the steel fence and realized, to his frustration, that he was trapped in here. It had been OK coming in, over the pallets, but it wasn't so easy to get back again. There was nothing to give him a leg-up now.

'Glenn!' he screamed, having no idea where his friend might be at this moment. 'Glenn!'

'I'm here, boss!' he shouted back, from – to Grace's immense relief – the other side of the fence.

'Give me a hand out of here!'

Moments later, Glenn was leaning over the top of the fence. Grace grabbed his strong hand and was hoisted up. He scrambled over the top and on to the tarpaulin over the first pallet. As he jumped down on the ground, the front of the dredger was drawing level with them.

'Is anyone at the lock gate?' Grace yelled.

Branson shook his head.

'We have to stop it opening!'

Grace broke into a sprint, with Branson alongside him. As they ran, Grace could hear a cacophony of police sirens approaching. They raced down the quay and reached the entrance to the gate. Red lights were flashing and a klaxon was sounding loudly. As Grace stepped on to the lock walkway, he felt it vibrating. He continued running, the gate juddering harder and harder beneath him. Then he reached the join.

Suddenly the vibration stopped. The gates had paused. He looked down and saw the boy beneath him. The helicopter was right overhead, Tyler clearly illuminated like some grotesque crucifixion figurine, water swirling wildly beneath him. He was about to be torn in half at any second.

'Stop the fucking gates!' Grace screamed at Branson, as he clambered over the top of the gate. He could see one end of the rope, tied around a wooden peg just below the top and frantically pulled at it.

A wild froth of water was building up beneath him. The gates juddered, the gap widening, inch by inch.

*

Branson ran on, over to the far side, the gate juddering more and more. He threw himself over the metal plates, pushed open the unlocked gate and then ran towards the control room. As he did so, he suddenly felt something wrap around his legs and he hurtled, face down, to the ground.

*

Roy Grace tugged again at the rope, which was getting tighter by the second. He could hear, above the roar of the helicopter and the wind and the rain and the klaxon, a muffled crying sound. Suddenly, an instant before the gates opened wider, the rope fell free.

The boy dropped down into the water and disappeared with a splash, as the gates parted, one of them swinging steadily away, out of sight to the left.

Grace dived into the mad, thrashing cold water. Bubbles exploded all around him. It was ten times colder than he had imagined. He burst back up to the surface, gulping air. In front of him, towering above him like a skyscraper, he saw the bow of the dredger, less than a couple of hundred yards away. He tried to swim, but the undertow dragged him back down. When he surfaced again, he was choking on vile oily water. He spat it out, then, despite the weight of his clothes, he swam with all his strength across the width of the lock, to the far side, where he saw a rope hanging straight down into the water from the gate.

He grabbed it and pulled, pulled as hard as he could, and after a few moments a deadweight surfaced. He cradled the boy's head in his arms, trying with his wet, slippery hands to pull the tape free from his mouth.

They both went under, then came back up again, Grace coughing and spluttering.

'You're OK! You're OK!' he tried to reassure Tyler.

Then they went under again.

They surfaced again. The dredger seemed to have stopped. They were bathed in a pool of light from the helicopter. The boy was thrashing, in wild panic. Grace struggled, kicking with his feet, trying to get a purchase on the weeds and at the same time hold the boy. He was shivering. He gripped a handful of weed and it held. The boy's head went under. He brought it back up again, then he clung on to the boy and the weed as hard as he could, his hand almost numb with cold.

*

Glenn Branson rolled over and saw a small man running towards the door of the control room. He scrambled to his feet, lunged after him and grabbed him just at he was pulling the door open.

The man turned and punched him in the face, then ran off down the dock.

The wrong way, Branson realized, dazed, but not so badly he couldn't think straight. He stumbled after him, then blocked his path as the man tried to zigzag back past him, forcing him close to the edge of the quay. The man tried a feint, to dodge round him, but Branson grabbed him. The man aimed a punch at his face. Branson, who had trained in self-defence in his former life as a nightclub bouncer, dodged the blow and swung his leg round in a classic kick-boxing manoeuvre, deadening the man's right leg. As he fell, Branson slammed a punch into the man's left kidney. He hadn't realized they were so close to the edge of the dock. The man plunged backwards, over the edge, and vanished under the surface of the maelstrom of water.

The helicopter beam momentarily swept over them. The man had disappeared.

Then he heard a voice shouting, 'Hey! Someone! Glenn! Where the hell are you? Someone get us out of here! Come on! It's sodding freezing!'

112

It was the first really warm day of the year, with the thermometer in Brighton hitting seventy-five degrees, and the beaches of the city, along with its bars and cafés, were crowded. Roy Grace and Cleo returned home after a short walk with Humphrey, mindful of the instructions of the consultant gynaecologist that Cleo was not to do too much exercise.

Then they sat on the roof terrace of her house, Grace drinking a glass of rosé, Cleo with an elderflower cordial and Humphrey gnawing on a chew.

'So what happens next with Carly Chase? Your suspect is presumed drowned in Shoreham Harbour and Tony Revere's mother is dead, right?'

'They're diving and dragging the harbour. But it's pretty murky down there. You can't see anything with underwater lights, so you have to do it all by sonar and feel. And there are some pretty strong currents. A body could get pulled out to sea very quickly.'

'I thought they floated to the surface after a few days?'

'Takes about a week for the internal gases to build up. But if they do surface, say at night, with the tide and wind in the wrong direction, they'll go on out to sea. Then eventually they'll sink again, and when they do, they'll get picked clean by fish and crabs and lobsters.'

'What about Tony Revere's father?'

'I've spoken to Detective Investigator Lanigan in New York. The guy who could be the problem going forward is his wife's brother – the dead boy's uncle, Ricky Giordino. With his father, Sal, locked up in jail for the rest of his life, realistically, it sounds like this guy is the one to watch. Lanigan thinks he's the man who probably hired the killer in the first place. We're going to continue with protection on Carly Chase and her family for a while, but I personally don't think the threat is as severe now.'

Cleo placed Roy's hand on her swollen abdomen and said, 'Bump's busy today.'

He could feel their child moving around.

'Probably because you just ate a chocolate ice cream, right? You said he always becomes energetic when you eat chocolate – and that he's probably going to become a chocaholic.'

'*He?*' she said quizzically.

Grace grinned. 'You're the one who keeps going on about all these old wives' tales, that if your baby's high up, or sticking out a lot, it's going to be a boy.'

She shrugged. 'We could easily find out.'

'Do you want to?' he asked.

'No. Do you? You didn't last time we discussed it.'

'I will love our child just as much whether it is a boy or a girl. I'll love it because it is *our* child.'

'Are you sure, Roy? You wouldn't want it to be a boy, so he could be an action man like my hero, Roy Grace? The claustrophobic who goes down a deep tunnel. The man who's scared of heights who climbs power stations? The crap swimmer who dives into a harbour and saves a boy's life?'

Grace shrugged. 'I'm a copper. Sometimes in my job you can't make choices based on what you're afraid of or not. The day you do is the day you wake up and know you're in the wrong career.'

'You love it, don't you?'

'I didn't love climbing down that ladder into the tunnel. And I was shit scared climbing up on to the power station roof. But at least young Tyler's going to be OK. And to see his mother's face when we took her to him at the Sussex County, where he was being checked over – that was something else. That's why I do this job. I can't think of any other job in the world where you could make a difference like that.'

'I can,' Cleo said, and kissed him on the forehead. 'It doesn't matter what job you do, you'd always make a difference. You're that kind of person. That's why I love you.'

He gave her a sideways look. 'Do you?'

'Yup.' She shrugged and sipped her drink. 'You know, sometimes I wonder about you and Sandy.'

'In what sense?'

'You told me that you tried for several years to have a child, without success, right?'

He nodded.

'If you had succeeded, what would have happened? Would you and I – you know – be together?'

'I've no idea. But I can tell you one thing, I'm glad we are. You're the best thing that ever happened to me in my life. You're my rock.'

'You're mine too.'

She squeezed his hand. 'Let me ask you something. Did Sandy ever call you her *rock*?'

Roy Grace hugged her. After some minutes he said, 'You know what they say about the past being another country?'

Cleo nodded.

'So let's not go there.'

He kissed her.

'Good plan,' she agreed.

113

'The time is 8.30 a.m., Wednesday 12 May,' Roy Grace read from his notes to his team in MIR-1. 'This is an update on *Operation Violin*. To bring you up to speed on the latest regarding the unknown suspect, missing, presumed drowned, this is the start of the fifth day of the search of Shoreham Harbour by the Specialist Search Unit. One development yesterday was the recovery of a Toyota Yaris car from thirty feet of water at Aldrington Basin, close to the location where Ewan Preece was discovered in the white van. The vehicle bears the last known licence plates of the suspect. It is now undergoing intensive forensic examination.'

Duncan Crocker raised a hand. 'Chief, we haven't heard anything from Ford Prison regarding the death of Warren Tulley. Has there been any progress in that enquiry that could shed any light on our suspect?'

Grace turned to Potting. 'Norman, do you have anything for us?'

'I spoke to prison officer Lisa Setterington this afternoon, guv, and to the West Area Major Crime Branch Team, who are investigating. They are preparing to charge their original suspect, Tulley's fellow inmate Lee Rogan.'

Grace thanked him, then went on, 'We are continuing to maintain protection on Carly Chase and her family for the time being. I'm waiting for intelligence from the US which may help us to decide how long this should go on and in what form.'

*

This intelligence came sooner than Grace expected. As he left the briefing, his phone beeped, telling him he had a missed call and voicemail. It was from Detective Investigator Lanigan.

As soon as he got to his office, Grace called him back, mindful that it was the middle of the night in New York.

Lanigan, as ever sounding like he had a mouth full of marbles, answered immediately, seeming wide awake.

'Something strange going on here, Roy,' he said. 'Might be significant to you.'

'What's happened?'

'Well, it's not like I'm shedding any tears, you know. Fernanda Revere's brother, Ricky Giordino – son of Sal Giordino, right?'

'The Mafia capo who's doing a bunch of life sentences?'

'You got him. Well, I think I told you, Ricky's the guy we reckon would have hired the guy who's been causing all your problems, right?'

'You did.'

'Well, I thought you should know, Ricky Giordino was found dead in his apartment a couple of hours ago. Pretty gruesome. Sounds like some kind of a hit. You know – wise guys on wise guys kind of thing. Strapped to his bed with his dick cut off – looks like he bled to death from that. Had it jammed in his mouth and held in place with duct tape. Also looks like whoever did it cut his balls off and took them with him.'

'Before or after he was dead?' Grace asked.

Lanigan laughed. 'Well, with a guy like that, I'd want the best for him, know what I'm saying?'

'Absolutely!'

'So let's hope it was before. Oh – and there's one other thing – this is why I thought you might be interested. The perp left a video camera running at the scene.'

114

Yossarian lay in his usual place, shaded from the midday sun, just inside the permanently open patio doors, dozing. Once a day he got interrupted by the woman who brought him food and changed the water in his bowl. He would eat the food, drink some of the water and then return to his dozing.

He missed his associate. Missed the runs up in the hills and the days out on the boat, when he got to gulp down endless quantities of fresh fish.

But today felt different.

There was a vibe. He felt excited. Every few minutes, after he woke from his doze, he'd pad around the inside of his home, then go outside for a few moments into the hot sunlight, then back to the shade.

He was just dozing off once more when he heard the sound of the front door opening.

It was a different sound from the one the woman made. This was a sound he recognized. His tail began to wag. Then he jumped to his feet and ran to the door, barking excitedly.

His associate was home.

His associate stroked him and made some nice sounds.

'Hey, good to see you, boy. How've you been?'

His associate put his case down and opened it, then took out a small white plastic bag. He walked over to the empty food bowl on the floor, in the shade, near the patio door.

'Bought you a treat!' he said. 'A special delicacy, all the way from New York. How about that?'

Yossarian stared at his associate expectantly. Then he looked down at his bowl. Two small oval shapes dropped into it with a soft *thud, thud*. He wolfed them down, then stared at his associate again, wanting more.

Tooth shook his head. He didn't do quantity.

He did quality.

115

The office of the Yacht-Club Rheindelta was a small white wooden building on the edge of the vast Bodensee. They were taking a week's vacation and she thought it would be fun if they did a dinghy-sailing course together. He had been really keen when she had mooted the idea.

The fit-looking young German manager behind the counter was pleasant and helpful.

'So, do you have any sailing experience?'

She nodded. 'Yes, my – my ex-husband was very keen. We used to sail a bit in England – off the south coast around Brighton. And we did a flotilla sailing holiday in small yachts in Greece once.'

'Good.' He smiled, and started to fill in a form on a clipboard. 'So, first the young man. He is how old, please?'

'He'll be ten, next birthday.'

'Which is when?'

'March, next year.'

The German manager smiled at the boy. 'So you have your father's sailing genes, perhaps?'

'Oh, he has a lot of his father's genes, don't you?' she said, looking at her son.

He shrugged. 'Maybe. I don't know. I've never met him.'

The smile momentarily changed to a frown on the manager's face, then he said, 'OK. So if I may have the young man's full name, please.'

She wrote down *Bruno Lohmann* and handed him the form back.

'Sorry, I need the full name. Does Bruno have a second name, perhaps?'

Sandy smiled apologetically. 'Yes, I'm sorry.'

She turned the form back around and in the space provided in the middle she wrote, *Roy*.

ACKNOWLEDGEMENTS

I try hard to get my facts right in every book. Most of the places named here are real, but just occasionally I've needed to make a street or a house number fictitious. The glorious house in the Hamptons is real, too, and it does have a bowling alley in the basement! But I should point out it is not owned by a crime family, but by the very delightful Jack and Jane Rivkin, who graciously allowed it to be the model for the Reveres' home in my story.

I owe huge thanks to very many people who so kindly and patiently put up with my endless questions and give me so much of their time. Most of all I owe an incalculable debt to Sussex Police. My first thank-you is to the Chief Constable, Martin Richards, QPM, not just for his kind sanction, but for the very active interest he has taken in my Roy Grace novels and the numerous helpful observations and suggestions he has made.

Roy Grace is inspired by a real-life character, former Detective Chief Superintendent David Gaylor of Sussex CID, my close friend and tireless fountain of wisdom, who helps me to ensure that Roy Grace thinks the way a sharp detective would, and to shape my books in so many ways.

Chief Superintendent Graham Bartlett, Commander of Brighton and Hove Police, has also been immensely helpful on this book, even taking my calls and responding with great creative suggestions while out on training runs for the Brighton Marathon! Chief Inspector Steve Curry and Inspector Jason Tingley have both been hugely helpful in so many ways, too. As have Detective Superintendent Andy Griffiths; DCI Nick Sloan; DCI Trevor Bowles; Senior Support Officer Tony Case; Inspector Gary Medland of Gatwick Police; DI William Warner; Sgt Phil Taylor; Ray Packham and Dave Reed of the High-Tech Crime Unit; Inspector James Biggs; Sgt Mel Doyle; Sgt Paul Wood; PC Tony Omotoso; PC Ian Upperton and PC Dan Pattenden of the Road Policing Unit; Sgt Lorna Dennison-Wilkins and the team at the Specialist Search

Unit – especially Critch, for his amazing bacon butties! – Chris Heaver; Martin Bloomfield; Sue Heard, Press and PR Officer; and Neil (Nobby) Hall, former Assistant Commissioner of Police for the Turks and Caicos.

Exceptional thanks are due to Colin O'Neill of the Road Collision Unit for helping so much with the details of the tragic fatal accident in the story.

Very special thanks also to the NYPD, to Detective Investigator Patrick Lanigan, Special Investigations Unit, Officer of the District Attorney, and to retired Detective Investigator Dennis Bootle, for their exceptional help and generosity of spirit.

A huge and very special thank-you to Ashley Carter for being the role model for Tyler Chase, and for so enthusiastically helping me on so many aspects of his character, and to his mum, Helene, for allowing me to roam their home.

And as always I owe massive thanks to Sean Didcott at Brighton and Hove Mortuary. Also to Dr Nigel Kirkham, consultant pathologist, Newcastle; Crime Scene Manager Tracy Stocker and Scene of Crime Officer James Gartrell; fingerprint analyst Sam Kennor; forensic archaeologist Lucy Sibun and forensic pathologist Dr Benjamin Swift; Michele Websdale of the UK Border Agency; Sharon Williams, Governor of Ford Prison; and Deputy Governors Lisa Setterington and Jackie Jefcut. And thanks to my terrific researchers, Tracey Connolly and Tara Lester, as well as Nicky Mitchell, and Sian and Richard Laurie for sharing the world and perspectives of pregnancy with me.

Thanks also to Juliet Smith, Chief Magistrate of Brighton and Hove; Michael Beard, Editor, the *Argus*; BA captain Wayne Schofield; Judith Richards and the staff of St Christopher's School; Dave Phillips and Vicky Seal from the South East Coast Ambulance Service; Consultant Obstetrician Des Holden; Les Jones; Rob Kempson; Sheila Catt at Brighton District Probate Registry; Mar Dixon; Danielle Newson; Hans Jürgen Stockerl; Sam Brennan; Mark Tuckwell; and David Crouch of the Press Office Toyota (GB) plc.

Shoreham Harbour, one of my favourite parts of the city, features prominently through the book and I'm immensely grateful to Rodney Lunn, CEO, Chief Engineer Tony Parker and Deputy Chief Engineer Keith Wadey. As someone who, like Roy Grace, is both scared of heights and claustrophobic, I'm also indebted to David Seel, James

Seel and Barry Wade of Rescue and Emergency Medical Services for coaxing me all the way down that 200-foot sheer descent into the tunnel beneath the harbour, and to Keith Carter and Colin Dobson of Scottish Power for giving me such a great tour and information about Shoreham Power Station.

Thanks as ever to Chris Webb of MacService, who has unlimited patience, for ensuring my Mac knows who is the boss . . .

Very big and special thanks to Anna-Lisa Lindeblad, who has again been my tireless and wonderful 'unofficial' editor and commentator throughout the Roy Grace series; to Martin and Jane Diplock, incisive new members of this team; and to Sue Ansell, whose sharp eye for detail has saved me many an embarrassment.

Professionally I have my publishing dream team to thank: the wonderful Carole Blake representing me; my awesome publicists, Tony Mulliken, Sophie Ransom and Claire Richman of Midas PR; and there is simply not enough space to say a proper thank you to everyone in Macmillan, but I must mention my superstar publishing director, Wayne Brookes, and editor, Susan Opie. And massive thanks are due to my wonderful PA, Linda Buckley.

Helen has as ever been tirelessly supportive, and my canine friends continue to keep me sane. The ever-cheerful Coco, lovely Phoebe and totally laid-back Oscar never let me put in too many hours without reminding me it's time for yet another walk . . .

Lastly, thank you, my readers, for the wonderfully enthusiastic support you give me. Keep those emails, tweets and blog posts coming!

Peter James
Sussex, England
scary@pavilion.co.uk
www.peterjames.com
Find and follow me on
http://twitter.com/peterjamesuk

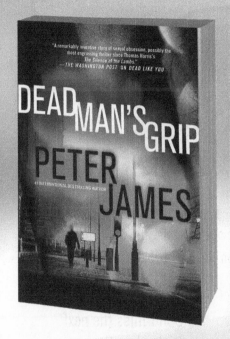